D0358545

The Marriage of Martha Todd

ALSO BY

DORIS LESLIE

Novels

FULL FLAVOUR
FAIR COMPANY
CONCORD IN JEOPARDY
ANOTHER CYNTHIA
HOUSE IN THE DUST
FOLLY'S END
THE PEVERILLS
PERIDOT FLIGHT
AS THE TREE FALLS
PARAGON STREET

Biographical Studies

ROYAL WILLIAM: *Life of William IV*
POLONAISE: *A Romance of Chopin*
WREATH FOR ARABELLA: *Live of Lady Arabella Stuart*
THAT ENCHANTRESS: *Life of Abigail Hill, Lady Masham*
THE GREAT CORINTHIAN: *Portrait of the Prince Regent*
A TOAST TO LADY MARY: *Life of Lady Mary Wortley Montagu*
THE PERFECT WIFE: *Life of Mary Anne Disraeli, Viscountess Beaconsfield*
I RETURN: *The Story of François Villon*
THIS FOR CAROLINE: *Life of Lady Caroline Lamb*
THE SCEPTRE AND THE ROSE: *The Marriage of Charles II*

The Marriage of Martha Todd

DORIS LESLIE

HEINEMANN: LONDON

William Heinemann Ltd
LONDON MELBOURNE TORONTO
CAPE TOWN AUCKLAND

First published 1968
Reprinted 1968

Printed in Great Britain by
Northumberland Press Limited
Gateshead

PRELUDE

On a day in the spring of the year 1880, a station fly halted at the door of Albion House, the Misses Merridew's Select Academy for the Daughters of Gentlemen, as displayed upon a plaque above their portals in the town of Dover, Kent.

From this conveyance two passengers descended: the one a young person in a grey mantle and a pork-pie hat: the other a portly individual, well-groomed and glossy, who bade the driver of the fly to wait.

Peering from behind the Nottingham lace curtains of the parlour window that overlooked a carefully tended garden with a far glimpse of the sea, Miss Emma, the younger of the two Misses Merridew, was in an evident state of perturbation.

Her sister, beak-nosed, hen-faced, fiftyish, and upholstered in black bombazine, sat confronting the window in a high-backed chair and motionless severity.

'They've come!' twittered Miss Emma, plump, pink, and of a faded prettiness as her gaunt elder sister was not. 'Just imagine!'

'Imagine what?' came stonily from the lips of Miss Merridew.

'That the new pupil is not the daughter of a gentleman, but the *wife* of one! Oh, dear!' Miss Emma, taken with the flushes, relinquished her stance at the window. 'I trust we have done right in accepting her.'

'WE?' capitalized Miss Merridew.

'I meant, of course, you,' quavered Miss Emma, 'I mean—'

'I am well aware of what you mean,' came the frigid

answer, 'and I beg you, Emma, to nurture no scruples or misgivings with regard to my judgement.'

'I don't – I won't – indeed, Laetitia, I do not. I never have and never would question your – whatever you decide is always for the best, and I do agree that in this case the circumstances, if peculiar, are—'

Further enlargement on the peculiarity of circumstances regarding the new pupil were terminated by the announcement of an aged parlourmaid:

'Mr and Miss Todd.'

Greetings were exchanged with effusion on the part of Mr Todd, with noncommittal chill from Miss Merridew, and from Miss Emma an over-zealous cordiality.

'Welcome to Albion House, Mr and, er, Mrs Todd. You have brought de*light*ful weather with you. It has been so cold these last few days though still a trifle breezy, which we must expect at this time of the—'

Cutting short her sister's disquisition on the weather, 'Pray be seated,' Miss Merridew indicated chairs, 'Mr and – Miss Todd.' An infinitesimal pause preceded the pronouncement of 'Miss', since thus, by request of Mr Todd and the concurrence of Miss Merridew, must the new pupil be addressed to circumvent importunate inquiry from her vestal fellow scholars.

The visitors sat, were offered tea – 'of which,' ventured Miss Emma, moving toward the bell-rope, 'you must be in need after your long journey.'

'No, ma'am, I thank'ee,' she was told. 'We had a cup at the station and I ave to catch the five forty-five back to Victoria and then on to Waterloo for Wimbledon, there being no through train from the terminus, so I shan't be Home till midnight.'

A certain misplacement of and emphasis on aspirates denoted Mr Todd's assiduous attention to the lack of them. 'I just wanted to make sure that my wife will not be put to Hembarrassment in the school, owing to er married state, and I must impress upon you ladies,' he bowed to each in turn, 'that she is only a wife in name, being and looking younger than er years. She – um – matured late, if you'll pardon me for mentioning it, with no intention of indelicacy, as she has no mother to mention it for her.'

Miss Emma blushed, Miss Merridew hemmed, and Mr Todd undauntedly continued: 'Moreover er Heducation aving been somewhat neglected – being orphaned, is the reason I decided to send her to your school – pardon – your Academy before she enters on the duties of married life.'

'We quite understand, sir,' Miss Merridew inimically assured him, 'and your wishes will be observed. Mrs – h'm – Miss Todd will be allotted a room to herself and given all the amenities accorded to other young ladies of her age, which you have told me is—'

A slight hesitation in recalling the age of the young lady was prompted by Mrs, or 'Miss' Todd, speaking for the first time:

'Sixteen.'

'Always providing,' Miss Merridew pursued, exclusively addressing Mr Todd, 'that her standard of general knowledge shall qualify her for a senior class. If not she will receive private tuition from me and my assistants until she has attained the required level of instruction.'

'She's well read,' pridefully stated Mr Todd. 'She ad a governess for a while, a Miss Hore, who left to be married. It was her who recommended me to your Academy. You'll not find er wanting in English literature nor French eether – I mean in speaking it, because er mother – I don't know as I told you this – was French born. She – she married an English gentleman of good family, a Mr – um – White. She was left with this little one,' he cast a doting look on this little one who sat, hands demurely folded in her lap and eyes downcast, while her husband provided the ladies with this gratuitous account of her antecedents. 'So then she, Mrs White, she came to us as Housekeeper, after my mother died for this Mr – White, he adn't much to leave his – widow, and she brought Martha along of her when she came to do for my father and me, so Martha has been with us ever since. We couldn't turn er out omeless, when her mother was taken, almost two years it is now, poor soul.' He dropped his voice, confidentially to mouth, 'Galloping. Lungs. I was made her legal guardian and that's ow I came to marry Martha, six weeks ago. You see.'

Miss Merridew, with a marked elevation of her eyebrows, saw.

'May I ask, in view of her maternal parentage, if Miss – if your wife is a Papist?'

'A Papist, ma'am?' Mr Todd exhibited shock. 'No, indeed she's not. Her mother was a Yougerno which is the same as Protestant with us.'

'Ah, a Huguenot.' Miss Merridew's tone expressed relief, and Miss Emma, who at Mr Todd's divulgation had deeply inhaled, exhaled as deeply on a rush of words.

'We do not encourage Roman Catholics in our establishment, since it is encumbent on all our pupils to attend morning and evening prayers in the school and Church twice a day on Sundays.'

'Which is as it should be,' assented Mr Todd. 'I don't old with Hidolatory, and you don't ave to worry about Martie's religion. She's been brought up C. of E., though I'm Chapel myself, not that it makes no difference so long as we ave naught to do with Popery and suchlike eathen practices. By the way, I forgot to mention that er name is Thereese Mart, as pronounced in French and spelt T.H.E. not T.H.A., but we prefer to call er Martha. We don't want to rub it in that she was born on the wrong side of the Channel though she's – she's on the right side o' of the blanket.'

At this information, accompanied by a slight reddening of Mr Todd's glossy cheeks, Miss Merridew retained increased refrigeration, Miss Emma's colour assumed that of an albino beetroot, and Mr Todd, rising, said:

'Well, I'll be getting along,' and served a hand to each sister. 'I must say I'm happy to be leaving my girl with you ladies. I've eard excellent reports of your school and I know she'll get all the advantages of Heducation that I've missed. I'm an Haddict,' he jocularly volunteered, 'to Heducation. Self-taught and self-made I am, and I'll spare no expense in giving my wife of the best. She must take all the extras, music, drawing – French she's well up in but she did ought to take French lessons if you ave a Mam'zelle to keep er up to the mark.'

Miss Merridew arctically admitted to a visiting French instructress.

'Good,' approved Mr Todd. 'This being a finishing school as your prospectus tells us, you would ave a Mam'-zelle but as for finishing Martha, why she's ardly yet begun! She don't know English grammar though she speaks it well enough – better'n me, come to that, reading so much and can write a good letter too, and – Ere! I was clean forgetting! Where's me head?' he tapped a finger to it. 'Wine. She's inclined, the doctor tells me, to anaemia, and he's ordered er a quarter to half a pint o' port a day. I'll have a dozen bottles sent from my Wimbledon branch. I deal in choice wines as well as in groceries. I've a good many shops in the London suburbs but I've not come to the counties yet, though I don't doubt your locals here sell Todd's Teas and Tasty Toasties, my special line in breakfast rusks. I could let you ave my Toasties and my best Darjeeling,' winningly suggested Mr Todd, 'at ten per cent discount if bought in bulk.'

At which offer, Miss Merridew, seemingly deaf to it, remained enthroned in ice; Miss Emma uttered a faint 'thank you, but we – I' – she gathered strength to say, 'am in charge of the catering, and the school is supplied with Lipton's teas and – and porridge oats for breakfast.'

'Fair enough,' assented Mr Todd, 'but you know where

to come if you want to give them something else – for a change. And now, Martie, my chuck,' he deposited a kiss on his chuck's averted cheek, 'mind you write me regular but no coming ome at half term. It might unsettle er, don't you agree?'

He appealed to Miss Merridew, the incline of whose head agreed. 'So goodbye, Martie, Gobless you. The summer olidays'll soon be Here. Goo'bye, ladies, and don't forget – ten per cent off all commodities if bought in bulk. I'll be sending you a price list so you'll see it's worth considering, along of a case of port for Martie and a bottle o' the best for yourselves. *Good*-day.'

Bowing profusely he backed to the door and was seen off the premises by the aged parlourmaid.

Having conducted the new pupil to her room and left her in the care of an elephantine personage in grey, collared and cuffed in white, presented to Miss Todd as 'Matron', Miss Emma returned to the parlour. Her state of perturbation had visibly increased. She spoke in hysterical jerks, escorted by a series of exclamation marks.

'He said – grocer! Shops! to supply us with – Bulk!' Miss Emma, who during this interview had held herself in, now let herself out. 'Trade! he's in *trade*! Groceries!' She became incoherently shrill. 'We have never – the daughter – I mean the wife – of a tradesman. Only professionals. One Q.C. and two Honourables – daughters of peers. And now – Todd's Tasty Toasties – Oh, *no*!'

'Beggars,' Miss Merridew unclosed her lips to say, 'can't be choosers.'

'Beggars!' Miss Emma's voice rose to a squeak. 'Laetitia, how *can* you! Will not the bank—'

'The removal by nervous parents of six pupils in as many weeks as result of diptheria in the town, has swollen our overdraft by another two hundred pounds and has caused the bank's refusal to accommodate us further until it is reduced,' was sepulchrally submitted.

'Mr Todd is paying highest fees for the privilege of "finishing" his wife.'

'Finishing!' cried Miss Emma. 'According to him she has hardly begun! As for his redundant revelations regarding her late maturity, I have never been more embarrassed. And he hasn't an aitch.'

'I was under the impression,' remarked Miss Merridew, 'that he has too many.' Behind her façade of frigidity there lurked a gleam of ironical humour. 'But let us not despise Todd's Teas or Tasty Toasties – at ten per cent discount – to say nothing of his fees that, with extras, will have much decreased our overdraft by the end of Miss Todd's first year.'

'"Miss" – oh!' A hand was clapped to Miss Emma's mouth. 'Suppose she should have a – a baby here by the end of *Miss* Todd's first year?'

'An improbable contingency if we may believe her a wife in name only.'

'*If* we may believe,' significantly repeated Miss Emma, 'which I do not. Shops! And trying to sell his groceries to us in our *par*lour! As for the girl, half French she may be and half-witted, I wouldn't wonder, for not one syllable did she speak more than "yes" and "no" when I took her to her room. Married or not, the situation,' Miss Emma deplored, 'is *most* irregular.'

But how irregular the situation would ultimately prove to be, neither the ladies of Albion House nor the new pupil could have possibly foreseen.

ONE

If Mr Todd had supplied the Misses Merridew with information concerning his wife that was not in strict accordance with the truth, we must excuse him since neither he nor the child, to whom he had given nothing more obligatory to their marriage than his name, had any certain knowledge of her patronymic descent. That her mother, a Mlle de Lamotte, had left her native France in the first year of Martha's life, and assumed the anglicized version of her baptismal name of Marie Blanche, alias Marie White, was as much a concession to English proprieties as to the nationality of Martha's unknown father.

Her earliest recollections of her mother were connected with, in fact inseparable from, a sewing-machine. She could exactly recall its incessant hum and, seen as in the fore-front of a faded tapestry, her mother's hands – like a mouse's hands, so small and thin – busy with yards of material. And, as in some woven fabric, colours, dimmed through veils of distance to pastel shades of silks and satins, or a sudden harsh crimson streak of velvet: or the whiteness of linen, a sheet, a pillow case to mend, embroider, or to edge with lace: or a gingham dress with the hem to let down, outgrown by Martha. Her mother 'took in' sewing. She also 'went out' sewing, to attend ladies in their homes by the day. On these occasions, Martha would be handed over to a Mrs Tripper. Her name was remembered because it rhymed with kipper, invariably linked with a smell of such, emanating from the basement of Mrs Tripper's house in Pimlico, where Martha and her mother lodged in a room on the top floor. It had a sloping roof, an outlook on a forest of chimneys, and a vista of windows below, often bedizened with washing: this the rear view of houses in the next street, their walls encrusted with the grime of ages and the smoke from Victoria Station.

Mrs Tripper, as Martha remembered her, was completely globular with a face like a red sun seen through fog: but all her memories of those early days in Pimlico were foggy, as if the smoke from the trains clattering in and out of the Station still clung to them. Nor was she ever quite clear how or when she went to school in one of those streets near by: a day school – 'pas une école commune,' her mother told her in the half English half French they spoke together. 'C'est une école très comme il faut. One pays deux shilling a week for zis school, vois-tu. You must learn to read and write en Anglais, car tu es demi-Anglaise, pauvre petite.' And her mother's sigh would turn into a cough and she would tell her to pick up the pins from the floor. There were always pins on the floor in that room. And Maman would cough again and rub her chest and say: 'Londres! C'est une morgue.' And Martha would ask: 'What is it, une morgue?' and Maman: 'Une maison des morts.'

'A house of the dead?' Always a stickler for information was Martha. 'Mais Londres n'est pas une maison. It's a town, and the people who live here they are alive, not dead.'

'They soon to be dead,' was the comfortless reply, 'ces gens who live en ce brouillard formidable! When I make money enough we go back again to France où est l'air si propre so I cough no more, and you, my little, you be not so pale. You grow big and strong. Mais – sur ces entrefaîtes, we go to school. . . .

There was not much to remember of this, her first school, more than a super abundance of children in a very large room where presided a very small lady called Teacher, whose hair was a dirty white strained back from a shiny forehead and done up in a netted bag behind. She was so small she had to stand on tiptoe to write letters on the blackboard. Martha soon learned to write those letters into words and to read them from a book. She learned so quickly that she won a prize, a story called *Alice in Wonderland* at the end of her third term. It was also the end of her schooling at that 'école très comme il faut'.

Of her schoolmates she could remember only that they made fun of and mimicked her for the way she spoke, and would sometimes follow her out of school, shouting after her: 'Froggy-Frenchy *Mar*tha! D'you eat frogs? Does your mother bake them in a pie, Mam'zelle French Frog? Frenchy-French-French Frog!' . . . Not, it would seem, such a 'comme il faut' school.

Thereafter it was as if a curtain had fallen to obscure these glimpes of her childhood, until the removal from the house of Mrs Tripper to the house of Mr Todd.

There had been a Mrs Todd, one of Maman's ladies, whom she visited to sew and mend, and attended during her illness, but Martha never knew her.

It is now that memories emerge from a background of vague figures that are gradually shaped to a more realistic design. At first these figures were inextricably a part of inanimate objects in the house above the grocer's shop at Dulwich where she and her mother went to live when Mrs Todd was taken to hospital and never came back.

At Mr Todd's, Martha and her mother occupied a room next the kitchen, which was upstairs, not down. An iron staircase led to the back of the shop into a vast apartment, as it seemed to Martha, whose previous habitat had been an attic room scarcely large enough for two with the bed, the ironing board, the table, the sewing-machine and the wardrobe for the dresses Maman mended or made for her ladies.

This back premises was contraband to Martha, who

would sometimes take advantage of her mother's absence when out marketing, to explore forbidden territory. It offered endless enticement of cardboard boxes, mysteriously labelled: Haricot, Sunlight, Granulated, Castor, Piccallili, Monkey Brand, to be carefully spelled and construed as: Beans, Soap, Sugar, Pickles and a smiling monkey holding up a frying pan, trademark of the powder used for cleaning pots, and there was always hereabout an intermingled, not unpleasant, smell of cheese and coffee, spices, bacon, cloves.

From this store-room a door gave access to a yard where vans, drawn by massive dray horses, waited while the heavy loads of boxes, cases, casks were hauled down, their contents to be served over the counter in the shop, but not by Mr Todd. He had three or four assistants to do that; nor was he there every day. He had other shops in other places, and was back and forth between them all, though he lived over the shop where Maman kept house for him and his father.

The elder Todd is a more significant presence than his son, who was often away in these, Martha's formative years. He is recalled as lean, blue-chinned, careless of his buttons, frayed about the cuffs and grey about the hair that lay in streaks across a balding patch on the top of an egg-shaped head. He had eyes set close together above an inquisitive nose, and those eyes, red-rimmed and indeterminate, were given to staring, nastily, at Martha during mealtimes, when he was not grumbling at Maman about her cooking or the food.

'This Frenchified soup – what-d'y-call it – consummay? – I don't like it and it don't like me. Gives me the gripes. Too much onion.' Or else: 'D'you Frenchies eat your meat raw? I like my beef well done, not all red and bleedin'. 'Ow much do they charge you for this sirloin? I bet they rooked you for it.'

And Maman, her eyes narrowed and up at him: 'Comment?' And he: 'Common's right. Not fit for 'uman consumption which this ain't – if butcher's meat at all. 'Orse or donkey most like.'

And he'd get up from the table and knock his pipe against the mantelpiece and refill it from the tobacco jar with the stuff he called shag, and say, grinning at Maman, as memory revived it: 'You'd be a bit of orlright, you would, if you 'ad more flesh on your bones. Not much of an armful, you ain't. My son Jo,' meaning the younger Mr Todd, 'takes after 'is Ma, the late departed. You know what a size *she* was – fourteen stone to my ten. I muss say I like a bit o' somethink to get 'old of and warm you up in bed – not but what I wouldn't make do with a feather weight like you – birds of a feather get together, eh? Not 'arf!' To this remark was added a wink that completely closed one eye. 'Better'n a stone 'ot water bottle to cuddle into of a col' night, what?'

If Martha understood but little of this, and her mother even less, it was not what he said but how he said it that made Maman look at him in the way she would look at Martha if she found her picking at the cake, fresh made for their Sunday teas: a look that meant a scolding. 'Mais! Ça c'est trop fort – what you do – go ruiner mon gâteau. Méchante, toi!'

They had meals in the dining-room that was also the parlour, much overburdened with mahogany: a sideboard, an overmantel, very high and heavy with a mirror reaching almost to the ceiling and brackets that held candles, never lighted, either side of it. There was a bookcase filled with books; and on the mantelshelf a black marble clock supported by pillars along with Mr Todd senior's tobacco jar, a pair of china dogs, a couple of green vases filled with paper flowers, and a photograph in a plush frame of the late Mrs Todd, wearing a wide-skirted dress horizontally banded with velvet. There were armchairs of leather, once red, now brown and rubbed shiny from long usage; there was a sofa of the same, and another photograph of Ted, a younger son, in a coat with bright buttons and a peaked cap; and this hung on the wall above the harmonium that since the departure of Mrs Todd nobody played.

Ted, as Martha came to know him, was ten years junior to his brother. There had been three others, two boys and a girl, who died in infancy, as she had been told. Ted, dark-haired, red-cheeked and jolly, was a welcome addition to the household when on leave from his ship. He was in the merchant navy and had all to say of his life aboard a liner. He had recently become an officer, just returned from a voyage to South America. He drew her a map showing the coastline of Peru with a lot of wavy lines in blue chalk for the sea.

'Look, see this? It's the Pacific. You've heard of the Pacific, haven't you?'

She hadn't but pretended that she had. She wouldn't have him think her stupid, 'a French Frog', as the girls at that Pimlico school used to call her and make fun of her French accent, which she was rapidly losing except for her R's.

Often, when his father was out for his evening stroll, which meant as far as the Red Lion at the corner, Ted would tell Maman while she darned socks or turned sheets sides to middle, how Jo had paid for his schooling – 'paid for everything, he did – for me and the old man too, who'd never done a day's work since Jo made good. He started in groceries at ten years old as an errand boy, worked his way up, and now look at him with half a dozen shops of his own! His boss died and left him the business. He's got a head for business has our Jo. I owe everything to him. Merchant Taylors school and my training ship. He paid for the lot.'

Maman, folding a sock and taking up another, said:

'He is homme de bien – a good man, your brother—' and shook her head at a great hole in the heel. 'Mon dieu! Do they walk on ciseaux in your ships, then, mon capitaine?'

'Not a captain yet,' said Ted with his wide white grin. 'I've a long way to go before that. And as for Jo being homme de bien, granted, but you're femme de bien – the way you run the house single-handed. There's more than enough to do to keep it ship-shape.'

'Mais non! Would I sit here – do nothing comme ça – like zis?' She let fall the sock and tucked her hands under her arms, and laughed, and fell to coughing; and Ted told her: 'That's a nasty cough you have,' and she: 'It is le brouillard – how you say – ze fog.'

'You should come for a sea voyage, you and Martha,' he said. 'Do you a world of good.'

Before Ted rejoined his ship for his second voyage to South America, he took Martha to the Opéra Comique to see a new musical play that was sweeping London; a great event this for her, whose entertainment had hitherto been limited to Penny Readings in the Methodist Church Hall, accompanied by Mr Toddy, as she called him – not to be confused with his father, the other Mr Todd – when she would be forced to endure dreary recitations of the *Village Blacksmith*, *Curfew shall not ring tonight*, or *The Boy stood on the Burning Deck*, infrequently enlivened by a Punch and Judy show at a street corner.

Ted, booking well in advance, had secured front seats in the Upper Circle, and Martha felt very proud to be seen with him appropriately attired in his uniform, for this was a Naval Occasion: a performance of *H.M.S. Pinafore*.

How amusing it all was with a ship, as near as might be real, on the stage! And how Ted roared with laughter at the old gentleman in a white wig, white stockings, knee-breeches, cocked hat and glistening with medals and gold braid . . . 'First Lord of the Admiralty,' whispered Ted through the yells of applause, and wiping his eyes for he had laughed till he cried at the First Lord's song with its rollicking chorus of Jack Tars.

Stick close to your desks and *never* go to sea,
And you all may be rulers of the Queen's Nav*ee*!

On the way home, by train and bus Martha had those tunes whirling in her head that she might sing them to her mother, especially the one sung by a fat lady who looked like a tub dressed up in a vast print dress and apron. 'Elle est si grosse, comme ça,' Martha described in the air a circle round her chest to show how fat she was, 'and she calls herself Little Buttercup'; translated to Maman as 'You know – cette fleur jaune, bouton d'or. I laughed – c'est à mourire de rire!'

Then Ted sat at the harmonium, which never was played till he came, and he strummed the tunes for her to sing them with him; and she made him teach her the notes so that she could play 'Buttercup' too.

After that, when Ted went back to his ship, both Martha and the house seemed lost and empty without him; but having learned the notes on the wheezy old harmonium she could amuse herself by playing by ear the tunes she remembered.

'She's got a taste for music,' Jo Todd told her mother. 'Picking it up so quick. She should have music lessons. We'll have to see about it.'

'Music lessons!' His father was sharp on that. 'Yes! And who's to pay for them? Eatin' us out of 'arth and 'ome as it is! And for gawd's sake, you!' he rounded on Martha who was playing and humming: '*Tum*diddle-um-tum diddle diddle *dee* – and we'll *all* be rulers of the Queen's Nav*ee*!' – 'Stop that caterwaulin', can't yer? Gets on one's nerves!'

And Martha hated him. She hated the way he sat smoking his pipe and staring at Maman, when not staring, nastily, at her.

Among the miscellany of books in the bookcase she had found three volumes of Shakespeare, illustrated: Carlyle's *French Revolution, A Children's History of*

England, The Family Doctor, Waverley Novels, What a Woman of Forty ought to Know, Foxe's Book of Martyrs, and *The Mystery of Man,* incomprehensibly subtitled *An Esoteric Anthropology;* most of them, in due course, to be sampled, discarding those she couldn't understand, in particular the *Woman of Forty* and *The Mystery of Man*. But it was the *Book of Martyrs* that chiefly engaged her attention. This also was illustrated with blood-curdling pictures of men being burnt at the stake, or hanged, their insides drawn out, as her mother would draw a fowl, and to which Martha would not have objected if done to old Mr Todd. Cet animal! Beast! Beast! So, watching from a window that overlooked the street, did she anathematize him as he went for his evening stroll to the Red Lion, pausing to light his pipe under a gas-lamp. She hated him because, for some inexplicable reason, she feared him. He gave her funny feelings when he looked at her, as if he could see through her to her bones. . . .

The winter of that year brought with it those fogs that her Mr Todd called 'pea soup', a thick greyish yellow, very like pea soup, that smarted your eyes and got into your throat and made her mother's cough much worse, especially at night. Once Martha woke up to see her leaning over a basin and blood coming out of her mouth. She was terribly frightened. 'Maman! Qu'est ce que tu as? Are you being sick?'

'Non, non, c'est rien.' It was her nose bleeding, she said.

But after that, so as not to disturb Martha if she coughed at night, she had a bed made up in the attic at the top of the house.

February came and the cottage gardens in the village heralded the spring with the first snowdrops and crocuses; and her mother was busy in the house, taking down lace curtains for the wash, cleaning the paint, polishing the brasses, and making a new dress for Martha from material bought at the January sales in Oxford Street on one of those rare occasions when Maman would take a day off to go shopping, and Martha would go with her and have tea out. Such pretty flowered stuff her mother had bought – 'bon marché,' she said, 'pour le printemps'.

* * *

Then came that awful, not to be forgotten day. A Sunday it was. Martha had peeled the potatoes ready for the oven with the joint, and her mother was rubbing the raw beef with garlic as she always did, and had put it and the potatoes in the roasting tin. She was singing, in her little thin voice, the song she liked to sing when she was cooking or working, or whatever:

Au clair de la lune
  Mon ami Pierrot
Prête-moi ta plume
  Pour écrire un mot
Ma chandelle est morte
  Je n'ai plus de . . . feu . . .

Then it happened. As she bent down to open the oven door she began to cough. She was shaken with the spasm that tore at her body so that she crumpled and fell in a heap with a trickle of blood at the corner of her mouth and her breath coming quickly, in gasps.

Martha flew to try and lift her, but her head slipped back. Her eyes were closed, her lips blue, and more blood trickling.

There was a step on the stair. Martha rushed to the door.

'Mr Toddy! Please!' clutching at his arm. 'Maman! she – she's—'

The doctor was sent for. They got her to bed – not in the attic for none knew she had slept there these last few weeks – but in the bed she used to share with Martha. She seemed to have recovered, and apologized to the doctor for being such a trouble – 'to give you the pain to come out sur le dimanche – on the Sunday.'

The doctor told Martha she mustn't sleep in the same bed with her mother, so she slept on the sofa in the parlour. The next day the doctor said Maman must go away to a sanatorium, which he explained to Martha's inquiry: 'Sanny – what?' was a house quite near to London on Hampstead Heath, where she could be visited from time to time.

Mr Toddy took her there in a four-wheeler. It came to the back entrance in the yard, and Martha saw her go, looking very well, she thought, and pretty, with a bright colour in her cheeks.

'Sois tranquille,' she said. 'Je reviens bientôt . . . soon . . . very soon.' And held her close and kissed her with lips that were hot and dry. Something wet dropped from her mother's eyes on Martha's face, but she couldn't speak for the ache in her throat.

She stood at the door to watch the cab drive off; saw her mother's hand – such a wisp of a hand – waving goodbye, heard her voice thinly floating: 'Je reviens!' above the dying rattle of wheels and hooves. . . . Then no sound more than the twittering of sparrows pecking at the shreds of straw in the gutter.

TWO

What shall be said of a child's grief, the agony of loss, despair, and desolation when she was told that her mother would never return? . . . 'Gone to a Higher Sphere.' Thus with much eye-blinking and clearing of his throat, did Jo Todd prepare her for that which in her heart she knew – and dared not know.

At first, shrinking from acceptance of it, she thought, or hoped, he meant that her mother had gone as housekeeper to another post. A better post.

'Am I to go with her?' Snatching at that furtive gleam of hope.

'Some day. Not yet.' He laid a clumsy hand on her downbent head. 'The Lord giveth and –' he cleared his throat again – 'and the Lord taketh away. We none of us'll go till we're invited.'

Her eyes were fixed on the carpet: a new carpet recently bought to replace the old one that had worn threadbare in parts. Very bright it was with colours of red, blue and green in squares, entwined with hideous impossible flowers, seen now to recede and swim in a mist which made them look even more impossible. Her mother had said it was a good carpet but du mauvais goût . . . Gone to a. . . .

Her tongue, tasting suddenly of lemons, went dry and stuck to the roof of her mouth. . . . Taken away. Why should the Lord give and take away? Ce n'est pas sensible, that.

Said Mr Todd: 'We all have our Cross to bear. Some has it early in life and some late. God's Will be done. Would you like a cup o' tea?'

Her tongue came unstuck to say: 'No, thank you. I . . . I'll . . . I must go and get the supper.'

'Unnat'ral I call it!' To his son, and not for the first time, did the elder Todd air his grievance as overture to the main theme involving the future of Martha. 'Unnat'ral to show no feelin', not even at the fun'ral which *you* paid for up to the 'ilt, and a pretty penny, too – finest oak, brass 'andles, kerridges, mutes, plumes, to say nothink of 'er mourning black. I'll be lucky if I get as good. D'you intend to keeper 'ere fr'ever? There's plenty of orphanages as 'ud take 'er. Them nuns – Sisters o' Mercy they call themselves what comes round collectin' – they'd find 'er a job as skivvy or somethink in their convent or send 'er out to work. The bit o' cookin' she does for us don't pay for what she eats, and as for bringin' in that char while the kid sits twiddlin' 'er thumbs – you've more money than wit.'

'Martha's a cut above a skivvy.' Standing, hands behind his back, legs apart upon the hearth-rug, his son glowered down on the bottle of port at his father's elbow. 'She's got breedin' every inch, and er mother, too. She told me once, Her mother did, what er maiden name was – dee something. You don't ave dee before your name in France unless you're top drawer. If you ever put your nose in a book you'd know that. You should read Carlyle on the French Revolooshun – I've got it here somewhere. All those Haristocrats who went to the gillerteen – they all had a dee or a la or both before their names. As for no feelin' – it's them that shows it least what feels the most. You've only to look at er – thin as a rake – don't eat enough for a bird. I'll ave to get the doctor to er or *she'll* go gallopin' same as er mother, poor soul.'

'You're barmy!' exploded his father. 'Breedin' be damned! The brat's a bastard like as not – born in France so she ain't even a British subject and livin' on English charity. *Your* charity.'

'Her father,' Jo said stolidly, 'was English.'

'So what? And where is 'e? Who was 'e – if 'er mother ever knew? Callin' 'erself a widow – save 'er face.'

'I'll thank you not to speak ill of the dead and' – with portentous significance – 'Martha's Here as *my* responsibility and Here she'll stay. If you don't like it you can lump it or get out.'

'Ho! Get out, is it?' pausing to refill his glass, Mr Todd imbibed simultaneously its contents with this latest information. 'A nice thing to threaten your father. *Your* responsibility! D'you set yourself up as another o' them philan – what's-its-names – like Lord Shaftesbury and his Benevolent Sercieties? 'E can afford to be Benevolent. You can't, or if you can, then Benevolent or Charity begins at 'ome.' . . .

While in some such fashion the Todds, or the Fates, decided the future of Martha, she, having laid the table for their mid-day meal, went in search of one Mrs Bilson. This lady, whose services had hitherto been rendered to the shop, before the doors opened to customers at 8 a.m., with an extension of bi-weekly assistance to the late Mrs White in the house, was now, by command of Jo, called upon to render similar services to Martha for four hours thrice weekly at threepence per hour, including her dinners and beer: a source of added grievance to the complaints of the senior Todd.

Martha found her in the scullery, wringing sheets through a mangle; it was washing day. Stout, hearty, lamentably deaf, Mrs Bilson was never seen about the house without a man's cap on her head, carpet slippers on her feet, a sackcloth apron round her waist – or rather that part of her anatomy that should have been her waist – and on her face a cheery smile, latterly exposing empty gums as result of sundry visits to the dentist.

Approaching her lips to Mrs Bilson's ear:

'Their dinner,' carefully enunciated Martha, 'is in the *oven*. Cottage pie, and spotted dog, if you wouldn't mind dishing up, and take yours first. I have had mine. I am going *out*.'

'Right y'are, ducks,' smilingly answered Mrs Bilson. 'I'll 'ang 'em out 'ere on the 'orse and iron 'em termorrer.'

'Will you dish up their *dinner* for me,' persevered Martha, 'and tell them I've gone *out*? You can have yours now if you like. I've had mine.'

'Termorrer.' Mrs Bilson cheerfully told her, 'I'll 'ave me new teeth in termorrer and be able ter swaller somethink more'n slops.'

And addressing herself to the mangle she burst into stentorian song.

> Ah'll be yer sweet'art
> If yew will be mi-ine
> All my li-ife I'll be yew-er Valent*ine*
> Blewbells I've gath*erd*
> Tyke them and be trew . . .

'I'd better write it on the slate,' Martha said resignedly; and having done so, and placed the message in conspicuous sight of Mrs Bilson, who was lustily assuring her that:

> . . . When I'm a man
> My-ee plan
> Will be ter marree yew . . .

she took herself off.

Her way led her through the village and into that which then was open country before London's suburbia had erupted in a rash of Victorian villas on field and meadowland. It was a blue and golden July day with bees in the clover and birds singing their paean of praise to the sun in every copse and hedgerow.

Often, when her Mr Todd was at the Dulwich shop, as now, she would seize the opportunity to escape from those purgatorial meals with his father, watching him shovel food in his mouth to deprive her of the little appetite she had; or having to hear him grumble at what she set before him. But worse than this, when she was alone with him, he would do beastly things to her, like pinching her bottom or sliding his hand up her legs; or he would pass frightening remarks with that leering grin of his . . . 'Comin' on a treat, you are. One o' these days you'll make a feller want to wring yer neck or tumble yer.' And although he would never do or say such things in the presence of his son, she welcomed the chance when he was at home to get out and away by herself. So seldom could she be alone, always having to wait upon or cook for the old man, whom more than ever did she hate . . . and fear.

On this day, when she had chosen to play truant at the risk of having to account to Mr Toddy for her absence, she had prepared him an excuse. She had been to the Dulwich Art Gallery to see the pictures, which he encouraged her to do, and would, if time permitted, take her there. Nor if truth, which she was not particular to tell, be told, did she suffer conscience qualms regarding this or any other moderate deception.

She was wearing an ankle-length black dress with a white turn-over collar, white stockings and black heelless shoes, and she swung by its black ribbons a wide-brimmed light straw hat.

Following a footpath between the springing grass and a lacy froth of meadowsweet, she found herself singing the little song her mother used to sing; then, as realization came to her with the remembrance of the last time she was ever to hear those words on her mother's lips . . . *Ma chandelle est morte*, she stopped short.

'No!' she cried aloud on a broken breath. 'No, not dead. Nothing dies, not a candle, for the wick remains. Not a flower, not a leaf that doesn't live again dans le printemps. . . . Yes, but people *do* die, and birds, and bees, they do, they do. . . . He, the clergyman, he said I am the

Resurrection and the Life, but there's no life now for her . . . or me. Maman!'

She flung herself down in the grass, her head buried in her arms, her little body heaving with the shock of memory.

It was then that the boy, on his way home from the College, saw her lying there. The russet brown tangle of her hair had fallen loose about her shoulders. He could not see her face but he could hear her stifled sobbing, had heard that pitiful cry but not the words that followed it.

The sound of his step on the footpath, no less than the tune whistled between his teeth that Ted used to play: *Stick to your desk and never go to sea* . . . abruptly halted at the sight of her, caused her to lift her head. She sat up, feet stretched out, her hands supporting her in the long grass. He saw her eyes, wide, startled, and of a dazzling blue in the warm pallor of her face. The sun glistened on her hair to make of it a bronze-gilded halo.

So they stared at each other, these two. She saw a long-limbed coltish boy in the College blazer, his brows raised and lips upcurved in a faun-like shamefaced smile. Nor neither knew that the eternal miracle had come to pass, urged by the same blind unconscious energy that implements the meeting of amoebae in a ditch. Yet, although he may have known something, if not all, about the sexual union of *proteus animalcule*, he would not have applied such a natural phenomenon to the meeting of himself with a girl in a shabby black dress, her mouth fallen open with the shock of surprise, and snivelling tears up her nose.

And in that moment's pause of naïve compulsions, he, the first to find his voice, vented it in an awkward inadequate croak:

'Hullo', which might well have finalized this briefest of encounters, for, even as he resumed his walk without another word or look at her who still sat staring in open-mouthed confusion, destiny had shaped their ends – by intervention of a cruising wasp.

A painful 'Ow!' swung him round to see her furiously attacking the marauder.

'It stung me!' she squealed.

At once he joined the fray, successfully to combat and vanquish the enemy.

'A queen,' he observed, surveying the corpse, annihilated by bombardment from his satchel and the grinding of his heel on the body in the path. 'A bit early for them, too. I expect there's a nest around here. Where did she sting you?'

'On my neck. It got under my hair. Ooh! it hurts.'

'I bet it does. Half a mo – let's have a look.'

He knelt beside her, peering, as she swept the fallen hair from her nape.

'Right,' he said, having had his look. 'I'll get it out.' And with sensitive long fingers he skilfully manipulated.

'Sorry,' he told her as she whimpered. 'Soon be done. . . . Ah, got it! It's a whopper.' He laid the whopper on the back of his hand for her to see.

She gazed at it and then at him in wonder.

'It's as big as a thorn. Fancy that sticking in me! However did you do it?'

'I squeezed it, but I ought to suck it now to let out the poison. D'you mind?'

She minded dreadfully, but regardless of her bleated objection, 'Oh, must you?' he resourcefully proceeded to operate.

'That's done it!' he announced, having sucked and spat, and sucked again to her increased embarrassment, nothing lessened by the unaccountable, yet not disagreeable, sensations aroused as much by his proximity as by his activities. 'Had to get rid of the poison,' he explained, rather red in the face, 'or it might set up toxaemia.'

'I see,' said she, who didn't; and, impressed by his handling of the situation and the long word he had used, 'are you,' she inquired, 'a doctor?'

'I hope to be.' He slithered down beside her. 'How does it feel now?'

'It smarts a bit.' Then, remembering her manners, 'Thank you very much for – for getting it out. You're at the College, aren't you?'

'Yes, till the end of this term.'

After that it was easy. He talked; she listened, noting the way his lips moved in his clear precise pronunciation of English as she knew it should be spoken, and as she seldom heard it spoken except, approximately, by Ted Todd.

He was leaving school, he told her, and going to Bonn in Germany in the autumn. 'I'm to live in the house of a doctor there to learn the language so that I can read German medical books which are better than ours. And then I shall be going up to Cambridge.'

'Fancy,' she murmured, visualizing that time, last year, when Ted, home on leave, had taken her to watch the boat race from Hammersmith Bridge. 'Shall you row in the race of the boats at Cambridge?' she asked.

He laughed round at her.

'Race of the boats – that's good. No, I shall have to swat for my M.B.'

'Em-bee? What is that?'

'My medical. I say, you speak with a sort of accent. Are you English?'

'I am half English and half French. I was born in France, but my father was English. I never knew him. My mother –' her lip trembled – 'was French. She died four months ago.'

'Oh,' awkwardly, 'I'm sorry.'

A silence fell between them, then:

'Have you,' she asked, 'a father and a mother?'

'My mother is dead,' she was told, 'and my father's in

India. He is a doctor, A.M.D., Army Medical Department.'

'Oh,'

Another silence, in which both took sidelong stock of the other. He reminded her of a picture she had seen in the Art Gallery of a godlike being with enormous wings, golden hair, and a clear pale face, only his face wasn't pale. It was pink, and his hair, ruffled in a breeze that had sprung up while they talked, fell over his forehead, and drew attention to a mark he had just above his eyebrow, a kind of deep white scar. She also saw that he had tiny bristly gold hairs on his chin that glinted in the sun. He was altogether rather hairy. His wrists, sticking out of his cuffs, which were a bit short for him as if he'd grown out of them, were also golden-hairy, and she guessed he'd have hairs on his legs. She had just started growing hairs on her legs, too, and . . somewhere else. And at that she flushed deeply, lowered her head and plucked a blade of grass to nibble it between her teeth. He, watching her, thought: a pretty kid. Extraordinary eyes. He'd seen that same startling blue in the eyes of those frightful cats his aunt went in for. Beastly things. Uncanny, more like monkeys than cats. And: 'How old are you?' he asked; not that he particularly wanted to know but for something to say. Couldn't sit there like a couple of stuffed owls. He wanted to get up and go but was equally inclined to stay.

Her eyes that had evaded his returned to him. She blinked them, and again he was reminded of a cat as she answered: 'How old do you think?'

'Eleven. Twelve?'

She frowned, pouting, sulky-mouthed. 'Always I am took – taken – to be so young. I am *not*. I'll be fif*teen* in November.'

A case, he thought superiorly, of arrested development. He had made inroads on his father's medical books, and had learned about puberty in girls. Earlier among natives and Latin races than in Nordic countries. She, being half French, ought not to be so kiddish at almost fifteen. Juliet was only fourteen.

She was asking him: 'How old are you?'

'I'll be seventeen in November. What day's your birthday?'

'The twenty-first.'

'So you're a Scorpion too.'

'A Scorpy *what*?'

'Scorpion. Scorpio is one of the signs of the Zodiac, meaning the stars under which we are born. Zodiac comes from a Greek word Zodiakos, an animal. Almost all the Zodiacal signs are animals. The ancients believed it to be an imaginary circle surrounding the heavens. It's what is called astrology.'

'Aren't you clever!' More than ever now was she impressed. 'Do you learn all that at the school – I mean the College? I wish I could go to school, a real school, not like the one I went to when I was young. Oh! la, la!' She put a hand to her neck. 'Ça me fait mal!'

'Hurts still, does it? It'll go off presently.' He turned sharply to look at her. 'I say – I suppose you speak fluent French. Are you bi-lingual?'

Such grand words he used! She felt shamingly ignorant. 'I spoke French with my mother – sometimes all French and sometimes a sort of half French and half English, because she wanted to learn English and she said that if we always spoke French together she wouldn't be able to speak English and nor would I, but she never spoke it properly, and I don't either, do I? Because of my R's.'

'I was wondering –' his brow wrinkled; she knew that he hadn't been listening, 'if – you see – my French is rotten. I know the grammar but my accent's all wrong and it's useful to be able to speak French decently if one has to attend a French patient who can't understand English – I'm talking about later on when I'm qualified.

I suppose you wouldn't like to meet me here again,' said he carefully indifferent, 'before I go to Germany? That will be sometime in September. We break up the week after next. Or perhaps you could come back here this afternoon? It's a half holiday today. If I could put in an hour or so two or three times a week and talk French with you it would help my accent. Our language master is English. No use at all.'

It was as if fireworks had flamed to light her up inside with showers of golden sparks. To meet again and talk to him in French! Not one word of French had she spoken except to herself since Maman . . .

'Oh, yes! I would! I never speak French now where I live and I don't want to forget it.'

'That's fine. Then what about later on today?'

Her face fell.

'I can't today. As it is I have gone out when I should not have gone, and I must get their teas. Mrs Bilson leaves at two o'clock.'

'Who's Mrs Bilson and whose teas do you have to get?'

'Theirs – Mr Todd's and his father's. And Mrs Bilson – she comes in to help and when she is not there I have to do the washing up. I always do the cooking. My mother –' controlling the shake in her lower lip – 'she was their housekeeper. I have lived with them since I was nine years old. But now . . .' she swallowed, 'I don't know if I will be there much longer. They may not want me . . . not now that she . . .'

His glance slid to her hands. She was twisting her fingers and biting her lips, looking down. Was she going to blub again? She couldn't, surely, he thought, be a servant. She didn't look or speak like a servant.

'Do you' – he reddened again – 'I mean do they, these Todds, do you have to work for them?'

'Only to cook and dust and sew on their buttons and the darning. And I make the beds and empty the – the slops.'

He stifled a laugh, and unconsciously drew nearer: his shoulder brushed hers, and, at that sudden contact and her swift response to his upsurged unvoiced demand, as instinctive as the mating of two butterflies hovering above their heads, his blood quickened. He leaned closer, out of breath. His mouth was poised an inch from her own and, involuntarily, her lips parted to receive him, when raucous interruption shattered that second's pregnancy to bring him to his senses and, in a scramble, to his feet.

A band of his fellows impinged upon his stricken sight their faces converging in one immense and loathsome grin.

Hell and damnation.

Paroxysmal fury possessed him, directed, inexcusably, at her. . . . She and her bloody wasp! This *would* happen.

Blast!

They were barging down upon the pair of them. What had they seen, or hadn't they?

They were kicking at a football. Seizing his satchel he made a dash for it to join them: and now they were one swarming indistinguishable mass of bodies, arms and legs entwined.

She had lost him, never to see him again, never to talk French to him. Gone. Kicking at that beastly ball with a lot of horrid yelling boys. Lost. For ever.

And she didn't even know his name.

Immeasurable emptiness engulfed her.

She died a little death.

'Is that you, John? You're very late!'

'Sorry, aunt. Just coming.'

He hung his cap and satchel on the hall-stand, went to the cloak room to wash, and presented himself brushed, combed and apologetic to his aunt, or rather his father's aunt, Flora.

She was the relict of Professor A. M. Ottery, M.P., one

time assistant Secretary to the Treasury (1855-1863), lecturer on political economy at Trinity College, Cambridge, author of *A Life of Pitt, the Younger*, *The Industrial Revolution*; two brilliant, if controversial Aristophanic satires or skits, and sundry philosophical pamphlets and essays.

A man of parts and not inconsiderable means, he had married, in his middle age, a young wife and after five and twenty years of marital incompatibility, had died, leaving her besides an ample income, his house and miniature estate at Dulwich.

When Surgeon-Major Herriott was ordered to serve with the Army Medical Department in the first Afghan war, he committed his motherless young son to the care of his Aunt Flora; and since her husband had been a governor of Dulwich College, the boy was removed from his preparatory school at Hastings to become a day boarder at the more conveniently situated Alma Mater of the late Professor Ottery.

With the ladies of her acquaintance, for whom Mrs Ottery had little use and no time, she had earned the reputation of an eccentric, who wore garments rather than gowns of bilious greens and yellows, with her hair flowing on her shoulders or done up in a Grecian knot bound with a fillet.

Her house was a rendez-vous for the latest disciples of the New Aesthetic Movement. Her patronage extended to the dying-hard remnants of the Pre-Raphaelites and the literary lions of previous decades, still lustily roaring their verse and prose to the *élite*, no less than to an astonished bourgeoisie. These, inspired by example, were tempted to fling to the winds, or the sale-rooms, their Albertian-cum-mid-Victorian hideosities of mahogany furnishings and wax fruit and flowers in glass cases in favour of wallpapers by Morris and the reproduced walnut of Annish days. They replaced their Stags at Bay and Monarchs of the Glen with Whistleresque riverscapes in greys and mauves, or Burne-Jonesy melancholic damsels climbing ladders. Their bookshelves, discarding Scott and Dickens, displayed the works of Walter Pater, urging long-haired pale youths 'to burn always with this hard gem-like flame'.

Mrs Ottery, whose eyelids were a little weary and her smile enigmatic, collected major and minor poets, poetasters, porcelain, the lame dogs of Bohemia and decorative cats.

His Great Aunt Flora's varied predilections were regarded by young Herriott with supreme contempt. Only under duress could he be persuaded to attend her conversaziones, those functions where she gathered together the embryonic stars of a galaxy that in a later decade would dazzle the world, and whose names, almost forgotten in the early twentieth century, would be reverentially remembered by a few left-over aged devotees, the Hot Gospellers of the Decadence, the apotheosis of *Fin de Siècle*.

On this July day in the late 'seventies, while John finished his luncheon served by an elderly butler, his aunt, who had recently become a vegetarian, toyed with a salad and said:

'John. I have had a letter from Herr Professor Schwarzkopf who writes that he will be in London next week and suggests you return to Bonn with him the week after. This I consider to be an act of Providence. I have abhorred the thought of your taking that long journey alone.'

'Why?' John tendered the look, half teasing, wholly fond, he especially reserved for her. 'Do you think I'll be seduced on the train by some amorous fat Frau who will change my langour and lilies of virtue for the rapture and roses of vice?'

'We are not amused,' his aunt said coldly, 'at your lamentable Philistinism that mocks at the exquisite voice of the Master. Have you been reading my advance copy of *Poems and Ballads* – recently published and inscribed to me by Him?' She spoke of Him as if He were deifical. 'Where did you find them?'

'Treacle tart or raspberry mousse?' was murmured in John's ear.

'I came across them –' said John, helping himself to liberal tart – 'this'll do to get on with, Simpson. I'll sample the raspberry thing afterwards if I've room for it. You want to know where I found this latest effort of your masterly Algernon Charles, Aunt? In the library when I went to look up the chapter on poisons in *Squire's British Pharmacopoeia,* and I came across your inscribed *Poems and Ballads,* bookmarked in purple satin at the page about Dolores, so I didn't have to read old Squire's poisons. A page or two of Dolores was enough to lay out a regiment. I felt as if I'd been forcibly fed a dozen cream buns plus roast pork stuffed with arsenic and those black sturgeon's roes you hand out at dinner parties. I've always wondered, by the way, which General Hamlet had in mind when he spoke of caviare. I suppose I'm one of the millions who *aren't* pleased because I was very nearly sick all over Dolores, but I managed to get out in time.'

'You disgust me.' His aunt eyed him with the utmost disfavour. 'I trust you will not give expression to these would be humorous vulgarisms at dinner tonight. Swinburne will be there and three others. I don't like odd numbers so I wish you to make a sixth at table. You will wear the new black velvet dinner jacket I have had made for you to take to Germany.'

'Oh, Lord, Aunt! Must I? What about my prep.?'

'Your prep., as you call it, can wait.'

'But,' he demurred, 'if I'm to go to Bonn with the Herr Professor the week after next – and that'll be just after we break up – I shan't get any holidays.'

'At your age,' his aunt told him in her silvery monotone, 'all of life is a holiday, a multiplied consciousness of new impressions in this short day of frost and sun between dawn's awakening and our long evening's sleep.'

To which John, in silence, submitted one epithetical word.

Rising from her seat, Mrs Ottery leaned over him to sweep aside a lock of hair on his forehead.

'Your father,' she said sighingly, 'should never have allowed you to jump five barred gates and follow hounds almost before you had lost your milk teeth. And now you will carry that scar to your grave as the token of barbarous blood sports. Don't bolt your food. I shall expect you to receive with me at seven o'clock tonight. What is it, Angel?' This to a fawn coloured cat with eyes of a startling blue set in a chocolate mask. It was uttering mournful banshee-like howls. 'Did it want its dinner, then? I hope cook saved the chicken livers for Angelico, Simpson?'

'I will inquire, madam.'

'Come with mother, darling.'

She wafted away followed by the demanding cat that cast baleful looks at the grinning John. He, having sampled the raspberry thing, got up and unfastened the two lower buttons of his waistcoat, breathing out.

'That's better. I'm full as a goat. I say, Simpson?'

'Sir?'

'Do you –' he walked to the french window that opened on to the terrace with steps down to the garden and, twisting the tassel of the blind in his fingers, asked casually – 'do you happen to know anyone of the name of Todd in Dulwich?'

'There's Todd, the grocers in the High Street, Master John. We gets our groceries from there. I don't know of any other of that name.'

'All right. Doesn't matter.'

He went out into the garden. Grocers. Probably their . . . No, but she *couldn't* be their servant, or could she? Anyway, just as well that he was going to Bonn earlier than had been arranged – week after next, so no chance of seeing her again and he didn't want to, except that it would have been useful to brush up his French. Yes, her eyes *were* like that beastly cat's, but actually she was more like one of those girls with a goitre Rossetti used to paint with that wiry hair and droopy mouth – only much younger, of course, than that model of his who was supposed to be his wife. Didn't she commit suicide or something? He'd heard Aunt Flora talking about it. She used to know Rossetti and his wife. Bit off the top. They all were. And now he'd got to go to that damn dinner tonight in a black velvet – Gosh! Good thing he was getting out of it. He'd bet those Germans didn't go in for that crackpot arty stuff. Lot o' – and again he repeated, but this time not silently, that same epithetical word.

John Herriott was not the only one that day to be interested in the name of Todd. When, having done justice to Martha's cottage pie and spotted dog, and while the elder Todd took his afternoon nap in his easy chair with a bandana handkerchief over his face and a bottle of port at his elbow, his son, in his office that adjoined the dining-room, was going through his weekly accounts.

To him came his manager, Button, a gloomy man of limited vocabulary, to present him with a card.

'Someone t'see you.'

Interrupted in his checking of a column of figures, Jo goggled at the card which read:

Messrs Chitterling, Bealby Son and Chitterling Solicitors
King's Bench Walk
London, W.C.

'What the – what's he want?'

'Didn't say.'

Jo exhibited unease.

'Solicitor, eh? Maybe something to do with that deal at Sydenham. There's a firm o' solicitors name of Todd in Garland Street, Soho,* acting for the vendor who sold me the lease of this property – sent one o' their partners here without warning. No relation of us. Tried to come it over me, and this is another of 'em, wouldn't wonder. Well, I've made my offer less two undred of the asking price. They can take it or leave it. . . . Oh, all right. Better show im in.'

A stout frock-coated gentleman with a brief case in one hand, a shiny top hat in the other, and an ingratiating smile on his moon-shaped face was shown in.

'Mr Todd. Mr Joseph Todd?'

'Yes. Well?'

'The name,' said the smiling gentleman, 'is Chitterling of Chitterling, Bealby Son and Chitterling, solicitors.'

'So I see.' Eyeing with suspicion the card he still held, Jo grudgingly indicated a chair. 'If it's to do with the executors' sale of the shop at Sydenham, I can tell you—'

'My dear sir,' suavely interposed Mr Chitterling, 'you are labouring under a misapprehension with regard to my visit.' Placing his hat on the floor and himself in the chair he opened his brief case, drew from it a file of documents and said: 'I am instructed on the part of a client to inquire on behalf of the daughter of the late – hem –' the smile suitably evaporated – 'recently deceased Mrs – ah – White.'

'Mrs White?' In Jo's repetition of the name, wonderment was diluted with relief that no attempt to 'come it over him' in his intended purchase of the shop at Sydenham appeared to be apparent. 'What do you want to know about Martha – that's to say er daughter?'

'The late Mrs White, as she chose to be named –' insinuated Mr Chitterling; and paused.

'What d'you mean *chose* to be named?' belligerently

* See *Peridot Flight.*

demanded Mr Todd. 'She *was* Mrs White – a widow, wasn't she?'

'No, sir.' Mr Chitterling assumed a far-away look. 'The deceased was not a widow. She was unmarried and her name was not – White.'

'Here!' Jo turned a dusky red. 'Unmarried, not a widow – a false name – what you getting at? I ope you're not casting Haspersions on that poor soul who can't defend erself.'

'Far be it from me,' he was pacifically assured, 'to cast equivocal reflections on the memory of that unfortunate lady who was the victim of circumstance rather than – ahem – unorthodox intent.'

To which Jo emitted a sound like a snort, while Mr Chitterling, adjusting spectacles upon his bulbous nose, referred to the file of documents.

'The lady known to you as Mrs White was a native of France as you are doubtless aware, and whose daughter, we understand, resides with you. Some years ago,' pursued Mr Chitterling, leafing through his papers, 'the lady, known to you as – hem – as Mrs White, was then living with her parents in the town of Orleans in France, where she made the acquaintance of a young gentleman who was at that time resident with a French family for the furtherance of his knowledge of the language, prior to his admission as an undergraduate of Oxford University. He was then – let me see – yes, eighteen years of age, a few months older than the young lady, Mademoiselle Marie Blanche de Lamotte, with whom our client became – enamoured. One must make allowance for the impulses of youth,' was the magnanimous suggestion, answered by a glare from Jo and the words:

'All right. Get on with it.'

Getting hurriedly on with it: 'That young gentleman, now our client,' said Mr Chitterling, 'on whose behalf we are called upon to act, is the son and heir of a member of the British aristocracy. The young lady, Mademoiselle de Lamotte, was the daughter of a reputable Huguenot family. The Huguenots, as you know, are French Protestants.'

This information which Jo did not know, was silently digested.

'The friendship between Mademoiselle de Lamotte and our future client—'

'Who *is* he?' came the inevitable question.

'His name,' Mr Chitterling said blandly, 'I am not at liberty to disclose. I was about to say that the friendship between these two ripened into a betrothal unknown to the young lady's parents. Their meetings, perforce, were clandestine for it seems that a marriage had been arranged by the lady's father with another suitor – of his choice, not hers. When in due course our client returned to England, a correspondence between him and his secretly affianced, ensued. Mademoiselle de Lamotte kept his letters of which we are now in possession. They express indubitable evidence of his intention to finalize the betrothal with marriage. The discovery of her likelihood to become a mother – pray hear me out, Mr Todd – occasioned a crisis in her family which resulted in her expulsion from the parental roof. It appears that the young lady had a small legacy bequeathed her by her grandmother, and on this she subsisted when she took refuge with an old nurse at Lille until, some few months after her daughter was born, she came to England. Her small means were soon exhausted, and, on her arrival in London, she made every effort to communicate with her betrothed at Oxford, who had failed to reply to her letters informing him of her condition and, ultimately, that he was the father of their child. Alas,' sighed Mr Chitterling, 'it is here that – hem – a – er – Nemesis, intervened—'

'A Mrs Who?' plunged in Jo.

'Nemesis,' Mr Chitterling indulgently explained, 'was the goddess of retribution.'

'I don't Hold with eathens,' muttered Jo.

'A mere figure of speech, sir. The young lady paid dearly for her – her indiscretion. The letters informing our client of her plight were not received by him. He had suffered serious injury in the hunting field and lay for some weeks at death's door in a coma.' Gazing over his spectacles at a point above Todd's head: 'The letters of his affianced,' said Mr Chitterling, 'were intercepted by our client's father who,' his tone held a note of near apology, 'had every reason to do so since, in the event of his son's recovery, the possibility of an action for breach of promise and the maintenance of a child of doubtful parentage might threaten his son's honour should the letters written by a Frenchwoman, of whom nothing whatsoever was known, be publicized to bring about a scandal attached to a famous name. Surely, Mr Todd, you can understand a parent's natural anxiety in these unhappy circumstances?'

'No,' said Jo hotly, 'I *don't* understand. When this son of his came out of his coma or whatever he was in, why didn't his father show him the letters and let Him deal with them?'

'Because, sir, our client's father had very properly disposed of the lady's letters, since, at the time of his son's recovery he was still a minor and entitled to his father's protection against that which, for want of evidence to the contrary, he believed to be an attempt to obtain maintenance, or marriage, under false pretences.' And as Jo opened his mouth preparatory to further heated intervention, 'However, these,' said the lawyer briskly, 'are but preliminaries to the main purpose of my visit.'

Resorting again to his brief case he produced a bulky packet tied with red tape. 'I have here –' he unfastened the tape, and took from it an envelope containing – 'the copy of a letter,' said Chitterling, looking over his spectacles at the glowering Jo, 'written to our client from the deceased – and – hem – let me see now. Um. Yes. In this letter which our client has translated from the French for our convenience, Miss da La – Mrs White, tells him that as she had received no acknowledgement to her previous communications advising him of the birth of their daughter, she had believed herself to be deserted. But knowing her end was near she again approached our client to entreat that he make provision for his child. She enclosed a photograph of the young girl taken about a year ago—'

Jo nodded. 'Yes, she did have her photo taken last year—'

'—and which,' continued Mr Chitterling, 'dispels any doubt cast upon our client's parentage. The likeness to himself is remarkable. This letter, the last before her death from Mrs – hem – White was sent to our client's College at Oxford, the address he had given her after his return to England from France, and was forwarded from there to the House of Commons. He,' said Mr Chitterling impressively, 'was elected a Member of Parliament in Mr Disraeli's ministry of 1874, and this letter and the photograph,' he laid a stumpy finger on the packet, 'were not received by our client until three weeks ago, because when they arrived he was in the United States paying a prolonged visit to his wife's parents. He is married to an American lady.'

Jo gave another snort.

'So he's married, is he? With no intent, seemingly, to right the wrong he done to that poor woman who he betrayed when she was little older than his daughter is now. Fine Member of Parliament, I'll say, and not much credit to the Tories.'

These asides on the part of Mr Todd, that had in them something of the nature of a Greek chorus, did not at all disturb the serenity of Mr Chitterling.

'Our client's private secretary opened the packet and, perceiving the – the intimate nature of the correspondence, he did not forward the letter to our client in

America lest it should cause embarrassment were it opened in the presence of his wife. However, immediately on his return to England, our client, having learned that his father had become possessed of and destroyed the letters the deceased had written to him during his illness fourteen years ago – for he, in his turn, had believed himself forgotten or his fiancée forced into a marriage arranged for by her father – he at once instructed us to make inquiries concerning the child whom Mademoiselle de La – hem – Mrs White had claimed to be his. She had given him your address, Mr Todd, with the result that our investigations have ascertained that the child has been in your care ever since her mother's death.'

'Investigations, eh?' Jo's eyes bulged. 'You've been having me spied on by detectives, have you? I thought I seen a big fellow with large flat feet anging about the shop last week and getting matey with my Hassistants.'

'We have our methods,' smiled Mr Chitterling, 'and I must tell you that our inquiries have satisfied our client that you, Mr Todd, are a suitable guardian for the welfare of the child whom he now acknowledges to be his natural daughter. This being so he has instructed us to draw up a settlement in her favour for the sum of two thousand pounds.'

'Two . . . Good life!' Jo, whose face at this staggering announcement was sterilized of all expression save that of incredulity, emitted a strangled echo of it: 'Two . . . thou . . .'

The return of Mr Chitterling's smile was beatific.

'The said sum to be held by my partner and myself as joint trustees of the settlement until the child shall become of age or, in the event of her marriage, then the capital under the present law that concedes no right of property to a married woman, will revert absolutely to her husband.'

'Well, I'm – Well!' ejaculated the dumbfounded chorus. 'She'll be a good catch for someone.'

'With the approval,' Mr Chitterling suavely amended, 'of whomsoever shall be her guardian should she still be a minor at the time of her marriage. It seems that the child's mother,' scrutinizing the letter he held, 'has expressed the wish that you, Mr Todd, will continue to undertake the charge of her daughter during her minority for she cannot bear the thought, she says – as translated by our client – "that my little girl be left homeless or placed in an orphanage".' He looked up at the goggled-eyed Jo. 'We are therefore further instructed by our client that the sum of one hundred and fifty pounds per annum be paid quarterly to you on his behalf, and—'

'A hundred and . . . Gawd!' came the chorused interruption. 'He must be another Lord Shaftesbury!'

'– for the upkeep and education of the girl, Thérèse Marthe de Lamotte, whose education, our client understands, has been, so far, elementary and, always providing that you, Mr Todd, agree to undertake the guardianship of this infant—'

'Infant!' burst forth Jo. 'She's rising fifteen!'

Mr Chitterling's smile expanded.

'She is still, in legal terms, an infant, but if you are not disposed to undertake such guardianship, then she must become a Ward in Chancery.'

'That! Never!' Jo banged a fist on the table to bruise his knuckles. 'While I'm Here Martha stays with me . . . Along of a undred and fifty a year,' was the silently gratified reminder of the chorus.

'There is just one more point – hem – ye-es,' Mr Chitterling refreshed his memory with a perusal of more documents. 'Regarding the child's education, we are instructed to secure the services of a governess to attend her daily, that is to say for five mornings a week. The allowance of one hundred and fifty pounds in addition to the interest derived from the trust should suffice to cover all expenses, including the salary of the governess. And we must ask you to render us a quarterly account of all expenditure incurred. The – hem – circumstances under which the governess is engaged by us on behalf of you, the child's guardian, must be, you understand, strictly confidential. We believe we can rely on your discretion.'

'I'm not one to blab about anything likely to do arm to Martha or her dead mother,' said Jo surlily. . . . Two – no, three undred and fifty – with the interest on it – should suffice, I should think so, and good luck to her! approved the silent chorus. We'll have to move from ere, Won't do for her to live over the shop. There's that premises at Wimbledon coming up for auction and a nice little ouse in a village nearby. Just do for me an Martie and the old man with a woman to live in. She'll not do no more cooking. A governess! But take it by and large that's the least he could do. . . .

'I think there's nothing more, at present to be discussed,' said Mr Chitterling, who was now returning his files to his brief case preparatory to departure. 'An agreement setting forth your acceptance of the charge of the child will be drawn up by us and will require your signature in the presence of witnesses, which, I suggest, should be signed at our office.' And he, who, during these transactions must have hemmed his throat raw, rose to his feet. 'You do understand – do you not? – that the utmost privacy must be maintained with regard to our proposal, and I must impress upon you that one of the conditions insisted upon by our client is that his daughter and yourself shall remain in ignorance of her father's identity. All communications now and in the future must be referred to us. I apologize for taking up so much of your time, Mr Todd, but these matters cannot be effected without – hem – the most careful consideration.' He retrieved his hat from the floor and held out his hand. Jo placed a sweating palm in it. 'You will be hearing again from us shortly. Good day to you, sir.'

Relinquishing the hand, Jo found voice to say:

'Will you take a cup o' tea before you go?'

'I thank you, but I am due back at the office. I have an appointment for five o'clock and am late as it is. *Good* afternoon.' With smiling affability he made for the door.

'I'll see you down,' said Jo.

THREE

The explanation offered to Martha by Jo Todd to account for her change of circumstances from an orphaned waif dependent upon charity to that of Mr 'Toddy's' ward, was received by her with the incurious acceptance of the very young.

'Your mother was always careful with her money – the French are, you know – and she saved enough with what your poor father left her' – this was near enough the truth to salve Jo's Methodist conscience – 'to leave you comfortable. See? And before she went to the Orspital she asked me to look after you should anything appen to her while you was what they call a minor, that's under twenty-one. And,' went on Jo, encouraged by Martha's wide-eyed silence, 'she also asked to have you Heducated – on what she's left you. See?'

'Not to school!' Martha's face crumpled. 'I don't want to go to school again. They didn't like me where I went to school in Pimlico because I'm half French.'

'You don't have to go to school if you don't want. We'll get you a governess.' Jo was thankful for this loophole to bring in the governess, for he had misgivings as to how she would take it.

'A governess – to give me lessons? Oh, Maman!' she covered her face. 'How she worked so hard to save for me!'

'Yes,' Jo breathed thankfulness, having cleared that hurdle. 'You was her one and only thought – to leave you comfortable and to know you'd be brought up ladylike. And I'm appy to have you to look after as if you was me daughter. So that's how it is, you see.'

And that's how it was; and if Martha were not quite so happy as Jo to be looked after by him as if she was his daughter, she continued to accept, as one accepts a climate, conditions that permitted no attempt at contravention.

But when the same semi-fiction was offered to the older Todd, his response to it was anything but happy.

'To think she'd been 'oardin' all this time and fobbed the kid off on us for board and keep and you payin' 'er twenty quid a year wages while most of 'em are lucky to get ten! 'Ow much did that lawyer feller say she left?'

'Enough to pay for the governess, and what's over won't put me out o' pocket,' Jo said equably.

His father slid him a narrow look.

'A lump sum, was it?'

'Yes, but she can't touch it till she comes of age or marries. It's in trust funds with the solicitors. It was left to her mother,' manufactured Jo, 'by her – by Martha's grandmother.'

'Trust funds, eh? Then it's somethink more than sixpence! I always thought that woman was a bit fishy. The French! Always out to do you down. Till she comes of age or marries, eh? If so her husband gets it. Come on. 'Ow much?'

Jo began to feel himself in deeper waters.

'Coupla hundred, maybe.'

'Coupla 'undred! What's that for her board and keep if it's invested? Ten quid a year. Fat lot o' use that! Won't 'ardly pay the char let alone a governess. Governess! The board school was good enough for me, and I paid a bob a week private for you and *that* didn't put you into grocery. It's brines what does it and not all the schoolin' or governessin' is goin' to get *'er* on in life, me lad. And if that kid's got to earn 'er livin' when she's twenty-one unless she marries—'Ere!' His father was off on another tack. 'Coupla 'undred, you said—'

'About that. Will isn't proved yet,' muttered Jo, sinking deeper.

'Well, then – might be more, and I bet it is. Blimey!' His father's head jerked up. 'If it ain't worth gettin' some of your own back to marry 'er yerself afore she's twenty-one sooner than let some Tom Dick or 'Arry collar the lot! Say it *is* only two 'undred – there's a nice little 'ouse advertised in this week's Mercury for twenty quid per annum and that 'ud pay ten year's rent – free!'

This suggestion concerning Martha's marriage had already crossed Jo's mind; and that the 'coupla hundred' was, in actuality, multiplied by ten, might indeed be worth getting his own back with a house rented at *twice* twenty pounds a year! That shop at Wimbledon – coming up for auction. No opposition there and a classy neighbourhood. In two years' time she'd be rising seventeen . . . a marriageable age. One could get a mortgage on the freehold and pay it off gradual with a tidy sum left over to rent that little house nearby. He'd had a look at it, going on a ninety-nine years' lease. Might be worth an offer to buy. . . . But even as the thought that had lain dormant in some dark recess of his inner man, reared itself to strike at him, he loudly refuted it.

Hot in the face Jo rounded on his father.

'You keep your big mouth shut! I'm Martha's legal guardian, signed and sealed, and until she comes of age she don't marry without my consent. Not one penny of her money, little enough though it is' – he edged that in to be on the safe side – 'will anyone lay ands on till I say so, see? I wish I hadn't told you now, only you'd be going on about the governess which these lawyers who are the trustees for the – the grandmother's legacy are to get for her and pay her salary out of the trust.' (Better not let on about that one fifty to be paid to him quarterly for her keep and extras, and *not* out of the trust.) 'So at that rate there won't be much left from that bit o' capital in six years' time. In any case I'd been thinking about moving from here. It's too small with only one living-room and Martha to have lessons in as well. I've heard of a freehold property at Wimbledon, and a nice little house at Coombe village near there, too. It's a leasehold up to 1977. You can always sublet a long lease.'

His father came out of his smoke screen to say:

'Wimbledon? You mean Sydenham, don't you?'

'Both,' said Jo shortly; and drawing forward a chair opposite his father, and leaning forward, he planted his hands on his knees: capable square hands with spatulate fingers. 'In this business it's expansion that counts. You can't make a livin' out of one or two shops in suburban High streets. No, nor a name, neether. You've got to ave a *name* in business – a name that everyone knows, and I'm out to make a name. I've got six shops and if I'm spared till the end o' the century and I'll only be in me fifties then, I'll have not six but six Hundred shops, and not only in the suburbs, but all over London, and in Liverpool, Manchester, Birmingham. There's money to burn in the Midlands and the industrial north. I'll be another Lipton before I've done. He started as an errand boy same as me, and now look at him! I'll have Todd's Teas and Toasties blazing on the buses and in every grocer's in the country. And when I'm gone my name'll live on. I'll be a company with a board o' directors and me the chairman, and the stock markets booming Todd's! There's no end to what you can do with a name and an – anitiative. I've got the anitiative and I've already got a name in my small way which'll be a big way in twenty years' time. I believe in aiming High.'

His father took his pipe out of his mouth to say:

'Them as aims too 'igh can overshoot the mark, and there's only one in a million 'its the bullseye. Still, it's none o' my business. This 'igh falutin' talk ain't my cup o' tea.'

'No,' Jo grinned at him. 'It's Todd's!'

* * *

It appears that Mr Chitterling found some difficulty in following his client's instructions to engage a governess for Martha. The various applicants who answered his advertisement for a daily situation in the neighbourhood of Dulwich and who were interviewed by their prospective employer, Mr Todd, declined the situation. The reasons given for refusal bore a certain similarity. None would undertake tuition of a child where no amenities, such as a schoolroom or private apartment set aside for lessons, seemed to be available. Moreover, and this the most serious deterrent, none would wish to have any connection with a grocer's establishment. One indignant lady of impeccable references, complained to Mr Chitterling that Mr Todd, having made an appointment for interview, had been delayed, and that a person who said he was Mr Todd's father had received her – in his shirt sleeves and smoking a disgusting pipe! She had not seen her prospective pupil, but was told that she would have to teach her in the room which was their parlour for there was no other, and that as he, this person, was at home, he said, most days, she wouldn't have to mind if *he* took lessons with her, too! A most unpleasant individual. Very common. Not at all what *she* had been used to.

'That settles it, then!' Jo decided, when Mr Chitterling informed him of these ladies' several objections. 'We'll *have* to move.' And even before the contracts for the property at Sydenham were exchanged, he at once made an offer, not only for the shop at Wimbledon, but for the leasehold of the house within easy distance of it, in the village of Coombe.

Three months later the Todds and Martha were installed in their new home that to her, accustomed to the cramped quarters of the house over the Dulwich shop, impregnated with the fumes of the elder Todd's shag, was paradisiacal.

Built of mellowed brick in the days of the second George it boasted six rooms and attics, a garden in front with a lawn the size of a pocket handkerchief, a long flower-filled garden behind with fruit trees where apples glowed among the leaves like little red moons, or so it seemed to Martha, and a rose-clad porch with a plaque above it bearing the name Rose Cottage, and the date, 1750.

Martha's bedroom communicated with what was to be her schoolroom, and the walls of both, as well as those of the two rooms on the ground floor, were panelled, and Martha had all to do to persuade Jo not to have them papered – 'or at least not mine. I won't have those ugly blue and red cabbages on my walls like you have in the parlour at Dulwich.'

'But,' objected Jo, 'I can't leave them all dirty and cracked. Those panels want plastering up. They've not been touched since the house was built more'n a hundred years ago.'

'Well then, have them painted,' Martha said.

'They'll look like an orspital,' demurred Jo; but he had them painted.

He had noticed, of late, indeed since she had come into her money, or more correctly since *he* had come into her money, that she was, as he put it, getting a bit above herself. 'Highty-tighty, if you please!' This he confided to Ted, home on leave shortly after the removal. She would have this or she wouldn't have that, but blood – he supposed – would out. To Ted, in strictest confidence, he had imparted the circumstances of her birth and the arrangements made for her by her natural father. 'One of the nobility, according to his lawyer, but don't you on your life, let on to the old man.'

'Not likely. It's funny, you know,' meditated Ted, 'I always thought there was something about her – *and* her mother. I guessed they came of good stock. I wonder who her father is. You'd think he'd want, at least, to *see* her, wouldn't you?'

Jo shook his head.

'He's married, and I expect he wants to keep it dark that he's got a child by another woman. How's he to know she wouldn't come forcing herself on him and his wife? Some would, when they're old enough.'

'Martha wouldn't,' said Ted.

Jo shot him a look. A fine figure of a lad – brown of face, sturdy, well-spoken – Jo must mind his aitches. They would keep on slipping. Ted spoke like a proper gentleman. Well, he was, wasn't he? An officer, if not in the Royal Navy as near as dammit. Mixing with all those swells on those liners. He'd be captain one of these days. Suppose he should take to Martha? Not as he did now, treating her like a kid, but – later on. Anyway no one, not even his own brother, could marry her without his consent before she's of age. Good thing he hadn't let on exactly how much the settlement amounted to, but he did let Ted know about the one fifty a year for her keep.

Ted had taken Martha to London again to see another of those musical plays. The harmonium had been moved into an attic, on Ted's advice, and he had actually bought her a piano! Got it knocked down to him cheap at a sale. Ted had always wanted a piano and could strum anything by ear. So could Martha; and there were the two of them at it, playing chopsticks, and Ted strumming tunes from one of those Gilbert and somebody's operas called 'Trial by Jury', and which, according to Ted, was all a skit about a breach of promise case. Not right for a child to know. And: 'Mind you get her a governess who can teach her music as well as the three R's,' were Ted's parting words to Jo; and he swung Martha off her feet and kissed her soundly on both cheeks, and said: 'Goodbye, little sister, for you are my little sister now.'

'Rum sort o' relationship,' grunted Jo. 'I'm not her father. Nor yours.'

'As good as – to both of us,' laughed Ted.

There had been no difficulty now since their removal to Coombe, in finding a governess for Martha. Jo saw to it that, during interviews with applicants sent by Mr Chitterling, his father should be invisible or at the Crown and Anchor to which venue he had gravitated as to a home from home.

A Miss Cecilia Hore was Mr Chitterling's final selection. The daughter of a clergyman, she lived in the village with her widowed mother, was in her late thirties, and had taught a succession of pupils during the last fifteen years of whom Martha was the fifth.

The elder Todd, who, despite his son's precautions, had encountered this lady on the first day of her tutelage as she left the house after morning lessons, had received a frigid reply of his greeting, 'Pleased to meet you, Miss. P'raps you could teach me a thing or two. I'm not too old to learn!' and gave jocular vent to his cronies in the Crown and Anchor of his grievance in that: 'She don't answer to 'er name. I'd 'opes of somethink spicy with the name of 'Ore! But there's as much spice in *'er* as in a dried 'addock!'

This went down very well with the bar but not so well with Jo, who happened to have seen and overheard his father's approach to the estimable Miss Hore.

'I told you not to show yourself or have any words with the governess. I'm not going to lose any more o' them because of you, and if she goes, then *you* go, see?'

Which threat sufficed for the elder Todd to keep out of the way of Miss Hore and seek consolation with one Florrie, who served the saloon bar at the Crown with their requirements and much diverting back-chat.

Miss Hore, daughter of the late Reverend Nicholas Hore, M. A., Cantab., one time Vicar of a good living in Kent, had acquired an education something more than was accorded to the average governess of almost a century ago.

She was sandy-haired, with high cheekbones, long teeth inclined to project, and her existence, when not centred on attendance to her *malade imaginaire* of a mother, was conscientiously devoted to imparting information to the young. She found in Martha an apt and willing pupil who imbibed knowledge with the avidity of a fledgling with an ever open maw greedily devouring the worms fed to it by its mother bird.

If during this current year Martha would sometimes wonder what had happened to the nameless boy who had treated her so kindly for that wasp sting – and how good of him to suck the poison out, causing her slight breathlessness at the remembrance – and it he were still in Germany, or where? And if she would ever see him again, which of course she never would now that she had left Dulwich; or if he had found some French girl to talk French to him only that it wouldn't be French in Germany; or if in daydreams, she saw herself walking hand in hand in an Elysian – or Dulwich? – field with a godlike being modelled on the image of Apollo, for she had delved into Lemprière with Miss Hore, she dismissed such idle fancies as unbecoming and silly for one who, at last, had become a young lady.

When this belated transformation occurred, of which she had been given no previous warning either by her mother or Miss Hore, whose instruction did not include the facts of life, she was terribly frightened and took her discovery to Mrs Bilson, for that lady had accompanied them from Dulwich to Coombe, which she was glad to do when approached by Jo with the suggestion, since, she assured him, she'd be doing Martha a good turn for it didn't do for her to live alone in the house with two men – not that she didn't think everything wasn't straight and above board but it was as well to have a woman about the place especially as Mr Todd's father – a knowing wink accompanied the unfinished innuendo.

So to Mrs Bilson Martha took her apprehensions concerning a 'something dreadful' that had happened to her, shouted into Mrs Bilson's ear, and having been reassured that: 'It's about time too, and you can read it in the Bible though why the Good Book calls it the flowers, dear knows.' And satisfied that she was not singled out for judgement, having read, as forbidden by Miss Hore, Shakespeare's *Venus and Adonis, Measure for Measure* and *Jane Eyre*, found among the miscellany of books in the bookcase, and much worse – for which God would surely punish her – she had sneaked out to the Fair on Wimbledon Common, Whit Monday, when there were no lessons, for Miss Hore had also taken a holiday that day; and when asked by 'Mr Toddy' where she had been all the afternoon, she said she had been doing her homework – writing an essay on Pope.

'On the Pope?' ejaculated Jo, profoundly shocked. 'Is Miss Hore R.C.?'

'Pope, the poet,' replied Martha, stifling giggles. 'I am writing an essay on the poets,' which was, regrettably, apocryphal: nor had she read more of Pope than a few quotations carefully selected by Miss Hore. 'He was a very great poet, although not in size for Miss Hore says he was a hunchbacked dwarf, and he wrote: "Know thou thyself, presume not God to scan, the proper study of mankind is man." I'm trying to know myself, only,' she innocently added, 'I've not much chance here, of knowing man – or men.'

And now what? Jo uneasily reflected. Proper study of mankind, indeed! So if *that's* what she learns from Miss Hore the sooner I make a change the better.

It seemed almost providential when Miss Hore's mother succumbed to her one illness that was not imaginary.

A month later Miss Hore apologetically gave in her notice. There had been 'an understanding' she conveyed with blushes, between herself and a cousin twice removed. He was a curate, and assisted the Vicar of St Saviour's, Brixton. While her mother lived she could not have left her, but now, she much regretted . . . if Mr Todd would excuse her . . .

Mr Todd did excuse her: and, if not quite so regretful as Miss Hore professed to be, he was in a quandary. Should he seek another governess or send Martha to school? The latter suggestion met with Miss Hore's approval, who recommended the Misses Merridew's establishment at Dover – 'which is in the nature of a finishing school, as the average age of the pupils is from fourteen to eighteen. Martha is well enough advanced now to enter as a senior pupil or parlour boarder.'

Martha rebelled. A boarding school! No. She didn't want to go to school again. Mr Toddy had promised, hadn't he? – that she wouldn't have to go to school.

So for a while the decision remained in abeyance.

Before Miss Hore left she advised Martha not only to continue her studies but to keep a journal.

'It will increase your powers of observation to write of daily happenings, no matter how trivial, and be a source of interest to you in future years. Although your spelling still leaves much to be desired, your essays show an aptitude for composition. I too,' confessed Miss Hore, 'keep a journal, and in the last century it was almost an invariable custom for young ladies to write what is called a Commonplace Book.'

Yet, as events transpired, Martha's journal plush-covered, supplied with a little lock and key and presented to her by Miss Hore as a parting gift, proved to be anything but commonplace.

* * *

She felt lost without Miss Hore, to whom she had become attached, and had enjoyed her lessons; but now she was again forced to endure the almost continuous company of the elder Todd. He, who during Miss Hore's governance, had been kept out of the schoolroom, would invade her sanctum and plant himself in an armchair while she endeavoured to obey Miss Hore's instructions to continue her studies; and, seated there, he would watch her and smoke his pipe and pass disturbing remarks, with that leering look of his, to the effect that she was coming on a treat, and 'ud be a plump little partridge to take a bite out of with more flesh on 'er bones than her pore mother ever 'ad. . . . 'A nice tasty little piece you'll be.'

And he would lean over her and fumble at her breasts, breathing in her face his foul breath that stank of tobacco and stale drink. And she loathed him, and would tell herself that she wished he were dead – or for preference that *she* were dead. For what had she to live for? Nothing and nobody. She didn't belong to anyone.

All very well for Mr Toddy to call himself her guardian, he was seldom at home, and if he were at home she couldn't talk to him of things that mattered like books and history – the Wars of the Roses or Christopher Columbus, or the Trojan wars, or anything she had learned with Miss Hore, for he was always full of his business, and when not talking to his father about his shops he was for ever arguing – the two of them together – on politics. During meals she would hear her Mr Toddy speaking of Lord Beaconsfield as if he were God and how he had been thrown over, as he said, 'for your mealy mouthed Gladstone who brought us to the brink of war with Russia, and his bribe to the voters to abolish income tax. 'And didn't your precious Jew,' this from old Todd, 'say he'd abolish the income tax and then put it up even 'igher!' – 'Well, we got to get the money somehow to pay for the Zulu war,' retorted Jo. 'Costing the country five hundred thousand a month, it is, and what if the income tax does go up to sixpence in the pound, better that than lose the war to a lot o' naked savages!' – 'So long as you can 'and it out to the Jew to feather his own nest and bolster up the Queen with a lot o' smarmy talk,' would be the answer to that, 'but he won't be in to talk much longer. 'E'll be out on his arse at the election.'

Which brought Gladstone in and threw over that extraordinary being whose political genius has never been surpassed and only equalled by another who, some sixty-five years later, was to suffer similar defeat from an ungrateful electorate to whom he, too, had brought 'Peace with Honour'.

It was a time of change, a perceptible determination towards a new democracy. Imperialism and the tremendous achievements of that mummified old man drifting slowly to his end at Hughenden, his black hair white at the roots, since there was no beloved Mary Anne to dye it for him, were forgotten, swamped by the 'Passionate Pilgrimage' as his formidable rival's electoral campaign was known in the Mid-Lothians. The Queen was shocked, horrified, disgusted to learn that a man who dared aspire for a second time to be her Prime Minister could address crowds from the window of a *railway* carriage! And that her people, her country, her Empire, had so treacherously abandoned her dear Lord Beaconsfield for *him*! . . . Oh, her dear, her good Lord Beaconsfield, so ill, unable to fight his enemies for her, his 'Faery Queen'! . . . 'When we come back from Osborne,' she wrote, she would see him and she begged him to be '*very* good and obey his doctors.' And when the letter was read by the dim old eyes, in which shone a tear behind the twinkle: 'This,' he said to the faithful Corry at his bedside, 'should be read to me by a Privy Councillor.'

Martha, the merest infinitesimal speck in the apostatic upheaval that had routed the Tories and brought in the Liberals for another five years, she too was aware dimly, half resentfully and wholly curious, of an equally apostatic change in herself. The Martha she had known all her life would, at times, become another person, so strange and unfamiliar that when this happened she had to run away from It, whatever or whoever it was, or tell It to *go* – or say anything to hear her own voice. This strangeness never lasted long, but long enough to make her think that she was not herself, *not* the Martha she had known all her life, but someone else, for whose thoughts and actions she was not responsible. . . .

She was also aware, unconsciously perhaps, of a more acute observance of externals. She reacted with emotional extravagance to the trivia of familiar impressions: the shrill green of budding spring on the Common, the marvel of light and form and pattern in the swansdown drift of cloud across a sky that had never seemed so blue before; ordinary accepted things presented a new and almost magical significance. The uplift of tall tulips unfolding to the sun; a thrush singing its heart out on a branch of cherry blossom in the garden would fill her with longings for she knew not what, unaccountable desires that urged her to break away from this daily tedium of nothingness in which she seemed to be so utterly alone and lost, a stranger among strangers; and so often that shadowy other person taking her as it were out of herself into . . . nowhere. She was sick to death of shouting in the ear of Mrs Bilson – poor Mrs Bilson so dreadfully deaf – and who would incessantly sing in her high cracked voice, alternating between being Martha's sweetheart and White Wings that never Grew Weary, and of which Martha had wearied until she could scream; and then those awful meals alone with the 'old Horror' as she named the elder Todd, whose son was away on business for days at a time. He had opened a shop at Clapham now and Martha was left more than ever alone with his father, by day and night. She would often take a packet of sandwiches and a bottle of milk to Wimbledon Common, sooner than have to sit with him at table.

Her journal, for the first few weeks of the New Year, reflects the daily monotony of her life and gives no glimpse of that strange 'outsideness' as she called that unaccountable experience of impersonality; but a notable entry in her Commonplace Book under February 14th 1880 tells us:

> Saint Valentine's Day and what a day or rather night because it went on until this A.M. . . . I don't know how I am able to write about it. It's too horrible. All that I had ever dreaded without knowing why or what I dreaded has happened. No one will ever see this I hope as I keep my journal locked in my desk in the schoolroom and have hidden the key but I have to write it because Miss H. said to write of daily happennings but she could never have thought of this as a daily or rather a nightly happenning.
>
> I had supper with the old man. Mr. T. is away at the Clapham shop and hasn't been home for two nights and I noticed that the Horror was staring at me more even than usual while I ate and he made some beastly remarks about my dress getting too tight for me across the Bust which he said shows I am ripening he called it and ready for plucking – I think he said plucking only it didn't sound quite like that. I am sure he had been to the public house for I could smell that nasty smell of drinking right across the table and he drank a lot of wine with his supper and then finished up with wiskey from the decanter on the side board. He asked me to have some I said no and got up to go to my room but as I passed where he sits to get out he caught hold of me and dragged me on to him and began slobbering kisses all over my face and mouth.
>
> I strugled with him and managed to get away and I dug my nails into his hands that were feeling me right up my legs under my petticoats and he said I was a little bich but that he'd learn me to like it. He was grinning and his eyes were all red and bleary. I was terrified and rushed up to my room and locked the door but forgot

that the schoolroom door that opens into it has no key. I sat up in bed doing the embroidry for the teacloth I bought Miss H. for a wedding present and then I got sleepy and blew out my candle and said my prayers and went to sleep. I don't know how much later it was before some noise woke me up. It must have been him rattling at the locked door and then I saw him standing in the doorway of the schoolroom. Although it was dark the moon was full and I hadnt drawn my curtains. I saw him there in the moonlight which made a path across the room. He was in his night shirt and I saw his long thin legs like the legs of a stork and – this is too awful to write but I must write it – he lifted his shirt and I saw – no I cant. And he was pointing at it and I screamed and then he came lerching forward and fell on top of me. I was sqwashed under his weight and he was pulling at the neck of my nightdress and tore it open and his hands were all over me. I went on screaming and trying to push him off and I heard him say Stop that do you want all the neighbours to hear you. I am not going to hurt you I only want to have a cuddle. Come on. Let me. You'll like it. And then he pulled up my nightdress and – no, I cant write it. I went on screaming. I was pettrified with fear and hit out at him but he caught hold of my hands and pushed his horrid smelly face on mine and then I bit him. Yes I bit him on his long stick out nose and he yelled and called me a bluddy something but it gave me the chance for him to let go of me so that I could scrambel out of bed and through the schoolroom and I locked myself in the lavatory. Thank goodness Mr T. had a W.C. put in the house when we moved. There was only one outside and that doesn't lock. I could have gone to Mrs. B. in the attic but as she is so deaf he would have heard me shouting at her to explain why I was there and might have come after me. I don't know how long I sat in the W.C. but I waited till I heard him go to his room which is across the landing. Then I heard him come out of his room and try the lavatory door. Finding it locked he shouted at me to come out but I sat there and prayed he would not break down the door. Then I heard him go back to his room. I waited till the sky was getting light so I knew it was morning. It was in my mind to run away but where could I go? I did think of going to Miss Hore who lives in the village but how could I tell her of this and bother her when she is so busy getting married.

So I went out before breakfast and stayed out all day. I bought myself a bun and glass of milk at that place on the Common and waited till evening when I hoped Mr Toddy would be back and he was. And the Horror has a plaster on his nose and Heaven knows what he has told about me having bitten him for Mr T. said in a way I have never heard him speak before I want a word with you young lady and then. . . .

The entry stops abruptly here.

The word that Jo demanded was less a word than a monological indictment in which she had 'gone for' his father like a mad thing and he, having heard her shrieking in what he thought to be a nightmare, had come to wake and soothe her out of it – 'to be set upon and pummelled for his pains and bitten – on the nose! You might have done him a serious mischief. A real savage bite it was! We'll have to call the doctor in if it don't heal up. Granted you were frightened by a bad dream there was no cause to attack him – an old man come to do you a kindness – unless you was out o' your mind. What have you to say for yourself?'

She had nothing to say for herself. She heard him in silence, seething, with no defence to offer against lies told by the father to the son and which so evidently he believed.

'Bad blood,' he muttered. 'There's bad blood somewhere – whoever he was,' he added incomprehensibly; and left her.

Long she sat there, shivering, stunned with the shock of this unexpected repercussion of that attack upon her to place her in the wrong who had every right to protect herself from – what? – something frightening and dreadful he had tried to do to her and showing himself and – It!

And now again the thought possessed her that she must run away from here, from this terrible old man – but where could she go? She might take a place as a servant, or, better than that, a nursery governess. She could still speak French as well, or almost as well, as she spoke English. She might find a place where the lady would want her children to speak French, only she might be considered too young for that. And she would have to go to London, and where would she live while she looked for a post? She couldn't go to Miss Hore and lodge with her while she sought a situation. Too near home. Besides she couldn't possibly tell Miss Hore why she had run away. It was something that couldn't be told. Anyhow she hadn't enough money to get her to London, let alone find a lodging there. She was allowed ten shillings a month for pocket money by Mr Todd, and almost a whole month's allowance had already been spent on Miss Hore's teacloth and the silks for the embroidery, and threepence for sweets, and another sixpence to a poor old noseless woman selling matches in Wimbledon High Street. She wondered if the Horror would be noseless from her bite! Then she fell into the giggles and couldn't stop until she pinched herself, in fright, because that 'outsideness' feeling had begun again. O God, don't let it happen. . . . And to prevent it happening she counted what was left of her money and found exactly elevenpence ha'penny left, and a lot of use that was! She put the sixpence and five pennies and the ha'penny back in the box and, still snivelling between giggles, bethought herself of Mrs Bilson. If only she were not so deaf . . . but if she could make her hear and tell her, she might believe her and then tell Mr Toddy what had really happened and why his father had that plaster on his nose. One could but try.

She went down to the kitchen. Mrs Bilson was cooking

their supper. She approached her mouth to Mrs Bilson's ear and shouted into it: 'You didn't hear me scream last night, by any chance, did you?'

'What, dear?'

'Last night something awful happened and I *screamed*!'

Mrs Bilson's face, red and sweaty from the oven and the heat of the airless kitchen, drew away from Martha. She said, offendedly: 'You don't have to scream at me. 'T'ain't my fault if my ears get stopped up with the wax.'

Martha caught at her arm.

'Mrs Bilson, try to hear me. . . . I want to tell you. Oh, please . . . *help* me!'

And now the aftermath of shock burst from her in a torrent of turbulent sobbing.

''Ere! Now then, now then!' Mrs Bilson expressed herself in a series of sympathetic clucks. 'What is it? What's all this about?'

'It's . . . it's the old man. He . . . he . . .' blubbered Martha, 'he came to my room last night and tried to . . . I think he was drunk. He's been telling lies about me. I bit him on the . . . Oh, please, do *hear* me. . . .'

Gradually by dint of shouting between the tornado of her sobs, Mrs Bilson was given account of the previous night's episode that at last succeeded in penetrating the walls of her deafness. 'And he . . .' yelled Martha, 'he says I . . . *attacked* him. It's lies! It was *he* who attacked *me* . . . You must tell Mr Toddy what I've told you. Please. He won't believe *me*, but he may believe you. Tell him what really happened. You can tell him you *saw* it happen even if you didn't!'

'The dirty old b——er!' declared Mrs Bilson, on whom light eventually had dawned. 'We all know what 'e is. 'E'd try it on with a mangelwurzel if 'e couldn't get anythink else. Now, lovey, you leave it to me. I know what I know and I seen 'im muckin' about with you and I knew what 'e was after. Bit 'im, did you? Yes! And pity it was only on 'is nose, the old basket! *I'll* tell on 'im – not 'arf!'

Exactly how much fiction was mingled with the facts of the case as presented to Jo by Mrs Bilson in one unpunctuated breath, can only be surmised; but it seems that she having been taken short in the night and had to go down heard loud screams to wake the dead coming from Martha's room and having tried the door and found it locked she went through to the schoolroom and saw with her own eyes Mr Todd's father as she would swear on the Bible in the Courts where he ought to be run in for assault as they call it on an innocent young girl which she knew all about with Bilson having been run in for the same but got off because the girl was no better than she ought to be as could be proved and as for *her* being innocent was all Mrs Bilson's eye and Betty Martin and having seen Mr Todd's father exposing himself if Mr Todd would excuse her speaking plain and trying it on that poor motherless lamb and as she was just going to tell him off Martha had got away and went screaming into the W.C. where she locked herself in and Mrs Bilson being in a hurry owing to that onion soup she went down outside and that was the Gospel truth of it and if he believed the old man's wicked lies. . . .

Here Mrs Bilson's breath gave out leaving Jo to extract from the Gospel truth of it enough with which to tax his father only to be told that if Jo could believe the word of that lying little bitch—

'Martha,' interrupted Jo, 'has never said a word to me about it. I repeat only what Mrs Bilson claims to have seen.'

'Which only goes to show them two 'ave put their 'eads together to get me out and if you can't see that Martha's a wrong'un through and through and makin' up a pack of f——n' lies against your own flesh and blood to serve 'er ends and be rid o' me so that she can go on livin' 'ere on the fat o' the land at your expense then,' exploded his father, 'you're no son o' mine.'

'In which case,' was Jo's answer to that, 'if I'm no son of yours I need no longer keep you here. You can go. I'm the child's guardian and whatever appened or didn't Happen that night is not going to appen again. So now you know!'

* * *

From her window Martha gleefully watched the exit of the Horror who, conducted by his son, was bundled bag and baggage into a fourwheeler and driven off to Clapham. Jo had dealt generously with his father in providing him with board and lodging in the rooms above the Clapham shop, which he intended letting furnished on a weekly rental, and which now would leave him out of pocket. In thus depriving himself of a source of income he may have salved his conscience for having dealt too harshly with the old man, as, on consideration, he inclined to think, in that he had believed Mrs Bilson's accusations without closer inquiry.

To his brother Ted, home on leave shortly after this, 'You know,' he admitted, 'I've only that woman's word against his. I could get nothing out of Martha more than that he did come to her room that night and that he frightened her. She confessed to having fought with him and that she bit him because she said he tried to *do* things to her – what things she refused to say. Mrs Bilson is deaf as a post so what could she have heard?'

'I'd not put it past the old man,' was the younger Todd's verdict, 'that he did try it on with the kid. You know he's always been that way, even in poor Ma's lifetime. I've seen him leching after barmaids and worse. Up West.' He looked Jo full in the eyes. 'I've seen you there too, and neither of you can say you haven't run the risk of what you may pick up with a tart. But there's no excuse for him. It's not like living in a ship and in hot climates. We dole out lime juice to the crew to keep down their nature when in port.'

Jo, white to the lips, moved his head as if about to duck.

'You – you dare accuse me of—' he stammered.

'I don't,' Ted said coolly, 'accuse you of anything more than what's taken for granted by most of us. One learns to know aboard ship the type that'll sing psalms and halleluias and go fornicating on the Q.T. with any bit of skirt while they damn to hell their daughters who may have run off the rails, and no matter whether they are first, second or third class, I've had to deal with that sort of thing on almost every voyage. So what are you going to do about the kid? You can't keep her here kicking her heels doing nothing now the governess has left, and no one to look after her with you away so much. She's growing up. You'll be finding her a handful. You'd better get her married.' Ted flushed to his eyebrows. 'I wouldn't mind marrying her myself – if it's all the same to you, and her. That is if she'd have me.'

He said it half jokingly but Jo had seen that flush. He had also seen Ted's eyes on Martha when they sat at meals, and the way they were for ever playing tunes together on the piano, and gallivanting to London with theatres and teas up West. And the presents he brought her! A gold locket and chain – real gold – and that Spanish shawl from South America. And he'd draped the shawl round her like the Spanish women wear them, he said, and told her she looked a knock-out in it. Knocked Ted out too, it seemed. Marry her! And her two thousand . . . Growing up. Yes, she was. Jo had noticed it himself. Still just a slip of a thing but she was filling out and as pretty a piece as you'd see in a day's march. He might certainly find her a handful, and him with his business taking up so much of his time. Ted was right. He ought to set about getting her married and be quit of the responsibility of being her guardian. But Ted wasn't going to marry her and cash in on that two thousand. Not if Jo knew it! He could do with that two thousand himself, not only to pay off the mortgage on the Clapham shop, but that double-fronted property at Herne Hill just in the market. No. Not Ted nor anyone else would lay hold of Martha's settlement. He owed a duty to her to see that whoever she married would use it right and proper for her good and in her interest. And what of this Married Woman's Property Act which was always coming up in Parliament and which would give to women the right to any property they had left to them by will or settlement both before and after marriage? The Act was more likely to become law under Gladstone and his Liberals than in Dizzy's time who himself had got a tidy bit out of marrying a rich old wife. And what of a rich young one?

The only way to keep some money-grabbing outsider off Martha and her bit of money *now* – before this Married Woman's Act became law – was to marry her to some decent man who had only her interest at heart. And who has or is likely to have her interest more at heart, God bless her, said Jo soulfully, than . . . me!

FOUR

Mr Chitterling placed his fingertips together, and leaning back in his chair, offered Jo, who sat facing him across his desk, the advice he sought.

'As guardian of Miss de Lamotte you are entitled to marry her although she is still an infant – hem – that is to say a minor, but she is now sixteen, and therefore of the age of consent.'

Jo, fidgeting and hot in the face, said:

'I was only wondering if her father might object to her marrying me, her being so young.'

'Her father,' he was told, 'has relinquished the entire responsibility of his natural daughter to you, Mr Todd, and if, as you say, you feel that you will be better able to guard her interests and protect her from importunate suitors—'

'My own brother being one,' broke in Jo, 'which would not be a suitable match for her as he's at sea more than half the year, and I don't think his pay is enough to keep her as she should be kept, and her av – Having to live alone except when he's Home on leave. And even my father—'

'Your father?' queried Mr Chitterling to Jo's pause.

'Yes, well even he did mention jokin' like, that he wouldn't mind marrying her himself and him old enough to be her grandfather – to lay hold on her bit o' money,' blurted Jo.

'I hope,' said Mr Chitterling severely, 'that you did not divulge to your father or brother the circumstances of Miss de Lamotte's birth and the settlement held in trust for her by us until she attains her majority or – marries?'

'No! Never! I never did,' prevaricated Jo, obliterating from his mind the confidences he had divulged, if not to his father, to Ted concerning Martha's birth and the settlement held in trust for her. But Ted was safe as houses. Or was he? No one's safe, thought Jo uncomfortably, where money's concerned. And, aware of a dampness on his forehead, he said:

'I don't think it right, me being away so much, for her to be left alone in the house except for our general servant, who's deaf as a post and is no fit person to look after Martha, now the governess has left. Besides, she's growing up and – and I'm not all that much older than her. I'm thirty-one,' Jo blatantly admitted, who was thirty-five. 'And people'll get talking with her living there alone with me. T'ain' – it is not,' he carefully amended, 'proper. As her guardian I must look after her interests and protect her from gossiping tongues. Besides which I – I've come to be – fond of her and not just as her guardian.'

'Quite,' noncommittally assented Mr Chitterling who had drawn his own conclusions regarding this avowal, which he believed had less to do with Mr Todd's fond attachment to his ward than to her marriage settlement.

'She's fond of me, too, I think,' Jo took out his handkerchief and mopped his face. 'Hot in here, isn't it?'

'Do you find it so? I will open a window,' suggested Mr Chitterling.

'No, thank you. I'll be going in a minute. I only wanted you to know that my Hintentions are Honourable and that I ope I'm not doing anything that isn't legal.'

'Perfectly legal.' Mr Chitterling darted a penetrating glance at Jo's red face. 'You are probably aware that on your marriage to Miss de Lamotte you become possessed of her entire settlement which, in such event, will be released from the trust and reverts to you as her – hem – her husband?'

'Which will be spent, all of it, on Her,' said Jo, breathing thankfully out. 'I wouldn't spend a penny of it except for er benefit.'

'Very praiseworthy, I'm sure,' was Mr Chitterling's dispassionate rejoinder.

'And what's more,' Jo warmly continued, who didn't much like this laconic reception of his benevolence, 'I intend to send Martha to a Highly recommended and Hexpensive school at Dover to complete her Heducation. I want her to stay there for at least two if not three years. Meantime she'll be my wife in name only.'

Plus two thousand pounds, silently supplemented Mr Chitterling. And rising from his chair, 'The settlement,' he said, 'will be released from the trust when the marriage has taken place. I shall wish to see the marriage certificate, that the necessary formalities may be concluded. You realize that the hundred and fifty a year allowed for her maintenance ceases on her marriage, of course?'

'Of course,' echoed Jo, a trifle crest-fallen. He had not realized it. He held out his hand to receive Mr Chitterling's dry palm in his moist one. 'I'll send you her marriage lines so soon as ever the marriage is over and done with. I'm not wasting any time. It'll be next month. Good day to you, sir.'

The sooner this Married Woman's Property Act becomes law, the better, was Mr Chitterling's inward comment as he bowed Mr Todd to the door.

On leaving King's Bench Walk, Jo hailed a hansom and drove to a house in Harley Street. It was not his first visit to this eminent consultant, to whom he announced his intended marriage and, more than ever red in the face – 'I just wanted to know if it would be right for me to marry now, or if I ought to wait a bit longer till that trouble you treated me for is – that I'm over it. You did say it was curable.'

The doctor referred to a case card.

'I see that in November of last year I prescribed a continuance of the mercury pills. Have you had a recurrence of the symptoms of which you then complained?'

'Nothing to speak of,' Jo again resorted to his handkerchief with which to mop his forehead. 'I only wanted to let you know that I want to be married and I ope you can give me a clean bill of Health.'

'As I think I told you when you first consulted me, your condition usually pursues a chronic course, and even if, or when, a cure is effected, it may be followed years later by a slight recurrence, or, more often, a nervous affection.'

'A cruel price to pay for one lapse,' muttered Jo.

The doctor cast a keen professional eye on his patient, whose mouth was twitching and who sat, one hand holding his bowler hat on a rigid knee, the other hand, its knuckles showing white, on the arm of his chair. The nervous affection, presumed the physician, might already be developing.

'You say you intend to marry. I would strongly advise you to postpone your marriage for at least two years, or else' – a pause before he added – 'to abstain, during that time, from cohabitation.'

'Which is what I intended to do in any case. She's very young. Only sixteen.' The doctor's eyebrows shot up. 'You see,' said Jo desperately, 'I'm her legal guardian and I'm marrying her to give her my name. She – she's Hillegitimate. I knew her mother but I've never been told who the father was. She has to be so much on her own when I'm away on business, and if I'm married to her I can keep her under my eye. I'm sending her to boarding school, but she'll ave to come ome for the Holidays and I wondered if – suppose I'm still infected

I,' his voice broke, 'I'd kill myself before I let er come to any Harm through me.'

'Well, now,' said the doctor, 'we'll see about that.'

After a thorough examination he, reseated at his desk to write a prescription, said, 'You are doing very well. The treatment I have prescribed for you gives every hope of a permanent cure.' He looked up to tell him, 'Don't take this too much to heart, Mr Todd. There are many in highest positions whose private lives will not bear scrutiny and who have passed unscathed. You have been unfortunate.'

'Only that once,' muttered Jo, 'and she wasn't a – not so to speak – a professional.'

'Those,' he was told, 'are the most dangerous.'

'I can tell you, doctor,' Jo rubbed a hand across his eyes, 'this has put me off aving Hanything to do with a woman for the rest of my life. As for the girl I'm marrying, she'll be my wife in name only – at least till she's older.'

He was handed a prescription.

'Have this made up. And don't worry or brood over it.' The doctor rose from his desk. 'You mustn't think yourself singular in this – just unlucky. You have learned the hard way, and if it has taught you self-discipline then you must regard it as a mercy rather than a calamity. Come to me whenever you need my advice.'

He gave Jo his hand. Jo, near to tears, grasped it. 'Thank you, doctor. You're very kind. I'm much obliged.'

* * *

Extracts from the Journal of Martha Todd:

April Fool's day and I thought he was making an April Fool of me when he said looking all ways at once and sort of shy which isn't like him that as my guardian I could not marry without his consent and that I had an offer of marriage which was very suitable. I must say I was surprized not ever knowing anyone who would want to marry me at my age and not seeing anyone except him and Ted and the old man so it couldn't be them but it was! Not Ted or the Horror but Him! Mr T! He said it would have been Maman's wish that he should marry me when the time came to find me a good husband and that he had grown to love me not just as his ward but with a warmer affection he said and that he would love and protect me better as my husband! I was taken as Mrs Bilson would say all of a *Heap*. It is intierly for your protection he said and you will only be my wife in name you are so young that until you are older I will not insist on my marrytal rights – whatever that may mean. Keeping house for him I suppose. He said I was to go to school again and come home for the holidays and all would be as before only that I would be married to him and be given his name and then he told me which upset me very much that my father had desserted my mother before I was born and that he wanted to give me his name because my name isn't White. He said Maman took that name from her Christian names Marie Blanche when she came to England. Her maiden name he said was de Lamotte. Of course I knew that and he said she and my father were to have been married but his father, another old Horror I suppose, broke it off. He was rather vaygue about this. . . . I didn't know you could have a baby without being married except in the case of Kings, like Charles the Second, and I suppose Kings don't have to be married to have one except to their Queens. Anyway I don't quite know what you have to do to have a baby unless its something to do with sleeping in one bed which thank goodness I shan't have to do because I asked him and he said I was too young yet and we would talk about that when I'm older. But however old I was I wouldn't sleep in one bed with him. Never. No. I'd hate to. . . .

April 12th

Mr T. says I needn't call him Mister any more now so I call him just Toddy as Jo sounds too familiar. He said he had been to see the school at Dover recommended by Miss Hore which he said is very High Class and I am to go there at Half Term, and that I will be very happy there and will only come home for holidays and we will live just as we always have except that you will be Mrs Todd and so as not to be different from the other girls I will be called Miss Todd there. He is buying me a whole lot of new clothes for school. We are to go to London tomorrow and buy them, so altogether I feel quite satissfied with the arrangement. Anything to get away from here for I am sick to death of being left so much alone with Mrs B. . . .

April 20th

Was married to T. at the Registary office at Wimbledon today. He said not to say anything to Mrs Bilson about it as he would tell her later when Ted came home and he hasnt told his father yet no need he said as it is only a matter of form and part of being my guardian. It was very short the service or whatever they call it in a registary office. No bridesmaids or clergyman or anything. Not like a proper wedding at all I didn't even dress up for it. I wanted to wear one of the new dresses he bought me but he said not as Mrs B. would be asking questions why I was dressing up to go to the station with Him as I do sometimes when he goes to the Clapham shop just for a walk. An old man with a bit of white stragly beard on his chin mumbled things I could hardly hear about taking this man to be your wedded husband and place the ring on your wife's finger which Mr T. did and then I had to sign my name on a paper as Thérèse Marthe de Lamotte and then I went home and he went off to Herne Hill where he is buying another shop but first he took the ring a plain gold one off my finger and said I will keep this for you. And so now I am Mrs Todd and his wife. It does seem funny being Mrs.

Later

He came back this evening and we had supper together as usual and he kissed me goodnight which he doesn't often do only on birthdays and Christmas and said God bless and keep you I will cherrish you all the days of my life and I went to bed but I locked my door just in case only there was no need and my bed isn't big enough for two

FIVE

The young ladies of Albion House were assembled in the Great Hall, as the one large apartment in the Academy was grandiloquently named. It had been built on to the house and had a vaulted timbered roof, three long leaded-paned windows and a stove with a chimney rising to the ceiling in the middle of the room. It was here that Miss Merridew held the first and second senior classes, and morning and evening prayers. Some five and twenty desks fronted a rostrum and behind them were ranged several rows of benches.

On this occasion Miss Merridew had called together the whole Academy, both juniors and seniors, the latter aged from sixteen to eighteen, the former from fourteen to sixteen.

As she rustled into the room the pupils stood while Miss Merridew took her stance on the rostrum.

'Young ladies,' she commanded, 'pray be seated.'

With one accord the young ladies sat; the seniors at their desks, the juniors on the benches. All heads were expectantly turned in Miss Merridew's direction.

'I am the bearer of news,' she solemnly pronounced, 'that has caused the shadow of mourning to fall upon the whole nation.'

A thrill of excitement passed through the seniors. The Queen! was the thought immediately uppermost. Dead?

'Our esteemed late Prime Minister, Lord Beaconsfield,' stated Miss Merridew, 'has passed peacefully to his last rest.'

A sound like a sigh, as of disappointment, went up from the desks. The death of an ex-Prime-Minister, or even a present one, was not nearly so important or exciting as the death of a Sovereign.

'I desire,' continued Miss Merridew, 'that the first seniors will write a tribute to the deceased Earl in the form of an essay on his life and political opinions. Our late Prime Minister, as you should be aware, if you have imbibed the knowledge I have been at pains to impart to you, who, until honoured with an Earldom, was known to the world as Benjamin Disraeli, first stood for Parliament in – what year, and representative of which party? . . . Janet? . . . Marion? . . . Clarissa? . . . Can none of you answer that in which I have endeavoured to instruct you concerning British politics of the past fifty years and which I consider to be a necessary adjunct to the general knowledge in young ladies of your age? . . . Yes, Martha?'

Martha, whose hand had gone up, rose to her feet saying modestly, with eyes downcast:

'Lord Beaconsfield, as Benjamin Disraeli, stood for Parliament three times. Once as a Radical, once as a Whig and was defeated on both occasions. He was elected as a Tory Member of Parliament in the year – I can't quite remember which year – about 1832, I think.'

'No, in 1837. Lord Beaconsfield, then Mr Disraeli, was elected Member of Parliament for Maidstone as co-candidate with Mr Wyndham Lewis in 1837. First seniors, make a note of that for your essay. Juniors, you may disperse.'

Thankfully the juniors dispersed. The seniors, eyes fixed upon Miss Merridew, poised pencils above their exercise books in readiness for their instructress's dictation.

'Since we have now covered the Regency and the reign of George the Fourth, we will proceed with the reign of King William the Fourth.' Miss Merridew moved to the lectern. 'Both first and second seniors attend, and do not interrupt me for queries in spelling. When you write me your account of today's lecture all spelling errors will mean loss of marks. Now, are you ready? . . . The late King William was faced with a heavy burden for his sixty-five years. The industrial revolution that, in the previous two decades, had been gathering impetus, was rapidly moving to its climax with the passing of the Reform Bill of 1832. . . .'

The class diligently scribbled, until at eleven o'clock a bell rang for break. The girls trooped out to partake of glasses of milk and slices of bread and butter served by Miss Emma at a table in the recreation room.

Said Clarissa, as she and Martha retired to a corner with their glasses of milk: 'I can't drink this. I don't know why the seniors shouldn't have tea for break. I'm going to throw mine down the closet. Will you? Come on.'

They came on to find the closet occupied. While they waited, making a pretence of drinking milk, Clarissa, plump, red-headed, rétroussée asked: 'Would you like to come to court when my papa is on a case in the High Court of Justice? He's a barrister and I'm allowed to bring a friend in the holidays so long as it isn't murder. I took Marion last time.'

'Does your papa try murders? How marvellous!' rhapsodized Martha, who in this, her first year at Albion House, had been taught not only to spell correctly but had also acquired a modishly gushful manner of speech. 'I'd love to hear a murder case.'

'Papa doesn't *try* anything,' Clarissa told her loftily. 'The judge and jury do that. He *conducts* criminal cases mostly, and sometimes divorces but he won't let me go to any of those. Oh, there's the plug. She's coming out.'

'Take my milk, too,' Martha said, 'and be quick. The bell will go any minute.'

Clarissa was quick, and as the girls filed back to class, she said: 'There haven't been many murders lately, but if there is anything exciting that I'd be allowed to hear, like breach of promise – which he wouldn't mind because of that Gilbert and Sullivan play, *Trial by Jury* –

I'll let you know. Besides, Papa is taking silk and—'

'What do you mean taking silk?' Martha interposed.

'It means he'll be Queen's Counsel and won't have so many cases. A Q.C. has to charge enormous fees, and people can't always afford to pay them. So we'll have two girls next term whose fathers are Q.C's. You know Maud's father, Sir Henry Doyle, is one of the leading lights at the Bar, so papa says. He does mostly murders. I wish girls were allowed to be barristers, don't you? Papa wants me to go to that new College for girls at Cambridge – Girton – when I leave here just to be able to call myself B.A.. Bachelor of Arts. Silly, isn't it for a girl to be a Bachelor! But better than being an Old Maid. I do hope I'll be able to get in – that's to say to pass the entrance exam, because I have a cousin up at Cambridge, and I'd get to know lots of undergraduates. There's the bell! How I *loathe* this dictation. I don't know how to spell half the words. Of course I'll never pass into Girton. What a bore having to do this essay on Lord Beaconsfield. . . .'

When the class had finished at twelve fifteen the seniors went for their morning walk before dinner which was at one o'clock.

They walked two by two in charge of one of the junior mistresses. Martha and Clarissa walked arm-in-arm together. Their way took them along the sea-front and on to the cliffs. The day was warm and sunny; the sea aquamarine, and below in the harbour the Calais-Dover boat was just steaming in.

'How I long to go to Paris again!' chattered Clarissa. 'Have you ever been there?'

'No, but I intend to go some day. My – my guardian has promised to take me. I am half French, you know.'

'Yes, that's why you speak so well. What a boon you are for helping in translation. I say, I'm to have a party for my seventeenth birthday in the summer holidays. Will you be able to come to it? You'd have to stay the night, but Mama said I could ask anyone from here I wanted to, and that they could stay the night if they didn't live in London. Only I don't want to ask anyone but you.'

'Thank you very much. I hope,' Martha said sedately, 'that I can, if my – my guardian will let me.'

'Why do you have a guardian?'

'Because,' Martha turned her head to look out to sea, for she felt her face reddening, 'I have no parents, and you have to have a guardian until – unless one is – married or twenty-one when their parents die.'

'Is he kind to you? Do you like him? Is he old?'

'Yes, he is rather old.' Still keeping her head turned, Martha said, 'But I don't see very much of him. He has to be away a lot at his – on business.'

'What is his business?'

'What a one you are for questions! Something to do with tea, I think.' And feeling Clarissa's eyes on her, she hastily added: 'I suppose, if you are going to Girton, that you will miss being presented to the Queen.' For she had learned from her schoolfellows that almost all were destined to 'Come Out', which meant that when they left school and put up their hair they would be launched on Society as débutantes and presented at Court.

'Of course I shall be presented – during vacation if there's a Court then. My sister was presented two years ago. She says it's awful. The Queen has no consideration for us. We're herded together like a lot of sheep and walk through endless state-rooms and no refreshment offered, and you have to be up at dawn because she *will* have them in the mornings. If it's hot some of them faint. Mama will present me. Who will present you? Have you any aunts or people who'll do it?'

'Yes. My grandmother. She is French, but she always comes from Paris for the London season. She,' romanticized Martha, 'is la Comtesse de Lamotte. I have very few relatives as neither of my parents had any brothers nor sisters and most of my family on my mother's side, being *les aristos*, were guillotined in the French revolution.'

'It is a bore having to be presented,' said Clarissa rather relieved at this revelation of Martha's aristocratic French ancestry, for she had been wondering if Mama, who was so fussy about knowing the right people, would have shied at a girl whose guardian was in business. Tea. . . . 'But one has to be presented because everybody who is anybody *is*. Mama is so dreadfully conventional and old-fashioned, although Papa is very modern in his outlook. He says all girls should have a career and not just to be married as if it were the be-all and end-all of their existence, that's why he wants me to go to Girton. He would have sent my sister, Hilda, there only she got engaged in her first season and is now married to Lord Aldeburgh and will be a Countess one day. Anyway she's such a half-wit she would never have passed her entrance exam. But what she lacks in brains she makes up for in looks. She's maddeningly pretty. I'm dreadfully jealous of her.' Clarissa squeezed Martha's arm. 'Do come to my birthday party. I'm going to put my hair up for it, only it isn't my coming out party. That will be a proper ball.'

If I do go to her party, Martha was thinking, I shall have to invite her back in return – to spend the day, at least. It would have to be when Toddy's not at home. She could not possibly let Clarissa meet *him*. And suppose it should come out that she was married to him! So far it had been easy to keep that a secret, at least from the school. She knew Ted had been told but not the Horror yet, and she hadn't seen Ted since her marriage as he had gone to Australia this time and would not be home on leave for ages. Oh, why did she ever let herself in for this! And all the girls here to be married by being 'presented'. She would never be given any such chance nor any choice. Married already. . . . O, God, she screamed within her, why didn't I kill myself before I let him do this to me? I know so much more about it now than I did then, and it isn't just having to sleep in one bed. It's something much worse than that . . . if one only knew exactly what.

'But Mama,' Clarissa was saying, 'is all against my going to Girton. She says men don't want a blue-stocking for a wife, though I think it would be fun if I can only pass my entrance exam because my cousin – he's my cousin once or is it twice removed? – his father and Papa are first cousins – he'll be up at Cambridge then and I adore him. I don't know if he adores me, but I'd give anything in the world if he did, only Mama wouldn't think him a good enough match. Now that Hilda has married into a peerage she'll want nothing less than a Bart for me. There's a silly ass of a boy – well, he's not a boy, he's twenty-one – who Mama says is paying me attention because he always calls on her days when I'm home for the holidays and he's a Bart and hideous with stick-out teeth and he's up at Cambridge too, so perhaps Mama won't mind so much if I *do* go to Girton because then I would see him there, only I wouldn't marry him, although he's awfully rich. . . .'

If you don't stop blathering, said Martha, I'll push you over the cliff. You make me sick. Marriage! That's all you, and all of you here, ever think about. And I *am* married. See? To a grocer! . . . I'd as soon be married to a pig! . . . But this she did not say aloud. What she did say was:

'It's lovely of you to invite me to your party and I would love to come and stay the night if my – guardian will let me.'

From the journal of Martha Todd:

Eaton Square,
August 5th

Well, here I am as guest in this grand house for Clarissa's

birthday tomorrow. T. gave me a guinea to buy her a birthday present so I bought her a bottle of Peau d'Espagne and a large cut glass scent bottle to put it in.

T. hired a brougham to bring me from Coombe. He said I must do it in style and will send it to fetch me home tomorrow morning. They have a butler and footmen and a French lady's maid who unpacked my bag. He has given me a lovely dress for tonight. White organza over pink satin with ruchings of organza round the bottom which just covers my ankles. He paid six guineas for it in Bond Street which seems an awful lot. The lady's maid whose name is Hortense was very pleased when I spoke French to her and we jabbered away together. I felt so sad speaking French again with a real French person other than Mademoiselle at school. Hortense asked, as I speak with no English accent, if I were French and I told her my father was English but I was born in France and that I always spoke French with Maman who was the daughter of le Comte de Lamotte, having told Clarissa that my grandmother was la Comtesse which I don't think is altogether a lie as my grandfather *may* have been le Comte as there is de before the name. I could see she was impressed.

I have come to the conclusion that Society, if that is what Clarissa belongs to, is very particular about Family and you have to be of Good Family if you want to be accepted. What would Clarissa's Mama say if she knew I am married to a grocer! I am thankful T. sent me to Albion House for at least I have learned to speak as they do although they tell me I still roll my R's.

I have been given a room next to Clarissa's. Such a pretty room all blue and white with touches of pink. The bed has white muslin curtains tied with pink ribbons and the wallpaper is blue and has a sort of satin stripe with a design of little pink flowers. Hortense curled my hair round her fingers and said Mademoiselle est ravissante, and went on about my eyes. Mademoiselle a les yeux magnifiques, et vos beaux cils, si longs. Maman had long eyelashes too . . . Oh, Maman, que je te manque tout le temps! They say time heals. It doesn't. It gets worse as time goes on. There is always this emptiness. One can't get used to it. I suppose cripples who have lost a leg or an arm do get used to doing without a part of them as I am getting used to being without her. I wonder if it's true, as he said, that she wished me to marry him. I can't believe she did. I think there must be some other reason why he married me. Was it something to do with the money he said she had left me? He seems to be spending a lot of money on me. Is it her money or his that he is spending? Clarissa will be here in a minute. I must put this away in the dressing-case, red leather fitted with silver topped bottles. He bought it in Bond Street when he bought the dress for tonight. He said I must have a dressing-case. He says all the Tip-Toppers as he calls them have dressing-cases. He is always reading books on social behaviour and he has been going to evening classes, so he told me. That's why he doesn't so often drop or put in an H. Poor Toddy! He tries so hard. Here is Clarissa. Quick. I must lock this up. . . .

'You look lovely!' exclaimed Clarissa. 'What a difference clothes make. Your dress is much nicer than mine.'

She was in white moiré with an overskirt of tulle. The closely fitted bodice accentuated the precocious curves of her over-ripened adolescent breasts. 'I wish I had your figure.' She surveyed herself in a cheval glass. 'This dress makes me look so fat. Mama says she was fatter than I am at my age and now she's as thin as a rake, but she takes care not to eat fattening things like puddings and sweets. How these new stays she bought me to wear with this dress do pinch! They are laced too tight. Have you got laced up stays or are yours buttoned ones?'

'Mine are buttoned,' she was told, with the mental reservation that henceforth buttoned up stays must be taboo.

'You oughtn't to be wearing buttoned stays – much too young for you,' superiorly said Clarissa. 'Come along to my room. We're to have sandwiches there as supper won't be served till half past eleven or twelve and the party goes on till two but there's a buffet if we want to eat before then. The grown-ups are having a dinner party first.' And coming close to Martha, she said: 'I've soaked myself in your scent – it's divine. It was lovely of you to give it to me and that beautiful scent bottle. Can you smell it?'

Martha ecstatically sniffed.

'Yes. Divine! I'm glad you like it.'

'I love it. John – my cousin – has sent me a *huge* box of chocolates for my birthday. Come on, let's go and eat sandwiches. I'm starving.'

Having taken their fill of chicken and ham sandwiches, washed down with lemonade, and sampled the 'huge' box of chocolates, they repaired to the drawing-room. It had been cleared of most of its furniture, and a drugget, well polished with french chalk, covered the carpet. Folding doors, now flung open, communicated with an equally large inner room where stood a buffet and several small circular tables.

'That's for us,' Clarissa said. 'The grown-ups will have champagne, but there's only claret cup for us except for John and the Bart as they'll be the oldest here. The rest are boys – at most eighteen. I'll try and pass the Bart to you for the supper dance. It would be a charity if you'd take him on. He's sure to ask for it and I want to have it with John. Shall we try the drugget to see if it's slippery enough? Play a waltz for me, will you?'

Martha seated herself at the grand piano and strummed the Blue Danube while Clarissa slid and slithered in the arms of an imaginary partner.

'Yes, I think it'll do,' was her verdict. 'Now let's see what's on the buffet.'

When the eatables had been inspected, Martha, a trifle overwhelmed by the sumptuous appointments of the inner drawing-room that had not been entirely divested of its furniture, the gilt, the marquetry, the pictures on the panelled wall and the two crystal chandeliers suspended from the ceiling of both rooms, affected, none the less, a casual indifference to this unaccustomed grandeur. One of the pictures attracted her attention for she had seen its original in the Dulwich Art Gallery.

'That,' she asked, 'is a Watteau, isn't it?'

'Yes – but it's only a copy.'

'I thought it must be. He wouldn't have painted two exactly alike.'

'How do you know it's a Watteau?'

'Because my grandmama has the original of this one in her château at Orleans, where I,' said Martha, unblushingly, 'was born'. . . . Well, almost, she told herself as a sop to God who always listened, for Maman was born in Orleans and for all I know in a château where there might well have been a Watteau.

'Listen! I can hear a carriage. That will be the first of the dinner party.' Clarissa darted to a window that gave on to a balcony where, under a red and white striped awning, seats had been placed – 'for the sitters-out,' Clarissa explained, 'only there won't be many to sit out as there are only fourteen couples, if they all turn up.'

They all, eventually, did turn up, and by half past nine the hired musicians, a pianist and two fiddlers, shielded from the rest of the room by a long coffin-shaped box filled with palms, aspidistras and hydrangeas, played the opening bars of the first dance: a polka.

The rout seats were now occupied by mothers and chaperones who complacently watched their young as they whirled in the arms of their youthful partners, most of whom, if not still at school, had but just left and were going up to Oxford, Cambridge, or Sandhurst.

The ladies, in full fig of fuschia reds and purples, emerald or sapphire, besatined, bejewelled, and discreetly perspiring for the night was hot, and their gowns, their bustles, their whale-boned corsets and such like impedimenta, were not conducive to comfort, fanned themselves and chatted together while their eyes scanned the revolving couples, marking each tail-coated boy as a future eligible or not. Since none of the girls was as yet presented they were therefore not members of the Marriage Market Hunt although, to their mothers, all were embryonic Dianas, and this little party a meet of the cubbing season. An astute observer might have discerned in the smiling masks of these matrons, a faint underlay of anxiety. . . . Would Alice, Anne, Cicely, Violet, run a suitable catch to the kill when out with the Hunt next year? Was Gladys too shy? . . . Was Olive too forward? . . . Would Dorothy ever be rid of that acne as the specialist called those abominable blackheads? . . . How *too* unfortunate! And she Coming Out in the spring.

Clarissa's mama in heliotrope, and her hair in a royal fringe, having received her young guests at the top of the stairs and left their fathers to their port and, later, to cigars in the smoking-room, heaved a sigh of satisfaction to see that Clarissa had been secured for the first dance by Rupert Goring and, she hoped, for at least four more . . . Thirty thousand a year, a castle in Scotland, that place in Leicestershire – falling to pieces, but it could be done up – and the house in Grosvenor Square. How ridiculous of Charles to want to send her to Girton. I shall forbid it. I *will* not . . . Heavens! there's the Ottery woman just arrived with John. I didn't invite her, and that ghastly gown . . . She rose to meet the newcomers. 'Dear Flora! Here's a charming surprise! I dared not ask you to come to this children's romp, but am delighted. And what a lovely gown! How well it becomes you . . . John! How good of you to come and help us out. Flora, do take this armchair. These rout seats are *so* uncomfortable.'

'I prefer a rout seat, and I adore a children's romp.'

Mrs Ottery, trailing clouds of green and yellow draperies, established herself between two stout well-bosomed matrons, and, lifting a lorgnette, gazed upon the now detached couples as the polka ended, 'Who,' she asked her hovering hostess, 'is that enchanting girl with the bronze hair and the Rossetti mouth?'

'Rossetti? Oh, yes, she is, rather, isn't she? A school friend of Clarissa's. . . .'

As the polka died on a flourish from the pianist, Martha's partner said: 'Thanks awfully. Shall we inspect the buffet? I rather fancy an ice. Do you?'

He spoke with a drawl, his voice seeming to come from the back of his throat; but most of them, she noticed – the few to whom Clarissa had introduced her – spoke like that. He had told her while they danced: 'You do this awfully well.'

'Do I? We have dancing classes at school. Do you?'

'At Harrow? No fear!'

He laughed voicelessly, through his nose. Sniggering. She felt a fool. Of course boys at Harrow wouldn't have dancing classes. He had tow-coloured hair and pimples on his chin that almost disappeared inside his high collar, and she thought his opinion of himself was equally as high.

'Were you at Lord's this year?'

'At . . . ?' Now what? House of Lords?

'No, were you?'

'Yes. I captained the team.'

Of course. Cricket. She knew that Eton and Harrow played each other at cricket and at Lord's, wherever or whatever that might be.

'How splendid.' That was safe, anyway. 'I wish I'd been there.'

'Do you live in London?'

'No. In Surrey. Do you?'

'Yes, but only in the season. Otherwise in Gloucestershire. The Cotswolds.'

After that conversation flagged, and they strenuously polkaed until . . . 'Thanks awfully!' and so to the buffet.

It was then, as they joined other couples similarly bent on refreshment, that she saw him standing in the doorway. . . . And suddenly the walls were in a curtsy and the floor was in a dip and that feeling of 'outsideness' came upon her.

'I . . . yes. I will have an . . . ice.' She had to say something to know herself still here and not . . . away. She dug her gloved fingers into her palms. Don't let it happen. Let him see me. Does he see me? Is this happening or am I . . .'

'Strawberry or vanilla?'

'Straw . . . berry. Please.'

'Martha, may I introduce you? Sir Rupert Goring. Miss Todd.'

Clarissa was at her elbow with a chinless young man whose teeth stuck out and who bowed jerkily, saying, in that back of the throat voice:

'May Ah hahve a dahnce?'

She handed him her programme on which a few illegible names were scrawled. He looked over the top of her head and said: 'Numbah thirteen?'

'Unlucky number,' laughed Clarissa; and, while he scribbled his initials, moved her lips in a whisper: 'Give him the supper dance.'

'We'll call it numbah twelve A, then, shall weh? Heh, heh!' He showed more of the teeth in a neighing laugh.

'I think,' spurred by Clarissa's nudge in her ribs, 'I – I'm engaged for number thirteen but number twelve is the supper dance. I am not engaged for that.'

She was back again now. The 'outsideness' had passed.

'Your ice.' The Harrovian presented a glass cup filled with a pink substance in rapid liquefaction. 'It's melting. We'd better take it on the balcony or else we'll have to drink it.'

'Yes . . . so hot in here.'

'John,' shrilled Clarissa, 'you must meet my friend Martha from Albion House.'

'May I have a dance?'

He had not even looked at her. He took her programme, wrote something on it and then . . . he did look at her and looked again.

'Haven't we met before?'

'Yes, I . . . yes, I believe . . .'

'Of course we have.' He was still holding her programme. She remembered his closed smile with lips curving up at the corners. 'You were going to give me French lessons.'

'And you cured me of a wasp sting.'

He was as he had always been in fleeting glimpses of memory. Taller, certainly, and more grown-up, the fair hair crisped and bleached almost white at the temples as if long exposed to the sun, and that same scar above his eyebrow. Nothing much had changed since that meeting, when? . . . In another life, and yet the whole of her life was here and now in this moment of recurrence. Nor did she know that in this very moment a child died to be reborn: a woman.

'You've met before!' Clarissa stabbed a glance of amazement from the pale young lady to the smiling young gentleman. 'You never told me.' She glanced accusingly at Martha.

'I didn't know.'

'What didn't you know?'

'His name.'

John said: 'A chance encounter. And I didn't know *her* name.'

'And what's all this about a wasp sting and French lessons?'

'She was going to give me French lessons and as for the wasp, that –' his eyes with a laugh behind them held Martha's – 'was all part of it.'

'Part of what?'

'Yes, and what,' demanded the Harrovian, 'about our ices?'

'I'm afraid,' Martha told him, 'that I'll have to let mine melt. I am engaged for this waltz,' which had just started.

'Yes, to me.' John, still holding her programme, returned it with an exaggerated bow. 'Mademoiselle.'

'No, not to. . . .'

'Me? But you are. See?' He had scored out a name and inserted his initials above it.

'John! You can't make her cut a dance!' cried Clarissa.

'Can't I? Isn't it done?'

'You know it isn't done.'

'Then we'll do it and . . . it will be done.'

Afterwards when all was over and all of them had gone, she, lying sleepless in her muslin-draped bed, relived that second 'chance encounter'. . . . Waltzing with him, to the strains of Strauss. They spoke no words, were lost, or *she* was lost, in an ecstasy of rhythm. The room with its whirl of harlequin colours, black coats, pastel flippancy of frocks, the aching scent of flowers fading on young discreetly veiled bosoms, the acrid smell from the sweating armpits of matrons, seated, monumentally watchful, on the rout seats; the whisper of gliding feet on the dusty drugget, all this, and all of him who held her, had a dreamlike inarticulate impermanence. Not until the waltz had sighed its lingering last note did he speak . . . 'The balcony. Shall we?'

No other couple was there. They had drifted to the buffet intent on claret cup, lemonade, or ices.

The still warm night wrapped the trees of the square in velvety dark shadows. The light of lamps in the empty street cast wavering metallic gleams of emerald on the full-leaved branches. The moon, like a yellow Chinese lantern, hung high above the rooftops, a harvest moon. They stood islanded in solitude in a world, it seemed to her, that contained none but themselves. The far off inexorable hum of the city, no more than the hum of a myriad bees, was a murmurous accompaniment to the undertones of voices in the rooms behind them.

Leaning his arms on the rails of the balcony he had turned his eyes without turning his head to look at her and say:

'I owe you an apology.'

'An . . .' she bleated . . . 'an apology?'

'I didn't turn up for my French lessons. You see I had to go to Bonn sooner than I expected. It was rather on my conscience that I couldn't let you know, but I didn't know your name or where you lived.'

Nor did he know her name now, not her – married name. He mustn't know. If he asked her she would say de Lamotte, the name she had signed on her marriage certificate, which *was* her name when she first met him. Her mother's name.

She sought about for something to say. How to talk to him who was the same, yet somehow, not the same, as the boy who had sucked . . . she felt herself go hot . . . And as if she echoed a question from a distance, out of the past, she said: 'Are you a doctor?'

'I hope to be,' and he added very quietly: 'It's happening again.'

'Yes.'

'Do you feel it too?'

She nodded. She couldn't just then speak.

He said, still very quiet:

'It's a curious phenomenon that comes to most of us at times, the feeling that some place, a room, a house, is familiar, or we are saying words spoken before that are being heard again. But actually what you and I have just said,' and this time he did look at her and forced her to look up at him, 'has really happened. You remember?' Again she nodded.

'So this doesn't apply to any sort of phenomenon. Because it *has* happened, to both of us. What I was going to say, though, is that this peculiar revision of –

something, might well be dimensional.' He was talking less to her now than to himself, and although his eyes met hers, she believed he was looking through her, not seeing her. 'We are conscious only of three dimensions, but there are others, a fourth, a fifth, who knows? It could, of course, be medically explained by a division of the brain.' He had come back, was no longer away from her, talking *to* her now, and between his bleached fair eyebrows was a faint frown of concentration. 'The brain is divided into two hemispheres, the cerebrum – the upper surface of the brain – and the cerebellum. I have a theory – I may be wrong – that when we feel this has happened before, or we have been here before, or can hear ourselves saying what we think we have said before, it is because one half of the brain receives that sight of something or hears words spoken, before the other half of the brain has registered them. It is only a split second, but in that second we can get the whole picture or hear words we believe have already been spoken at some previous time. Am I clear?'

'Yes, and is that why. . . . Sometimes I get a feeling, but this has nothing to do with the feeling of things happening before. It is difficult to explain. It's a feeling as if I were no longer me, *myself*, that's to say not me in my body. Outside of it and not belonging to me. Is that feeling of outsideness something to do with the brain receiving sight or sound before the other part receives it?'

He said, thinking it over: 'It could be, but not entirely. It is indicative of super-sensitivity, and more common in children, who are usually more receptive than adults to impressions. That, too, could be dimensional. Yes, I know what you mean.'

'Have *you* had it?'

'Not so much now. I used to, as a kid. "Outsideness",' he smiled reassuringly, 'explains it very well.'

A lengthy pause ensued while she savoured this admission. He knew! And now when it happened she need never be frightened of it. And sliding a look at him, she rushed in with:

'Do you still live at Dulwich?'

'Yes, until my father comes home. He's in the Transvaal at present. He was at Majuba, which ought to see the last of this hellish little war. He . . .' she saw his hand clench on the rail of the balcony, 'he's in hospital now. He was wounded.'

'I'm sorry.' How inadequate. So much easier to feel sorry in French – comme c'est affligeant. Sorry is a silly word.

'Is he badly wounded?'

'His leg. Lost it. Still, it's not like losing an arm. It won't prevent him carrying on as a medico. And do *you* still live in Dulwich?'

'No, I . . . we moved to Coombe, near Wimbledon.'

'Who's we?'

'My . . . my guardian and I.'

'Who is your . . .'

'I say! You two!' Clarissa's voice broke in upon them in a series of staccato jerks. 'You! Both of you. Been cutting dances. You've been out here for ages.' Her face was all puckered as if she were about to cry, but her eyes seen in the light of the street lamp below were hard and shining, not with tears. She was furious. She had pushed herself in between them where they stood. 'And as for you, John, you've cut my dance – monopolizing Martha the whole evening.'

'Not the whole evening, surely.' He was laughing below his breath. Teasing her. Making it worse.

'Yes, and now it's the lancers and I kept it for you. Of course if you don't *want* to dance it with me—'

She tossed her head like an angry pony, and Martha thought: She'll paw the ground in a minute; a bubble of laughter rose up. She tried to stop it and couldn't. Clarissa said: 'Very amusing!' And the laugh froze in her throat as John edged away from her and offered his arm to Clarissa, saying with that same exaggerated bow as when he had taken her to dance: 'I wouldn't miss the lancers with you for all the tea in China.'

Or Todd's tea, silently supplemented Martha and began to laugh again . . . idiotically.

She watched them go, and lose themselves in the lancers.

Her journal gives us something, not all, of that night's entertainment.

> . . . and fancy meeting him again and that he should be Clarissa's cousin! We danced, only once, and then talked on the balcony. . . . He understands everything about outsideness. Clarissa was rather annoyed, said he had monopolized me and took him away. I didn't see him after that, not to speak to. His aunt, a funny old thing in a cloudy sort of dress, all greenery yallery Grosvenor Gallery like in Patience which Ted and I went to last holidays before he sailed, called out soon after eleven that they were going home. So he didn't have the supper dance with C. after all. She had it with that Sir Rupert something and I had it with the tow-headed Harrow boy. We sat at one of the tables with a girl in pink and another boy, a suet faced boy. He's at Eton. I wasn't a success. None of them seemed particularly anxious to dance with me. My programme was only half full. I can't say I enjoyed myself. Was very out of it, not being able to talk to those three at supper. They all came from the same county – Gloucestershire – and talked about hunting most of the time. When they found I didn't hunt they hardly spoke to me . . . What a mercy C. interrupted us just as he was asking who my guardian was and even now he doesn't know my name because C. told him only Martha. He could ask her, of course, but I don't suppose he will. Not interested enough. Never even looked at me again. . . .

Jo was waiting for her when she got home and wanted to hear about the party, with whom she had danced, and if she had been paid 'great attention, for I'm sure there wasn't a young lady in the room to hold a candle to you.'

'On the contrary,' she smiled at him with lips turned down, 'I was extinguished in the blaze of their candles that quite outshone my very dim light.'

'That's what you say. Never one to blow your own trumpet. I bet you ad – Had the gentlemen buzzing round you like flies round a jam pot.'

'No, I didn't – or they didn't. I sat out four dances with two or three girls who didn't take, either.'

'What d'you mean, didn't *take?*'

'The flies didn't buzz round me. I couldn't have had enough sugar in my jam.'

Jo chuckled. 'You're having me on! I'll have to watch out or they'll be queueing up here asking my permission to pay court to you, and then what'll I do, eh?' he pinched her cheek. 'Nem' mind. You've got your feet well in with the tip-toppers now, and by'm by when you leave school we'll give a proper ball for you in London at one o' them – one o' those grand hotels to celebrate our wedding. It'll be time then to announce it. And *then,*' he puffed himself out, 'I'll be able to put you where you belong among the Highest. We've got a future together, you and me, my girl. You with your looks and your book learning and me with my business expanding Hand over fist – I made a clear thousand profit this year – so I'll be able to get you away from Here and into a House in Town. I'm thinking of renting one of them nice little beejoo – as they call them – residences off the Buckin'am Palace Road. They're small, but big enough for us so long as we don't, um . . . but plenty o' time for that. Smart address too, a stone's throw from the Palace. I'm not going to let you ide your light under a bushel. We'll Hexpand together, you and me. I'll be in the West End before long, but first – the City. Once I'm in the City I can rise to greater igh – greater Heights. I got my eye on a freehold – at a price, mind, but worth it on a mortgage – in Liverpool Street, City o'

London. High class grocieries. The big business men coming home will be buying something for their wives, preserved fruits, ginger done up in Chinese jars, Todd's Teas in fancy tins, money's no object to those Stock Exchange blokes, and they don't all have their carriages to fetch them. Got to take the train. Liverpool Street Station. It's all on the way from Throgmorton Street. And once I'm there, well – there's no knowing where I'll end. Alderman, likely. And Lord Mayor in my old age, if I've made money enough. Better than going in for yachts like Lipton's Shamrocks. Anyway, we're Here for the time being and—'

'And I hope,' Martha, who had let him go on, now brought him to a halt with a quiet, 'that here we'll stay. I like this little house. I don't want to live in London. Ever.'

'We'll see about that. We might be able to live in London and here as well. Meanwhile, there's no arm in lookinga-Head.'

SIX

Martha remained at Albion House for another two years, during which time she had acquired sufficient poise and education to 'take her place', as Jo pridefully admitted, 'with any lady in the land'.

Soon after her nineteenth birthday, Jo informed his father of his marriage, with reservations concerning the time and place of this event. It may be premised that the announcement was received at first with astonished incredulity and, when the truth had penetrated, with explosive execration.

We have no record in the Commonplace Book of this scene, since it took place in the house above the Clapham shop where the elder Todd was comfortably lodged, but that the grievance he had fostered against Martha after his eviction from Rose Cottage, had increased in malignancy cannot be doubted for he would often repeat to his son his determination to – 'get his own back on 'er, the artful little bitch, for wheedlin' round you to 'ave me out and 'erself in where I belong. And as for the money you said was settled on 'er by 'er father and you don't even know who 'e is – a nice feather for your nest and just in time afore this married woman's act comes in so you can collar the lot! There's no flies on you, me lad, nor on me, neether, as you'll see and live to regret 'ow you deceived me, your father – your own flesh and blood. Married! And not a word to me until it's done. For why? Because you knew I'd put me foot down to stop the match, a f——in' dirty trick to play on me!' And so on, intermittently recurring.

Martha, all unconscious of these smouldering eruptions,

was now installed as mistress of Rose Cottage, the acknowledged wife of Joseph Todd. The journal presented to her by Miss Hore had long been filled; another that she had bought herself had also been completed and a third begun in the year 1883.

She had persuaded Jo to postpone his plans for removal to a larger house in London. She did not want to leave Rose Cottage, which she had come to regard as her home. She took an interest in the garden, under the guidance of one O'Ryan, who gave her a bitch puppy of doubtful breed that, he assured her was the pick of the litter and her mother a near champion. She, who in O'Ryan's vivid Hibernian imagination may, or may not, have been a near champion, had untimely escaped his vigilance to receive the attentions of the father of the pup, bore him a litter of seven, and Martha became the happy recipient of one to be noteworthily entered in her journal as:

> . . . a darling and so well behaved. She doesn't need to be taught to be clean in the house, she asks to be let out. She is only eight weeks old but looks much older. She is going to be a big dog, part retriever and part spaniel, I think. I am grateful to have her, apart from the companionship, because T. had been sleeping in what used to be my schoolroom with the door open between us so that Mrs. B. wouldn't wonder why we do not what he calls co-habit, and now he keeps the door shut so as not to hear her bark to be let out in the early morning and wake him up. I have named her Lorna because she looked so forlorn when O'Ryan brought her to me, I expect she was sad at leaving her mother, but I couldn't call her Forlorna so I have shortened it.

Mrs Bilson accepted the advent of the puppy with the same equanimity as she had accepted Martha's marriage.

''E done the right thing by you an' that's all what matters. I said to meself when you come 'ome from school it wouldn't do for you to be livin' 'ere alone along of 'im, guarjon or no guarjon people 'ud get talkin', but what I'm wonderin' –' here Mrs Bilson lowered her voice, the high monotone of the deaf – '*is* if there's not somethink wrong with 'im. You're old enough now to be – you know.' A drooping of an eyelid accompanied this suggestion. 'To be sleepin' in two rooms don't seem right to me. Not nat'ral to my mind.' Mrs Bilson pointed this remark with another conspiratorial wink and a question, slightly more direct: 'Does 'e ever – you know?'

'Ever what?' Martha coldly inquired.

'Do as a 'usband ought, if,' chuckled Mrs Bilson, ' 'e's got anythink to do it with. Not that you're missin' much if 'e don't.'

There is no mention in the journal of a continuance of friendship with her erstwhile schoolmates, but we learn from an entry under February 1884, that:

> The Times announces Clarissa's engagement to Sir Rupert Goring, Bart, so she didn't go to Girton after all. I never thought she would. Her mama was all against it. There is a report in the Times of a murder case where the husband was accused of shooting his wife in their country house gunroom. Mr Herriott Q.C. defended and won the case. He was acquitted. There was some doubt about whether the gun went off accidentally or not. Poor man. I pity him having to face an awful charge with no real proof against him. Toddy read it at breakfast and said there would always be suspicion that he was guilty as the verdict gave not sufficient evidence. . . .

And under July, 1884:

> Clarissa's marriage is announced in the Times and Illustrated London, a very grand affair with a list of titled guests. Have never heard anything of her cousin. Suppose he is still at Cambridge. . . . Am going to visit Miss Hore at Brixton this afternoon. I simply can't think of her as Mrs Grimsby. T. has hired a carriage to take me there and back. He says he will keep a carriage when we move and

it will be useful for him to drive to his various shops. I don't want to leave here but it looks as if we will have to. He has bought another shop, at Richmond. . . .

Her visits to Cecilia Grimsby provided her with periodic though brief enough respite from the daily monotony of what now was her existence. Mrs Grimsby and her curate lived in a shabby genteel small house hard by the vicarage, scarcely large enough for the son and daughter with whom she had dutifully presented her husband and whose joint ages had not then attained three years.

To Mrs Grimsby Martha had confided her secret marriage before Jo had given her permission to do so. We are told little more from the journal than:

> If Miss Hore – I really must remember to call her Mrs G. – was surprised she didn't show it, at least not in words. She went rather pink, and said she hoped I would be very happy and allow me to congratulate you, and was about to say something else but the baby began to cry and she said it was his feeding time and went out of the room with him. I wonder what she really thought about it? . .

On this occasion of Martha's visit to Brixton, Mrs Grimsby received her alone. The babies, Jonathan, now two and a half and Joanna, fifteen months younger, were taking their afternoon outing in a perambulator attended by their sixteen year old nursemaid; and Mr Grimsby was visiting parishioners.

Over the tea-table further confidences were divulged, while Mrs Grimsby pressed her former pupil to partake of seed cake, cucumber sandwiches, and macaroons. Between intervals of masticating Martha brought herself to ask: 'Is it usual for people who are married not to share a room? I mean a bedroom?'

Cecilia, greatly taken aback, sought for a suitable reply, discreetly to achieve:

'It is not usual but in some cases it might be considered more convenient if the husband is detained late at night on business and would not wish to disturb his wife.'

'I see. Yes, he is often detained late, and still more often doesn't come home at all. He sleeps in the houses over his shops unless they are let. He has quite a lot of shops now and is talking of opening one in the City.'

Another slice of seed cake was offered and refused.

'It is delicious, but I can't eat any more, thank you. . . . So I suppose that is why we have separate rooms. Not that I *want* to share a room with him,' Martha hastened to add. 'We never have and I would hate him to sleep in my bed.'

Mrs Grimsby, turning distinctly pink at this, managed to convey a gentle reproof.

'It is a wife's duty not only to honour and obey but to concede to her husband his marital rights.'

'I have never really understood what his marital rights are.' Martha stared beyond the pinkened Cecilia to concentrate on the Monarch of the Glen that hung on the opposite wall. 'Of course when I was at school and only came home for holidays, it was different. I still had my own rooms – the schoolroom and my bedroom as always, but he told Miss Merridew, when he first took me there, that we were married in name only and that I had to be called Miss and not Mrs. He didn't tell his father for ages and I don't know why he told Miss Merridew and Miss Emma, except that he may have wanted to make sure that they would take me if I *were* married. None of the girls knew.'

Looking down into her empty cup Cecilia, although scandalized at these further revelations, again achieved restrained comment.

'One can appreciate Mr Todd's discretion in observing secrecy regarding your marriage, because you were so very young.'

'Yes, but,' persisted Martha, 'I'm *still* his wife in name

only and we've been married four years. I do know now –' under the table she flexed her fingers – 'at least I think I know what a proper marriage means, and I'm thankful mine isn't a proper marriage. I've been reading a book I found in his bookcase. It's called *Esoteric Anthropology* or *The Mystery of Man*. I looked up esoteric in the dictionary and it said for the initiate, taught to a select few, but I always thought that anthropology was to do with apes, not man.'

'You are confusing it with anthropoidal, as applied to the higher apes,' Cecilia, reverting to type, welcomed this side issue. 'Anthropology is the science of man in its highest sense.'

'That's more or less what the book is about, at least what I imagine it's about. None of it is very clear. It seems chiefly concerned with what to do to have or *not* to have a baby. It is all rather vague but I have read enough not ever to want a baby though I would love to *have* a baby but not if I had to go through what I think one has to go through to get it, yet I suppose *you* had to didn't you? And have you had to prevent having any more? The book, or as much as I could understand of it, tells you how to – prevent it, I mean.'

'I think,' said Cecilia faintly, 'that my husband has just come in. He is home earlier than I expected.'

And which brought to a thankful close this embarrassing anthropological discussion.

The entry of the Reverend Paul Grimsby, spectacled, stooping, painstakingly drudging, suspended further intimacies concerning the marriage of Martha, whom he greeted with polite cordiality; and while his wife went to the kitchen to make fresh tea for him and to recover from the shock of these divulgements, he helped himself to a sandwich, inquired after Mr Todd, and remarked upon the weather. 'This drought must be causing havoc to your garden. Even our small patch of lawn and our one hydrangea have sadly suffered.'

'Yes, hydrangeas need a lot of water. I wish it would rain.' Then Mrs Grimsby came in with fresh tea and the talk turned to General Gordon's mission to the Soudan, the siege of Khartoum and the urgency for a relief expedition.

'I read the report in *The Times*,' Martha said, 'of the letter General Gordon sent to Sir Evelyn Baring saying they were kept at Khartoum because the Arabs shut them in and won't let them out.'

'Yes, I fear the situation grows more and more serious.' Mr Grimsby sampled the seed cake. 'An acute observer, Father Ohrwalder, a missionary, who had been taken captive by the Mahdi, considers General Gordon's position to be hopeless.'

'Toddy – my husband – says it is all Mr Gladstone's fault, and that if Khartoum falls and the General and his garrison are massacred, it will be a blot on Mr Gladstone and the Liberals for ever. . . . Oh, there's the carriage. I am *so* sorry not to have seen the children.'

'Can you not wait a little longer?' Mrs Grimsby asked. 'They should be back very soon.'

'I'd love to, but he – my husband – will be home this evening so I mustn't be late. Goodbye, Mr Grimsby, so nice to have seen you both.' And as Cecilia walked with her to the door, 'I do like coming here. It makes a change. I never see anyone I can talk to but you, because Toddy is so often away, and except for Mrs Bilson – and you know how deaf she is, one can't talk to her – I go for days without speaking to a soul.'

'Come as often as you can,' Cecilia said, as she kissed her goodbye. 'You are always welcome.' And to her husband, when she stood at the window to watch the carriage drive away: 'That poor child! What an unfortunate marriage. It hurts me to know how she is wasted on that man. She is so young still for her years. That is one of her most endearing qualities. Such intelligence and yet she is so – ingenuous. It never occurred to me, when I was her governess, that Mr Todd had any intention of marriage. But I always felt there was a mystery attached to her birth, and to his guardianship.'

'You mustn't take other people's troubles too much to heart, my dear,' was her husband's advice. 'So long as her husband is good to her, and he seems to deny her nothing, she should not be unhappy or unfortunate.'

Cecilia refrained from telling her husband why Martha's marriage was, to her mind, unfortunate, and, with the return of their young, the subject was dismissed and, until some future date, forgotten.

When she arrived home Martha found not only Jo waiting for her, but – a joyful surprise – his brother Ted.

He had made the voyage in record time and was a week in London before he had let them know he had landed, having been held up with various commitments at the head office.

'Or with the ladies, God bless 'em?' was Jo's jocular insinuation.

Evading an answer to that, Ted went on: 'I had in mind for you and Martha to have a week's holiday with me at Brighton. You both look as if you needed a whiff of sea air. And as for you, Jo, you're yellow as a guinea.'

'I've not been too good of late – a bit of stomach trouble. Livery. And I've got to have some of me teeth out. The doctor here says I should take up horse-riding, but a fat lot o' time I have for that, even if I knew how to sit on a horse,' chuckled Jo.

'All the more reason why you should take a jaunt at Brighton. If you don't go horse-riding, you can at least go walks on the downs or come out in a row-boat. That'll exercise you – brace up your muscles. What do you say?'

What Jo said, with a shake of his head was: 'How can I spare a week away from business? I'm up to my neck in a deal for a Liverpool Street property.'

'Liverpool Street!' ejaculated Ted. 'You are going it, by Jove! The City now.'

'Yes,' Jo complacently nodded, 'I am going it *and* while the going's good. It'll make our fortune, won't it, Martie?'

Martha's face that had brightened at the thought of a whiff of sea air, darkened as Jo made attempt to pinch her cheek, which she wished he wouldn't do or call her 'Martie'. As for looking yellow, she had noticed that herself, and he was always complaining of indigestion, wouldn't eat this or couldn't eat that and taking quantities of pills and medicines before and after meals. His teeth too . . . Either they or his indigestion made his breath smell awful if he kissed her, which, thank goodness, was not often.

'It'll cost you something,' Ted was saying, referring to the Liverpool Street project. 'How much?'

'Money and fair words,' Jo cautiously replied, and, his flabby cheeks expanding to a smile, he handed him a box of cigars. 'Have one of these Coronas.'

Ted took one, smelled it carefully, removed its band and applied a match. 'Well, and what about Brighton? This is a jolly good cigar.'

'So it ought to be. I bought five un – Hundred of them from Hanson's in Paragon Street *and* at a jolly good price. As for a week at Brighton – not for Jo! But there's no reason why you and Martie shouldn't go for a week or longer if you want. And it's my treat, see? I'll book rooms for you at the Old Ship. A week at Brighton 'ud do Martie a power o' good. She's looking a bit peaked. It's this Heat wave, so soon in the year.'

'I had thought,' Ted said, uncomfortably, 'of asking Pa to come down with us. What do you think?'

Although he spoke to Jo, it was Martha who answered, close-lipped.

'If your father comes with us I won't go. Take him, by all means, if you wish to, but not with me.'

Ted removed his cigar from his mouth and looked not at her but at its glowing tip.

'Hasn't that old feud gone on long enough for you to forget it?'

'Not long enough for me to forgive.' Martha moved to the door and turned to say over her shoulder, 'even if I could forget what he did – or tried to do to me.'

'We must forgive them that trespass against us,' said Jo sententiously, 'as we hope to be forgiven. . . .'

'Spiteful little bitch!' Thus the elder Todd to Ted, who had unwisely suggested to his father before he had mentioned it to Jo, that he would like him to come with them to Brighton. 'A nice thing for me daughter-in-law to refuse to 'ave me in me own son's 'ouse so I'm 'ounded out of it like a leper and won't even let me 'ave a bit of an 'oliday along o' you. I blame you as much as Jo for this. Givin' in to a bastard brat 'oo don't even know 'oo 'er father was.'

It rankled. It ate into him. He brooded on it, until it became an obsession to bear poisonous fruit.

Jo saw his wife and brother off in the train at Victoria station, bidding them: 'Enjoy yourselves and better without me than with me. I'm not so young as you two to go gallivanting, bathing and rowing – my stomach won't stand a row-boat even if the sea is like a millpond.'

Martha did thoroughly enjoy her brief holiday with Ted. Together they wandered through the halls of the Pavilion that had been an Aladdin's cave of treasures when that greatest of Corinthians had achieved the impossible, the capture and retention of a dream.

Surrounded by a gaping horde of sightseers, Martha, wonder-charged, was lost in 'another world, another life,' she whispered to herself. 'So far, and yet so near in time to us.' And to Ted: 'There must,' she said, 'be some old people left who used to see him driving along the Marine Parade in his tilbury. It is little more than half a century ago since he died.'

Ted slid a glance a her and the thought came to him, who was nothing if not a sentimentalist: She's like a butterfly caught in the clutches of a stag-beetle. Trust Jo to know what he was about when he made sure of her and her money before she was out of the schoolroom. But what sort of marriage was this? How would it end? They still occupied separate rooms and he'd swear she was a virgin. If *he'd* been given half a chance . . . yet what life could he have offered her living half of his life at sea? Even if she'd have taken him, which ten to one she wouldn't. Though why, in God's name, had she taken Jo? Didn't realize what she'd let herself in for, poor kid. . . . And looking down at her when, in the music room, she stood enwrapt, up-gazing at a giant lotus flower that swung from the ceiling, its leaves of vermilion tipped with frosted glass, his heart twisted. So young, untouched and . . . Ted reddened, untouchable.

Glancing round and up at him she tucked her arm confidingly in his: 'I could tell you lots about the Regent,' she said. 'Miss Merridew had a *penchant* for him. We were crammed full of him but she never let us have the spiciest bits. I have ferreted those out from the heaps of memoirs written by his contemporaries.'

Ted, whose ears were hot, and, aware of discomfort in his intimate parts removed himself from propinquity, mustered a laugh, and said:

'Let's hear the spicy bits!'

'I'll tell you as we go down to bathe. I must have a bathe before we leave here. We used to bathe at Albion House – we had a private beach, but you won't be able to bathe with me as I'll have to go in the ladies only. I must go to the hotel and fetch my bathing dress. You've brought one with you, I expect.'

And while they walked back to the Ship, Martha told him: 'Three of the Prince's greatest friends were the Barry brothers. They used to come here with him when Brighton was just a fishing village called Brighthelmstone

– but the Prince – he wasn't Regent then – called it Brighton for short. It was said that one of the Barrys – not the Prince though I expect he was in on it – rode a horse up Mrs Fitzherbert's staircase. She had a house here too. They were always rather drunk. And what do you think the nicknames of those Barry brothers were?'

Ted hadn't an idea, but he enjoyed to hear her talk in her cool clear voice, with its very slightest foreign intonation, never entirely lost, and bubbling with laughter. She, whom he knew, so seldom laughed.

'The eldest of the three, the Earl of Barrymore – I got this out of one of the journals of the time – *he* was known as Hellgate because he had such an awful temper. Then there was his brother, Henry, he was called Cripplegate, because he had a club foot. Another brother – he took Holy Orders, but there was nothing very holy about *him*. He'd been in and out of prison for debt over and over again. They said that nearly every gaol in the Kingdom had received him, and so that's why he was called Newgate, which was supposed to be the only prison he never was in! And their little sister, Lady Caroline, who used the most shocking bad language, *she* was known as Lady Billingsgate! How I wish I'd lived in those days, don't you?'

Ted agreed that he certainly did – 'much more free and easy.'

'So free and easy,' Martha said, on a sigh, 'that one could be married in haste with no time to repent – at leisure.'

'Do you repent at leisure?' was on the tip of Ted's tongue to ask, but the eyes she raised to his, so deep a blue, as if – he thought, they had each caught a bit of the sea that was almost a Mediterranean blue today – held no laughter now: and her lower lip was in a tremble. Then, as they went in at the door of the hotel, one, standing by the reception desk accosted Ted with:

'There you are! And 'ere am I. I guessed you'd be stayin' at the Ship, you bein' a sailor!'

There was no bathe for her that day or any other day. Her brief holiday was ended. 'The Horror', as her journal invariably names him, having followed herself and Ted to Brighton, decided her to return to Coombe the next morning while Ted stayed on at Brighton with his father for another week.

Back at Coombe, she must face the monotony of her daily life, made increasingly dismal by Jo's home-comings that, of late had been more frequent. Not often now did he stay overnight at his various shops. She dreaded to sit with him at table and watch him eat, or listen to his complaints of his stomach and his bowels, of which he would spare her no intimate details – 'as between usband and wife'.

It was a month or two after the Brighton episode, when Ted had rejoined his ship, that Jo came to her with a long face and longer tale.

'I don't want to believe anything wrong of you and me own brother, but something has come to my Hearing that I want to have put straight.'

He stood before her, his head outthrust, his little beady eyes, slightly bloodshot, stared at her haggardly.

A coldness came upon her, and almost before he told what he had to tell, she knew. She had been prepared for this from the moment his father had descended upon them at Brighton.

'My father has reason to warn me that you and Ted have –' the words dried in his mouth; he looked about him, drew forward a chair, sank into it. His thick heavy hands were splayed out on his thick heavy knees.

'Go on,' she heard herself say, 'and tell what your father has reason to warn you about.'

He licked his lips that held a bluish tinge.

'I booked rooms for the two of you at the Old Ship,' he said, 'and I understand you registered there as Mr and Mrs Todd.'

'As so we were. What of it?'

'Not separately but as Mr and Mrs.' And again his tongue came out to wet his lips.

'Yes, they asked us to register and I did for both of us while Ted was seeing the porter about the luggage. Is that all your father has to tell – or warn you of? Did he come there to spy on me?'

Her tone was like a whip-lash, and Lorna, who had been stretched on the hearthrug, rose up and stood beside her, stiffening; and from the unflinching challenge in the eyes of girl and dog, Jo's own eyes fell.

'You were given a room with a double bed next to the single room where Ted slept.'

'Yes, I was given a double room because they had no other single room vacant. And they only charged you single price for it.'

His hands were clutching at his knees.

'Would I care what they charged? That's not the point. It's this – that Ted was seen going in and coming out of your room in the middle of the night – the night before you left.'

'He was seen, was he?' Her words dropped like crystals of ice. 'Your father must have been waiting to catch us in what is called *flagrante delecto*, or in other words flagrant delight.'

'In –' Jo started up. His face became a mottled red. 'Why, you brazen hussy! Standing there shameless to admit your sin of adultery – and with me own brother! You admit it – that he came to your room that night and that intimacy took place between you?'

'Certainly I admit that he came to my room.' Behind her frozen calm a tumult was rising. It rose, in a hurricane of demoniac wrath, and her voice rose with it. 'Yes! Ted did come to my room that night. I called him to open my window. It had stuck. And if you can believe that he and I – what your beastly old father would have you believe – his filthy lies –' her face was transfigured with uncontrollable passion – 'if you can believe *that* of me and your brother who is worth a dozen of you – you smug, clumsy, self-satisfied fool— Yes! you're a *fool*!' inexcusably yelled Martha, 'with no idea in your head beyond your groceries and tea. All your talk of education—'

She was sobbing now in her fury. Tears of anger trickled down her cheeks; her whole body trembled, while Jo, whose eyes were bolting and whose face had changed from red to dusky white, stared at her in startled incredulity as Balaam might have stared when his ass turned to speak to him. That this unsuspected personality, transformed in one apocalyptic moment from a gentle submissive young lady on whom he had lavished much of her – of his money; this girl he had taken nameless to wife to bestow upon her his name, his pride in himself and her, could stand there, shameless as any harlot and admit—

'How do you suppose I can endure to live with you – you— Oh!' She came at him hands fisted as if to strike. Jo ducked. 'And no one to talk to except a deaf old hag – I might as well be a Trappist. And you with your stomachaches and constipation when it isn't diarrhoea – and now –' chaotic speech poured from her between her sobs – 'your dirty minded old father who hates me because I bit him when he tried to— Oh, why did you marry me? Why did you take me when I was too young to know what it would mean? I've done with you – I've finished. I've borne enough. I'll leave you. I'll go away – anywhere to get away from *you* and this hell that is my life! I wish – I wish I were dead!'

And with that she was out of the room like a rocket with Lorna bounding after her.

'Who'd have thought it?' demanded Jo of the empty

air. 'Such a temper! That's the French in her, I suppose. Well, I'm blowed.'

It was the best he could do to restore his shattered self-esteem. What had he done to deserve it? He, who had sheltered her, guarded her, given her an education on a par with the ighest of the gentry. No father could have done more. Yes, he had been a father to her in resisting the rights of a Husband for her sake, because of a past – mistake, for which he had paid too dearly. But he'd resist no longer. The specialist had told him at his last examination that he was safe now to . . . but not to overwork. He must take a holiday.

Nervous exhaustion. That's what the doctor had said, and that his complaint often left that effect. Nerves. Upsetting his stomach. A holiday? How could he take a holiday with this Liverpool Street deal hanging fire? He wasn't going to lose it to a higher bid. Nervous. That's why he couldn't sleep, never a good night's rest. Those pills, too, didn't help. Mercury was too bracing, and this scene had made him feel all of a twitch. Did she really mean that she would leave him? No. Just her temper, though he never knew she had a temper, except that time when she'd flown out at the old man. . . . Still waters run deep. Yes! she *was* a deep one, she was. Could he believe there *had* been nothing between her and Ted? They'd always been matey together, playing the piano, going to theatres. He ought never to have let them go off to Brighton without him. Asking for trouble. And what did she mean, 'might as well be a Trappist'?

He got heavily out of his chair and went over to the bookcase. Taking down a dictionary he sought under the T's and found Trappist. Monk of an order noted for silence. . . . Not much silence about her just now, he thought grimly. *What* a vixen, eh? Needed a good iding, that's what she ought to have. Little devil! But perhaps he *had* left her too much alone. If she had a child . . . well, maybe she would have one now. No reason why not.

Not necessarily inherited, the doctor said. Perhaps this outburst was all for the best. He could make it up with her and lead a normal life and God willing, perhaps he would have a son to carry on the business. . . .

Still all of a twitch he mounted the stairs. Her door between their rooms was locked, but the outer door that opened to the landing was not. He went in. She was lying on the bed, her head buried in her arms, with Lorna on the floor watchfully beside her. At his entrance the dog sprang up, and Martha, raising herself turned to ask, in a frozen voice:

'What do you want?'

'I want to speak to you – to apologize.' It wasn't easy to bring himself to tell her who looked at him in cold surprise as if at a stranger's intrusion on her privacy. 'I shouldn't,' he blundered, 'have said what I did – have called you what I did—'

'I've forgotten what you did call me –' the faintest grin appeared across that icy mask, like the flicker of light on stone – 'a harlot, wasn't it?'

She had uttered his very thought of her. He recoiled, shocked.

'For shame! Are you lost to all decency?'

'It all depends on what *is* decent, or rather how *you* would define decency,' said she meditatively solemn. 'If you mean respectability, I am inclined to think that respectability is a kind of penance – the hair shirt of the hypocrite.' Her grin, more pronounced, was impish now. 'That's rather good, isn't it? And all my own. But it's not you who should apologize for calling me whatever it was – or wasn't – but for believing your disgusting old father's vile accusations against me and his son. It's he, that old Horror, who should apologize, and you must make him.' She got up and went over to her dressing table. She spoke to him, whom she could see behind her in the looking-glass, while she ordered her hair.

'I want,' she said in that cool clear voice of hers, 'a

written apology from your father. A verbal one won't do. He would refute it and go on telling lies about me. But if I have it in writing – and he will have to say he was mistaken and that I have been most wrongfully accused by him, or words to that effect – and if he refuses, then I will leave this house and you, and take Lorna with me and never come back. So you can tell him this from me. And now, please go. I don't wish to see or speak to you again until you have that written apology from your father for the wicked mischief he has made. If Ted were here he would not have dared, but he waits till he's at sea, and can't defend me, so I must defend myself. It is slander, you know, and I believe one can sue a person for slander. I've read cases of slander in the papers.' And leaning closer to her dressing-glass, 'How vexing,' she murmured, 'I seem to have freckled. That's the worst of a sensitive skin. A written apology, or else—'

She left the remainder of that unfinished.

* * *

Extract from the journal of Martha Todd:

. . . I managed to get that written apology from his father by telling him I would leave him if I didn't get it. I made him have two copies of it *printed* and I have locked them away in the drawer of the bureau. He has also given me a diamond ring to celebrate our marriage, he said. Oh, God, our marriage! He . . .

Another abrupt ending, but later we learn:

I have not been able to write of it before. It was too near. He told me he wanted a child and that the time had come for our marriage to be consummated. I want a child, too, but I didn't realize exactly what I – or rather *he* would have to do to give me one. It happened almost a month ago and I haven't written anything in my journal since. I've been going about in a kind of daze, a continuous sense of outsideness. It is as if another person, not me, went through that awfulness with him. This book about the mystery of man, esoteric anthropology, doesn't explain what to expect. It is written for women who *do* know what to expect. If I had known I would never have let him . . . I must be very unintelligent about the facts of nature although I read so much. Of course I *ought* to have known. Even though the Horror tried to – that time when I was only fifteen, I didn't realize – even then. When T. talked about Ted coming into my room and intimacy I didn't really know what intimacy meant and although I would love to have a baby, something belonging to me and to whom I belong – the only thing to whom I belong and belongs to me is a dog – but if I don't have a baby and if he insists on making me go through that again I shall kill myself. Take poison. I know it is wicked to think of such a thing but it was so dreadful that I would rather die than live my life with him under the conditions of what he calls his marital rights. He made me go through it twice with two hours interval between to make sure, he said. He told me he had got something from the chemist to strengthen him. He said he is not very virile and has never been robust. I think there is something wrong with him. Apart from his fussing about his health, I have noticed lately that he seems so strange. When he is at home he sits and stares in front of him as if he is seeing things. And he says such strange things, too. About mesmerism. He had been reading a book, he said, by a Swiss doctor in the last century who claimed to be able to mesmerize people – making them give up their will to another. I almost said, but didn't, that I hoped that he was not going to mesmerize me to go through *that* again with him. How can women endure it? All women have to if they want children. Maman, Mrs Grimsby, the Queen – imagine the Queen! But then she adored the Prince Consort, so I suppose she didn't mind. If he were young and attractive, if one were in love – even then it would be awful but not as it was with him. His breath! And his teeth all black and decayed and the way he – I can't think about it. Suppose nothing comes of that ghastly – I mean suppose I don't have a baby. I am due this week. If I miss

I may be going to have one. I read about it in the Family Doctor. If not. . . .

Yet another halt here, until under August 20th, 1884:

> Have missed two months. The doctor says I *am* going to have a baby! Now I need never go through *that* again. He has promised me we will live together always as before. My life will be endurable now with this to look forward to. A baby of my own. I'll try and forget he had anything to do with it. He, or she, I don't care whether it's a girl or a boy, will be mine entirely. All mine. Oh, it was worth it, all that awfulness – for this!

* * *

During the months of her pregnancy, a frequent visitor at Rose Cottage was the Reverend Albert Dixon with whom Jo had become acquainted by attending the Wesleyan Chapel at Coombe of which Mr Dixon was the minister.

A sober-minded elderly young man, this Mr Dixon, of medium height, with carefully trimmed whiskers, a black walrus moustache, and a pallid skin that exuded a perpetual shine; not a prepossessing personality, yet Jo, who seemed to have conceived an admiration for this gentleman's scholarly, though not exceptional, achievements – he had obtained a degree at Aberdeen University – had devised a plan by which Martha, no less than himself, might benefit from this new-found friend's tuition.

'It would help you while you're carrying to take lessons with him,' he told her. 'He suggests you should learn Latin, and he'd be glad to teach you.'

Martha thought she would like to learn Latin, which she knew was at the root of French and Italian – 'and even some of our English words,' she said, 'those that don't derive from Anglo-Saxon. Actually Miss Merridew was beginning to teach Latin to the first seniors during my last two terms there, and I have got through most of the verbs.'

Willingly, at a fee of five shillings an hour that he was loth, or appeared loth, to accept from Jo and which was a grateful addition to his meagre stipend of a hundred a year, did the Reverend Mr Dixon attend Martha at Rose Cottage two or three times a week. She proved, as her former instructors had found her, an apt and intelligent pupil and had soon mastered not only the intricacies of Latin irregular verbs, but at Mr Dixon's further suggestion, the rudiments of Euclid.

So, on a warm October day, we find her on Wimbledon Common seated on a bench with her nose in a lexicon, and Lorna's head sharing her knee with a book containing excerpts from the Latin Masters of verse and prose.

'Now, Lorna, let's see if I can construe this bit of Cicero he has set me. We are getting on fast, aren't we?'

Lorna, who appeared to take as great an interest in Martha's studies as Martha herself, although she evinced a marked indifference to her mistress's tutor that bordered on contempt, wagged her feathery tail in agreement while Martha laboriously pronounced:

'"*Quod enim munus reipublicae afferre majus, meliusve possumus, quam si docemus, atque erudimus juventutum?" Enim* – what's this? I don't want to cheat and look it up but I can't make sense of it here – ah, wait a minute, I've got it – What greater gift or better – that's rather a free translation, isn't it? – And now where are we? What greater gift or better can we offer, *reipublicae* – to the republic? No, to the State, but either will do because Rome *was* a republic at the time of Cicero, than *erudimus juventutum?* – than to teach, or instruct youth. What's the matter, Lorna?'

For she had got up and stood, nose suspiciously pointed, in the direction of one who leisurely approached. On sighting Martha, he increased his pace effusively to greet her:

'Good morning, Mrs Todd! And *what* a good morning. Quite summery.'

'Yes, Mr Dixon, it is a lovely day. Sit, Lorna.' Whose reception of the newcomer was accompanied by a low-throated growl.

'Your dog guards you well but he ought to know by this time that I am no stranger,' gingerly Mr Dixon stooped to retrieve Martha's lexicon, fallen from her knee, while Lorna, obeying orders, sat, yet still maintained a distinctly belligerent attitude towards his reverence. 'Does he bite?' somewhat nervously inquired Mr Dixon.

'She,' Martha coldly corrected, 'would never bite unless under provocation.'

'Then,' Mr Dixon exhibited a row of gleaming white porcelain teeth in an ingratiating smile, 'I must take care not to provoke him, or should I say *her*? But I am prone to regard the canine species as exclusively male. I see,' he returned to her the lexicon, 'that we are improving the shining hour. And how are we getting along?'

Seating himself beside her on the bench he took up the book of excerpts from the works of the Roman Masters, open at a page under Cicero. 'A great orator was our Cicero; the father of his country as he was called. And have you construed the passage I marked for you from the *De Devinatione*?'

'I was beginning to construe it,' she told him, 'just now.'

'Very well, then,' more show of the teeth. Martha could not help but think him a study in black and white, so black his clerical clothes, so black his moustache and whiskers, so very white those teeth, even whiter than his dog collar. 'Let us,' said Mr Dixon, who, by adopting the plural, inclined the better to identify himself with his pupil, 'hear what we have so far made of this excerpt.'

Dutifully Martha gave him what she had made of it.

'Excellent,' approved Mr Dixon. 'And, indeed, most apt. What greater gift, or benefit, since we are making free of our translation, can we offer to the state, and not only to the state but to him who is privileged to teach and guide the young? I consider it the greatest privilege – he edged closer to Martha on the bench as he spoke – 'that I have been chosen as Mentor to such a receptive Telemachus.'

Somewhere in the distance a church clock was striking. 'Dear me!' Mr Dixon drew from his pocket a ponderous gunmetal watch. 'Is that eleven o'clock? I have a funeral service at eleven-thirty. I fear my watch is slow. I must be gone. I will be seeing you tomorrow. Your good husband has kindly invited me to stay and dine with you in the evening after our lesson.'

He rose from his seat and bent to bestow a timid pat on Lorna. 'Good doggie, you wouldn't bite me, would you?' Lorna rather looked as if she would. '*Au revoir*, Mrs Todd, and tomorrow we will discuss the statesmanship of Cicero, one of the most brilliant and accomplished men of letters in those stirring days of the republic. We will enjoy, will we not, to delve into the political activities of this great orator, who was also a great pleader of causes, or as we would call him today, a barrister, an advocate. So, *au revoir* again. Parting is such sweet sorrow we could say goodbye,' the teeth were more than ever now in evidence, 'until – tomorrow.'

And lifting his hat he took himself off.

On the way home, with Lorna racing ahead to investigate delicious smells where sheep had strayed, Martha savoured the beauty of that mellow autumn morning, so near London, yet so far they seemed, those grassy spaces of commonland interspersed with cornfields, shorn now of their harvest, and meadows where pied cows grazed; for here was a farm from which Martha bought fresh butter and eggs and, rising above the trees of a coppice still full leaved but stained with amber and an occasional smear of crimson rowan-berry, the windmill that had stood there, she had heard, for generations, stayed unstirring in the quiet air under a flax blue sky. She would be sorry to leave Coombe for a London house, yet it seemed certain that when her baby was born she would have to go. Not only because *he* was determined to live within easy driving distance of the City in the carriage on which he had set his heart but, and this a more pressing consideration from her point of view, his father had expressed the wish, or as she surmised, had made it a condition in return for his written apology denying those accusations against her, that he should again share their house at Coombe so soon as her baby was born. That – never! The cottage would be too small, in any case, for the baby, a nurse, and the 'Horror'. No, she would have to leave here and if it must be London, she would see that a house was found still too small to accommodate him.

Calling Lorna to heel, she came out on to the lane that led to the cottage, and, as she neared the gate she saw the station fly drive up. It halted and out of it slowly alighted – her father-in-law.

She stood stock still. Why had he come, he whom she had refused to see or speak to since the night of his attempted assault upon her almost three years ago? That his eviction from the house as a result of it had brought upon her his unending vengeance she was well aware, but having been given alternative accommodation and an ample allowance to support him in the rooms above the Clapham shop, he had so far adhered to the arrangement, and kept himself well out of her way. He could not, surely, mean to enforce the conditions of his apology now – before her baby was born! If so, she would leave at once. She would go to an hotel in London, or find rooms somewhere. To have to share the cottage with him in her condition would probably bring on a miscarriage.

Lorna, sensing her apprehension, looked inquiringly into her face. She laid a hand on her collar.

'He hasn't brought any luggage with him,' she whispered, 'so he can't have come to stay – at least not yet.

We'd better go and find out what he wants. And don't go for him, Lorna, will you? You've never seen him, and you are sure to hate him at sight.'

She watched him ring the bell and wait, and ring again. She knew Jo would not be home until the evening, and Mrs Bilson might not hear the bell, in which case he would have to go away. While she stood uncertain whether or not to go in, she saw O'Ryan come from the back garden wheeling a barrow, and heard:

'Is anybody 'ere? I've rung twice.'

'Have you now? Will it be the master you was wantin'?'

O'Ryan knew him, and may also have known that he was not welcome at the house, and the reason why. Mrs Bilson might have told him. He had been gardener there ever since they had come to the cottage.

'I must see one or other of 'em. I've 'ad bad news about my son Ted.'

That, seemingly, decided O'Ryan, for he said, 'I'll go round and open the door for you.'

Martha, with a clutch at her heart, went forward and into the house.

He was standing in the parlour, his back to the fire, his long lean face, pinched and sharp, had a greyish tinge with its bristles of two days' growth of grey unshaven beard. His balding head showed streaks of sparse grey hair. His head was sunk, but at her entrance he stared up and at her from his pale bleared eyes. In his scraggy neck, rising above his collar, the prominent Adam's apple moved as he swallowed, with the words:

'Jo's out, is 'e?'

'Yes. Why have you come?'

Her disgust of him filled her with nausea, yet so bowed, so stricken and so old he looked that, despite her fear and loathing, she felt a twinge of pity and knew before he spoke what he had to tell.

'I've 'ad one o' tham telegraphs. I went to the Wimbledon shop to see Jo but they said he 'ad come 'ome 'ere. I 'ad to see 'im. As next of kin they sent the telegraph to me – it's from Port Said. It's knocked me clean out.'

His hand went groping for a chair.

She pulled one forward.

'Sit down. Is it – is it Ted – ? Is—' The words stuck in her throat.

He tottered forward into the chair. She went close to him, and laid a hand on his shoulder. He put up his hand and clutched it, raising his head. She shuddered away from his drink-sodden breath.

'I've got the wire 'ere.'

He fumbled in his pocket and produced it.

Dazedly she read: *Regret to inform you . . .*

'I feel queer,' she heard him say, ''Ave you a drop o' somethink?'

She brought him the whisky decanter and a glass, watched him pour himself a stiff dose and drink it down. The effect of it induced a storm of maudlin tears. She, tearless, stood while she fought against the impact of shock that overswept her. 'Stay here,' from out of a dry mouth she heard herself say, 'and wait for Jo. I expect him home at midday. I . . .' Her words dwindled into nothingness, and, with Lorna at her heels, she left the room.

On her bed she lay, stunned in a stupor of no-feeling. Ted. Gone. How did he die? That message. So cold. Impersonal. *Regret . . . your son . . .* He, so full of fun and vitality. Must one lose everyone and everything one loves? Only Maman and Ted in all her life, except Lorna, to love. And now, both gone. Lost. Dead. She had loved Ted as if he were really her brother. . . . His image came to her, rolling in his seat with laughter at the droll jokes in *Iolanthe,* the last Gilbert and Sullivan opera they had seen together. The words of the song he used to play danced before her closed eyes, white letters on a black wall. *When you're lying awake with a dismal headache, and repose is tabooed with anxiety, I conceive you may use any language you choose to indulge in without impropriety.* . . . And now, never to see or hear him laugh again. Dead. Finished. Gone. Where? How?

Then, for the first time, she felt within her the stirring of her child. 'You,' she whispered, and laid a hand with a protective gesture against her body, 'I have you. I won't lose you . . . ever.'

SEVEN

The old man had come to stay. 'We can't send him back to live alone with his sorrow,' Jo had said. 'There's his room empty and waiting. Just till Baby comes, then we'll move. I know of a good apartment house in a classy neighbourhood where we can stay till we find a home near to Eaton Square where your swell friends live who've dropped you like an ot brick. You're not good enough for them who move in High Serciety, eh? Well, we'll see. We'll be even with 'em yet. I'll have you driving in your carriage in the Park before long, and a House with three or four servants – one o' them neat little ouses Victoria way with a mews at the back for the carriage. I can easily sublet this cottage on so long a lease. So you must let bygones be bygones and umour me father for he mourns his loss deeply.'

Martha, for the sake of peace, was over-ruled; but she stipulated that Jo should sleep in his own bedroom as before, and that the schoolroom should be hers again, thus to give her privacy for her studies with Mr Dixon which also provided her with excuses for avoiding the elder Todd. But if Jo were at home she would be forced to tolerate his father's presence. Then, while she sewed her baby's clothes, he would sit by the fire in the parlour, smoking his noisome pipe, and lamenting the loss of Ted.

'It's an 'ard blow to a man as 'e gets on in years to lose a wife and son, left 'omeless, dependent on charity. Shockin' that one case o' smallpox should cause an outbreak aboard ship and that my boy should 'a taken it. The Captain wrote so 'ighly of 'im, too. My poor lad! To think 'e should die in a foreign land among a lot o' stinkin' Arabs away from kith and kin in that Port Said which I've 'eard tell is full o' bad 'ouses –' he dwelled with relish on this – 'where them native touts grab 'old of innercent young English fellers to entice them with dirty pictures and nasty ways o' fornicatin' with 'ores so they'd pick up some 'orrible disease. But my poor Ted, 'e was clean livin' as 'is father before 'im and as Jo always 'as bin, ain't you, Jo?'

'Will you have a cup of tea before you go to bed?' Jo hastily invited.

'No thanks. Tea keeps me awake. A drop o' Mother's Ruin' – with a ghastly grin – ' 'ud do me nicely, if you've got it.'

Jo handed his father a liberal glass of gin, hoping to stem the tide of this discomfiting monologue, which, however, had little desired effect.

The visits of Mr Dixon when, at Jo's invitation he often dined at Rose Cottage, afforded some relief from that dreary trio in the parlour. Then the conversation, led by the Reverend Albert, would range from the ever burning topic of the day, the siege of Khartoum and Mr Gladstone's dalliance in sending forces to the aid of General Gordon, and so to more intimate discussion.

According to Martha's account in her journal of these talks, Jo would air his singular views on matrimony, voicing his opinion that a man should have two wives – 'one for use and one for companionship', and he would add, with an anxious eye to the minister's reaction to this startling heterodoxy, 'those Biblical kings were allowed more than one wife, so why aren't we?'

'There is nothing in the New Testament,' was Mr Dixon's pontifical answer to that, 'which encourages or condones polygamy. The Judaic laws concerning marriage were, to say the least, elastic.'

'What about the ancient Greeks, then?' Jo glanced aside at Martha who sat sewing in the window seat. 'I've heard you teaching my wife, when I've had time to listen to her lessons, about those ancient Greeks. Didn't they go in for – what is it – pol*oh*gamy?'

'Polygamy,' pronounced Mr Dixon, 'was not practised by the Greeks who, despite their worship of heathen gods were immensely civilized and cultured. But although monogamous in practice they, for the most part, chose their wives solely for procreation and the management of their households and enjoyed the – ah – the – concubinage – that is to say the society of the more intelligent hetaerae.'

Jo blinked.

'Hetty – what?'

'Hetaera,' Mr Dixon patiently explained, 'is the Greek word for a superior type of – of courtesan.'

'In other words,' Jo doggedly pursued, 'a sort of concubine as the Old Testament calls these extra wives. So why shouldn't we be allowed to have more than one wife, whether you call them concubines or Hetteary or whatever – one for work, and –' knowingly he winked – 'one for play?'

'Your opinions, sir, are no matter for jest,' said the minister severely, having noted that insinuating wink and its accompanying chuckle. 'In all civilized countries marriage is a sacrament and should be regarded as such by Christians. But, reverting to the ancient Greeks, their attitude to life was largely influenced by Socrates, the greatest philospher of all antiquity, and whose most ardent disciple was Plato.'

Then, aware of Martha's attention, he proceeded as if delivering a lecture to a roomful of students instead of to an audience of three, one of whom was nodding in his chair between replenishment from the bottle at his elbow: 'Plato's system of philosophy followed the metaphysical theories of Pythagoras and the morals of Socrates. Plato acknowledged, and was indeed the first to acknowledge, the immortality of the soul, and he believed and did instruct his followers to believe in an immaterial love, irrespective of sex, which we, of a later civilization, call,' here Mr Dixon gave a glimpse of the teeth before he came out with, 'Platonic love. The existence of the human mind which we know to be the emanation of God Himself, must never be subjected to the baser passions, as Plato declares, and—'

''Ere!' the elder Todd, waking from a doze, drained his glass and heaved himself out of his chair. Focusing an eye on Mr Dixon, who, at this interruption returned him a look of the utmost contumely, 'I'm orf,' he said. 'Got ter see a man – hic – about a dog – hic –shou' say an' 'orse. An' if you take my tip,' he placed his hands on the table and leaned confidentially towards the confounded Mr Dixon, to tell him: 'Don' back Play Girl – hic – that filly ain't in the runnin'. 'Ad it straight from the 'orses mouth – hic – hee, hee! Pal o' mine. Goo'-nigh'.'

He lurched out of the room.

Jo broke the silence that followed his exit by offering – 'another glass of wine, your reverence?'

His reverence thanked him, 'No,' and rose. 'Your father it would seem, is labouring under some misapprehension if, indeed, he is in a condition to understand my allusions to the Master. I, too, will bid you goodnight. We will,' he turned to Martha, who was in the giggles, 'resume our dialectics at our lessons tomorrow, when we will study the Socratic Dialogues. Goodnight, Mrs Todd.'

He offered her a damp hand: the perpetual dew on his face and brow seemed always to have oozed into his palms; and with a bow and a wider exposure of those dazzling teeth, he was seen to the door by Jo.

Said he, returning after having conducted the minister to the gate:

'He's very learned – a bit too much for me, although if you come down to brass tacks he's hit the same nail on the head as I'm driving at. Platonic love, he calls it, and I call it companionship between man and wife which I have with you. And as for one o' them Hetteary – I mean if the law allowed it – the only use, so to speak, I'd have for her is in the bed. But you needn't think that I'll go trapesing after another wife, in bed or out of it –' he pinched her cheek which she hadn't time to dodge – 'while I've got you. Give us a kiss.'

He pushed his face at her; his foul breath was in her mouth. She hastily drew back, and folding her baby's garment put it away in her work basket.

'I am tired,' she told him. 'Goodnight.'

Followed by Lorna, she went upstairs, and hearing him lumbering after her, she locked both the doors of her room.

* * *

From the Journal of Martha Todd:

> Xmas Day. Have spent it in bed. Have a cold. Said I did not feel like getting up. Just couldn't face the Horror, making merry. He got drunk last night, and was disgusting. Mr Dixon was invited to Xmas dinner with us but had to go to see his mother at Ealing. T. came and sat with me most of the afternoon. Talked a lot about mesmerism. He seems to have an obsession about it. Wanted to mesmerize me to get rid of my cold in case it affects the baby. He calls it auto-suggestion. Is still fussing about his health. Is very odd at times. Imagines things. Say he has worms crawling up from his inside into his mouth. Makes me feel sick. I suppose it is all part of his nerves. Have noticed lately that he has developed a twitch. He twitches his mouth and blinks his eyes while he sits and stares – at nothing! I asked the doctor about it, and he said it is a nervous tic and that he should take his advice and go for a long holiday, but he won't leave his business. The Liverpool St. deal has fallen through which has upset him. . . . Only three months now before my time. The doctor says all is going well.

And all did go well until we are told in a hasty pencil scrawl:

> Am having my baby any time now. The midwife, Nurse Jennings, was not due to come till next week. Mrs B. sent for the doctor when I had pains this morning and he wired for the nurse at once. She is here now. T. is at Dulwich. I told him not to send for him. He is not coming home till tonight so hope the baby will be born before he comes. . . .

The window framed a wind-torn sky with the slice of a new moon drifting through a beggar's cloak of cloud. She had told the nurse not to draw the curtains . . . 'I like to see the hours fly across the sky . . . but not the moon . . . you mustn't look at the new moon through glass . . . unlucky. . .'

She watched herself writhe in mounting orgasms of pain, seen, strangely, in colour, curious colours and shapes. There were dull cubes of pain and sharp streaks of pain, storm-tossed like the sky, shot through with flashes of crimson lightning, and pain presented in steps, opaque, moon coloured, up which one seemed to float through violet mists of no-feeling, and then a scarlet tongue of torment curling round her . . . and an intermittent numbness.

She watched the convulsions of her body as if her astral counterpart, her 'outside' self hung aloof, took no part in the shame of this abject, piteous thing that shrieked and heaved and doubled absurdly in acrobatic contortions and then, at last, after one tremendous tearing apart of all of herself, came blessed, dark oblivion.

There was no moon in the sky now. The clouds had gone, and with them, the torture; there was sunlight, a blueness where the clouds had been, and a treetop bowing to the window; and the doctor at her bedside with a hand smelling of carbolic on her forehead.

His face, large, red, comforting, bent down to her.

'That's better. Now we'll do.'

'Do what? My baby – where's my baby? Have I had my baby?'

The doctor took her hand and told her: 'Yes, my dear, your baby is . . . has been born.'

She tried to struggle up. 'I must see my baby'.

Both he and the nurse were holding her hands now.

'You are very weak,' she heard the doctor say, 'and it is better you do not see your baby yet.'

She was in no fit state, he informed the sobbing Jo, to be told of that still-born birth.

'A – boy, too,' blubbered Jo. 'I wanted a son. What went wrong? How? Why?'

Carefully the doctor explained how and why . . . Mr Todd would be advised not to see his wife for a day or two. After so protracted and critical a labour she was utterly exhausted. A most difficult birth.

And a slow recovery.

She had no wish to live. 'I did so want my baby. Why could I not have died with my baby'. . . Over and over again, during the following weeks would she unburden to Nurse Jennings who stayed with her during her convalescence until the spring was well advanced. A couch had been brought into the garden, and there with tall vari-coloured tulips in the borders and a riot of wallflowers and may blossom scenting the warm air, she would lie, listless.

'You are so young, dear,' the nurse said soothingly, 'you will have plenty of time to have more babies.'

'No!' she lifted herself up from her cushions, her face encrimsoned with the vehemence of her reply. 'No! never again. I wouldn't go through *that* again. Not with him. You don't know what I – I can't tell you – I couldn't have believed—'

From such remarks as these and others more direct Nurse Jennings drew her own conclusions.

So, in one stroke, as an axe fells a branch from a tree,

did Martha, crippled of hope, adjust her broken life to face the empty years ahead. Even could she have forced herself to 'try again', as urged by Jo, the doctor had said that were she to conceive, another birth might prove fatal both for her and the child.

Lonely and disconsolate through the ensuing weeks and months of her bitter disappointment she suffered, to what depths only her own soul knew, for she hid despair behind a mask of cool indifference that gave Jo to think – 'as things have turned out,' he told his father – 'that she's likely thankful to have lost our son.'

His father looked down his long nose.

'You may well say so, seeing as 'ow my poor lad is gone and will never know – what I know.'

'Now, see here,' Jo spat out the words at him who had risen to knock the ashes from his pipe against the edge of a spittoon, 'I'll not have you casting any more Haspersions on my wife. We've been through this before and you've apologized for your ugly suspicions. Ted isn't here to speak for himself and her, and if you think—'

'I'm thinkin' nothink,' said his father, with his back turned, 'only that it was about the time she and Ted went to Brighton together that she got in the family way but – I'm thinkin' nothink' came the muttered repetition accompanied by a slow half turn across his shoulder, 'only that it's funny-like considerin' what I saw with me own eyes.'

'What you saw,' shouted Jo, 'was in your nasty mind and nowhere else. And if I hear any more of this from you – apology in writing or not – out you go! I'll not have you under the same roof as my poor girl to slander her and make her life a misery, so now you know. And you'd better keep your big mouth shut or take what's coming to you!'

The threat sufficed to keep his father's mouth, which was not big, but small and pinched, close shut on that subject until such time as it was opened wide.

The doctor had advised a completion of Martha's convalescence by the sea, and accompanied by Nurse Jennings she went to Dover where Jo joined them later. He had secured lodgings on the sea-front and had taken a season ticket to enable him to go to and from London by an early morning train and back on the same night. Under these conditions Martha was free of his presence, save at week-ends, when more often than not he would arrive with Mr Dixon who would come on Friday evenings and return the next day in time for Sunday's services.

The nurse stayed with her at Dover until the doctor pronounced her well enough to dispense with her attendance. Martha was sorry to lose her. Friendless, save for Cecilia Grimsby, and too seldom did she have the chance of seeing her former governess, she had found in the nurse a friend in whom she could confide.

With Nurse Jennings and Lorna, who much to her disgust had travelled to Dover in the luggage van, Martha took her daily walk down to the beach.

'I am glad, in a way,' she said, the day before the nurse was due to leave, 'that the doctor says I mustn't have any more babies. I couldn't go through *that* again – with him.' She drew a hissing breath; and at the nurse's quick look at her, 'I mean – in order to have another baby. Nurse, have you ever read a book called *The Mystery of Man* by a Doctor Nichols?'

No, Nurse had not read that book.

'Then I'll lend it you. It's Toddy's. You can glance at it tonight before you go. I'd like your opinion of it. It is mostly about how to avoid having babies, not by what this doctor calls contraception, but by total abstinence or what the Catholics say is the safe period. But no period is completely safe, is it? And that is how my husband and I have lived together, except to give me the baby. I hated it – I loathed it, and perhaps that's why my baby was born dead.'

'Oh, no, dear,' replied the nurse disguising dismay under professional tact, 'that was not the reason at all.

Your baby was still-born because he was lying in the wrong position. And I don't think you should read those kind of books which are written solely for the medical profession and not for young wives who cannot understand them.'

'But that is just why this book was written,' persisted Martha, 'to help married people and wives in particular. Not that it will help me as I mustn't have any more children. I will have to make do with dogs.'

'The sea looks quite rough today,' Nurse said with sprightly cheer. 'I don't envy the cross-Channel passengers.'

'Yes,' Martha nodded, 'the sea is showing its teeth. Those white crested waves are very like teeth – grinning teeth, or Mr Dixon's exceedingly white false ones. You have met Mr Dixon, haven't you, Nurse? What do you think of him?'

'I have only spoken to him once or twice,' was the evasive answer. 'I gather he is – scholarly.'

Martha wrinkled her nose.

'Very scholarly. He rams his knowledge down my throat, not only when he is supposed to be teaching me Latin and geometry, but whenever he can show off his scholastic achievements to Toddy, who hangs on his every word . . . Oh, Lorna!' who had laid at her feet the stick thrown for her to retrieve from the sea. 'Don't shake yourself all over me! Do you want to go in again? All right, fetch it, then.'

She got up to fling the sodden stick for the joyful Lorna and resuming her seat beside the nurse:

'What do you think Toddy told me?'

'Well, dear,' apprehensively, 'what?'

Martha took a pebble in her hand, and staring down at it: 'Such lovely colours these stones have. At first they look all drab and grey, and then if you look closer you see all kinds of tints and patterns in them. Like people. Some people appear dull and colourless and suddenly you perceive a richness, a warmth, a pattern quite different from what you thought they were. Miss Merridew at my school here in Dover was like that, only she wasn't dull or colourless. She was sharp and pointed like this one.' She took up another stone. 'I liked her more than I liked her sister, Miss Emma. . . . I've gone right away from what I was about to say. He, Toddy, told me he was going to make a second Will, in case he dies, suddenly, or soon. He said he had made the first one when we were married leaving everything to me – this is what he told me in front of Mr Dixon – on condition that I never married again, when I would lose, he said, every penny of it. And then he told us – Mr Dixon and me – that this second Will which he intends to make would leave everything to me absolutely so that I could marry again if I want to and still have his money, for a man can't take his wife's money now that this Married Woman's Property Act is made law. I said I wasn't interested in his Will or how he left his money, and I do wish he wouldn't keep on about dying because lately he does talk as if' . . . She let fall the stone she held and gazed out at the crested sea. 'He is confident he has a growth. He is always reading medical books and imagines he has everything under the sun, and I do think he ought to see a doctor. He is getting so very *odd*. It worries me. Have you noticed anything odd about him, Nurse?'

'I have not observed him sufficiently to pass an opinion,' was the careful answer to that. 'I think Mr Todd has probably been overworking and that he needs a complete rest from the anxiety of his business.'

'I know, and he doesn't come every week-end any more – only if Mr Dixon will come with him from a Saturday till Monday if he can get another minister to take his service on Sundays. Toddy adores him. They have started calling each other by their Christian names now and Mr Dixon began calling me Martie. I hate being called Martie and told him so and now he calls me Birdie, which is worse. You haven't heard him call me that, have you? – because you don't sit with us in the evenings when he's there. Oh, I do wish you weren't going to leave me. I don't know how I shall bear it when you go. . . .

'I do miss Nurse so much,' she tells her journal, 'but she has promised to come and see me sometimes between her cases. T. is getting worse. Complains of pains in his stomach and looks awful but refuses to see a doctor. Says if there is anything seriously wrong he would rather not know . . . Am calling on the Misses M. today. Thought I had better go and see them before I leave here.'

'My dear Mrs Todd, what a pleasant surprise!'

Miss Merridew, unchanged, if slightly greyer and more gaunt, and Miss Emma in the flutters and looking, Martha thought, rather like a pink fondant in the process of disintegration, inquired severally after her health, how long she would be staying in Dover, and if she were still living in Dulwich.

'No, we have moved to Coombe, in Surrey, near Wimbledon,' they were told, 'but my husband wants to live in London, so we shall be moving again very soon.'

'And your husband – is he keeping well?' twittered Miss Emma.

'Not so well as I would wish. He has been overworking. His business takes up so much of his time.'

'And,' with some lack of originality Miss Merridew asked, 'are you keeping well?'

'Thank you, yes. I am better now. I have not been very well. My baby,' Martha set down her cup, 'was born dead, two months ago. My first baby. I almost died too.'

'How very sad. Pray accept my condolences. I am deeply grieved to hear of your loss,' said Miss Merridew, with no apparent evidence of grief. And Miss Emma, busy with the tea-pot, chorused: 'It must indeed have been a bitter loss. May I refill your cup?'

'No, thank you. Yes, it was a great disappointment, especially as the doctor says I mustn't have another baby. I had a very difficult labour and another would probably kill me. I had a hospital nurse – my midwife – with me here until last week.'

'Pray take another macaroon,' offered Miss Emma, to whom these intimacies concerning the birth of Mrs Todd's baby had caused a recrudescence of the flutters.

'No, thank you.'

'And do you see any of your former school friends?' inquired Miss Merridew.

'No. I have not seen any of them since I left Albion House. I saw the announcement of Clarissa Herriott's marriage, but I was not asked to the wedding.'

'Sir Rupert Goring is a charming gentleman, we understand,' gushed Miss Emma, 'a baronet and a great property owner.'

'From what I know, or knew of Clarissa, I don't suppose she would allow herself to be included in his ownership of property, nor did I find him particularly charming when I met him at Clarissa's birthday party during the holidays while we were still at school. He had stick out teeth, a deficiency of chin and an equal deficiency of brains, so far as I could judge after one dance with him.' And before Miss Emma could recover from this denigration of an ex-pupil's husband, and a baronet – 'Pray excuse me,' Martha said, 'I must be going now. I promised Lorna I would not be out long.'

'Who,' inquired Miss Emma, 'is Lorna?'

'My companion,' explained Martha, pulling on her gloves.

'Oh,' again from Miss Emma, in titillated curiosity, 'so you have a companion?'

'Yes, I have a companion. She,' Martha innocently added, 'is a bitch. . . .'

And all the way back to her lodgings she laughed to herself at the remembrance of Miss Emma's reaction to that unmentionable word applied to her companion.

'To think,' gasped Miss Emma, watching Martha's exit from behind the window curtains, 'that a pupil of ours could have deteriorated and to such extent. Close association with the grocer husband to whom she is evidently no longer a wife – in name only – has had a most deleterious effect. Such shocking language! Doubtless learned from him.'

'I am inclined to suspect,' Miss Merridew smiled with half of her lips, 'that she was alluding to a female of the canine species with deliberate intent to shock, not me whom long custom has enured to shock from former or present pupils, but you, Emma, who are essentially a shockee.'

'Laetitia! to make a jest of it! That disgraceful word. And even if she were speaking of a lady dog she surely need not have used a term that is only permissible in a kennel. But what can one expect of the wife of a grocer? Todd's Teas!'

'It is very good tea,' Miss Merridew reminded her. 'And he still allows us discount for buying it in bulk.'

'You surprise me, Laetitia. I thought Martha's manner almost – insolent. And the way she spoke of Sir Rupert Goring!'

'Which,' reflected Miss Merridew, 'from my momentary introduction to him at the wedding, was not, I think, entirely unjustified.'

'Of course.' Miss Emma's blonde white curls jumped to the toss of her head. '*You* went to the wedding. We were both invited, and I had to stay as your deputy here. But Martha always was a favourite of yours. I never understood why.'

'She was not a favourite of mine for it is my policy, as you should know, to preserve a strict impartiality toward our pupils, yet I confess to an appreciation of so receptive a mind as hers which was a pleasure to instruct, despite a somewhat too vivid imagination.'

'She was not truthful, if that's what you mean,' retorted Miss Emma. 'I often found her out in the most barefaced falsehoods.'

'Prevarications, rather, shall we say?' The clangour of a bell brought Miss Merridew to her feet. 'Will you take prayers?'

'Must I?'

'I have letters to write,' said Miss Merridew, 'and the reports to send out.'

Miss Emma took prayers.

* * *

Although the Reverend Albert Dixon, was unable to spare more than a day or two from his ministerial duties to visit the Todds at Dover, Jo would write frequently to him, of which correspondence the following letter has been preserved.*

Dear Albert,

Permit me to say I feel a great pleasure in thus addressing you for the first time. To me it is a privilege that I am allowed to feel towards you as a brother and I hope our friendship may ripen as time goes on without anything to mar its future brightness. Would that I could find words to express my thankfulness to you for the very loving letter you sent Martha today. It would have done anybody good to see her overflowing with joy as she read it whilst walking along the street, and afterwards she read it to me. I felt my heart going out to you. I long to tell you how proud I feel at the thought that I should be soon able to clasp the hand of the man whom from his heart could pen such noble thoughts. Who can help loving you? . . . Looking towards the future with joyfulness,

I am, yours affectionately,

Joseph.

* This and the answer to it are excerpts from the originals.

To these effusive expressions of friendship the Reverend Albert as effusively replied:

My dear Joseph,

Thank you very much for the brotherly letter you sent me yesterday. I am sure I respond from my heart to your wish that our friendship may ripen with the lapse of time, and I do so with confidence, for I feel that our friendship is founded on a firm, abiding basis, trust and esteem. . . . Yet I ought to confess that I read your warm and generous letter with a kind of half fear – a fear lest you should ever be disappointed in me and find me a far more prosy and matter-of-fact creature than you expect. . . . I am looking forward with much pleasure to next week. Dear old Dover, it will ever possess a pleasant memory for me, and a warm place in my heart.

With kindest regards,
Yours affectionately
Albert.

It is unfortunate that there is no record of the letter from the Reverend Albert to Martha which caused her such an overflow of joy, but it is possible that her joyous reception of it as observed by Jo while she read it 'walking along the street', may have been an overflow of hysterical laughter, for according to her account of this interchange of correspondence:

I laughed till I cried. It is incredible that a man of his intelligence could write such drivelling sentimental rot. His letters both to me and T. might be written by a sixth form schoolboy in the throes of a first calf love. Not that I think he is in love with me – God forbid! Actually it is T. who is infatuated with him *vide* that Platonic love Toosie-pegs (alias Dixon because of the teeth) is always so full of, like David and Jonathan, 'the love that surpasseth the love of woman'. T. calls him Prince Albert now! . . . We are leaving here next month. T. has let the cottage furnished while he goes house-hunting, and has taken rooms in Clarendon Place not far from where we used to live when

I was little, but as T. says in a 'much classier neighbourhood' than Pimlico. This borders on Belgravia. It is the drawing-room floor with a balcony and communicating bedroom. I intend to buy one of those new divan beds that look like sofas so that I can sleep in the drawing-room. No one would know it was a bed. . . . Toosie-pegs has moved to Putney and is minister of a much larger chapel. Says he will be able to visit us more often from here for my lessons, as it is no distance in the train. Unfortunately. However I am thankful for one thing. The Horror will have to go back to Clapham. . . .

As the winter advanced with the November fogs, Jo presented Mr Dixon with a season ticket from Putney so that he could stay the night in London, for Jo would not allow him to go back and forth by train in what he called these 'dangerous pea-soups'. On such occasions, and at Jo's expense, he was provided with a bedroom by the accommodating landlady, Mrs Bridges, where he kept a change of clothes.

It was on an evening when the Reverend Albert was invited to dinner after giving Martha her lesson, that Jo came out with:

'I've made that new Will which I told you I was going to do, leaving everything I die possessed of to my wife, and I've appointed my general manager, Button, and you, Albert, joint executors.'

'I am more than honoured,' Mr Dixon exposed his teeth in an elaborate smile.

'As I am not long for this world,' Jo lugubriously pronounced, 'I felt bound to lose no time in having everything fixed, fair and square so's Martie will be provided for and that you –' he applied a toothpick to a molar – 'these dratted teeth o' mine or what's left of 'em – full of oles! – that you, who I trust Himplicitly as my dearest friend and minister of God, will protect and love my girl when I'm gone.' And he added with emotion, 'I leave er as sole legacy to you.'

'Rest assured, my dear Joseph,' was the reply with equal emotion which may have held a lurking disappointment that this sole legacy did not indicate a more lucrative beneficence, 'that in the sad event of your predeceasing me, I will never fail your trust.'

'I know that.' A tear from Jo's eye trickled down his nose. 'My Prince Albert, my brother, my more than brother, a David to my Jonathan.'

Martha got up from the table.

'Will you excuse me if I go to bed? I have a splitting headache.'

'A headache?' Mr Dixon sprang to his feet. 'Poor little Birdie. I trust you have not strained your pretty eyes with too eager attention to your studies. *Æmulus Studiorum et laborum*.'

'Better see an oculist,' said Jo. 'She mustn't strain her eyes.'

'No, indeed she must not. Goodnight and God bless you.' Mr Dixon opened the door for her and taking her hand bestowed a fervent kiss upon it. 'My precious little Birdie.'

To Lorna who had followed her she whispered: 'The next time that grinning ape calls me Birdie, will you oblige me by tearing out his tongue?'

She wiped the hand that he had kissed, to wipe away the dampness he had left there. Then, as she turned to go, she halted, and Lorna, who was panting with excitement as if in anticipation of the pleasure of demolishing Mr Dixon's tongue, if not Mr Dixon, halted with her.

'Now what?' murmured Martha, for she had heard:

'I didn't want to say this before Martie, but since we are all in God's Hands—'

'Amen to that,' from his reverence.

Martha crept to the door and laid her ear against it.

'– and as we never know how soon we may be called, it is my dearest wish that you should take her for your own when I'm no more. That's why I said I leave her to you – not in my Will, but as a solemn trust. I think I am right in believing that you love her, not just because she is my wife nor as a pupil who you find, as you tell me, a joy to teach, but,' Jo's voice broke, 'as a – Husband.'

'Oh, my God!' breathed Martha.

'My dear, my dearest friend,' was the lachrymal answer, 'I have no words to express how deeply I am moved by this most sacred endowment. If it be the will of Almighty God to receive you into Eternal Life before I, howsoever unworthily, may be called to join you later, I will deem it not only my bounden duty to observe your wish, but as I think you have sensed as only two persons who are in complete spiritual accord as are we *can* sense, that it would be the fulfilment of my heart's desire to love and cherish her in memory of you, dear friend. . . . Forgive me. I am overcome.'

Said Jo, also overcome: 'I'll tell Martie when the time is ripe to – to – tell her of my wishes – and – and yours, my friend and more than ber-ber-brother, but I think she'll need no telling. Her wer-wer-woman's instinct will have told her ow-ow-How you feel. Let me fill your glass and we'll drink to you – and her.'

'They've had more than they can hold already, and the princely Albert,' said Martha below breath, 'can't carry more than a thimbleful. Come on, Lorna, let's go for a walk. I must get some air or I'll choke.'

She went to the bedroom used by Jo, that opened on to the landing by a second door other than that which communicated with the sitting-room; and hatless, wrapped in a cloak, she tiptoed softly out. The recent fogs had cleared; the night, still young, was moonlit with a scurry of cloud in the dark river of the sky, star-studded, between the high roof tops.

Her way took her to Eaton Square, hard by. The light of street lamps shone on the bared tree branches where the last bronze leaves of autumn clung or lay on the narrow pavement under the garden railings like piles of new-minted pennies. The policeman on his beat, who knew her by sight for she often walked Lorna round the Square at this time of the evening, greeted her with a cheery 'Goodnight, Miss.' There were few pedestrians about. A courting couple stood, in heavy breathing silence, strained each to each against the wall of the shadowed archway to a mews; and a hansom, a four wheeler and a brougham or two, passed her as she crossed round and over to the other side of the square.

She was thinking, while indignation mounted with disgust. But of course, even if he *does* die before his time, which he won't because if they are always talking of dying, as he is, they never do – I'll probably go long before him – but if I don't and Toosie-pegs should also not have gone before to join him in Eternal Life above – or below – then nothing and no one on earth can make me marry him! I'm of age, or will be this month, and if I were not it wouldn't have made any difference. I was sixteen when Toddy married me, which is, I believe the age of consent – if only I had known! I need never have consented. What a fool – what a stupid ignorant fool I was to have let myself in for it. And now to dispose of me, handing me over to him as if I were a packet of his tea!

She had come to the house where the Herriotts lived, and as she paused allowing Lorna politely to use the gutter, a carriage and pair drove up. Lorna hastily rose from her squatting position to the safety of the pavement. . . . Might have run over her. Beasts! Martha voicelessly addressed the coachman and cockaded footman who came down from his perch to hand out the occupant of the carriage.

The street lamp shone full on her as she alighted, assisted by the footman to whom she said:

'Call back for me at ten o'clock.'

'Very good, my lady.'

Clarissa! Visiting her parents?

Martha stood uncertain whether to make herself known

or to pass on, but Clarissa had seen and recognized her under the light of a street lamp.

'Good heavens! Martha – it *is* Martha Todd, isn't it? How extraordinary. Fancy seeing you here. Were you coming in? You're not – are you – invited to dinner?' Her glance swept her from top to toe, and rested on Lorna. 'And with a *dog*?'

Martha smiled.

'No, I am not coming in nor am I invited to dinner, with or without a dog. I just happened to be passing.'

Clarissa, in a fur-trimmed velvet mantle that only partially concealed the sheen of her modish satin gown the train of which was caught up by one gloved hand, evinced astonishment, not altogether unsuspicious.

'Passing?'

And Martha, interpreting Clarissa's involuntary recoil that her presence, loitering, and with a dog, had been misunderstood, for she had heard from Mrs Bilson who used to warn her of the dangers of walking with Lorna after dark, even at Coombe – 'for them street-walkers often take a dog out with them. It's a kinda 'all-mark –' did not, mischievously choose to enlighten her.

'Yes, I pass this way almost every evening.'

Suspicion was now paramount.

'Whatever for?'

'Exercise for my – dog.'

'But you – do you live in London?'

'I do now.'

'You used to live in Surrey.'

'Yes.'

'Well, I – I mustn't stay talking. I am dining with my people.'

'And how is your husband?' Martha asked, deliberately detaining her.

'So you know I am married.'

'I saw it in the paper.'

'And you –' still uncertain what to make of this hatless,

smiling, and possibly disreputable Martha Todd, Clarissa asked doubtfully – 'are *you* married?'

'Oh, yes. I'm married.'

'To whom?'

'I married my guardian.'

'Your guardian? I remember now, you had a guardian. Isn't he much older than you?'

'Quite a lot older.'

'Have you any children?'

'No. I had one. Stillborn.'

'What a shame,' said Clarissa vaguely. She was thinking: Martha always was unconventional. But it is really rather going to extremes to walk about alone, dog or no dog, and no hat at this time of night. And: 'I really must go in now. I am late for dinner as it is. You know,' she laughed, a relieved little laugh, 'you haven't changed much since we were at school – what ages ago it seems. Do you live near here?'

'We have taken rooms in Clarendon Place while we are searching for a house in this neighbourhood.'

'Clarendon Place? That's just off Errington Street, where John lives. You remember my cousin John? He is qualified now. He passed all his doctor's exams in record time. His father died, and his aunt – that crazy old Mrs Ottery – bought him a partnership in a fashionable practice. I really *must* go in. Mama has some old fogies to dinner and I promised to help her out. Nice to have seen you. I will be in London for the next few weeks at Grosvenor Square. I'm at home every third Wednesday if you care to call.'

'I accept your apologia,' Martha smiled.

'My what?'

'Never mind. Goodbye.'

She watched Clarissa go up the steps where the footman, who had rung the bell, stood waiting for the door to open. A white-haired butler, the same butler as on the night of Clarissa's birthday party, admitted her.

'*O tempora, O mores,*' whispered Martha.

When she returned to the house Mr Dixon was at the open door preparing to depart.

'My Birdie! I thought you had gone to bed. Have you been out – and alone?'

'Not alone. I have Lorna with me.'

'Good doggie.' He stooped to pat her who darted past him into the hall, and stood bristling.

'You are leaving early,' Martha said. 'It is only nine o'clock.'

'I have to prepare my sermon for tomorrow –' it was a Saturday night – 'but since I am early shall we run through our excerpt from Horace? Our dear Joseph is not feeling too well, so I have packed him off to bed, where you, dear child, ought to be.'

'I have done nothing yet of Horace that you set me, so it is no use your coming in.'

Martha walked past him into the house and was about to close the door, but he, hastening after her, closed it upon them both.

'Never mind. We will refresh ourselves with a resumé of Ovid's *Amorum . . . Quod non licet acrius urit. . . .* How,' panted the minister, following Martha up the stairs who was taking two at a time, 'I agree with the Master . . . that which is denied us . . . is the most . . . to be desired.'

The maid had cleared the table in the sitting-room and made up the divan bed where Martha slept. Mr Dixon placed his hat and overcoat on a chair and himself in another by the fireside. As Martha knelt on the hearth-rug to warm her hands at the low burning coals, for she had gone out gloveless as well as hatless, Mr Dixon leaned forward, pulled her head against his knees, and turning her face upward, planted his mouth and his moustache on her forehead, and then, before she could avoid him, his lips on hers.

'My dearest little Birdie,' he whispered, 'if you could only know how I desire the – the most desirable . . .'

'Mr Dixon! Please! Are you – have you – gone mad!'

Indignation was mingled with disgust as she made attempt to free herself when, just at that moment the door opened, and Angharad, the little Welsh maid known as Annie, who attended to the drawing-room suite, came in with a scuttle of coals.

Martha was scarlet; Mr Dixon unembarrassed, and still seated, bestowed upon the maid the full exposure of his teeth.

'I was just about to give Mrs Todd her lesson.'

'Pardon me, sir. I will come back again,' said Annie with a sniff.

'Mrs Todd,' Martha told her, deadly calm and on her feet, 'is not having any lessons, so you may bring in the coals. And give Mr Dixon his hat and coat.'

'Tomorrow, then?' Still unabashed he got up, to receive his hat and coat from Annie and from Martha a stabbing look that from one less pachydermatous might have drawn blood. 'Perhaps it is rather late to attend the Master, and you are tired, so – shall we say Monday, when you will have prepared me our Epilogue, Book One? Goodnight, my child, God bless you.'

'There is no lie I am telling you, ma'm, may the devil fly off with me if what I saw is not the truth and him with her head on his knees and myself stood there in the door and no shame in them, and him a minister, look you. Lessons he will be giving her, is it. There is fine lessons, indeed!'

This, Annie's report to Mrs Bridges below stairs of what she had witnessed above, to which Mrs Bridges, if shocked, showed admirable restraint and, reminded of prompt payment by the drawing-room, bade her:

'I don't wish to hear tittle-tattle from you about my guests. Hold your tongue, girl, if you want to hold your place or I'll send you back to Wales. And why did you bring down the coals?'

'I was not wishful to stay, look you, ma'm, and there is two of them bold as brass and her saying to leave the coals and me not liking to put her and the minister out by staying to mend the fire, mind.'

'You can take the coals up again. Was madam's bed made ready in the drawing-room?'

'Yes, ma'm, and the sheets turned down and the hot bottle in and Mr Todd in the bedroom snoring to be heard through the door. There is true I have told you, ma'm, and not to be sent home to Ebbw Vale, is it?' said Annie with her knuckles in her eyes. 'My father he will hide the skin off me if I am sent to be home and seven of us younger than myself to keep and him only now out of hospital with his broken leg when the mine fell in and killed a dozen. There is sorrow in the Vale for us all, indeed. Thank you, ma'm. I will take up the coals.'

Martha, having duly noted in her journal the conversation overheard between Jo and the Reverend Albert, gives a brief account of the latter's repulsed demonstrations. . . . 'anticipating, I presume, the aforementioned legacy (me) bequeathed to him by T. Luckily Annie came in or I would have set L. at him. How much longer must I endure the pair of them? I dread my lessons with him now' . . . And of her meeting with Clarissa we are told:

> . . . Because I wore no hat and appeared to be strolling, I could see she thought I was not respectable. *She* is eminently respectable, has made what her mother would call a most suitable match. Carriage and pair, footman, all very stylish . . . . When I said I was married, which I think relieved her mind concerning my apparently disreputable character, she asked me to call on one of her 'Days'. Shall do nothing of the sort. She is not of my world, nor I of hers, I, who belong to no world.

And to this she adds a laconic rider:

> N.B. She says her cousin John is a fully fledged doctor now and has a practice in Errington Street. As he lives so near wonder if I shall see him again sometime. . . .

The next morning, Jo, who on Sundays allowed himself what he called his 'lie in', which meant that he stayed in bed until ten or eleven o'clock unless he went to Chapel at Putney, had breakfasted alone, for Martha had gone to Church at Holy Trinity. This, much to Jo's disapproval. 'Might as well be R.C. Anglo Catholic they call themselves. All that incense and images and what not. . . .'

'I want to speak to you,' she told him when she returned to find him still at breakfast.

'Speak away.' Jo unfolded a Sunday newspaper and read the headlines. '"Lord Randolph Churchill appeals to the Whigs" – that's an old fashioned word for the Liberals – "to coalesce with the Tories", and it says that "Lord Randolph made a stirring speech advocating measures to quell a socialistic tendency." That's what we're coming to under Gladstone – Socialism. But this election will throw him out. The whole country and his own lot too'll never forget what he did to General Gordon. Ole – Wholesale massacre, that's what it was.'

'Have you finished your breakfast?' Martha asked.

'Yes, that was a prime smoked haddock. I will say these Bridges do us well – at a price, but it's worth it. Best quality food though Todd's do a better back of bacon than theirs.'

He seated himself in an armchair by the fire and was once more immersed in his paper; and when Annie had cleared the table and taken down the dishes, 'Well,' Jo wished to know, 'what does our little Birdie want to speak to me about?'

'*Don't*,' she spun round, 'call me Birdie!'

'Aren't you our little Birdie – Albert's and mine? He's written a poem about you. He showed it me. To Birdie.'

'A poem – to *me*? Oh, God!'

'I'll not have you take the Almighty's name in vain, and on the Sabbath, too. Is that what they teach you in your High Church? Yes, a poem to *you*. I've got it here somewhere.' He felt in his pocket, and brought out a crumpled paper. 'Albert gave me a copy of it. Shall I read it to you?'

'No, give it to me. I'll read for myself.'

She took it, went over to the window, and without looking at him, said:

'I happened to overhear what you told Mr Dixon last night about your Will – and me.'

'So you were listening were you? Eavesdropping. Listeners never hear good of themselves. but this time you did, didn't you, eh?'

'No. I did *not* hear good of myself. I heard that you have left me to your precious Albert,' she gave a little shiver, 'as a legacy if, or when, you die.'

A dull flush suffused his flabby cheeks.

'And isn't that good Hearing? But there's nothing of it in writing – not in my Will. I've made him an executor and when I'm gone I've left you in his care as you was left in mine at your mother's wish, and it is *my* wish that he will guard and protect you and – take you to wife.'

She whitened.

'So you think you can dispose of me as if – as if I were your chattel or an – an animal to be cared for, given a home, is that it?'

'No, a husband, who I can trust to look after you. There's no one in this world,' said Jo, solemnly, 'that I'd give you to with a more willing Heart than him. I know he's sweet on you, and I know you like him not only as a minister of God but as a man. I'd die happy to know that you and Albert was made one flesh in Oly matrimony which is what you and I has never been. You read that bit of poetry and you'll see how he feels which is his nice way of putting it to you, and which is why he gave it me to read, and to tell you of his feelings. Go on, read it.'

She read it, her lips moving to the words:

> 'Who is it that has burst the door,
> Unclosed the heart that shut before,
> And set her queen-like on its throne,
> And made its homage all its own –
> My Birdie.'

There was more of it in similar vein, but Martha, who had got so far, read no more of it for the hysterical laughter that seized her.

'Good heavens! Is it possible that he, who has a certain knowledge of the classics and a university degree – I can't believe it! The man's a lunatic. Such drivel – worse than that sentimental slush he wrote in his letter.'

'I think it expresses a warmth and a true love,' said Jo, offendedly, 'which I see you can't appreciate. I'd have thought you had better taste than to laugh – to mock at a good man's love.'

'Oh, shut up! You make me sick, both of you! And for you to encourage him in this – this inane, this –' she tore the sheet of paper across and flung it on the floor – 'this twaddle, I – I'll –' her voice failed her. She raised her hand as if to strike at some unseen face, and then with a sudden fierce gesture brought the back of her hand to her mouth and dug her teeth into it. 'I'd *kill* him – or my*self* – or *you* – sooner than have him, or either of you, *touch* me!'

And with that she dashed through the folding doors into the next room.

Lorna who had been lying on the hearthrug leapt up and followed her. The communicating door was slammed.

'What d'you think o' that?' muttered Jo. 'I've had a taste of her temper before, but this takes the cake!'

He rose heavily out of his chair and, flinging open the door, went in to see her on her knees by the bed with her arms round Lorna and her face buried in her neck. She was sobbing.

'Now then, now then, this won't do,' said Jo, clumsily attempting to soothe. 'You won't have me and Albert touch you but you'll go cuddling a dog. Come on, you know I love you even if you don't love me – not as a wife should love her husband.' Placing his hands on her shoulders he dragged her to her feet and held her against him, breathing haddock at her. 'I've no thought but for you, Martie, and if I've not been to you all that man and wife should be to each other except that once to give you our child, which it was God's will to take from us, there was a – a reason why I denied myself what is nature's right. But there's no reason now – for the short time left to me on earth – why we shouldn't be together as we was meant to be.'

In a risen gust of passion he bore her down upon the bed, sprawling on her; his fingers fumbled for the fastenings of her bodice. 'You excite me,' he said hoarsely. 'You're lovely in one of your tempers. I'm going to have what's mine before I'm called. I'm not long for this world and I want you and I'm going to have you—'

'No! *No*!' Her voice, terror-bound, was a whisper. 'I can't – I won't! I don't want—'

'I'll make you want. I'm up and ready and I'll make *you* ready! I'll take care you don't conceive. I know what to do.' He pulled her bodice off her shoulders and was mouthing at her breasts. I'll have what's mine before Albert has you – when I'm gone.'

A dizziness overswept her, but she had strength enough to raise her hands and tug at his hair, saying in that screaming whisper, 'If you do – I – I'll *kill* you!'

'Then we'll go together. I'm going to have you – now!'

'Talking all the time of dying! *You* won't die. Let me *go*!' Releasing his hair, her nails sought to claw his face, when –

'Jo! Jo? Are you in there?' was heard outside on the landing.

'It's your father,' she said weakly, as Jo, startled, withdrew himself. 'Go to him,' she gasped. 'He has never been so welcome. Go!'

* * *

It was some three weeks later that Jo returned unexpectedly from business in the afternoon complaining that he felt ill. He had been violently sick. 'It's my stomach again. Same old trouble.'

'What did you have for your midday meal? You may have eaten something to disagree with you.'

'Only a ham sandwich and a glass of beer, and I brought it all up.' He sank into a chair. 'I'm in awful pain and – here! I'm going to be sick again.'

Rising unsteadily he made for the door into the bedroom. She heard him retching and groaning, and when she went in she found him lying on the bed. His face was bathed in sweat. His eyes, terrified and blood-shot, stared up at her. 'I'm dying,' he muttered, dry lipped. 'I've got cancer. I know I've got cancer. I read it up in *The Family Doctor*. I've all the symptoms of cancer of the stomach.'

'Of course if you will go reading those doctors' books, you'll imagine you've got every disease there is.' She laid a hand on his forehead. 'You feel rather hot. I'll take your temperature. . . . I'd better empty this. Can't ask Annie to do it.'

Shuddering with disgust at the contents of the chamber-pot, she carried it into the lavatory, and came back to him. Nurse Jennings had given her a clinical thermometer. She fetched it from the medicine cupboard where he kept his collection of pills and drugs.

'Under your tongue – don't bite it.' She watched the clock and took it out. 'Yes, it is slightly up. A hundred point one. I think you ought to have a doctor.'

'Don't want a –' he retched again. She flew for a basin and held his head over it, to no purpose.

'I've brought up everything inside me,' he moaned. 'There's nothing left to come. And I won't *ave* a doctor. I know what he'll tell me. Cancer. And cut me up. I won't have an operation. I won't!'

'Oh, for goodness sake! It's probably no more than an upset stomach from all those pills and medicines you take. But I am sending for a doctor, if only to put your mind at rest. You're *making* yourself ill – imagining things. I'll ask Mrs Bridges who her doctor is.'

She left him still hanging over the basin that she had left by the bed.

Mrs Bridges, when asked if she could recommend a doctor – 'to see Mr Todd. He has a bilious attack, and a slight fever –' obligingly sent the boot boy for Dr Ellis.

'We have had him for years. He is a very good doctor. I am sorry Mr Todd is unwell. Pray do not hesitate to order whatever you wish for his diet, but if he is bilious I expect the doctor will order beef tea or chicken broth and no solids.'

'Yes. Thank you.'

She went back to Jo; he told her he had been sick again. His scared eyes sought hers. 'It's cancer right enough. I've had it coming on for the past six months. All these pains and now – this!'

'Oh, do stop it!' cried Martha, on edge. 'Wait and hear what the doctor says.'

'You've never called in a doctor!' he jerked himself up, 'I won't see a doctor.'

'Yes, you will. He is on his way now.'

The boot boy had returned with a message that Dr Ellis was not available but that his partner would come directly. She went into the drawing-room, and called to Jo: 'Annie is bringing tea. Will you have a cup?'

'Don't suppose I can keep it down,' came the muffled answer, 'but – if you like.'

When the tea had been brought and she was about to pour a cup for him the door opened and Annie announced:

'The doctor is here ma'm.'

'Show him up, but first take this tea to Mr Todd.'

The afternoon was closing in with shadows. Below in the street the lamplighter was busy with his pole. She went to draw the curtains. The room glowed warmly in the firelight. Hearing Annie leave the bedroom and go downstairs, she lighted a table lamp and, taking a taper, stood on a footstool to light a gas bracket when Annie announced:

'Please, ma'm, the doctor.'

She turned.

Some seconds passed while, still standing on the stool, the taper in her hand, she stayed transfixed. Then:

'I have been called to see Mr Todd.'

Coolly professional. . . . He had not recognized her, or was she changed in – how long? Four – five years?

She stepped down from the stool; her heart was beating a tattoo against her ribs so loud that he must hear it, but, as cool as he, she said:

'Are you a . . . the doctor?'

If he had not known her at first he knew her then, to tell her:

'I had hoped to be, and am. This is the third time. You remember?'

'Martie!' Jo called from the bedroom, 'if that's the doctor I don't want to see him.'

Up went John's eyebrows. 'My patient?'

'Yes, and – my husband.'

'Your – ? I have never known your name, other than Martha. I came to see a Mr Todd.'

She said quietly: 'I am Mrs Todd. I married my – my guardian. Please go to him. He is suffering from a bilious attack and has a temperature. He imagines – or perhaps he *is* seriously ill.'

'I can't believe,' he told her with a puzzled measuring look, 'that you are married. You still have that dryad quality. . . .' And with reversion to the strictly professional, 'But what about the patient? Of what does he complain?'

'He thinks he has cancer.'

'A not uncommon obsession. Give me this before it burns your fingers.'

He took the taper from her and blew out the flame.

'Well?' Martha, who had brought him to Jo's bedside and left him to make his examination, waited in the sitting-room for his return. He was gone more than half an hour. 'Is it – cancer?'

'No, it is not cancer, as I have attempted to convince him, but I don't think he believes me.' Seating himself at the table, from which the tea had been cleared, John took a prescription pad from his medical bag and a pen from his waistcoat pocket. 'He has sub-acute gastritis aggravated by mercurialism.'

'Mercurial – what is that?'

He did not immediately answer, and rising, he handed her the prescription. 'Have this made up at the chemist's and give it to him last thing at night.'

'Is he – *is* it anything serious?' she asked anxiously.

'I can find nothing of a serious nature. Tell me,' he gave her another searching but entirely impersonal look, 'is he in the habit of taking mercury pills?'

'Mercury pills? Is that what you call mercurialism?'

'His symptoms rather point to it.'

'I don't know if he takes mercury pills,' she said, 'but he is always taking different kinds of pills and purges.'

'It might well be mercury. I have noticed a blue line round the edge of the gums which is symptomatic of the effects of mercury.'

'Why should he want to take mercury? What is it for?'

To that question he made no direct reply. He put

his stethoscope into his bag, closed it and said:

'His general condition is one of extreme nervous prostration, probably induced by hypochondriacal fantasies. He complains of sleeplessness. Do you know if he suffers from insomnia?'

'No. You see we don't – I mean I sleep in this room. We have never –' under that cool inquiring gaze of his the colour rushed to her cheeks – 'I wouldn't know. I do sometimes hear him moving about in the night.'

And now the veneer of professionalism slid from him to be replaced by the well remembered faun-like smile that regressed him to the schoolboy of seven years ago.

'So you married your guardian. When?'

Her heart missed a beat, but she replied steadily enough:

'I married him when I – before I went to school. I was married when I met you at Clarissa's party, but I wasn't – we were married in name only.'

He seemed not to have heard her, or if he did he made no comment. He said reflectively: 'The long arm of coincidence is not an infallible platitude. It does sometimes apply, although I hold no brief for coincidence. Fate, accident, or – the Moving Finger decides the cycle of our destinies.'

Her eyes evading his, she said low-voiced: '"The Moving Finger writes, and having writ, moves on: nor all thy piety nor wit shall lure it back to cancel half a line."'

That sudden smile came back again upon his lips.

'So you know your Omar, but, of course, you,' he slightly stressed it, 'would. Yes, we are as powerless to control our destinies as are ants when trodden under some clumsy human hoof while they go about their lawful and laborious occasions, and then their brethren come to bear away their dead and repair their devastated earthworks. Do you ever observe ants?'

'No.'

'I have often thought that when the Almighty made

man He may have experimented first with ants and bees, gigantically fashioned and endowed with an intelligence far above the rest of His creatures, until He decided upon – us. We, arrogantly believe this world to be the only inhabited and highly evolved planet in the universe which, however, may contain innumerable worlds beyond the limited perception of the human mind, wherein are greater beings, vastly superior both mentally and physically to our puny selves.'

'Do you believe, as some people do believe, that Mars is inhabited?'

He shrugged a shoulder.

'Who knows? Least of all we who inhabit this earth and are finite and destructible, "cast into the Universe and why, not knowing, whence like water, willy-nilly flowing".'

'I see you, too, are a disciple of Omar.' Her smile answered his. 'I have only just discovered him.'

'And with him,' said he, 'the new sophistication, an awakening of the social consciousness that is over-burdened with maladies of the soul's unrest. This *fin de siècle* of ours will see a demanding revolt against stuffy Grundyism as personified in our admirable and rigidly orthodox dictatress, our ageing Queen Bee of the Imperial hive. The end of every century sees the overthow of preconceived shibboleths, a rebirth, regeneration, which is discernible now with the first labour pains of the child in the womb of the twentieth century.' He glanced at his watch. 'I must be off. I'll take the prescription to the chemist on my way to my next case. I have to pass him, and it will save time. There are one or two other things I want to send round to Mr Todd.' He took her hand and with it the prescription she offered him, in a firm warm grasp. 'Don't worry about your husband. His condition is chiefly in his mind.' He turned to go, and Lorna, who had come up from the basement, since Mr Bridges with whom she was a favourite had taken her for a walk, pushed open the door which had been left ajar, and came to him with every evidence of welcome.

'Is this yours?' he stooped to pat her, who wriggled her body in delighted response.

'She is mine and – all I have.'

She half whispered it, and he:

' "The more I see of men the more I admire my dogs." Do you know who said that?'

' "*Plus je vois représentant du peuple, plus j'admire mes chiens.*" Lamartine said it to Count D'Orsay, didn't he?'

'Who quoted it *ad nauseam* as his own. We seem to have a similarity of taste in literature and or – what?'

'The Moving Finger or – coincidental?' Those amazingly blue eyes of hers, upraised to his deprived him, momentarily of breath.

'I'll call again in the morning,' he said, and was gone.

A jingle of bells below the window caused her to open it and step out on to the balcony. In the light of the street lamp she saw a private hansom drawn up at the kerb, and a top-hatted coachman on the box. John, who wore a cloak that he had left in the hall and carried his hat in his hand, gave a direction to the driver: 'Stop at Rogers the chemist, then on to – fifty five, Belgrave Square.'

The light shone on his uncovered head, gilding the fair young hair. She had noticed the scar on his forehead, now fading but still discernible. He looked older, yet still the same, long-limbed, and taller, certainly. He must be well over six feet, for she had to look up to him from her five feet five inches. Had he found her changed, she wondered? Four or five years makes a difference when one is very young.

The Moving Finger writes and, yes, had written. From that second meeting at Clarissa's party she had known, deep within her, that her life and his had met to be . . . star-crossed.

EIGHT

From the Journal of Martha Todd:

December 18th, 1885

. . . Dr Herriott says T. is in no danger of dying, that his condition is chiefly imaginary and that his teeth are the cause of his toxaemia and must come out. But he is so strange in his manner. The latest is that he imagines he has worms crawling all *over* him! And is so depressed and talks so much of death and wanting to die that I am afraid of what he might do to himself by taking an overdose of those sleeping draughts the doctor gave him. I told Dr H. of my fears and he said not to leave any medicines or sleeping draughts within his reach. . . .

I wouldn't want anyone to see what I have written about T. and me nor about his father. For T's sake I wouldn't want anyone to know about that. Mrs Bilson knew, of course, but I heard, only last week from the people who had taken the cottage, and her with it, that she had suddenly died of a heart attack, poor old soul. So I am going to take out those pages about his father and seal them in an envelope and I shall put them in Maman's tin box where she kept her trinkets and things she brought from France. I have found a loose board in the attic where our trunks are stored. It came up quite easily, and when I have finished writing this I am going to bury the box under the board and hammer down the nails, and when we leave here I can take the envelope out again. . . .

The Horror has been coming to see T. every day but the doctor says he must not be worried by visitors talking to excite him. It is difficult to tell his father so. He was furious when I told him what the doctor said. I shall have to write it to him. He thinks I am keeping him from seeing T. out of spite – the old beast, or perhaps he thinks I am responsible for his illness by giving him the wrong medicines or something. Heaven only knows what he thinks! If only Ted were here. It is such a responsibility having him like this and his father so hateful to me. I have had his bed brought into the front room which gets more sun and have put the divan into the bedroom, but for these last two weeks he has made me sit up with him at night. If I try to have an hour's sleep in the other room he gets up and walks about calling for me and makes me hold his foot under the bedclothes. Goodness knows why his foot and not his hand! Says it soothes him. So I have to sit in a chair by his bed and mustn't move. He keeps waking up, But between his short sleeps I manage to doze on the sofa. . . .

His 'Albert' also comes – almost every day, and despite the doctors orders, he sits with T. and gets him all worked up, talking about those idiotic ideas of his, and Platonic love, and all the rest of it. Yesterday T. made him *kiss* me! 'Kiss her,' he said, 'she is as much yours as mine now, and will be all yours soon.' D. kissed and slobbered over me and called me his 'Beloved little Birdie', in front of T. who looked on smiling in a silly and rather frightening way. Yesterday when I had tucked him up for the night he pulled me down to him and *he* began kissing me and saying 'I am not going to let Our Prince Albert have what is mine while I am still here to enjoy you!' And he got himself out of the bed and pulled off his shirt. It was awful but I managed to quiet him by saying that he was not well enough yet to do anything like that. He looked very strange and his eyes were all blood-shot, his breath too horrible – that's his teeth. Thank God he is going to have some of them out on Thursday. Poor dear, I do so pity him. It is awful to see him so changed, so rapidly deteriorating. The doctor says he is not in any pain although he insists that he is. . . . Now I am going to hide these pages under the board in the attic.*

Directly old Todd had heard of his son's illness, reported

* A tin box containing some yellowed pages covered with writing in faded ink was discovered by workmen some seventy years later during the demolition of certain houses in a bombed area that were being rebuilt as a block of flats.

to him by Button, Jo's manager, he hurried to Clarendon Place and was admitted to the sick-room by Martha. He had called daily after that, but was not allowed to see his son more than three times a week, and then only for a few minutes.

'It's a mystery to me,' he told Martha, 'why he should be taken ill all of a sudden like this, with sickness and diarrhoea. Never a day's illness, more than a cold, in his life. Looks like 'e's been poisoned.'

The insinuation behind this remark, not the first of its kind, was made with a roving eye at the ceiling.

'Dr Herriott,' she smothered indignation in a voice, steel-edged, 'considers his toxic condition is due to his teeth that are in a dreadful state, which, he says, might well be the primary cause of the trouble. The doctor has arranged to take him to the dentist.'

'When?'

'Tomorrow.'

'Well, whatever 'e '*as* got is somethink worse to my mind, than what the doctor makes out.'

This conversation took place in an ante-room on the ground floor used by the guests of the house as a smoking-room and which had been placed at the disposal of visitors inquiring after Mr Todd. Moving to the door, Martha said:

'I will be obliged if you will leave me now. It is time for his medicine.'

'*I'll* give 'im 'is medicine,' said his father pointedly.

'I would rather you did not. He is suffering from insomnia, and talking doesn't help him to respond to sedatives. The doctor gave him an injection of morphia this morning to induce sleep, and says he must be kept quiet.'

'What time is 'e going to the dentist termorrer?'

'At eleven o'clock. The doctor is taking him and bringing him back.'

'Then I'll come 'ere early in the afternoon to know the

result.' And he stared at her now. 'I 'ope this doctor knows 'is job. I'd like ter see 'im and ask 'im what 'e's doin' of givin' 'im morphia which is poison – leastways I've always 'eard so. If 'e ain't better when 'e's 'ad 'is teeth out I'll get another doctor in to see 'im.'

'I have every faith in Dr Herriott. He is a very careful and highly qualified physician.' A bell rang loudly in the basement. 'That was Jo's bell. Excuse me.'

It was after this that Martha, seeing the effect his father's visits had upon Jo, encouraging him to think himself much worse than he was, refused to allow old Todd's admittance to the sick room. However, she sent him several notes reporting on his progress; but when he insisted he should be permitted to see his son she wrote:

'You are welcome here when I invite you but at no other time. I am sorry to have to speak so plainly but I have neither forgotten nor forgiven the past . . .' And she adds: 'You seem to forget that I have not been to bed for thirteen nights, and am consequently too tired to speak to visitors.'

Far from inducing sympathy for Martha, this letter determined the old man's decision to demand further medical advice, even though the visit to the dentist corroborated that the patient's condition was largely due to his teeth, which were described as being in 'a shocking state'. Jo refused to get up although the doctor told him he could find no reason why he should not, and took him sternly to task.

'You must get up and go out. You are perfectly well enough to go for a walk or a drive in the park. You are doing yourself no good by lying here.'

But Jo remained obdurate.

'If I get up, Doctor, it will kill me,' he whined. 'I know I am dying whatever you may say, and I'd sooner die here in my bed.'

'You are no more likely to die before your time, which

is not now, than I am or anyone of us.' John was losing patience. 'And if you won't take my advice I will refuse to treat you. Not that you need any more treatment than to get yourself out of this bed, and out of the house and go back to your business. So – get up!'

Jo took this greatly to heart.

'A most unsympathetic doctor,' he complained to his father, who unknown to Martha, had come to see him when she was out with the dog. 'He wants me to get up and go back to my business.'

'He told me you should go for a sea voyage,' said his father. 'Fine sort o' doctor to want to send you on a sea voyage and you weak as a rat.'

'It's my stomach,' groaned Jo, 'and the wind in my bowels, and I feel like as if I have worms crawling up me. If I could only get a good night's sleep. I never sleep!'

To Martha, who had nursed him incessantly for more than two weeks, day and night, John was equally blunt.

'He's a hypochondriacal hysteric, and you must not give in to him. The more you fuss over him the worse he will be, and you must go to bed and get some sleep.'

And she: 'What is the use of my going to bed? If I do lie down in the bedroom he gets up and prowls around fidgeting and won't sleep a wink unless I sit with him and hold his toe.'

'His toe!' ejaculated John.

'Yes, his toe –' an unexpected smile lightened her face – 'or his foot, under the bedclothes. He says my touch soothes him.'

'I never heard such nonsense. What he needs, as I have already prescribed, is a sea voyage – alone, with no one to pet and slavishly wait on him – holding his toe!' John took up his medical bag and walked to the door. 'As for you, if you don't get some rest away from him, you'll be my next patient. I won't call again until the end of the week unless you send for me.' At the door he told her: 'Do have some sense about this. I mean it.

You will crack up if you don't take my advice.'

No sooner had he gone than old Todd came puffing up the stairs and waylaid her on the landing.

'I saw that doctor o' yours gettin' into his private 'ansom all togged up in a cloak and topper more like a masher than a doctor. What's 'e say now?'

'He says that Jo is quite well enough to get up and he repeats his advice that he should go for a sea voyage – alone.'

'Keepin' on about a sea voyage – in his state o' health, and alone!' exploded Todd. 'Does 'e want to kill 'im? Sayin' there's nothin' the matter with 'im more'n his teeth and a fat lot o' good pullin' 'em out 'as done 'im! I want another opinion. I'll 'ave a 'Arley specialist to 'im, and you can tell the doctor that from me. I want to get to the bottom o' this and know what *is* wrong with 'im. Givin' 'im morphia!'

'He hasn't had any morphia for these last ten days,' Martha said, inwardly fuming, outwardly calm, 'but if you want another opinion, by all means have one.'

'Yes, and let's 'ave no more muckin' about with that young know-all. Send a note round to ask 'im to call back tonight and give us the name of a specialist.'

'If you wish, but I think a specialist is a needless expense.'

'Expense! When my son's life is at stake? Is that all you care about – savin' 'is money so there'll be more for you when 'e's gone? You do as I say, my girl, or it'll be the worse for you, if,' said Todd meaningfully, 'anythink 'appens to 'im.'

That same evening John, having received a note from Martha asking him to call – 'I will explain why when I see you' – came at ten o'clock and was received in the room set aside for visitors.

'I must apologize for bringing you out at this time of night, Doctor,' Martha said – it was always 'Doctor' and 'Mrs Todd' between them – 'but there is something I have to tell you and I would rather it were told in the presence of my hus – of your patient. Will you please come to him?'

'You look worn out,' John said brusquely. 'I will give you a tonic, and you really must have some sleep.'

'Perhaps tonight,' she smiled a thin little smile, 'if he will let me.'

'No question of his letting you. It is what I prescribe for you, and that's an order. Understand?'

To which she made no reply, and, after a pause while their eyes met and, meeting, seemed to find it difficult to disengage, 'I want you to know,' she said, 'that what I have to tell you, or what *he* tells you, is nothing to do with me. It's – his father. Please to come upstairs.'

Leaving his hat and cloak on a chair, John followed her to Jo's room.

'I'm sorry, Doctor,' mumbled Jo, 'to have dragged you out tonight. It's because my father,' he glanced aside, 'is always interfering – and no offence meant, but he, my father, wants another doctor to see me. That is if you don't object.'

'By all means,' said John easily, 'call in as many doctors as you will.'

'It's because of my father,' Jo repeated. 'He's not friendly to my wife. Never has been, and any doctor *she* calls in he'll be sure to find fault with. I'm quite satisfied with all you've done for me, and if I don't feel as well as you say I am, I expect it's my own fault – not taking your advice and getting up. But my father, he says he wants a specialist to see me.' Jo rose up from his pillows, his mouth twitching, his face flushed. 'I've every faith in you, sir, and I'll see any gentleman *you* choose to have see me for a second opinion, and I'm only agreeing to that for my wife's sake. My father's always pestering and bothering her – thinks she isn't doing what's right for me or following your orders, and what not. And he doesn't agree with your treatment so – there it is!'

'In which case,' said John equably, 'I will make an appointment at once with Dr Gardiner of Harley Street, the eminent neurologist.'

'Neurologist – that's nerves, isn't it? He's not a brain specialist, is he?' asked Jo, alarmed.

'No, he is not an alienist – that is to say a brain specialist. He is a general physician, specializing in neurology.'

'So you think it's me nerves, do you?' Jo gave him a bolting look. 'I know what you doctors think of nerves. The beginnings of madness, that's what nerves are. And it's not me nerves, it's me stomach – some sort of growth. It says in *The Family Doctor* that anyone who's had a good digestion which I've had all my life suddenly suffers from pain after meals and vomiting with flatulence – which is how this started – that it's a sign of cancer of the stomach. As for these sleeping draughts you gave me they don't send me right off, I keep waking up. They're not strong enough to be any use.'

'I will give you nothing stronger, and I must ask you not to impose upon your wife's rest by demanding that she spends her nights at your bedside. Do have some thought for her, Mr Todd, and less of yourself. You have no symptoms of malignancy as I am sure Dr Gardiner, when he examines you, will agree. Goodnight.'

'I will see you down, Doctor,' Martha said; and when they were out of earshot: 'Do you think his condition *is* only nerves?' she asked anxiously. 'He does so incessantly complain of pains and imagines all sorts of horrible things. He told me the other day that worms are eating him. "A taste," he said, "of what he'll have when he's in his grave." Is he going out of his mind?'

'No. Nervous hysteria aggravated by egocentric morbidity. I insist,' he told her, taking his hat and cloak from the hall stand, 'that you do not give in to him. Leave him alone at night and go to your bed. I'll have a message sent to Dr Gardiner in the morning and hope for an appointment the next day. When we have had his opinion, which I am sure will endorse mine, I trust your father-in-law will cause you no further annoyance.' And noting shadows like faint bruises underneath her eyes that made them more than ever an astonishing deep blue, 'I am more concerned about your condition than your – than the patient's. You *must* have some sleep, otherwise you'll be heading for a breakdown. And if there is anything troubling you,' he added as she opened the door for him, 'I want you to know that whenever you wish to consult or – confide in me, I am always at your service not only as a doctor, but as your – friend.'

'Thank you, I know and I . . . will.'

Tears stung her eyes as she watched him go down the steps and into the hansom that waited at the kerb. She heard him give a direction: 'Rogers, the chemist,' and as he took his seat she saw his hand raised, less in salute, she thought, than in benediction.

Dr Gardiner was unable to make an appointment until three days later. After a thorough examination of the patient, whom he found to be suffering from nervous depression and melancholia, he saw no reason to advise any alteration of the treatment prescribed by Dr Herriott. He assured Jo that he was physically sound and that the best advice he could give him was, as already suggested, to rouse himself, get up from his bed, go for a walk or drive every day, and directly after Christmas take a holiday at Torquay, for preference, with its mild winter climate.

While the doctors consulted together downstairs:

'What an ill-assorted couple,' Dr Gardiner remarked. 'How on earth did that lovely girl come to marry such an oaf?'

John paused for a second or two before he answered:

'I understand he was her guardian and married her when she had reached the age of consent.'

'I wonder she did consent. Probably didn't understand

to what she was consenting. She still seems to be, though not in years, a child, and much above the intelligence and breeding of that fellow she has married. Keep on with the bromide and get him off that bed.' Then, as John went with him to the door: 'Congratulations on your Membership, Herriott,' he said. 'You will have your Fellowship ten years before I did.'

And covering his head with a shining top-hat he walked down the steps to his carriage.

* * *

From the Journal of Martha Todd:

Christmas Day, 1885

A more than ever dreary Christmas. Wanted to go to Church but T. very tiresome, said he could not be left so long without me. Still refuses to obey the doctors and get up and go out. They say there is nothing the matter with him. It is only his nerves. I did, however, persuade him to leave his bed for Xmas dinner of which he ate heartily, in spite of being almost toothless. He went to bed immediately afterwards and lay munching sweets and talking about his pains and those worms and a buzzing in his ears and then he fell asleep and snored till teatime so that I was able to lie down in the bedroom and doze for half an hour until he woke me up calling for me to put him on the commode. After tea, at which he stuffed again and ate almost half of Mrs B's Xmas cake, as well as crumpets and scones – truly a remarkable invalid – I played a nocturne of Chopin for him and he sat there smiling foolishly, and presently burst into tears and said he was positive this was his last Christmas on earth. Then he suddenly got up and came over to me, crashed my hands down on the notes, and began fumbling at the buttons of my bodice and trying to undress me and – no, I can't go on. It was too horrible, but I managed to stop him by reminding him that he had 'given' me to his precious Albert and that it would be wrong to do what he wanted to do, besides being bad for him in his state of health. . . .

And: 'What am I to do with him?' is the despairing cry in her Commonplace Book. 'How to quiet him and prevent these increasingly frequent demonstrations of – one cannot call it love. Is it wicked of me to pray God that He will let me die? How am I to face my life with him for *he* won't die. I can't go on like this. I can't . . . I can't!'

Boxing Day.

His adored 'Prince Albert' came today. He had spent Xmas with his mother at Ealing and hurried here as soon as he could. The same performance from T. 'Go on,' he said, 'kiss her – she's yours as much as mine and all my money, too. And if anything happens to me it is my earnest wish that you two should come together! By which he means that if he dies I am to be married to that creature! They seem conclusively to have disposed of me between them. Then Dixon, urged by T., who appears to get a vicarious sort of pleasure in watching his 'familiar's' revolting attempts at courtship, began fondling me disgustingly, but I got away from them and took Lorna for a walk. It was about six o'clock and had begun to snow, so I could not take her far, although I was in half a mind to pack my bag and go off – run away, Lorna and I. How easy to catch a train to Dover and then to Calais and – France! But, of course, I wouldn't and couldn't. How could I leave my poor sick T.? Not sick in body but in mind. So back we went again and up to my room. . . .

Later. Midnight.

Toosie-pegs has gone. T. very talkative and restless. He asked me for a book he said he had bought some years ago, called Companion to the British Pharmacopoeia. He said I would find it in his trunk with some of the other books he had brought with him from Coombe. I found it, after turning everything out, but by that time he had dozed off. So I laid down on the sofa and began turning over the pages. There was a book mark in the page that tells of the effect of chloroform when administered as an inhalation and in small quantities. If I could get some and let him sniff it, either from the bottle like smelling salts, or sprinkled on a handkerchief, I wonder whether it would make him less – amorous. He keeps on about his 'Rights' and that I am not fulfilling my wifely duties by denying him. What am I to do, and how can I bear what he is trying to *make* me do? Help me, God, help me, for I cannot help myself. . . .*

On the following evening Mr Dixon called again to see Jo, and met Martha in the hall going out with Lorna as he went in.

'Where is my Birdie off to so late?' he tenderly inquired. 'Her little head should be tucked under her wing for beddie-byes. . . . Good gracious! Why is the dog growling and showing his teeth at me?'

'She is a sad mimic,' smiled Martha.

'Mimic? What is she mimicking?' nervously he backed. 'A nasty tempered animal, I fear. He looks as if he wants to bite me. Bad dog! Don't growl like that, you naughty boy. Naughty! Really, he looks quite savage.'

'She rather objects to being called a boy. There is nothing epicene about her. She is a great feminist. Will you please come away from the door, Mr Dixon? I want to catch the last post.'

She had written a letter of thanks to Cecilia Grimsby for her Christmas gift of carefully selected Shakespeare's Sonnets.

'Not *Mister*. Why so formal?' he writhed at her. 'Am I not your Albert?'

For answer she pushed past him and opened the door. Fastening the lead to the disgusted Lorna's collar: 'Will you go upstairs to Jo,' she said, 'he is expecting you.' She closed the door after her – and was followed.

'I cannot allow you to go alone to the post,' panted Mr Dixon, hurrying down the steps. 'It is quite a way to the pillar box and there are ugly customers about during

* The pages of this entry, torn from her journal, were subsequently found with others during the demolition of the house in Clarendon Place.

the festive season, even in this fashionable neighbourhood.'

'There is no necessity to accompany me. Nor am I going only to the post. My dog is in need of a walk.'

'And so am I,' said Mr Dixon, with another writhe. 'That is to say, a walk – with you.'

It was then that she was prompted, as she afterwards admitted in her Commonplace Book . . . 'by the devil, who must have put the thought into my head for why should I have asked *him* of all people, to do that which I could and should have done for myself?'

'Mr Dixon,' she turned on him who was sidling up to take her arm; she shook him off, 'can you tell me where or how I can obtain a bottle of chloroform?'

'Of what?' exclaimed the minister.

'Chloroform. My husband is so restless and sleepless, and – hysterical. None of the sleeping draughts the doctor prescribes for him seems to quiet him sufficiently, and Dr Herriott refuses to give him anything stronger, so I thought a little chloroform might soothe him. He is convinced he is suffering from some internal disease and says he is in continuous pain. I have read in a book on pharmacy that chloroform, if sprinkled on a handkerchief in small quantities – not as is given for an operation – but just enough to relieve his pain would help him to sleep.'

'Surely,' Dixon protested, 'the doctor would have prescribed this had he thought it necessary?'

'No, he says he must not be encouraged to take sleeping draughts and that he should have as much natural sleep as possible, but he is wearing me out. I can't get any sleep myself while he – Please, Mr Dixon—'

'Albert to you – my love!' he murmured, and stopped beneath a street lamp to display his teeth with a languishing look.

Ignoring this she continued, 'Please do what I ask. If I don't get some rest I shall go – mad! I can't go on like this having continuously to sit up with him all night.'

'Surely the doctor,' he began again, feebly, 'would give you the prescription if—'

'No, I can't ask the doctor. He wouldn't give it to me. He doesn't know I have had experience in the use of chloroform. Nurse Jennings,' barefacedly she lied, 'showed me how to use it in my – when I was having my baby, so that if she were out of the room and I needed to deaden the pain I could use it myself sprinkled on a handkerchief. Just a whiff is very soothing – makes one sleepy. I would be more than grateful,' and now it was she who took his arm, 'if you would buy a bottle of it for me.'

'H-how – wer-where am I to obtain it?' he stammered.

'At a chemist, of course, and in your own neighbourhood, not here, for they would wonder why the doctor didn't give me the prescription.'

'And how can *I* get it without a prescription?' asked he, greatly flustered, yet none the less gratified that she should have appealed to him, and happily conscious of the squeeze she had bestowed upon his arm.

'Any chemist would give it to you as a clergyman. You can say you want it to remove grease stains. I am told that chloroform is excellent for that and has all sorts of uses and none is harmful. They wouldn't use it for operations if it were.'

'Is it costly?' was delicately suggested.

'I shouldn't think so. I don't know exactly because Nurse Jennings used to buy it for me, but I can't ask her to get it now as she is in – America.' Which was a further fabrication, unashamed. She took her purse from the pocket of her muff. 'Here is a sovereign. That would more than cover it, and I understand Jo owes you five pounds for your season ticket from Putney which is overdue. He told me he was sending you a cheque for it.'

'My season ticket costs nothing like as much as five

pounds, and I would not dream of accepting so large a sum.' was the somewhat unconvincing reply as he pocketed the coin. 'It irks me to accept his generosity.'

'Don't let it irk you,' she said coolly. 'It would irk him more if you refused it.'

'I will bring you the change from the purchase of the – of what you want.'

'You don't have to. Buy yourself a New Year's gift with it – from me.'

'My sweet little Birdie!' he regained her arm that she had withdrawn from his. 'You are the only gift I want. You!'

'Plus,' she murmured, 'all my worldly goods.'

'You said?'

'That here is the post box. Oblige me, please, by going back to the house. I will walk Lorna round the square.'

'No, I cannot allow—'

'Yes, you can. Go to your Jonathan. Go and hold his toe!'

On returning to Clarendon Place, Dixon found Jo tearful and much more depressed than on the previous day. He therefore thought it wiser not to tell him, which he was inclined to do, of the commission Martha had persuaded him to undertake.

That same night, when he went back to his lodgings at Putney he wrote a note to a medical student of his acquaintance asking him to send him a bottle of chloroform. After posting the letter he believed he had addressed it wrongly, having remembered that his friend had removed to another lodging and that he had now mislaid the new address. Fearing the letter would be undelivered he decided he had better not wait for a reply that might never arrive.

As he had pledged himself to oblige his 'Birdie', and hopeful of more encouraging favour as reward, he went to three different chemists, two at Wimbledon and one at Putney. Although it was now past eleven at night, they were still open and at once supplied him with his requirements. He bought four ounces all in one ounce bottles. Each was labelled 'CHLOROFORM. POISON'. On returning home, he removed the label from one of the bottles, stuck it on to a larger six ounce bottle, and poured into it the contents of the four smaller bottles.

It had been surprisingly easy. No questions asked, for he was known to all three chemists, two of whom had been members of his congregation at Wimbledon. He told them he required the chloroform for removing grease stains from a suit.

Having made his peace with his Maker for this mild deception – 'to give my Birdie a good night's rest, O Lord' – he went to bed and slept the sleep of the just.

The next day he took the bottle of chloroform to Clarendon Place but had no opportunity of giving it to Martha until later, as Button was visiting Jo. He therefore suggested that she should take a walk in the park with him – 'on this pleasant afternoon—' 'So long as she is back here to give me my tea,' said Jo.

'He seems much brighter today,' remarked the minister as they walked in the direction of Hyde Park Corner.

'Yes, he is better. He went for a drive this morning, his first outing, except to the dentist, since he was taken ill. Have you managed to do – what I asked you to do?'

'I did. There is nothing in the world,' was the fatuous reply, 'that I would not do for my Birdie.'

Passing St George's Hospital, they waited for a traffic halt before crossing into the park. The lowering sun, red as a holly berry, stained the wintry sky with crimson. A bluish mist clung to the skeleton branches of the trees. Martha unleashed Lorna and let her run ahead. Stepping over the railing on to the grass, she walked briskly on, leaving Dixon hurrying to keep pace with her.

'Why such haste?' he panted.

'It is too cold to dawdle.' The crisp air had whipped some colour to her pale cheeks. There were few people about. Occasional nursemaids with their young; strolling couples, engrossed with one another; a stray park keeper alert for loitering tramps. The parade of Fashion when, behind the barriers of the Ladies' Mile, carriages, phaetons and horsemen lined up to exchange greetings with acquaintances or make secret assignations with their latest *innamorata,* did not frequent the park at this hour of the day.

'Well?' she turned on him sharply. 'Have you the – medicine?'

'Yes, I have it here.' He drew the bottle from his pocket.

'Give it to me.'

He passed it to her and she slipped it into her muff. 'Thank you. This will quiet him and give him some sleep. He refuses to take what the doctor prescribes. He is suspicious of all medicines now that his horrid old father keeps on telling him he is having the wrong treatment. In fact he as good as told me I am deliberately trying to *make* him ill!'

'Good heavens!' ejaculated Dixon, 'but this is scandalous!'

'Yes, and might get me into serious trouble if the old devil goes about spreading such wicked reports about me. He hates me – I can't tell you why – but he does and there are no lies he wouldn't tell to injure me.'

'Not while I am here.' He sidled closer, with an arm round her waist. She released herself and hurried on. 'Not –', he repeated, regaining her side, '– while your Albert is here to protect his little Birdie.'

This with full exposure of his teeth.

'Will you not –' she stopped short; the frosted grass crackled to the stamp of her foot – 'call me Birdie!'

'Time will be, pray God, when I may call you – wife!' He clasped his hands, gazing heavenward. 'May God forgive me for presuming to pre-ordain that which is the dearest wish, not only of our beloved Joseph but of me, to whom you are promised should our dear one be received in his heavenly home before ourselves, who are his—'

'Lorna!' she called. 'Come along. Come!'

The dog came bounding, straight as a dart, for Dixon. He, in terror, backed. 'You had better go,' said Martha, deadly calm, 'or you'll miss your train to Putney.'

'But I am staying to supper.'

'Not tonight. Jo has had enough of you today, and so have I. He must get some rest and your presence excites him, so please to go.'

'I cannot let you walk unaccompanied through the park in the dusk of the late afternoon.' His ungloved hand sought in her muff hers that clutched the bottle. 'Dearest,' he pleaded, 'be kind to me. Do not send your Albert from you. How can you be so cruel, so heartless, so indifferent to my adoration? *Injuriae potentiorum sunt!*'

'Oh, go to – hell!' cried Martha; and taking to her heels she ran from him, dragging the unwilling Lorna who evidently thirsted for his blood; nor did she stop until she reached the entrance gates, leaving him dolefully to make his way to the station. There he found he had missed the four-thirty train and must wait three quarters of an hour for the next. He sat in the buffet drinking tea and eating stale buns while he brooded on his wilful love's contrariness.

That evening, after Button had left him, Jo, who appeared to have benefited from his business discussions with his manager, sat up in his dressing-gown for supper, which he seemed to enjoy, and talked cheerfully of his visit to the dentist on the morrow.

'Four more to come out, but they'll be easy. Almost out already, and when the last of them is gone – that's a stump and will have to be taken out with gas – Dr Herriott says I'll be a new man. And you –' he pushed aside his chair and rising went to her – 'you'll be my new woman, my wife in *more* than name. We'll have our honeymoon, too long delayed. We've not had any honeymoon yet. We'll go to Torquay together and I'll have, at last, what's been denied me. But I'll not wait for that. Come to me now!' He pulled her on to the bed. 'I can't have enough of you to make up for all I've missed.'

Panic seized her. She struggled. 'No! Not yet – not now. Annie will be in to clear the table. You must wait until you are quite well again and then—'

'How can I wait? You've never had it yet – not as I can give it you. Being a virgin when we had it that time it didn't half hurt you, did it, little Birdie?'

'No!' she screamed, 'no! Don't *you* call me that – as well!'

'You won't have anyone but him call you that, will you?' he pinched her cheek. 'Nem' mind. It won't hurt you this time and you'll not find me wanting in how to make you like it. You'll enjoy it that you'll be so randy you'll be wearing me out.' He chuckled, gloatingly. 'Come on. Let's have a go now.' Unfastening his dressing-gown he began peeling off his nightshirt. 'How,' he repeated, 'can I wait? Look! See how I am up and ready – for you!'

He bore down upon her. She tore at his hair.

'I won't – you mustn't – it's bad for you. Besides it would be wrong, as you say you – you've promised me to Albert. Please, *please* – you mustn't! It's not right – you're not well enough—' gabbling, she strove to save herself. 'Let me give you your – your sleeping draught.'

'I won't take it.' He stared at her. He was smiling, open-mouthed; his furred tongue sucked at his empty gums. His eyes were blood-shot, wild. She closed her own against the look in them, and thought: He's mad, and grinning as his father grinned when – O, God, have pity!

'I'm not taking any more of that young feller's sleeping draughts.' He withdrew from her, suddenly calmed. 'I've got those belly-aches again. Thought I was feeling too good to last. My John Thomas isn't up to the mark after all.'

Thank God. I thank you, God, her heart whispered as she helped him into bed, saying: 'That's a good Toddy. Try to go to sleep.' She spoke to him as to a child, and like a child he obeyed her.

'You won't leave me alone, will you?' he asked piteously. 'I can't sleep if you're not with me. I like to know you're with me.'

'Of course I'll be with you – all night. I always am.'

He turned over on his side, and soon was snoring.

The final appointment with the dentist had been made for four o'clock on the last day of December.

It had been snowing hard and flakes were still falling when Jo, muffled to the ears with a woollen scarf and a Balaclava helmet pulled over his head, was accompanied in a cab by his wife and doctor to the house of the dentist in Ebury Street.

Although in a far more pitiable state of nerves at the ordeal before him than at his previous visits to the dentist – possibly because he knew that this final extraction would necessitate gas – Jo had fortified himself with a prodigious dinner of jugged hare and half a dozen oysters. Martha, hoping to distract him who was shivering with fright, talked cheerfully to John during the short drive in the cab of their proposed holiday at Torquay.

'My husband says it will be a second honeymoon for us, won't it, Toddy? Just as if we were being married all over again.'

John, glancing at the palely smiling Martha, said with supplementary tact:

'Which will prove to be a better cure than anything I can prescribe.'

To these pleasantries Jo's reply, scarcely audible through his swathed wrappings, was to the effect . . . 'remains to be seen . . . if I ever am cured.'

The tooth having been extracted, and Jo recovered from the gas, Martha took him home in a hansom. He seemed disinclined for bed and insisted on sitting up for his supper.

Mrs Bridges, who came to inquire how he had stood the operation, found him in good spirits.

'I'm thankful it's out and now I'll be meself again. That Dr Herriott, young though he is, knew what he was about when he ordered my teeth to be got rid of. Poisoning me, they were. And with this last of them gone, I'll be fine.'

'Could you eat something, Mr Todd?'

'Eat? Yes! I can eat now – not Half! Have you any of those oysters left?'

'There's still a dozen waiting to be opened – fresh as daisies,' was the beaming answer.

'Let's have them, then. That was a prime Hare you gave me for my dinner. I could do with three such dinners a day, but I could fancy those oysters – they don't need chewing, they slip down easy – and some of your mango chutney with a bit o' cheese 'ud do me proud.'

'I'll have your supper sent up to you at once.'

Mrs Bridges bustled away to give orders; the table was laid, the meal set before him, and Jo set to with gusto devouring oysters, mango chutney, bread and butter, cheese, and cake.

'Just imagine what bad teeth will do,' said Mrs Bridges who, at Jo's invitation, had seated herself to watch him eat. 'Now they are all out you're right as rain. You've not enjoyed a meal like this for weeks. But, Mrs Todd, you have eaten nothing.'

'She's never been one for her food,' said Jo, leaning back in his chair with a gratified belch. 'Pardon me, that chutney repeats. Come on, Martie, have a slice of this cake.'

'No, I – I'm not hungry.'

'Let me boil you an egg,' suggested Mrs Bridges.

'No, thank you, just this cup of tea is all I can – all I want.'

Mrs Bridges regarded her with kindly concern.

'*You'll* be our invalid next,' she said. 'You look thoroughly worn out.'

Jo belched again and explored with a finger the empty socket of his vanished molar.

'Gone – for good! And my pains all gone too, praise be! A bloody marvel – excuse my French, ma'am, but I'm not choosey of my words tonight, being dragged from the grave, so to speak, to begin a new life with – you!' He leaned towards Martha, sitting silent and pale beside him, to bestow a slobbery kiss on her cheek.

She jerked away from him and got up.

'Don't you think you had better go to bed now?'

'Bed? I've had a bellyful of bed. You know,' he told the landlady, who had also risen and was standing preparing to leave, 'that gas – I didn't go under, the doctor said, as quick as I should have done. Have you ever had gas, Mrs Bridges? Sit down again, do.'

Mrs Bridges obediently sat.

'No, I have never had gas,' she replied, 'but I did have chloroform once.'

'Chloroform?' Martha looked up sharply. 'What sort of effect did it have?'

'It was so long ago, I can't remember, except that when I came to I was very sick. It was given me when I had my first baby – and a bad time I had with her, too. They had to do an operation on me to deliver her. Caesar – something or other – they called it.'

Staring down into the untouched cup of tea offered her by Mrs Bridges: 'How,' Martha asked, 'did they give the chloroform?'

'I really don't know. They put some rubber gag or something over my face, I believe, but I couldn't say for sure. It's more than five and twenty years ago, and my girl's married now with two of her own.'

'That's got it!' A further exploration of Jo's toothless gums produced a piece of chutney on his finger-tip. 'I could fancy an addock for my breakfast, Mrs Bridges, if it's all the same to you,' said he, swallowing his find.

'By all means, sir. I'll tell Annie to go round to the fishmonger's before they close.'

'Good Lord!' Jo heaved himself out of his chair. 'I'd clean forgot. It's New Year's Eve.'

'And may there be many more New Years for you, Mr Todd,' said Mrs Bridges with smiles. 'No, Annie,' as the maid entered to clear the table, 'I'll see to this. I want you to run round to the fishmonger and buy a nice smoked haddock. Tell him to put it down to my account.'

'Yes, ma'm.' And when Annie had gone, and while Mrs Bridges busied herself with the table, 'I'd ask you, sir, and your good lady,' she said, 'to see the New Year in with us if it's not too late for you.'

'I think it would be,' Martha answered for him. 'The doctor said he ought to go to bed early after the gas.'

'Yes, I think I'd better get to bed,' agreed Jo. 'Don't want to overdo it just because I'm coming out of the wood. But I thank you all the same, ma'am, for the invitation. And the compliments of the season to *you*. Let's ope it'll be a Happier New Year for all of us – better than the last when we gave General Gordon to a pack of Howling Eathens, thanks to the Liberals, and old Mealy Mouth, Mr G.'

Mrs Bridges, whose husband was a staunch disciple of 'Mr G.' folded, simultaneously, the table cloth and her lips at this unseemly allusion to the Prime Minister and, wishing them: 'Goodnight to you, sir and ma'am, and may the coming year be happier indeed for all of us,' she took the tray and departed.

Martha undressed Jo, who was now yawning, put him to bed and gave him a clean nightcap and the mouth wash given him by the dentist with which to rinse his gums; having been made comfortable he lay relaxed but talkative over the extraction of his tooth and the administration of gas.

'The doctor said I took four minutes to go under, didn't he? Which is longer, seemingly, than is usual. I'm not an Haddict to – what do they call 'em? Soap somethink or other – sop – what is it?'

'Soporifics. Toddy, I – I have something to tell you.' She knelt beside him, steeling herself to say: 'I wasn't going to tell you but I can't keep it to myself. You must forgive me. I can't do what I meant to do – not without you knowing.'

'Why, wha – what's this?'

Jo sat up, the tassel of his nightcap wobbled over his nose. 'Drat the thing!' He tore it off. 'Fidgets me. What did you mean to do? Run away – leave me? Go off with Albert, or what? You've been carrying on something cruel when I ask to have what I ought to have, instead of living like a monk, though not,' he chuckled, 'a monkey. See them in the Zoo – they're at it all the time when not fiddling with themselves.'

'Toddy, please. You *must* hear what I have to tell you . . . Wait a minute.'

She went into the bedroom and took from a drawer the bottle of chloroform Dixon had procured for her. She brought it to Jo, held out for him to see.

'What the –' he snatched it from her, reading the label. 'Here! this – why it's *poison*!' His mouth fell open. He blanched, shrinking from her, terrified. 'So you were going to poison me! That's why my father was so against you nursing me. I wouldn't believe what he was getting at. He wasn't so far wrong after all. My God!'

'No, no! Listen.' Again she knelt, taking his hands that were blindly groping in mid-air as if to grapple with someone or something horrific: unseen. 'It is chloroform to soothe you and help you to sleep. I meant to sprinkle a few drops of it on a handkerchief so that you wouldn't want – wouldn't try to make me do what you are not well enough to – do. Besides, you know the doctors said I mustn't have another child. It might kill me and the baby, too. I can't risk losing the baby. I don't mind about myself.'

'There's no risk. I'd not let you have a baby.' He sounded relieved. 'You did give me a turn when I saw that label. If that's why you've been fighting shy of me, there's no need. I've got preventives. Bought a packet of them before I got ill – just in case. There's no reason now why I shouldn't have what I ought to have, though there might have been in the past.'

'The past? Why – what do you mean?'

'Nothing. Just – well – you were too young when I married you.' His eyes slid away. 'That's all I meant. But you're not too young now.' He began feeling her breasts, 'not now.'

She drew back, pushing him from her.

'Please – no!' She rose to her feet, saying wildly, 'it wouldn't be right. You know you have promised me to – to your Albert, so you—'

'Be damned to that! I'd got it into my head I was dying and wanted to leave you in good hands with one I can trust to look after you and the money that'll be yours when I go, which should be ten thousand at least, plus the business. You'll be a good match, my girl, and I wasn't going to have what I've put by for you, squandered by some Tom, Dick or Harry. But I'm not *going* to die. Not yet. And no one's going to have you but me. Come on, let's have a go now – for luck.'

He flung off the bedclothes and went to the wardrobe, fumbling in the pockets of one of his suits.

'Can't find them now,' he muttered. 'But I promise to be careful.'

She said peremptorily:

'Go back to bed at once. I will not allow – you mustn't – especially after what you have been through today.'

'I see.' He turned on her drawing a long breath. 'It's all lies about trying to soothe me – send me to sleep. Yes! To sleep, never to wake. I'm not a fool though you think I am. You hate the sight of me – want to kill me off, sooner than be a wife to me.' He stumbled back to the bed and got into it pulling the bedclothes up to his chin. His eyes sought hers piteously. 'Is that it?'

'My poor Toddy!' She took his hands that were clutching the sheet. 'I ought never to have told you. I only wanted to give you some sleep. None of the doctor's medicines helped you. I thought just a little whiff of it would give you a good night's rest which you have not had for weeks, but I couldn't do it. I had to tell you. I couldn't keep it to myself. I wanted you to know and then if you agreed – I wouldn't have given it you without your knowledge.'

'So that's it, is it?' Indignation, for an instant, blazed. 'I was to agree to be drugged – but you've got it wrong, my girl. I'm taking nothing from you – no medicines or chloroform – and from now on I won't take a drop to eat or drink that you have brought me. Understand? Give that to me.'

She had taken the bottle from him; he made a grab at it. 'If anyone's going to give me poison, I'll give it to myself.'

'No, Toddy!' she was in a rare fright now. 'I'll throw it away!'

'Oh, no you don't. I'll keep it here to show the doctor and ask him if it'll do me any good. I'm not having you mucking about with poisons. You might do not only me a mischief but yourself too. Chloroform! I thought you had more sense. Here you've been nursing me like an angel all this time—' tears welled; his voice broke. 'I've been a selfish brute,' he blurted, 'making you sit up with me every night – but I'll not let you do it no more. Things'll be different now I'm better, see? And I'll look after you instead of you looking after me.'

Her heart was wrenched.

'You forgive me? Say you forgive me. It was wrong of me to try and do what only a doctor should have done, but if I had told him and asked him to prescribe it, I would have had to explain why – not only because you are sleepless but because,' she faltered, 'of your demands on me.'

'I'll never take from you what you don't want to give. My little Martie, little angel – that's what you are – too good for me. I should never have taken you to wife, so young as you were, even though my wife in name only and making you out as three years older than you were on your marriage lines, so's not to have it known there's all that difference in our ages. You're far above me, in breed and everything, my little one, my baby.' He slid an arm round her shoulders. 'I love you, not just as a man wants his woman, but as a father for his child. And so, please God, I'll be your father *and* your husband if you – just for this once – I won't ask it again unless you come to me of your own free will – just to let me have you. It'll send me to sleep better than any medicine. Come on, let's have a go.'

Hot with desire his mouth found hers, sucking, slobbering. She tasted the blood from his oozing socket.

'No!' she shrieked, clawing at his face, 'Don't – not now! Don't make me.'

His gust of passion passed.

'Am I so ateful to you – scratching me like a wildcat? I could and I would make you and and I *will* – or put an end to this sham mock of a marriage. What sort of life is it for me to have a wife who is no wife – who wants to be rid of me even if it runs to – killing me?'

'You don't believe that!' Fear paralysed her voice to a whisper. 'I would sooner kill myself – if I dared face everlasting torment which could not be worse torment than this living hell!'

'With me? Is your life a living hell with me? Is it?

Is it? Then, by God,' he took her by the throat, 'I'd choke the life out of you, I would – if *I* could dare.' He turned from her, dragging the disordered bedclothes over his head. 'Leave me,' he muttered, 'get away. I don't want you. I'm better without you. Go on. Leave me be.'

She leaned over him, stroking his greasy hair.

'My poor Toddy, please don't take it so to heart. I'll not leave you. Go to sleep – you'll be able to sleep after that gas. And I'll sit up with you till you do.'

'Don't want you to sit up with me,' came the mumbled answer from under the bed covers.

She drew them back and tucked them round him, saying, 'I always do sit up with you and I will – especially tonight, New Year's Eve.'

'A bloody Happy New Year, I'll say!' His eyelids sank. 'That gas – you're right. It's having its effect so you don't have to drug or – poison me. You go and get some sleep yourself, and I will too.'

There came a knock at the door. It was Annie with the coals and a bowl of the beef tea he always took last thing at night.

'I'll make up the fire,' Martha told her, 'and I think Mr Todd will not be needing his beef tea tonight. He is half asleep already, and I don't want to wake him to take it.'

Annie, with a glance at the huddled figure on the bed, carefully deposited the coal-scuttle by the fender, and with a hushed 'Goodnight to you, ma'm,' left the room. Martha, having previously placed the bottle of chloroform on the mantelpiece, went to the bedroom, took off the dress she had been wearing during the day, and her corsets, and put on the loose gown she wore when sitting up with Jo at night.

When she went back to him, having been gone half an hour while she changed her clothes and brushed her hair, she found him sleeping soundly.

She drew up a chair to his bedside and lit a lamp well

shaded from him, but with sufficient light for her to write in her journal:

New Year's Eve

I have told him about the chlor. He took it very well, considering that at first he thought I had bought it to poison him! . . . I think the shock did him good. He talked more sensibly than he has since the first days of his illness. Perhaps it is all for the best that I did tell him although he showed a fit of temper before he quietened . . .

That Outsideness came on me again while I was undressing. It is ages since I had it last. I had to walk about in and out of his room and bite my fingers to bring myself back to me. I can't remember what I was doing or . . . what I did. It lasted a long time, longer than usual . . . too long.

The clock in her bedroom struck the half hour to midnight. From below she could hear the sound of a concertina and the murmur of hilarious voices. Mr and Mrs Bridges were entertaining guests to see the New Year in.

The fire burned brightly, casting a flicker of flame like ripples of red-gold water in the depths of a mahogany wardrobe. She must go through his clothes tomorrow, they would need pressing and buttons sewn on if he were to be up and about again. If . . .

She buried her face in her hands. God, she prayed, forgive me for what I might have done. Save me, God, save me from . . . Yes, and he would be wanting some new shirts. She had noticed his cuffs were frayed.

Her eyes voyaged slowly to the bottle on the mantelshelf. Was it in the same place where she had left it when she went to change for the night? Or nearer to the bed? But he couldn't have reached it even if. . . . Did I want him to reach it? O, God, what possessed me to tell him, giving him ideas. He might try to drug himself to sleep. She leaned over him again. He is snoring very heavily. Why did I leave it there? Could he have . . . ? No. He always snores when he's fast asleep. So very fast asleep. Must be the gas.

She slid her hand under the bedclothes and felt for his foot. She had better hold it for if not, when he awakened he would get into a state, would think she was neglecting him. He is still unbalanced. This insistence on her holding his toe. . . . Laughter surged up in her. . . . This won't do. She checked herself. We can't both go . . . mad.

In the basement the voices were more noisy. Some man was singing *Champagne Charlie,* amid roars of applause followed by a sudden quiet while the bedroom clock struck the first note of midnight.

Then was heard the chiming of church bells in the distance and a loud chorus from below of *Auld Lang Syne* and a general shout of 'Happy New Year!'

And at last Martha slept, exhausted.

When she awakened the house was silent, the guests had gone. Jo's watch, on the bedside table, gave the time as half past three. Down in the street was heard the occasional rattle of wheels, the clatter of hooves, as late revellers returned to their homes.

She was aware of pins and needles in the hand that had been holding Jo's foot, and withdrew it gently for fear of disturbing him. She saw he had altered his position and was now lying face downwards. She turned him over. His jaw had dropped, and he had ceased to snore.

Fear clutched at her. Was he breathing? She laid her ear to his mouth, could detect no breath. She unfastened his shirt, felt for his heart, and then his pulse . . . no movement. She flew for the bottle of brandy in his medicine cupboard and tried to pour some down his throat; it spilt, unswallowed, running down and on to his unstirring naked chest.

'No!' she whispered. 'No, God, no! Not – *this*. Did I . . . did he. . . ?

The bottle of chloroform was still on the mantelshelf. She sniffed at his fallen lips, no smell more than the spilt brandy that dripped from them.

His heart! The doctor. . . . She must get the doctor. Neither he nor the specialist had said there was anything wrong with his heart, but perhaps the gas . . . he was so cold! The fire had burned low. She replenished it into a blaze to warm him.

Her knees trembled; the room swayed, a darkness overcame her. She mustn't faint . . . too long without food. Taking the bottle of brandy she swallowed some; it steadied her and, lighting a candle, she ran upstairs to the fourth floor where the servants slept. She knew which door was Annie's. She went in.

'Annie!' She shook her awake. 'You must get up – get *up*! Mr Todd is – is ill. You must go for the doctor – at once!'

Annie, rubbing sleep from her eyes, blinked at her.

'What – why, ma'm – what—'

Martha took her by the shoulders.

'Hurry. Get up. Go and fetch the doctor – Dr Herriott. Dress yourself quickly. Make haste.'

She tore down the stairs to the Bridges' room and knocked on the door. Without waiting for an answer she burst into the room.

'Mr Bridges, please! Will you come to Mr Todd? I have sent Annie for the doctor. I think . . .' her voice dwindled, 'I think my husband is . . . dead.'

* * *

When in the dawn of that New Year's Day John arrived at the house in Clarendon Place, he confirmed at a glance Martha's fears. She, who had hoped against hope to believe Jo in a coma as result of a stroke or heart attack, heard the doctor's verdict, gently given: 'There is nothing I can do, my dear. He is gone.'

She sank to her knees by that motionless figure on the bed, over which John had drawn the sheet, and, at this climax to the strain of the past few weeks, her defensive self-control was shattered in a storm of weeping.

John raised her up and led her to the inner room, sat her in a chair and waited for the paroxysm to pass.

'Why – how–' she managed to find voice to say, 'did he – die? He seemed much quieter, less nervous when he went to sleep.'

'At what time was this?' asked John.

'Just after midnight.' She could speak more calmly now. 'But why,' she repeated in her numbed voice, 'is he . . . dead?'

'I am unable to tell you until a further examination has been made.' He drew another chair to sit beside her, and taking her hand he held it fast. 'Can you bear to answer a few questions?'

She nodded; her eyes in the pallor of her face were dark pools from which all blueness looked to be lost.

'You say he went quietly to sleep.' John felt her small cold fingers flutter in his hand like the wings of a frightened bird, and he tightened his hold on them. 'Did you give him a sleeping draught?'

'No, he slept without any, but he was snoring – more than usual, more heavily, I thought.'

Her hand stayed in his, unstirring now, almost lifeless, as if the blood in her veins had ceased to flow.

'Before I treated him he was in the habit of taking pills and various medicines, was he not?'

Again she nodded.

'Could he,' pursued John, chafing the cold little hand in both of his, 'have inadvertently taken something that would act as a poison – in an overdose?'

She dragged her hand from his. Her eyes were wide with terror.

'Poison! No, oh, no! He couldn't possibly – not without my knowing.'

Said Bridges, hovering inquisitively in the doorway:

'I noticed a peculiar smell when madam called me to – the deceased. I knew he was dead as soon as I touched him.'

Martha made her voice firm to say:

'I tried to pour brandy down his throat, but it spilt – you might have smelt that.'

'No,' asserted Bridges. 'It weren't brandy, more like ether. And,' he added, 'the fire burned bright as if it had been made up within the last half hour, but the body was cold.'

'He has been dead about two hours,' John said curtly, and turning his back on Bridges who was agog with self-importance, he told Martha:

'You wait here while I search his room. I want to find out what he may have kept stored away somewhere among his various medicines.'

'There was also a wine glass on the mantelboard, Doctor,' vouchsafed Bridges, puffing out his chest on an exhalation of breath redolent of the night's imbibations, 'and I noticed a tray by the bed with a water jug and tumbler on it and some white powder at the bottom of the glass.'

'You may go,' John said, but:

'No, sir, if it's all the same to you,' Bridges doggedly replied, 'as being my house and any question of the poor gentleman having taken something he didn't ought, I'd like to be with you and help in the search – if you don't mind.'

With every indication of minding very much, John said: 'If you wish,' and leaving Bridges to follow him he went into the front room.

'I should take a lie down if I was you, madam,' said Bridges with a sour look as he closed the folding doors behind him.

Starting from her seat Martha went over to a tallboy, took from its hiding place where she kept the key of the drawer that contained her journal, unlocked it and searched among her handkerchiefs and other intimate possessions for the bottle she had hidden there before she sent for John. Suppose they should search this room, find the drawer locked and ask for the key! That bottle must not – must never be found. Where to hide it? For the present she slipped it under the mattress of the bed and was back in her chair when the door opened and John returned to tell her:

'There is nothing of any suspicion in his room, unless this.' He held out to her an empty bottle of chlorodyne. 'What was it doing on the mantelshelf within reach of the bed?'

'It was given him by a dentist to use as a mouthwash. He always kept it on the mantelshelf.'

She was surprised to hear herself speak without a tremor though her knees felt weak as water.

'Chlorodyne,' John was saying, 'could be harmful if swallowed in excess by mistake.'

She said from a parched mouth: 'I think there was very little left in the bottle.' And, on a caught breath, 'Will there have to be an inquest?'

'There will have to be a post-mortem.'

'A – oh, yes,' she moistened her lips, 'there must be. Will it be soon? It must,' she was insistent on a rising note, 'be *soon*.'

'Just so soon as a pathologist is available.' John eyed her keenly, saw her at breaking point and asked:

'Would you rather not stay here? I do advise that you come to my aunt's house at Dulwich until the – these formalities are over. She would be only too glad to make you welcome and to look after you. My aunt, Mrs Ottery – I believe you met her at Clarissa's party.'

'It is very kind of you,' her voice faltered, 'but – I must – I want to stay.'

Later in the morning Todd arrived, having received a telegram from John, sent on behalf of Martha, to break the news of his son's death. He appeared less grief-stricken than accusative, directing the full force of his suspicion upon Martha.

'I knew 'ow it would be. I seen it comin'.' Although he spoke to John, he pinioned Martha with a look of inconceivable malice. ''E's been poisoned – 'ow or 'oo by I'm not sayin'. I leave that to them 'oo'll be makin' the inquiries – but I know what I think and I'll 'ave it proved as to 'ow my poor boy died for no reason – all of a sudden – when 'e was gettin' better, s'far's I was *told*. And now I'm goin' to get the truth of it. I must 'ave a post-mortim.'

He turned upon Martha who sat as if carved from stone, and pointing a long finger at her said with ominous significance: 'I'm sendin' for my solicitor to be 'ere when they do the post-mortim on 'im that 'e may 'ear the verdic' and take what's ne'ssry steps. Why – but *why*—' and now for the first time he broke, tottered to a chair by the table in the smoking-room where this scene took place, and bowing his head, bald in parts and sparsely covered with streaks of grey, he sobbed uncontrollably – '*why* should 'e be taken – like this? Both of 'em gone, Ted and Jer-Jo, and 'ere am I – left.'

John laid a gentle hand on the scraggy shoulder.

'Rest assured, Mr Todd, that everything within medical knowledge will be done to ascertain the cause of your son's death, of which, until an examination has been made, none of us can be certain.'

The old man raised his head; his meagre mouth, sucked in, looked to be lipless. His dry leathery skin and those narrow darting eyes venomously searching hers, reminded Martha of a lizard's. She thought: I have never seen him reptilian before, but, of course, he is. And she shivered. He got up and, leaning his hands on the table, dark veined and scaly, their nails engrimed with dirt, he said:

'Doctor, I want to see my son. Will you take me to 'im?'

John, with reluctance, agreed: anything to get him away from Martha.

When the old man entered the room where the covered body lay, he dragged the sheet from the face, and after kissing and blubbering over it, he smelt the dead lips.

'They stink of poison – per – prussic acid,' he said between sobs. ''E's been poisoned!'

'Of which there is no evidence whatsoever,' John told him sternly.

Todd glared at him.

'I don't care what you say, I'm goin' to 'ave me own doctor present at the post-mortim and if any other doctor must be there I won't 'ave you or that specialist what you called in to see 'im. Done to death 'e was – I *know* 'e was.'

'Your accusations, or implications,' John said, with ice, 'are purposeless and unjustifiable. But all necessary arrangements will be made to accede to your request. I will at once contact Dr Chance and his assistant, Dr Manners, pathologists of Guy's Hospital, to conduct the post-mortem; yet both myself and Dr Gardiner, the physician I called in consultation to your son, must be present at the examination.'

'Well, if you must – you must,' surlily capitulated Todd.

While another search, which took some time, was made in the inner room, Martha wrote two telegrams to be despatched by Annie, one to Button and one to Cecilia Grimsby, telling them of her husband's death and asking Cecilia to come to her.

She was there before noon and at once suggested that Martha should return with her to Brixton.

'Not yet,' she was told, 'not until they – after the post-mortem. I must wait for that.'

'My poor child! What a dreadful ordeal for you – but I am not leaving you here alone. I will telegraph my husband to tell him I shall not be back tonight. Perhaps your landlady can oblige me with a room?'

Mrs Bridges readily obliged. 'And thankful to have someone to take over the responsibility of *her*,' she told Bridges, 'him dying like that and no one knows how.'

'We'll know how,' was the dark response, 'when the pathologists have made their report. And the sooner we get her out of here, the better.'

Martha had managed to have a few words apart with John on his return in the afternoon to say that the post-mortem would take place the following day.

'It is very kind of you,' she told him when he repeated his previous invitation for her to stay with his aunt, 'but my former governess, Mrs Grimsby, is here and has asked me to stay with her and her husband at Brixton. He is a curate of St Saviour's Church.'

'Just as you wish, but please believe that I speak for my aunt. I know she will be happy to receive you. I want you to remember that if – at any time – you would wish to come.'

His eyes held hers with that in them to bring a hurry to her heart and warmth to her cold cheeks.

'Thank you. I – I will remember.'

Dixon was the last to hear the news of the death in a brief note from Martha.

The minister came hurrying by an early train the next morning and was met by Martha in the smoking-room, attended by Cecilia, who had gone with her the day before to buy her mourning.

Her widow's black made her appear very young, the merest slip of a girl, her face bereft of colour save for the pale rose of her lips and the vivid blue of her eyes, like the staining on a wax-white mask.

With every evidence of woe, even to an inch-wide black bordered handkerchief purchased on the way and applied at intervals to his apparently streaming eyes: 'My precious little Birdie,' Dixon uttered between sobs, ' "Blessed are they that mourn for they shall be comforted".' He made as if to clasp her; she effectually dodged, and:

'How,' he asked, 'did this happen? What cruel misfortune struck him down? When I last saw him two days ago, he seemed to be well on the road to – to – recovery.'

Said Cecilia in answer to an imploring look from Martha:

'We cannot know the cause of death until after the post-mortem.'

'The –' his mouth fell open – 'post-mortem? Why should there have to be a – and when?'

Taking Martha's hand in hers, Cecilia led her to the door saying:

'This afternoon at two o'clock. I must ask you to excuse us now, Mr Dixon. Mrs Todd requires rest.'

'Yes, yes, of course ber-but why,' blubbered he, whose gleaming teeth, in the throes of his emotion, had dropped from his upper jaw, hastily to be replaced with a click, 'cannot the doctor tell the cause without this – this sacrilegious interference with the – dead?' And receiving no answer, 'My own bereaved beloved little Birdie!' he made another attempt to embrace her, circumvented by Cecilia, to whom he tearfully appealed: 'May I be permitted to see him? He was –' again resort to the black-bordered handkerchief – 'my dearest friend, my more than ber-brother.'

'No, sir,' Cecilia told him firmly, 'you cannot see him. Dr Herriott who is in charge of the case, is preparing the room where the – the examination will take place.'

'Not,' moaned Albert, 'to be allowed a last sight of the dear departed. I will wait here. You cannot,' Cecilia was favoured with a glance of the utmost contumely, 'refuse me to wait that I may hear the result of this – examination?'

'It is not for me to refuse that you wait. And now, again, pray allow me—'

With Martha in tow, she passed, or more correctly pushed by him who would have barred their exit.

'Keep him away,' Martha whispered as they went upstairs, 'I can't bear him near me. Don't let him come near me.'

'He shall not if I can help it,' said Cecilia. 'And now, dear, I am going to see that you have something to eat. I am sure you have had nothing all day.'

'I can't eat.'

While Cecilia besought her to partake of the meal provided for them in Mrs Bridges' private parlour below, the ubiquitous Mr Dixon had gone out to buy himself a packet of sandwiches and sat munching them in the visitors' room above, to all appearances a male Niobe. Yet he seemed sufficiently recovered to inquire of Button, who had arrived in answer to Martha's telegram, if 'the dear departed had left that poor broken-hearted child well provided for?' And evinced considerable relief, and thanks to God for befriending the widowed and fatherless, on hearing that the net income apart from the business and the dear departed's capital investments, would give her something in the region of several hundreds a year; and that the goodwill of the freehold shops, if sold, would fetch anything from five to ten thousand in cash, but that she would be advised not to sell. He, Button, as one of the executors – 'and yourself, Mr Dixon, as the other, will agree that the business should remain as it is, with me as general manager of the whole concern.'

'Quite so,' Mr Dixon fully agreed, since rapid calculation possessed him when married to his Birdie of an income which would offer opportunity of taking a postgraduate course at Cambridge, so to become a Doctor of Philosophy instead of a mere B.A.

Martha having sipped a few mouthfuls of chicken broth and declared she would choke if made to take more, she and Cecilia went upstairs to be met by old Todd coming down. He, who, on his account, had been making investigations in Martha's room, stopped her on the landing.

'Well, it's to be 'oped you're satisfied. You've got all my poor boy's money and 'is business,' he, too had made inquiries of Button, 'and what's to become of me? No 'ome, no money. Thrown out. Done for. Finished – to end me days in the work'ouse.'

The slow painful tears of old age trickled from his eyes, red-rimmed with weeping and, at the sight of them, all Martha's hate and fear of him dissolved. For the first time in her life she voluntarily touched him. Slipping an arm round his neck, she said:

'You will never want – never. I promise you that all shall be as it has been. You shall have as much or more than he ever gave you. I don't want it – only just enough to live on.'

'So you say.' He looked at her aslant and cunningly. 'I'll 'ave that in writin' before I'll believe it, and not even then.'

'You shall have all,' she said wearily, 'all that was his if you wish it.'

She had pity for him who had none for her.

When the grisly task of the post-mortem was done, John, whose part in the proceedings had been confined to taking notes, summoned a meeting in the drawing-room, the body having been removed to an upper room set apart for the pathological examination.

The company, other than the doctors, consisted of Dixon, the deceased's father, his solicitor, Martha and Cecilia, while John at the request of his colleagues, acted as spokesman.

'These gentlemen wish me to state we are unable to detect any pathological cause – that is to say any obvious natural cause – of death. The contents of the stomach are, however, suspicious, and we have preserved them for further analysis. There was found to be a pungent smell that in my opinion might be due to chlorodyne, but is attributed by Dr Chance to chloroform.'

At which Dixon, who had sat hunched in his chair slumped forward, deathly white, but Martha, with

Cecilia's hand in hers, showed no emotion whatsoever, staring unseeingly before her with a look on her face as of a deaf-mute.

John, having forced the half fainting Dixon's head between his knees, said low-voiced to Cecilia:

'Will you please take Mrs Todd to her room?'

'I am taking her home with me, Doctor,' he was told.

It was then that Dr Manners, the assistant pathologist who had been conferring in an undertone with Todd's solicitor, said:

'Mrs Todd would be advised to leave her handbag –' which was on the table – 'and her cloak. The rooms are to be locked and the keys handed to the coroner pending the inquest.'

'No need for her to leave her cloak,' Todd intervened. 'There's no pockets in it, and nothing in her bag of any use to you. I've had a good look.'

John turned indignantly, but Martha, icily composed, said:

'I will not take my bag or any of my belongings other than my cloak, my dog, my purse, and necessary night wear.'

She took her cloak that had been thrown across a chair presumably by Todd after his search of her room, and with a slight bow to the doctors she went to the door followed by Cecilia. Todd stayed her, a hand on her arm.

' 'Ere, don't take me wrong. I only wanted to 'ave a look to see if you'd been givin' 'im somethink to make 'im sleep which might 'ave upset 'im knowin' 'ow restless 'e was, and—'

She shook his hand away and passed him by, leaving his attempted apology frozen on his lips: and with that same unseeing look she left the house, never to return to it again.

NINE

At the end of that dismal day, the Reverend Albert, in his lodgings at Putney, passed a sleepless night of terror, beset with dire forebodings directed at himself for having bought that fateful chloroform.

The next morning, after detaching the labels from the four empty bottles, he threw them in a gorse bush on his way across Putney Heath to officiate at Sunday service in his Chapel. Then, having ascertained from Mrs Bridges the address of the Grimsbys, he hastened off in the afternoon to Brixton.

He found Martha alone, and without any preliminary greeting, at once demanded:

'What, oh, *what* did you do with the chloroform you made me buy?'

'I did nothing with it,' he was told. 'I didn't have occasion to use it. The bottle is unopened. I brought it with me when I left the house.'

'They searched your room before you left,' he pointed a shaking finger at her who sat gazing not at but through him as if he were a window, one hand resting on Lorna's head, who at Dixon's entrance had risen from the hearth-rug and stood, hackles up, nose quivering. 'Do you not realize –' his voice cracked – 'what the purchase of this chloroform may mean to – *me*! The doctors already suspect that he was poisoned and one of them thinks by – chloroform! No natural cause of death, they said. Oh, God in Heaven, what have you done?' He sank into a chair and buried his face in his hands. 'Why – *why* did I succumb to your – your request! See what it has brought me to! The devil prompted me and I obeyed – against my better judgement! I must have been mad. You will have to confess—' he raised his sunken head; his horror-stricken eyes sought hers. 'I must *know* what you did with that bottle. Did you administer a dose as you said you would to make him sleep – and gave him an overdose by mistake? It must have been by mistake. Did you? *Did you?*'

His voice was a hushed scream.

'I have told you I did not.'

He sank on his knees clutching at her skirt. Lorna uttered a deep growl and made as if to spring at him.

'Down. Quiet. Down,' Martha whispered and the dog flopped at her feet, while the craven object grovelling at Martha's rose to his.

'I have loved you,' he quavered, 'have thought and dreamed of you as no sane man should dream and keep his senses. I have been your dupe, betrayed by my love – by my Birdie!'

'Don't!' And now the scream in *her* voice was not hushed. 'Don't call me Birdie.'

'But,' came in a repetitive whine, 'I must know what you did with that chloroform.'

And her frayed nerves torn to shreds she lost control to flare at him:

'Oh, *damn* the chloroform – and you! Go! Go *away*!'

It was at this moment that Cecilia, who had been out with the children, came into the room, and whether or not she had heard Martha's outburst, said:

'Mr Dixon, we did not expect you here today, and I must ask you to be so good as to leave. Mrs Todd is in no fit state to receive visitors.'

'My God!' he was heard to groan as he tottered to the door, 'I am ruined – a ruined man!'

'What,' asked Cecilia, as she watched him go down the path to the gate, 'was all that about?'

'I haven't the least idea,' was the mendacious reply.

'more than that he seems to be in a fuss over the inquest. He is afraid he will be called as a witness because he thinks he was the last person to see my husband alive – other than myself.'

Which sufficed, *pro tem,* to satisfy Cecilia.

However on the following afternoon he was back again and met Martha and Cecilia setting out for the station. John had sent a message to Martha to say that in view of the approaching inquest, he wished to be put in full possession of the facts as to how she had found her husband when she presumed him dead or dying, that he might make a clear statement to the coroner at the inquest.

It was snowing hard, and Dixon, determined not to let Martha out of his sight, offered to fetch a cab and accompany them to their destination. This Cecilia refused, but accepted the cab to take them to the station, and upon arriving there intimated that as they were going on a shopping expedition his attendance would be superfluous. None the less, having managed to discover they were bound, shopping or no shopping, for Dr Herriott's house, he went after them and was shown into the waiting-room where Cecilia stayed during Martha's interview with John.

Unable to contain within himself what he called his 'guilty secret' Dixon blurted out to the horrified Cecilia how, against his better judgement, he had been persuaded by Mrs Todd to procure for her a bottle of chloroform that she might alleviate the pains of an internal complaint from which she alleged his 'dear friend, the late lamented' had suffered agonizingly and with heroic courage for many years; and also to give him his much needed sleep an embellishment of the statement he had prepared in advance to support his excuse for his part in the transaction, if called upon to do so.

Cecilia, recovered from the first shock of his narrative, delivered between sobs and some misbehaviour of his teeth that necessitated re-adjustment, coldly suggested he should repeat to her husband that which he had conveyed to her.

Martha, meanwhile, was undergoing a gentle cross-examination by John.

In answer to his questions as to how and in what condition she had left her husband when she retired to her room to change her dress for the night, she could only repeat that she had left him sleeping, that she too had slept, and woke to find him – 'Not, as I could dare to think – dead, but as I have already told you, in a sort of coma.'

'And,' with a searching look, 'is that all you have to tell me?'

'What else can I tell you? He had no poisonous drugs nor any medicine except what had been given him – unless he had some hidden away. He couldn't have reached the chlor – the chlorodyne.'

How was it possible to speak calmly with her heart pounding at her ribs. And the doctors had mentioned – chloroform. Help me, she screamed within her, help me, God, to tell him. I must *tell* him! . . . But he, seeing her so white, and fearing he had tried her too far, went to a cupboard, took from it a decanter of sherry, poured a glass and bade her: 'Drink this, and then go home with Mrs Grimsby and rest.'

She received the glass from him and put it to her lips; her hand shook as she sipped the wine, but she swallowed a few drops, set it down and faltering, said:

'Thank you, Doctor, I will rest. I need some – sleep.'

If only it could be for ever. . . .

Cecilia had arranged for Martha's trunks to be collected and brought in a cab to John's consulting rooms; but although Dixon followed them out when they left the house, Cecilia again made it clear that his company was superfluous. She told Martha nothing of the extraordinary revelations imparted to her by Dixon in the waiting-room, and immediately on their arrival at her home she packed Martha off to bed. Yet her manoeuvres to be rid of the adhesive Albert were of no avail. He was there on the doorstep when Mr Grimsby returned, and begged to be allowed a word alone with him. The word, or series of words, delivered in an hysterical monologue, were a repetition of the tale he had already unfolded to Cecilia.

Paul Grimsby, having heard from his wife that one of the doctors conducting the post-mortem had inclined to the belief that chloroform might prove to be a cause of death, let him go on uninterruptedly but with growing disgust – 'and her husband, my dear friend, the late lamented to whom I was devoted, deliberately threw us together in consequence of which' – the black bordered handkerchief was here in much display – 'I formed an – an attachment to the lady who encouraged my advances and attacked me on my weakest side. I have been duped,' wailed Albert, 'grossly deceived, and involved in what may prove to be a – a – a criminal offence by an unscrupulous woman's wiles. May God forgive me! But I intend to make a clean breast of it if called as a witness at the inquest.'

Said Paul, hard put to disguise his repugnance of him who cringed before him: 'As it is not yet ascertained that chloroform was the cause of Mr Todd's death I recommend you to keep silence until the report from the Home Office has been received.'

He had invited Albert to be seated while he stood, and walking to the door he opened it, saying:

'I must ask you to excuse me. I have much to do and a sick bed to visit.'

Albert slunk out and Paul went in to tell his wife, after giving her a résumé of the interview – 'How I kept my hands off him I do not know! He deserves to be horse-whipped and I would derive considerable satisfaction from doing so – if,' he added with a rueful smile, 'I had a horsewhip.'

Greatly perturbed, Cecilia asked:

'Do you believe he was speaking the truth about buying the chloroform for Martha?'

'She may have wanted to procure some sort of anodyne to alleviate the pains of which the poor man complained – entirely imaginary – for you have told me Martha reported that both Dr Herriott and the consulting physician said he was hypochondriacal.'

'But why could she not have asked Doctor Herriott to give him something to soothe him?'

'I have no doubt she did, but nothing seems to have had any effect.'

'Yes,' Cecilia said, doubtfully, 'and the poor girl was herself sleepless and worn out with nursing him. Probably in desperation she thought chloroform might help to give them both a night's rest. Will this abominable Dixon have to give evidence at the inquest?'

'Possibly, but if he is in the state he is in now, any evidence he may give will not be well received. Don't you worry, my dear, your little Martha will be safeguarded. Have you induced her to go to bed?'

'Yes, and she seems more rested now. Do you suppose *she* will have to be called as witness at the inquest?'

'If so, I am sure she will conduct herself with the same courage and fortitude she has shown all along. And now, pray, my love, do not distress yourself. Let us dismiss from our minds this fellow Dixon's tales – told by an idiot.'

However, when the coroner's court assembled, the hearing was of the briefest. Old Todd was called, much to Cecilia's dismay, but Martha remained apparently unconcerned. Todd deposed that until his son had been taken ill shortly before Christmas he had always enjoyed the best of health. His daughter-in-law objected to his visiting him during his illness and – 'kicked up a fuss, refusing to let me see 'im more than three times, sayin' as 'ow talkin' tired 'im – not allowed to see me own son – and then 'im goin' off like that so sudden in the night bein' well on the way to recovery the doctors said and one of 'em sayin' 'e'd no right to be lyin' there dead, a strong 'ealthy man like 'im which was why I insisted on a post-mortim bein' done by a doctor or doctors 'oo 'ad nothing to do with 'im before and to find out exactly why 'e *should* 'a died for no reason as fur as anyone could tell and so—'

'Thank you, Mr Todd,' came the suave interruption. 'You are excused.' And dismissed, while the coroner, Mr Hicks-Johnson, announced that the inquest was adjourned until Dr Stevenson, the Government analyst, would deliver his report.

Martha, who, with Cecilia beside her, had sat through the hearing pale but wonderfully composed, watched old Todd shamble out, and while Dixon, anything but composed, his face lemon-coloured that he looked to be in the last stages of jaundice, hovered at the exit to waylay them, Cecilia told Martha that she had some shopping to do at Gorringe's. 'So if you will wait for me at the confectioner's – I saw one almost next door from here – we will have a cup of tea before we go home.'

As they passed out of the parochial board-room where the inquest was held, the sickly Dixon intercepted them, caught Martha's arm, and hissed at her:

'I must – *must* speak to you!'

'Not now. We are in a hurry.'

'God send,' murmured Cecilia as they hastened away, 'that he doesn't follow us.'

But follow them he did, saw Martha deposited at a corner table in the confectioner's shop and, Cecilia gone, presented himself to her saying:

'You can't escape me like this. I hope you realize to what extent you have incriminated me by making me your dupe – an accessory to the purchase of a poisonous drug – that chloroform! O God, what have I done –' his voice rose to a squeak.

'If you don't incriminate me,' Martha disgustedly told him, 'I won't incriminate you. Now please leave me. I will not have you forcing yourself upon me like this. Go, I tell you!' But as he showed no intention of going, she, with an excuse to the waitress who came for her order – 'I am sorry. I have left my umbrella—' she rushed from the shop and stood waiting at the entrance of Gorringe's, where presently Cecilia found her.

'Quick!' she tugged at the sleeve of Cecilia's mantle. 'He came to the shop and began at me again. Look! There's an empty hansom – we must take it! See! He's coming out of the shop. He'll be after me. Cabby!'

The hansom halted at the kerb and Martha hustled Cecilia into it. The cabman, directed to Holly Road, Brixton, and urged by Martha to hurry, whipped up his horse and drove off in as great a hurry as the traffic would permit, leaving Dixon, who had seen their departure, to take himself, also in a hurry, to the station and thence to Holly Road.

The little maid who combined the services of nurse to the children and 'general' to the household, recognizing him as a previous visitor and a clergyman, admitted him to the parlour where the Grimsbys, with Martha, sat at tea.

'I offer my apologies for this intrusion,' was his announcement, 'but I have that to say which *must* be said.' And in extremest agitation he said it. Pointing a finger, clothed in a black glove, at Martha, and disregarding the Reverend Paul's injunction – 'Pray, sir, do not incommode Mrs Todd, who has had a trying day, by this importunate visit—' 'You!' he declared. '*You* are the instrument of my – my defalcation. You have ruined my ministerial career. I will have to resign. You prevailed upon me against my will and better judgement to buy that chloroform— Yes!' Dixon turned to Cecilia, 'I say it before you, madam, and you, sir,' to the outraged Paul, 'as my witnesses, that I was tempted by the artifice of a deceitful—'

'Will you be silent, sir, and leave my house,' said, or rather shouted, Paul, who had risen to his feet.

'I will not be silent!' again the finger, shaking now, was pointed at Martha. 'I wish to know what you – *you* whom I trusted and – God help me – loved—' his teeth clicked to the sob in his thoat – 'what,' he screamed it, 'did you do with that *chloroform* which, if proven that you—'

'Very well, then!' she flung at him, 'you can say I gave it him, if that's what you want!'

Cecilia gasped. Dixon turned an even more than ever sickly lemon. Paul removed his spectacles, wiped them, replaced them and put a hand to his dog collar as if it were about to throttle him.

'Well?' demanded Martha, 'Isn't that what you *want* me to say?'

'N-no, no, God forbid! I didn't – you couldn't – you— Did you?'

'I did not. How many more times am I to tell you so?'

'But what did you do with it?'

'I threw it away. Will that satisfy you?'

'Never, unless I know where and when you—'

'Mr Dixon!' Paul, having now perceived Martha's declaration to have been made in a burst of excusable temper, said: 'I must ask you to discontinue this distasteful discussion and also your equally distasteful visits, not only to me but to Mrs Todd, my guest.'

And once again he was seen to the door and off the premises by the Reverend Paul, who had much to do to restrain his foot from the miserable Albert's backside.

* * *

Extract from the Journal of Martha Todd:

Devonshire Street, London, W.
January 12th, 1866.

Well, here I am. I did not intend to start another Commonplace Book – what a misnomer! – for there is nothing commonplace about what has happened, and *may* be going to happen – to me. But it helps to pass the time while waiting for the inquest which has now been adjourned for three more weeks. I am afraid the dear Grimsbys were rather hurt that I insisted on leaving them, for one thing I just couldn't let them go on boarding and keeping me, and Cecilia refused to let me pay – I know how hard up they are – and also I didn't want them to be burdened with me if the inquest goes unfavourably against me which it well may do should that Creature D. give evidence and make what he calls a 'clean breast' of his share in the buying of the chloroform. The pathologist said there was a smell of chloroform when they made their examination, but Dr. H. said he thought it was chlorodyne. Pray God they find it is chlorodyne . . . Anyway here I am and here I will stay till this ghastly business is over and done with. They are very nice rooms. Dr H. found them for me, they were the consulting rooms with the suite above occupied by a doctor friend of his who has moved to Harley Street, close by, and is letting the furnished suite which I have and is a bachelor suite – because he is getting married and it is not large enough for two. Today I took the bottle, which I told D. when he kept pestering me at the Grimsbys that I had thrown away, and I have emptied the beastly thing in the W.C. How I wish I had never asked him to get it for me. I must have been mad. . . . I took the empty bottle into Regent's Park and threw it in the canal. I had removed the label which had poison on it – yes, Poison! – I had rinsed it well so that if anyone finds it floating about they could never smell what it had contained for there was no smell when opened to the air. . . .

January 22nd.

Consulted Dr H. today about those headaches which I have had ever since that awful night. Also I can't sleep –

keep waking up and if I do sleep I have horrible dreams. I suppose all that time I nursed him I had got used to dozing and waking and never had a good night's rest. If only I could remember what I did that night when I . . . my mind is a blank about it. A void. An emptiness . . . He, the doctor, tested my eyes for the headaches and said I must see an oculist, probably needed reading glasses, and then he told me he had some good news for me. That the report of the analyst had been received and I would be glad to hear that no trace of poison had been found which he said should set my mind at rest. It was chloroform that had been found. Had it been one of those secret and rapid poisons which he might have taken unwittingly, suspicion might have been directed at me! I felt quite sick when he told me that and sort of gasped out, for I could hardly speak, that I wished anything but chloroform had been found. He looked at me in that quiet searching way of his as if he could see through me to my bones and asked, 'Why do you wish that? If there is something you want to tell me – tell it me now.'

And so I told.

'But why did you not tell me all this before?' John asked when she had finished.

'I didn't like to. It was so – intimate.'

He walked over to the window, pulling at the tassel of the blind.

'There is nothing too intimate for you to tell me – your doctor.'

Her recital had been delivered in a quiet monotone, seated where he had placed her in a chair before his desk, but now her enforced composure gave way. She rose, went to him and laid a hand on his arm. 'Please, *please*!' convulsively her fingers clutched at his sleeve. 'I am – afraid. What if he – the coroner finds out that I *had* this chloroform? You know how that hateful old man, my father-in-law, was always hinting that I – I was giving him poison which was the reason why he had been taken ill. You know how he made you call in another opinion. Will the coroner believe I tried to poison him?'

He took her hand in his and held it closely. 'No. They can never believe that if I tell them – the coroner's jury – what you have told me. That which you intended to do and did not do, even if carried out, could not possibly have caused his death by inhalation.'

'But you say chloroform was found inside him. How did it get there? How?'

'That is for pathological evidence to decide. Be of good cheer,' he smiled down at her, feeling anything but cheerful. The fact that she admitted to having chloroform in her possession might require a more convincing explanation than she had given to him. He implicitly believed her but – would the coroner and his jury? What a damnable coil! And going back to his desk, he gestured her again to be seated.

'There is no need for you to fear the inquest, although you may have to give evidence, but it will be very brief and not alarming. It is likely that you won't be called as a witness at all, but in case – have you consulted a solicitor?'

'A solicitor?'

Her eyes, ink coloured in the whiteness of her face, widened, fear-haunted.

'I think you should be represented by a solicitor, or better still a barrister-at-law. I recommend you to Sewell and Sewell. They are my family's solicitors. I was up at Cambridge with a son of the head of the firm, and I feel sure they will advise you to be represented at the inquest and will brief Counsel for that purpose. Will you leave all this and – everything to me?'

She nodded.

'I will do whatever you say. I have nobody – no one – only you to advise me. I wouldn't wish to worry Cecilia – Mrs Grimsby – any more. She and her husband have been worried enough by me already and – and him, who –' she stopped herself. She had said she would not incriminate Dixon; but would he incriminate her?

John was writing a prescription.

'I want you to take this three times a day after meals. It will strengthen you and help you to sleep. And now,' he got up, 'my hansom is at the door. I am due in Harley Street to meet a patient for a consultation. So may I drive you back to your apartments?'

The talk between them on the way to Devonshire Street was monosyllabic on the part of Martha, and entirely non-allusive to their recent discussion on the part of John. He spoke of the recent General Election that, for the third time, had brought in Gladstone as Prime Minister – 'but the Liberals,' he said, 'will never stay the course, fought and won on Home Rule alone.'

'Oh?'

'I take it you are not,' he glanced aside at the so pitifully young face under the widow's bonnet, 'interested in politics?'

'No.'

'The time is not far distant when all women of intelligence who wish to be regarded as something more than the female of *Homo sapiens* endowed with charming imbecilities, will demand that they have the right to express themselves as individuals and to vote for their political opinions.'

'Really?'

They had now arrived at Grosvenor Gate, having come through the Park to be held up in a traffic jam when John, leaning forward, exclaimed – 'and here is one of them whose interest is less centred, as formerly, on the aesthetic movement as exemplified in *Patience* than in the Franchise movement, as exemplified in women's suffrage.'

A brougham had halted alongside John's hansom. At the carriage window a face with rouge in its wrinkles and remarkably crowned in a green velvet toque adorned with ostrich feather tips, appeared. A hand in a purple glove studded with green sequins beckoned; a languid high-pitched voice hailed him:

'John, why did you not come to my dinner last night? I was most anxious for you to meet Mrs Pankhurst. We had a marvellous meeting.'

'Hallo, Aunt!' was John's reply to this. 'Where are you off to?'

'To beard William Morris in his lion's den. He refuses to speak to me since I bought this gown from Worth in Paris. You perceive it is in the colours of the Cause. Purple and green. No, I think, after all, I will not go to see Morris. I will take you to tea at Gunter's. You have a companion?' A lorgnette was levelled. 'Will she come too?'

'Thank you, Aunt, I think not. I have an appointment and—'

At this moment the traffic disintegrated: the brougham went on, John's hansom went with it, and passed out before it at Grosvenor Gate.

But Mrs Ottery had given orders to her footman: 'Follow Dr Herriott's hansom. I wish to speak to him.'

Thus it was that, as they drew up at Martha's lodgings in Devonshire Street, the brougham containing his aunt simultaneously arrived.

Mrs Ottery, continuing the conversation through the carriage window as if it had never been left off, said, 'You should have been there, John. Speranza, Oscar's mother, came and that explosive young Irishman with the sandy hair, Bernard Shaw – so rude and clever – and Oscar, too, an hour late so there was no dinner for him only dessert but he didn't mind – said he was thinning – in a wig. I am sure it was a wig – of Neronian curls and a violet velvet smoking jacket and—'

The lorgnette was raised again. 'Who is this?'

John effected introductions.

'Of course! The Rossetti girl. I could never forget those

eyes – my poor darling Angelico's eyes – and in weeds! He died of eating rat poison. If I could find the criminal who murdered him – but why in black? You are too young to be in mourning for your past so you must be in mourning for your future.' She unwrapped herself from a sable stole and consulted a diamond bow watch pinned to her purple mantle. 'It is now four o'clock. We will go to Gunter's. Did you say Todd? One of the Leicestershire Todds? Gunter's,' to the footman; and to John, 'bring the Blessed Damozel to dine tomorrow if you can't come to Gunter's now, but not in those macabre trappings. Something diaphanous and aquamarine. *So* beautiful and sad.'

As Martha watched the brougham drive away, a laugh, the first that had escaped her – for how long? – John wondered, lightened her face; and holding out her hand, 'Thank you,' she said, 'for – everything.'

'Will you be brought to dine with my aunt tomorrow?' he asked, retaining her hand. 'She is a perpetual entertainment and I feel sure you would be a welcome guest if you could be persuaded to stay with her until or after the inquest.'

But she was not to be persuaded.

'I would rather remain here, although it is so kind of you to suggest it. In any case I can't leave Lorna, and I think your aunt would not welcome *her*.' Releasing her hand from his that seemed reluctant to let it go, 'I have thought a lot about Lorna. Suppose,' her voice trembled; 'suppose if the – the jury won't believe that I did *not* use that chloroform and – if I have to be sent – somewhere, would you – is it too much to ask of you that you will take care of Lorna for me?'

'There is nothing,' he said, 'too much that you can ask of me. And should you have to move from these apartments to others,' he spoke easily, with deliberate misunderstanding of the implication behind her request, 'where dogs are not permitted, for there are very few rooms or hotels in this part of London that will allow dogs, then I will be only too glad to have her.'

'That is a great weight off my mind,' she said. 'Lorna is very fond of you. She doesn't like men as a rule; but you are a favourite of hers.'

And with the smallest of smiles and without another word she left him and went into the house.

From the Journal of Martha Todd:

I have read somewhere – I forget where – that an inquiry about death is torture to the living but a source of enjoyment to persons not involved. I was reminded of this today when I saw a crowd of people, mostly women, who had come to the Court room to hear and watch this second inquest as if it were a play. The newspapers who were not much interested in the other inquest were now full of it, with reporters scribbling away at their table. My name, of course, was prominent, as the widow of 'the deceased'. But the torture is prolonged. It is again adjourned.

Mr Ellis is the barrister representing me, recommended by John's solicitors. John had said I must tell him exactly why and how, and from whom I had procured the chloroform – which I didn't use – I was emphatic about that, and I am sure he believed me. Mr Ellis is very nice and sympathetic, looks rather like a bulldog, square-faced with a heavy turned-up jaw. He refused to allow me to give evidence until the Home Office pathologist, Dr Stevenson, had been heard. But the Coroner, Mr Johnson-Hicks – he looks like a goat – I seem to find an animalistic likeness in all these legal gentlemen – he has a little beard under his chin and that sort of un-smiling smile on a thick lipped mouth that goats have – well, he said he could not compel me to come forward but my Counsel must understand that the jury would draw an unfavourable inference from such refusal. I went quite limp when he said that but J. who was sitting beside me held my hand tightly and said not to worry, that he had his reasons which were all to the good. Then Dr Stevenson gave evidence and said death was due to a fatal amount of chloroform which had been found in the stomach. I had been prepared for this by John, and that is why I told him I wished that *any*thing but chloroform had been found, and the reason for asking Dixon to buy it for me. He said then that even if inhaled on a handkerchief it could not have caused death, so that when I heard the pathologist's report I was not too agitated. But Cecilia, sitting on my other side, went very white. I looked across at Dixon – *he* was pale yellow and looked about to faint. He wasn't called to give evidence either. I wonder what he would have said if he had!

Then John was called. After today we are more than doctor and patient. He is my strength, my hope and – my salvation. One could almost be thankful that all this has happened as it has given me, through him, the only real happiness my life has ever known. For even with Maman – living as we did with the Todds and no home of our own we were not really happy except that we had love for each other. I know now what 'Perfect love casteth out fear' can mean. I have no fear, not any more. . . .

J. had to repeat what I had told him about having that chloroform in my possession. This caused a sensation in the Court room, heads nodding, whispers flying, all eyes directed at me, but they couldn't see my face as it was swathed in my crape veil. John was perfectly calm, cool, impersonal . . . He asked leave to be given time to consult his notes before he could fully report on my talk with him relating to this question to which the Coroner agreed and so the inquest was again adjourned.

John drove me back to my rooms in his hansom. We hardly spoke at all. He held my hand all the way, pouring his strength into me. When we got back to Devonshire Street, he said he wanted to speak to me so we went up to my sitting-room. I asked him if I would be accused of giving T. the chloroform. He said again that even if so it is virtually impossible for chloroform to be given by the mouth. There would have been excruciating pain and signs of burning. If, under the influence of the drug he could have taken it himself, the pain would have been lessened, but it is highly improbable that it could have been self-administered, though not impossible.

'You don't believe I gave it to him?' I asked. He said

quietly, 'I know you did not.' I then reminded him of something that had been troubling me – that feeling of 'outsideness'. 'Suppose,' I said, 'in a moment of – not knowing what I was doing – if I had been outside of me – I was in such a state of anxiety about him that night, and trying to prevent what he was trying to do to me – suppose I had unknowingly, when outside of myself, for I don't remember anything about it after it had happened—'

He seemed not to be listening and without looking at me he said in his most professional manner: 'You made an appointment with my man-servant for tomorrow for another consultation. I shall be obliged if you will cancel it.'

I felt very dashed. 'Certainly,' I said, as professionally as he, 'if it is not convenient.' 'It is not,' he said, 'convenient and will never be convenient. I cannot be your doctor because – I want to be your lover and I can't be both. It would be – unethical.'

And then – No, I cannot write what then. It is too precious.

But this I can write that when we, or I, came down from a seventh heaven to a sixth, for I, and I think he, too, was lost to all sense of time in that one long timeless moment, I told him I have always hoped – deep within me – that this would happen since that very first day I saw you when—' I was half laughing, half crying – 'when you cured me of a wasp sting. Do you remember?'

He said, 'How could I forget? That was no chance encounter between a boy and girl. It was pre-ordained, the linking of a kind of spiritual umbilical cord that joins us together, and I have the strangest notion that if it were broken I would bleed internally. Eternally. But it never will be broken. I am yours utterly now and for ever. As for curing that wasp sting—' And then we were both laughing, although I was in tears – one *can* have tears of happiness, I never knew it before. He kissed them away saying, 'Henceforth, even if I can no longer be your doctor, I will cure you of all stings – and slings and arrows of whatever outrageous fortune might be yours if you will come with me and be my love. You see what you have done to me that I can only speak to you in misquotations.

So, is this love between us? Is it – will you – can you –' and he was blushing like the schoolboy that he used to be, for he is very fair of skin; his hair, too, is like a boy's so very fair. I brushed that lock from his forehead, the same lock which always will fall over to hide that deep white scar, and told him: 'Yes, I can and will. . . . God willing.'*

At the resumed hearing of the inquest a week later the statement of Dr Herriott was read in the Coroner's Court, after which the Reverend Albert Dixon was called to give evidence.

So thoroughly did he carry out his threat 'to make a clean breast of it' with reiterated emphasis on how he, the innocent victim of an unscrupulous woman's beguilements in persuading him to procure the chloroform for a medicinal purpose, that the foreman of the jury announced they were all of the opinion that Mrs Todd could no longer be at liberty. A gasp of horror, disbelief and, from several of the female spectators, excitement swept the Court when Mr Johnson-Hicks, Martha's 'goat' man, readily agreed to the decision of the jury.

Martha, as before, sat through the proceedings apparently unmoved by them. She showed no emotion whatsoever at the foreman's announcement and more concern for Cecilia beside her than for herself. With John, on her other side and her hand in his, she had no fear.

'I expected this,' she whispered to the pale Cecilia. 'I am – upheld.' And to John, who sat there with a face of stone, 'I am glad you told them everything. Now they know the facts they will, they must know – that I –' and for the first time her voice broke—

'—to break my heart,' Cecilia told her husband when rendering him an account of the inquest and its result. 'And I know, what anyone except those fools of jurymen and the coroner must and *will* know, that she is no more guilty of deliberately giving him a fatal dose than you

* This is the last entry in her Journal, dated February 4th, 1886.

or I or – or Dr Herriott. And then,' Cecilia went on, 'they took her away in a police van – my poor darling – taken away! It was that man, that minister of God as he dares to call himself, who brought her to this. All he can think of is how to save his skin, he has no thought for *her*. And what will they do to her?' wept Cecilia. 'I can't bear it – I can't!'

'Have no fear, my love,' said Paul, drying her eyes on his handkerchief. 'Justice will be done. She will never be charged.'

But on the following day before the magistrate at Westminster Police Court, charged she was with causing the death of her husband by poisoning him with chloroform. Whereupon formal evidence of arrest was given, after which she was remanded.

The same fate overtook the wretched Dixon, when the coroner's jury returned a verdict of wilful murder against Thérèse Marthe Todd, and found the Reverend Albert Dixon an accessory before the fact.

A month later both prisoners were committed for trial at the Central Criminal Court.

TEN

'No! Oh, *no*!' squealed Miss Emma from behind the newspaper she was reading at the breakfast table. 'A pupil – I should say an *ex*-pupil of ours to be accused of – tried for – No! Oh! I knew – I *knew* we should never have accepted her!'

Every curl of her now almost white hair was a-bob. Her face, still pink but faded as a rose-petal that has been pressed between the pages of some forgotten book, crumpled in horrified excitement as her eyes ravenously devoured the headlined news of the murder case that was equally imbibed at half the breakfast tables in the kingdom.

'To which of our ex-pupils do you allude?' queried Miss Merridew, buttering toast.

'Oh!' wailed Miss Emma, 'it is too, *too* dreadful. What a calamity for the school! Have you not seen the report of the inquest in *The Times*?'

'Since you have monopolized *The Times* I have had no opportunity of seeing it,' was Miss Merridew's acidulous reply.

'Then see it now.' Miss Emma passed to her *The Times*. 'I am immeasurably shocked – too frightful! The Old Bailey! Read it.'

Putting on her spectacles, Miss Merridew read, and in the breakfast parlour of that Select Academy no sound more than the ticking of a long-case clock and the hurried breathing of Miss Emma could be heard.

'Well?' she exclaimed as her sister laid aside the paper and applied marmalade to her buttered toast. 'Is it not too terrible? Can't you,' she demanded, '*say* something? Martha Todd committed for trial – charged with murdering her *husband*! Oh!' Miss Emma wrung her hands. 'We shall lose all our pupils – never lift up our heads again. To think we have harboured a *murderess*!'

'Which,' Miss Merridew said, whose face had turned a marbled grey, 'is as unthinkable as it is unlikely.'

'I can't believe it!' Clarissa Goring, also at breakfast, which was served to her in bed on a tray, called to her husband through the half open door of his dressing-room. 'Never Martha Todd!'

'Never who?' Sir Rupert appeared in the doorway with lather on his chinless chin.

'Martha Todd – I was at school with her. She married a grocer. Just fancy – a grocer! I never knew he was a grocer and she's to be tried for having murdered him!'

'How very sensational.' Drawled Rupert Goring. 'Todd? And a grocer? Dear me.'

He returned to his shaving-glass.

'I always guessed there was something queer about her. But – a grocer! So *that's* what she married. Oh, Rupert! . . . John! It says here he was their doctor. How *a*wful for him. I can't – I simply can't *believe* it!'

'Not the Rossetti girl?' Mrs Ottery at her breakfast table, for despite her age she refused, unless compelled by illness to breakfast in bed, glanced over *The Times* at her nephew who had driven to Dulwich the previous night. 'Todd – a grocer! If it's *our* grocer in Dulwich who sells such abominable tea he deserves to be murdered. Surely she didn't marry *him*! Orange juice, Simpson. Do you recommend orange juice, John? My doctor – that new Harley Street man – says we should all drink the juice of oranges and black currants, so good for the – no butter, Simpson. I want to see *you* in Harley Street – and rusks. Must you really go?' His aunt stretched a claw-like hand to John, who had risen. 'I don't see you often enough but – murder! Of *course*! You know her.'

'Her husband was my patient. Don't be alarmed if you see my name called as witness.'

'Good heavens! Do you mean to tell me *you* are mixed up in it!'

'In so far as I will have to give medical evidence.'

'I *knew* she was reincarnated from the Renaissance, so like one of the Borgias or Rossetti's wife, only hers was suicide. I am tremendously thrilled. She didn't do it, did she? Or did she?'

'She did not.'

John bent his head to receive his aunt's kiss, warm and dry, on both his cheeks that in the last few days had thinned. There were hollows under his eyes; his face, set and stern, had lost its boyishness.

'It will be a good advertisement for you,' said Mrs Ottery – 'no sugar in the orange juice, Simpson, you know I mustn't, I'm slimming – but far better to be talked about even in a murder than never to be talked about at all and doctors aren't allowed to advertise. So unfair when you think of the money spent on advertising soap. Come to dinner tomorrow and meet that young Sidney Webb. So enthusiastic and invigorating. I shall come to the trial with Oscar. He will write a play about it and Gilbert too, such an opportunity for him to satirize the law only that he has done it already in *Iolanthe*. . . .'

Half fashionable London, including Lady Goring and Mrs Ottery were among those who crowded the Court at the Old Bailey for the memorable trial of Thérèse Marthe Todd on that April morning in 1886.

When Martha, still composed but deathly pale, was brought to the dock by two female wardresses, a buzz like the humming of bees came from the female element of the numerous spectators; for despite the photographs blazoned on the front pages of the national press, none had thought to see a girl, so young, nor, spitefully went the whispers among not a few of the ladies . . . 'so actressy. got up for the part . . .' 'But she would have to be in black though why no hat?' . . . 'To show off her hair, my dear. . . .'

'Lovely young creature,' dispassionately murmured Mrs Ottery to John beside her. He sat leaning forward, his hands knotted together on his knees, his face colourless, immobile. 'You look so like Millais' Knight Errant, and she is La Belle Dame sans Merci. This is *too* melodramatic. Oscar should have been here but he said he coudn't bear to see beauty pilloried. How he knew she is a beauty I can't imagine, for the pictures of her are quite libellous. Who is defending her?'

John unfastened his taut lips to say, 'We have retained Sir Henry Doyle.'

'We?' Lowering her lorgnette that had been focused on the small black figure in the dock overpowered on either side by the two massive women, her wardresses, Mrs Ottery turned her head to ask: 'Why *we*? *You* don't have to be defended.'

'Her solicitors, to whom I recommended her as she has none to advise her, have briefed him.'

'Henry Doyle!' exclaimed his aunt. 'I didn't recognize him in that wig and all those chins and so fat in that black gown. He comes to my meetings. Very pro *us*. Who is prosecuting?'

'The Attorney-General,' muttered John.

'The Attorney – Never Froggie Fennell! Very oily but hard as a rock. Doyle is no match for *him*.'

To Sir Henry's daughter, Maud, next to whom Clarissa was seated – a plain dumpy girl with a face like a pie, she thought – and said: 'Does your father think she did it?'

'He doesn't discuss his cases with me,' tritely replied Maud, who was up at Girton studying medicine and had come to London for this first day of the trial.

'What a nasty little man this clergyman looks,' whispered Clarissa, 'he is supposed to be an accessory after – or is it before the fact? I never know the difference. They say they were having an affair. I'd as soon have an affair with a black beetle. I was at Albion House with her – you left the term before she came. She was an awful little liar – always boasting about an aristocratic French grandmother who didn't exist. What a shock for the poor M's. I am so disappointed Papa isn't in on this but he is defending the woman in that big divorce case. I'm allowed to hear divorces now I'm married and I hate having to miss it – very *spicy*! Only murder is much more exciting especially as I used to know . . .'

Suddenly the murmur of voices and Clarissa's sibilant monologue ceased. An expectant hush descended on the packed Court as the great doors opened for the entrance of the Judge, and the vast assembly stood.

A wizened little man, dwarfed in scarlet robes, his heavy wig falling either side of his narrow old cold face, he enthroned himself beneath the Royal Coat-of-Arms, and the trial, that was to be the *cause célèbre* of the year, began.

It began with a surprise that shook the Court and many representatives of the law to whom it was as unexpected as to the person concerned, the Reverend Albert Dixon. Standing in the dock, his face, decorated with its heavy black moustache, that of a cadaver, he heard his Counsel, Mr Griffith-Hughes Q.C., address the Judge.

'May it please your lordship, before the Court proceeds to arraign the prisoners – both having pleaded not guilty – I appear before you on behalf of the prisoner Albert Dixon, with the application that they be tried separately.'

Whereupon the Attorney-General rose to announce that as there was no case to be submitted to the jury upon which they could convict Mr Dixon, he proposed to offer no evidence against him. At which his lordship, in his cracked old voice, directed the jury to find Albert Dixon 'Not Guilty'.

After the necessary formalities had been dealt with the Judge declared that as there was no case against Mr Dixon he was entitled to his discharge. Although he had still to face the ordeal of giving evidence, and if his ministerial career, as he had feared, might well be ruined, he had escaped the gallows, and with fervent inward prayers of thanksgiving, he was joyfully conducted from the dock.

Sir Rodney Fennell, Attorney-General, who had earned the sobriquet of 'Froggie', owing to a marked similarity in the protuberant eyes, wide mouth and receding under-jaw, to a certain species of amphibian, then, in mellifluous tones, opened the case for the Crown.

'Gentlemen of the jury,' he turned his black-robed person in the direction of those twelve; and to her in the dock whose eyes were fastened on them seated there to decide whether she must live or . . . die, their wooden faces looked to be merged into one monstrous face as that of some fearful unknown god, condemning . . . 'the prisoner at the bar,' solemnly pronounced the representative of the Crown, 'is charged with the murder of her husband, that murder, if murder it were, having taken place on the night of December the thirty-first, last year, or the first morning of this present year. The name of the deceased was Joseph Thomas Todd. The maiden name of the prisoner at the bar – for she is a native of France – was Thérèse Marthe de Lamotte. After their marriage, which occurred,' Sir Rodney referred to his notes, 'in the year 1880 she went or, more correctly was sent, by her husband to school to complete her education, her age at the time of her marriage being, as she averred, sixteen. Yet her marriage certificate gives her age as nineteen.'

Sensation among the ladies at this revelation of the prisoner's age, and some titters at the Attorney-General's would-be facetious remark: 'But we know it is not unusual for the age of a wife to differ on her marriage certificate from that on the certificate of her birth.'

Having shown himself to be indulgent to feminine foibles and, despite that he was prosecuting the prisoner for the heinous crime of murder, that he would prove to be a man of sympathy for and understanding of the frailties of woman, he proceeded to describe in detail the married life of the accused which was, to say the least, unusual, since the prisoner maintained that she and her husband, the deceased, did not cohabit save on *one* occasion *only*.

'That one occasion, gentlemen,' the frog-like eyes of the Attorney-General travelled slowly to scan those twelve expressionless faces, 'resulted in the birth of a still-born child. We have no authority, other than of the accused, to ascertain that this – ah – platonic relationship between the husband and wife continued throughout the years of their marriage, yet it appears that in spite of these singular conditions the couple lived together on amicable terms. There is no suggestion of any quarrel between them, but there is evidence of a somewhat hostile attitude on the part of the prisoner toward her father-in-law.'

At this point the prisoner was seen to raise her head, her pale lips parted as if on a sharp intake of breath; and her eyes of a startling blue, the only colour in her wax white face, were veiled by their long dark lashes. . . .

'Put her in the box,' muttered a briefless young barrister to his equally briefless young colleague beside him, 'and there'll be an acquittal. It's always one up to the defence when he's got something as pretty as paint to hand out to 'em.'

'Doyle'll never risk it with the Frog to make mincemeat of her,' was the answer to that from a corner of the mouth. 'Not a leg to stand on if it were Venus herself in the nude!'

On and on droned that lubricated voice, drawing the attention of the transfixed jury to an important event in the lives of the deceased and the prisoner at the bar. . . . 'That event, gentlemen, which occurred early in the year 1885, was the acquaintance of the Reverend Albert Dixon, Wesleyan minister, whose chapel the husband and wife attended while living in the village of Coombe, near Wimbledon. This acquaintance soon ripened into a friendship of close social intimacy between the married couple and Mr Dixon, whom the deceased engaged as tutor to his wife, and continued when the deceased and the prisoner at the bar moved from Coombe in Surrey to furnished apartments in London. In September of that year, 1885, the deceased made a Will leaving everything of which he should die possessed to his wife. There is no doubt,' here a significant pause, 'that the prisoner at the bar was aware of the contents of the Will. Now, gentlemen,' that amphibious gaze was directed to the ceiling as if the gentlemens' decapitated heads had been conveyed from their bodies to cluster there attentive, 'we come to the illness of the deceased, when he requested Dr Herriott, attending him, that another physician should be called in consultation, not in any way detrimental to his own medical practitioner's treatment of his illness, which he had diagnozed as nervous prostration and subacute gastritis, but to allay certain doubts, suggested by the father of the deceased, who was not satisfied that the prisoner had been following the doctor's advice and he believed she was giving her husband a – ah – injurious medicines – shall we say? Therefore, to protect his wife from any such suspicion, a second opinion was invited.'

Having by this time set the Court in a buzz of expectation, Counsel brought his narrative down to the convalescence of the deceased, who had so far recovered that he was pronounced well enough to take a holiday in Torquay before returning to his business.

'So now, gentlemen,' still addressing the ceiling, 'I refer you to December the twenty-seventh when, despite her husband's recovery to almost normal health, the prisoner approached Mr Dixon to obtain for her a quantity of chloroform that she might soothe, she tells him, the frequent paroxysms of pain he suffered due to an internal complaint of some years' standing; yet neither the doctor attending him nor the consultant called to give a second opinion had found him suffering from any such complaint. The prisoner told Mr Dixon she was well used to administering chloroform for the alleviation of pain, and that chloroform had previously been obtained for her by the midwife who nursed her in her confinement. This as will be proven, was entirely untrue, but it served to dispel any doubt on the part of Mr Dixon, who meekly yielding to her demand, procured and duly delivered to the prisoner a four-ounce bottle of chloroform on December the twenty-eighth. . . . It would appear,' added Counsel, after another significant pause, 'that the prisoner seems to have exerted a considerable influence over this unfortunate gentleman.

'On the thirty-first of December, the last day of his life, the deceased ate a hearty evening meal with evident enjoyment. It was New Year's Eve and in that house the landlord and landlady were entertaining guests to greet the New Year with the customary jollifications – a New Year which the deceased was not destined to – see.'

Here the carefully modulated accents achieved a noticeable break; the almost lidless protuberant eyes blinked as if to dispel from them a moisture as he watched the effect of his words on those twelve who sat dutifully imbibing each syllable, but never a look did he give to the old man, seated above in his red enermined robes, impervious and enured to the Attorney-General's subtle histrionics.

'During and after that evening meal – his last meal on earth –' the oily voice with pointed emphasis continued, 'the deceased appeared to be in uncommonly good spirits, notwithstanding that he had paid a visit to the dentist in the afternoon, to have a tooth extracted – by gas. He retired early to bed. Since his illness the deceased had slept on a bed in the drawing-room, communicating with the bedroom, and the prisoner at the bar slept in a chair or on a couch at his bedside. You will hear how the prisoner dozed in her chair with her hand resting on her husband's foot and woke to find him – cold.'

A truly dramatic pause here for that to sink in.

It sank.

'The prisoner at once roused the landlord, Mr Bridges, the time being about four o'clock in the morning. She expressed alarm. She told Mr Bridges she feared her husband was dead. The doctor was sent for and confirmed those fears. The deceased had been dead about two hours.'

After describing the events of that morning, followed by the post-mortem the next day and the details of the ensuing inquest, Counsel created a considerable stir when he told of the report issued by the Home Office analyst which ascertained the presence of chloroform in the stomach. 'Meanwhile, gentlemen, the prisoner had revealed to Dr Herriott a statement of the most extraordinary and intimate nature.'

If any of those present had eyes or ears for other than he, who with due solemnity had made this pronouncement holding his audience spell-bound, it would have been seen that she in the dock swayed where she stood, that her eyes were lifted, seeking, till they found those of a young man seated at the back of the Court, and that between them passed a look, a message, unuttered, unheard save by these two, and that from him she seemed to have derived some strength, for the colour that had fled from her face returned, as a sun-shaft piercing the leaded panes of a window set high in the massive wall, lighted it and burnished as if with a halo the glowing bronze of her hair.

'You will hear,' those twelve were told, 'how when the doctor informed her that chloroform had been the cause of death, the prisoner replied, in evident distress, that she wished it had been anything but chloroform. . . . Gentlemen, the prisoner did not appear before the Coroner at the inquest. She was there, yet she did not tender herself to give evidence, but I would not have you to understand from this that any inference is or ought to be drawn against her despite, as result of the inquiry, the coroner's jury found a verdict of – wilful murder.'

Like two stones dropped in a stagnant pool those words fell upon the silent Court. The red-robed figure on its throne twitched a pinched nostril; his hands, withered as autumn leaves, fumbled among the papers before him; he peered down at them, and up again to stare at the urbane countenance of the prosecution who, with marked emphasis, proceeded to draw the jurymens' attention to the fact that the prisoner admitted in her statement to Dr Herriott to having had chloroform in her possession on that fatal night which, according to pathological evidence, had found its way into the stomach of the deceased. 'But . . . how did it get there? So far as could be known there were only three ways in which it could have got there. The first being that the deceased took the chloroform intentionally with a view to self-destruction which, when the full facts had been heard, nothing would be found to support the possibility of any such suggestion.

'The deceased was in the best of spirits on that last night, and looking forward to a holiday.' The voice of the Attorney-General gathered impetus to impress upon his listeners: 'There is no reason whatsoever why he should have contemplated suicide. As to a second hypothesis, that he could have taken it accidentally, having poured the contents of a bottle of chloroform into a glass in mistake for a sleeping draught or any other medicine, such a mistake would have caused him excruciating pain which could not have failed to attract attention by his outcries of agony. The third, and in the opinion of eminent medical men, the *only* reason would have been by oral administration made by . . . someone else. You will say that the same acute pain and outcries would have followed, but not if that administration were preceded by external inhalation or application of the chloroform, sufficient to stupefy the sense of pain.

'Gentlemen of the jury,' those tones, no longer lubricated, swelled in volume to the warning, 'you must not find the prisoner guilty unless the result of the evidence against her is proved beyond all doubt – beyond,' was weightily repeated, 'all possible and *rea*sonable *doubt*. . . . Gentlemen, I have discharged my duty in so far as it is to be discharged at this stage. It now remains for you to consider the evidence which will be placed before you.'

And with the air of a leading actor delivering his final speech before the curtain falls on the first scene, and in a silence that, were the crowded Court an auditorium would have been succeeded by a round of applause to raise the roof, Counsel for the prosecution sat; Mr Grice, Q.C., assisting the Attorney-General, stood, and the first witness for the Crown was called:

Mr Edward Todd.

As he entered the witness box, his lean shoulders bent, his sparse grey hair receding from a parchment-coloured forehead, his eyes red-rimmed as if from recent weeping, he presented a spectacle of pity for a bereaved father forced to give evidence for the murder of his son.

With every consideration due to such an ordeal, Mr Grice questioned him with careful sympathy. . . . Yes, he was a carpenter by trade but owing to his age and his rheumatics he could not carry on his regular work, only odd jobs here and there. . . . Yes, he lived with his son and his – the prisoner – till he was turned out.

'Turned out?' repeated Mr Grice, in evident surprise.

'She, the prisoner, she took against me and wouldn't 'ave me live with them – said there weren't room in the 'ouse for me.'

'You having lived with your son and the prisoner for many years?'

'Yes, and when 'er mother 'oo was our 'ousekeeper died, my son – 'e give 'er a 'ome, and then 'e – well, 'e married 'er.'

'You were not, I think, present at the marriage of your son?'

'No, I weren't.'

'And after the marriage did you know that your son sent his wife to a boarding school for – how long?'

'About three years an' no money spared on 'er, neether.'

'Did the prisoner reside at this school and come home for the holidays living with your son as a married couple – as man and wife?'

'S'far as I know.'

'Do you remember the birth of a still-born child?'

'Yes.'

'When was this?'

' 'Bout two years ago.'

'What had been the condition of the health of the deceased, during his married life?'

'Never a day's illness – always strong and 'ealthy until them last three weeks of December, just afore Christmas.'

An interval allowed for the application of a rather dirty handkerchief to the snuffling nose of the witness, who replied to Counsel's next question that he went at once to see his son when he heard he was ill.

'And on that first visit of what did your son complain?'

' 'E told me –' here the witness was seen to draw himself up and pointing his pink-tipped nose in the direction of that crimson-robed figure on high ' 'e told me as 'ow the doctor 'ad said 'e 'ad poison in 'im – mercury – and my son, 'e said 'e 'ad mercury in 'is mouth.'

'How did your son appear to be when you saw him, Mr Todd?'

'Well,' laboriously, ' 'e looked like 'e was under a – a nartock-tick.'

'A *what?*' from above.

'A narcotic, my lord,' was apologetically explained.

'That's right,' from the witness. 'I get me words – them doctor's words – wrong. 'E looked dazed like – not so sharp and fresh as 'e used to be.'

'How many times did you see your son while he was ill?'

'About three times. She – 'is wife – she wouldn't let me see 'im more'n that.'

'While your son was ill did the prisoner write to inform you of his condition?'

'Yes.'

'Are these the letters she wrote?'

Which when handed to the witness he confirmed that they were. Six short letters were then read by the Clerk of the Court, the last of them undated.

Mr Grice: 'There is an allusion in this letter,' referring to it from the packet handed back to him, 'I do not quite understand what it means, "I have neither forgiven nor forgotten the past".'

Witness, mumbling: 'Must I go into all that?'

'Go into all what? Speak up,' from the Judge, whose head was poked forward and whose eyes, amazingly shrewd under their wrinkled lids, were fastened, with gimlet penetration on the witness who, thus commanded, spoke, jerkily, up:

'It's about some unpleasantness to do with – with

Ted, my younger son. 'E's dead, too, both of 'em gone.'

Mr Grice, compassionately: 'I will not press you further on that point. I gather it relates to an old matter irrelevant to the present case. I think you next received a telegram informing you of your son's death?'

'That's right.'

Asked to describe what he did when he arrived at the house in Clarendon Place on receipt of the telegram, witness said he went into the room where his son lay dead, kissed him and smelt his mouth.

'Why,' he was asked, 'did you smell his mouth?'

'Well, I – I thought 'e might 'ave been given somethink – prussic acid or somethink – to go off sudden like that when I'd been told 'e was better – and goin' for a 'oliday.'

'Did you detect any such smell?'

'No,' reluctantly, 'I never. Must 'ave passed off by then – whatever it was.'

'At that time was any mention made of a post-mortem?'

'Yes – me – I made mention – I arst for it.'

Witness was then questioned if the prisoner were with him when the result of the post-mortem had been heard.

'Yes, and the doctors 'oo did the post-mortim was there and one o' them 'e put 'is 'and on my shoulder and said Jo, my son, 'ad no business to be lyin' there, dead – a strong man like 'im.'

'Did the prisoner hear this remark?'

'Yes, she 'eard it all right.'

A venomous look accompanied witness's reply, darted at the girl in the dock who stood so still, so white she might have been carven from marble.

'And,' continued Mr Grice, 'did she then leave the house?'

'Yes, she was told to go.'

'Who told her to go?'

'One o' the doctors an' 'e told 'er to leave 'er bag and 'er cloak be'ind.'

'She said goodbye to you?'

'No, I said goodbye to 'er and kissed 'er.'

A document purporting to be a will made by the deceased was now produced and shown to the witness, who was asked if he recognized the signature as that of his son, to which he replied he wasn't sure – couldn't swear to it . . . 'bein' different some'ow to what I seen 'im write.'

Had he ever seen the document before?

After some hesitation he said that he had seen it.

'Where did you see it?'

Witness, uncomfortable: 'I – I seen it at Somerset 'Ouse.'

The will, dated the third day of September, 1885, was then read by the Clerk of the Court.

> 'I, Joseph Todd will and bequeath all my property and everything I possess to my wife, Martha Todd, for her sole use, and appoint Albert Dixon, B.A., a Wesleyan minister, and James Button, my business manager, to be my sole executors.'

The Judge, to whom the will had been handed and after remarking that the signature looked to have been written backward instead of forward, which occasioned some titters, announced that the Court would adjourn for a short interval.

'Is there enough time for us to go out for coffee?' inquired Mrs Ottery of the pallid John.

'Certainly time enough for you, though not for me. I may be called any minute.'

But he was not called any minute for when the Court reassembled and Mrs Ottery, hugged in her sables, returned after refreshment – 'at a *dreadful* little place – a kind of bar for cab-drivers, and poisonous coffee – no, that is rather too apposite –' Edward Todd was recalled for cross-examination by Sir Henry Doyle, Q.C.

In direct contrast to the Attorney-General's manner of address was that of Counsel for the defence. Cumbrous framed, with three chins and eyes under beetling brows embedded in fat, his tone was neither dulcet nor mellifluous. It boomed. It thundered. It struck terror in the heart of his witness, to whom Sir Henry showed no consideration whatsoever for the father of a son alleged to have been murdered by his wife.

'You have said you were not present at the marriage of the deceased? Did you disapprove of that marriage?'

'I didn't much approve of it.'

'Why?'

'Well, to begin with she was a forriner.'

'A foreigner?'

''Er mother was French.'

'And your son's wife was left an orphan at – what age?'

'About fourteen.'

'You say your son gave her a home – for how long?'

'Till 'e married 'er.'

'Was there not a marriage settlement made upon the defendant?'

The 'defendant', it was noted, and not the 'prisoner' as markedly referred to by the prosecution.

'Not as I know of.'

'May I enlighten you? There was, I understand, a substantial marriage settlement made to the defendant by her father on the occasion of her marriage to your son?'

'She never 'ad no father, or if so she never knew 'im.'

'That is not the question, nor,' said Counsel sternly, 'does it cast discredit on the defendant that she did not know her father, since dead, and who made a handsome settlement upon her when he discovered that a daughter had been born to him by the young gentlewoman to whom he was affianced in his youth and was by tragic circumstances prevented from marrying.'

Having thus directed the sympathy of the Court and the jury from the bereaved parent to the prisoner, victim of a tragic and romantic birth, Sir Henry boomed on:

'Now, Mr Todd, you say the defendant went to school after her marriage and that your son spared no expense on her upbringing and education.'

'That's right.'

'Did you know that the fees for a daily governess and later of the school, were paid by her father from monies deposited with your son for that purpose?'

'No, 'e never told me nothink o' that. 'E paid for 'er board an' keep out of 'is own pocket after 'er mother died – that I do know.'

'And she was sent by him to an expensive boarding school almost from the Church door, as it were. She remained there, you have said, for about three years. What was the date of this marriage?'

'I'm not much good at dates – I forget.'

'I will refresh your memory. This marriage of a man in his early middle age to a child of sixteen, in the year—'

'She was nineteen when 'e married 'er.'

'Do not interrupt me. We have her word for it that she was sixteen years of age when the marriage took place in the year, which you have forgotten and of which I will remind you, was 1880, three years before the Married Woman's Property Act became law.'

'Sir Henry, I fail to see,' from above, 'the significance of all this.'

'With every respect, my lord, it is of vital significance, in that, as your lordship is aware, until the Married Woman's Property Act became law, any property or settlement made upon or owned by her could revert to the husband, which, in this case, when the deceased married the defendant it did so revert and by which he was enabled to expand his business.'

'Very well, Sir Henry,' croaked the old voice. 'Proceed.'
Sir Henry, ponderously, proceeded.

'Shortly after Mrs Todd left school and came to live with your son did you write an apology for certain allegations of a serious nature that you had made against her?'

'Yes, I did. I signed an apology but I never meant it. I knew it was false.'

'What!' thundered Sir Henry. 'You signed an apology knowing it to be false?'

Witness, stammering: 'I – I signed it to – to make peace with my son, because Martha – the prisoner – was on at 'im to make 'im – make me write it.'

'To *make* you write it?' echoed Counsel; and producing a sheet of paper, 'I will read this apology you were *made* to write – and which you signed.'

Counsel, reading:

' "Having made statements reflecting on the character of Martha Todd, the wife of my son Joseph, which statements I have discovered to be false and untrue, I hereby withdraw all such statements and express my regret for having made them. I also apologize to Mrs Martha Todd and to my son Joseph Todd and acknowledge all such statements are unfounded and untrue". . . .

'Was that the apology you signed in the presence of your son's solicitor?'

'Yes, to make peace and because it 'ad to do with my other son, Edward. 'E was younger than Jo.'

'Do you mean to say,' exploded Counsel, 'that these false allegations made against Mrs Todd were also made against your younger son, Edward, whom you have told my learned friend is dead?'

' 'E weren't dead then. 'E died out East after 'e'd sailed – gone back to 'is ship.'

'So that he could not refute these allegations?'

No answer.

Sir Henry now applied the screw to another vital point.

'Did you know if the deceased, your son, had any exceptional ideas on married life?'

'No, 'e used to chaff and joke about such things – that was all.'

'What used he to say?'

' 'E said a man ought to 'ave two wives – one to do the work an' one fr'is pleasure. Same as I 'eard a man larss' night say 'e could do with forty wives like that.'

Loud laughter, suppressed by the Judge.

'This is not an occasion for levity. If these unseemly demonstrations occur again I will be obliged to clear the Court.'

Stifled giggles from the ladies, while Counsel admonished witness to: 'Keep your mind on the subject of this remark made by your son and of which you say he "chaffed and joked". Did you not think it a very curious observation?'

'Not partick'lerly.'

'Mr Todd,' was the next question hurled at him, 'did your son ever speak to you about mesmerism, or being mesmerized?'

'Never. It was always business – nothink but 'is business.'

'Except when expressing his views on polygamy?'

'Pardon? Polly – 'oo?'

This occasioned more giggles, unhushed by the Judge, whose wrinkled cheeks expanded in the fleeting semblance of a grin.

'On the subject,' explained Counsel, also conceding himself some mild amusement, 'of a man having more than one wife?'

'I never 'eard 'im say anythink else about that.'

'You say that when you saw him after he was taken ill he appeared to be labouring under a narcotic. Was he subject to depression?'

'Not afore 'is illness. 'E was a bit low then.'

'Did he tell you he knew he was going to die?'

'No, never.'

'Try and recollect. You are on your oath, remember. Did he not tell you,' ruthlessly pursued his inquisitor, 'that no man could feel and be so ill as he, and live?'

'Might 'a done – bein' low.'

'You have said that after the autopsy –' and at witness's goggle-eyed query, ''oo's Topsy?' – 'after the post-mortem,' was the explanatory substitute amid renewed titters from the Court, 'you were summoned to the drawing-room with Mrs Todd. Did she say anything to you of a kindly nature on that occasion?'

'I don't think she ever said nothink at all that day.'

'You have told the coroner she said this,' reading from his notes: '"She put her arm round my neck and said it will make no difference to you" – presumably referring to your financial position – "it will be just the same as if Jo were alive." Did the defendant tell you that?'

'Well, if she did, she did. Can't be expected to remember everythink – bein' shockin'ly upset at my son's death at the time.'

More tearful snuffling into the handkerchief, while Sir Henry, entirely unaffected by this display of paternal grief, went on:

'After the post-mortem you have said that one of the doctors told Mrs Todd to leave her bag and her cloak. Did you say there was no need for her to leave her cloak because there was nothing in the pockets?'

'It didn' 'ave no pockets.'

'No pockets? Then I take it you had attempted to search in, or for, the pockets of her cloak?'

'I was only 'avin' a look round.'

'A look round for what – and why?'

'To make sure that she wasn't takin' nothink away that she didn't ought to take.'

'And this on the day that she had spoken kind and reassuring words with regard for your future welfare?'

No answer.

'When you went to see your son on the day of his death, you say you smelt his lips, suspecting poison – prussic acid?'

'Yes,' defiantly, 'I did.'

'On what grounds?'

'Because 'e said 'e 'ad poison in 'im – mercury – an' I thought as it might 'ave been somethink else.'

'What else did you think it might have been?'

'I thought as 'ow 'e might 'ave got lead poisonin'.'

'But you have just said you were sniffing, or smelling him for prussic acid.'

'Well, I didn't know quite what – I thought pr'aps 'e might 'a got lead poisonin' from tastin' 'is teas.'

'Surely, sir, you do not suggest that your son sold, among other commodities, poisonous teas?'

Gusts of laughter rippled through the Court, checked by a sharp rap on his desk from the Judge's bony knuckles and further admonishment: 'Must I again remind you that I will not have this hilarity or it will be treated as contempt of Court!' while in the ensuing silence witness was heard to mumble: 'I was thinkin' 'e might 'a got 'old of some lead out o' the tea-chests.'

'Come, Mr Todd, was your son in the habit of tasting the tea-chests as well as the tea?'

The Court, in stifled mirth, held its sides; and Sir Henry, releasing his victim, said: 'I thank you, Mr Todd,' and let him go.

Somewhat resembling a rat that had been mauled by a ferret, witness went, or rather tottered, from the box.

The Court adjourned.

After an interval for luncheon Edward Todd was recalled for re-examination by the Attorney-General.

'Mr Todd, my learned friend has mentioned an apology

written and signed by you. To what does this apology refer?'

Witness, with relish: 'Somethink very bad.'

'Something,' persuasively dulcet, 'reflecting on the character of the defendant?'

Sir Henry, ballooning up: 'My lord, I object!'

The Judge, having eaten heartily of steak and kidney pudding and more inclined for a doze than a hearing, gave it as his opinion that witness must state what he had to apologize for.

'Well,' thus encouraged, his eyes still red but more now from liberal refreshment than from recent weeping, witness in a voice a trifle slurred, replied:

'She, the pris'ner – she went off with my son Ted – Edward – to Brighton an' stayed with 'im a week – alone. I went after 'em and – hic – an' caught 'em at it.'

From Sir Henry in a thunder-clap: 'Caught them at what?'

'Well,' shrinking beneath galvanic bombardment, ' 'er – the pris'ner – and my son Ted – an' 'im goin' into 'er room in the mil' – the mill'le o' the night.'

'Your son Edward whom you say is dead?'

'Yes, but that was afore 'e died.'

'I am not suggesting you saw your son go into the lady's room after he died.'

Subdued laughter from the Court, and from the Attorney-General a glare at his learned friend as, slightly less honey-mouthed, he continued:

'Was your son Joseph aware that the prisoner and his brother went to Brighton together and – alone?'

'No, 'e weren't. 'E didn't know.'

At this the prisoner was seen to lift her head; the colour rushed to her face, her lips parted as if to speak, but no sound came from them more than her hurried breathing heard only by the two stout women guarding her.

By Sir Henry: 'Was it not at your son Joseph's suggestion that his brother should accompany his wife to Brighton, since she was in need of a holiday and her husband unable to accompany her, owing to the demands of his business?'

'No,' defiantly, 'it were Ted 'oo sud-suggested it – 'e wanted me to go with 'em but she wouldn't 'ave *me* – an' it weren't the firss' time, neether, that they went off together. They was always gaddin' about when 'e was 'ome-hic-on leave.'

'With the knowledge and approval of the deceased, your son Joseph?'

''Ow should I know?'

'You are not,' boomed Sir Henry, 'here to question me.'

The Judge, swallowing a yawn and repetitive steak and kidney: 'Sir Henry, I cannot see the point of pursuing this matter of apology which Mr Grice has already said to be irrelevant to the present case.'

'With every respect, my lord, it was my friend, the Attorney-General, who has just referred to the apology signed by the witness.'

'And which was read by you. I have a note of it.' The skeletal fingers fumbled at the sheaf of papers before him. 'Is there anything further,' the tired old voice asked of Sir Rodney, 'that you wish to pursue?'

'No, my lord,' with a bow, 'not of this witness. I thank you. Mr Todd,' not quite a bow to him but something near it, 'you may step down.'

Mr Todd stepped, somewhat unsteadily, down, and the next three witnesses, James Bridges, landlord of the house in Clarendon Place, his wife, and their maidservant Angharad Williams, were severally called. Each gave evidence as to the hour in the early morning when Mrs Todd had roused them to send the maid for the doctor, to tell Mr Bridges that she feared her husband was dead, and Mrs Bridges to recount the conversation relating to chloroform while she served supper to the deceased the night before his death. She told of the hearty meal he had eaten and that he seemed more cheerful than she had seen him since his illness.

Bridges, questioned by Mr Grice, told how he had gone into the room where the deceased lay dead and had seen the fire burning brightly as if it had just been 'packed', inferring that the prisoner had not, as she declared, been to sleep and had just awakened to find her husband cold, but that she had been up all night.

The frightened little rabbit of a maid, asked if, while in waiting on Mrs Todd during the visits of Mr Dixon, she had ever noticed anything unusual, replied:

'No – yes – one time,' thin little hands twisting and writhing, her voice in a bleat, her lips in a tremble, 'on the floor.'

'On the floor?' quacked the Judge.

Terror held Annie speechless.

'You were saying,' coaxed Mr Grice, 'on the floor. What did you see unusual on the floor?'

'The mistress did I see on the floor and her head –' a terrified halt.

'Yes, Miss Williams?'

'Her head it was on his – the Reverend's knee and then –'

'What then?' urged Mr Grice.

'That is all. And then I – I went away, not wishful to be awkward, mind.'

By Sir Henry, surprisingly douce: 'Had you been summoned to the room when you went into it, Miss Williams?'

'Yes, she – Mrs Todd, she rang the bell, look you, and I,' more hand-twisting, 'went up with the tea.'

Asked by Mr Grice if Mrs Todd were wearing the same dress as she had worn all day when witness was called by her to fetch the doctor in the early morning of January the first, witness said it was the same dress as she always wore when out walking with the dog.

Sir Henry: 'Are you sure it was the same dress – a walking dress – she was wearing when she called you?'

'Yes, sir, I think—'

'Now, Angharad, think carefully. Was she not wearing a loose sort of negligée, a kind of dressing-gown, having retired for the night?'

'No sir – yes, sir, I misremember. She had a many dresses, mind. . . .'

The briefless young barrister, to his colleague, 'I bet she never retired for the night or went to sleep. Doyle can't get away with that.'

'Doyle,' said the other, 'will get away with – murder. You'll see.'

'What'll you have on it? A fiver that he don't?'

'Double or – Here! Grice has done with this poor little beast. Now for Dixon, and when Doyle gets his teeth in *him*, he'll –'

'Shut up! I want to listen.'

The whole Court, on tenterhooks, was listening to this most important witness for the Crown, who understandably appeared more confident than when, a few hours since, he had stood in the dock arraigned as accessory before the fact. He looked, indeed, as self-assured as if about to address his congregation from the pulpit.

To Mr Grice, again examining, he answered readily: Yes, he was a Wesleyan minister and Bachelor of Arts. . . . He had made the acquaintance of Mr Todd during his attendance at his chapel in Coombe, and the acquaintance was continued after the removal of Mr and Mrs Todd to London. . . . Yes, he had agreed at the request of Mr Todd, to instruct Mrs Todd in Latin, history and mathematics.

'Were you on intimate terms with the deceased and his wife?'

'Yes, I was a friend – I may say an honoured friend of both Mr and Mrs Todd.' As, with becoming modesty, he admitted this, the whiteness of his teeth became visible.

contrasting sharply with the heavy black moustache and the sickly lemon yellow of his face.

'You visited Mr Todd and the prisoner when they were at Dover?'

'I did, at Mr Todd's invitation.'

'And while you were there you wrote to him and he to you?'

'Yes.'

Letters exchanged between the deceased and witness were then read.

'These letters,' said Mr Grice, 'express Mr Todd's feeling for you as that of a brother and in your reply you say you respond from your heart to his wish that "our friendship may ripen with the lapse of time". That lapse of time was not destined to last for long?'

'Alas, no, sir.' A sigh, an upward roll of the eyes accompanied a doleful shake of the head. 'He, my dear friend whom I, too, loved as a brother, departed this life within the year, to my abiding sorrow.'

Counsel, consulting his notes: 'On the occasion of one of your visits to the deceased during his illness, do you remember a conversation you had with the prisoner about her husband's health?'

'Yes,' with unhesitating eagerness came the reply. 'It was on December the twenty-seventh when I met Mrs Todd going to the post. I walked with her to the post box. She told me she was anxious to obtain chloroform to relieve her husband's pain and his insomnia which had latterly increased. She said he believed himself to be suffering from an internal disease.'

The Judge, peering forward:

'How was this chloroform to be administered?'

On being told that witness understood it was to be sprinkled on a handkerchief and inhaled, 'Then why,' queried his lordship, 'did she not obtain the chloroform from the doctor attending her husband?'

'That was what I wanted to know, my lord,' was the

eager self-confident answer to that, 'and she said as the doctor was unaware she had been used to administer the drug in the past, he might not have allowed her to do so. She said she had previously obtained it from the nurse who attended her in her confinement.'

Questioned concerning the purchase of the chloroform, witness said he had bought four one ounce bottles at three different chemists' and poured the contents into one larger bottle.

'Why four different bottles and at three different chemists'?' demanded his lordship.

To which witness, with somewhat less self-confidence, replied that he thought he would not have been granted so large a quantity from one chemist without a doctor's prescription.

'Then why did *you* not obtain a doctor's prescription?'

'Well, I – I,' gulped Mr Dixon, 'I did write to a medical friend for a prescription but had unfortunately mislaid his address, and because Mrs Todd had told me she was anxious to alleviate her husband's suffering and sleeplessness, I was persuaded – injudiciously, I fear – to oblige her, my lord.'

'Most injudiciously,' commented his lordship. 'Proceed, Mr Grice.'

Mr Grice, proceeding, extracted from his witness that on the day following the purchase of the chloroform he had given the bottle to Mrs Todd while out walking with her in Hyde Park. . . . Yes, he had seen the deceased once more after that, on New Year's Eve. 'This,' with suitable woe, 'was the last time I saw him alive.'

'Did you see Mrs Todd again?'

Yes, witness had visited Mrs Todd at the house of her friends, the Reverend Mr and Mrs Grimsby, and asked her what she had done with the bottle of chloroform he had bought for her. 'I was, naturally, very – perturbed, having heard that the pathologist conducting the post-mortem had failed to find a cause of death, but that chl-

chloroform,' another gulp, 'was – suspected as a possible cause, and that specimens would be sent for – for analysis.'

'What was Mrs Todd's reply to your question concerning the bottle of chloroform?'

'She replied that she had not used it and that the bottle was still unopened. I visited her again on the next day and told her –' witness lowered his head – 'that I was a – a ruined man for having acceded to her request. I repeated that I must know what she had done with the bottle of chloroform if she had not used it. She became very angry and stamped her foot at me.'

Mr Grice, persuasively: 'But what did she say?'

'She said – I hardly like to repeat it,' uttered witness, eyes to heaven, 'she said – we must excuse her, my lord, she was going through a critical time – she said –'

'Don't keep on saying she *said*,' was the croaking admonishment, '*What* did she say?'

Witness with a haunted look above 'She sa – "Oh, go away. Don't bother me!" She meant about the chloroform, my lord.'

'I did not presume you were telling me to go away and not bother you.' Sycophantic titters at his lordship's little joke. 'Is that all?'

'Ner-not quite all, my lord. She sai – she – I much regret she said, "Oh, damn the chloroform!"'

Loud laughter silenced by his lordship's thump on the table and the words:

. . . . 'until tomorrow morning. Ten o'clock.'

* * *

Outside the Old Bailey a surplus crowd had gathered, waiting for a chance to get into the Court, already packed to capacity with spectators eagerly expectant of this second day of the trial that had been given nation-wide publicity; and now the latest witness, the Reverend

Albert Dixon was called for re-examination by Mr Grice.

In reply to Counsel's question as to what he had done with the bottles of chloroform he had bought . . . 'those four empty bottles', witness broke out in a visible sweat. Having been found not guilty of any murderous intent and discharged from the case, he was asked to give evidence concerning those accursed bottles that well might implicate himself. Counsel, he thought frantically, might be *cross*-examining and not *ex*amining.

'They,' his forehead shone with a slimy dew as he answered, 'as far as I remember they were at my – my lodgings in Putney.'

'It was on Monday, January the fourth, before the inquest, that the four bottles were at your lodgings?'

'Er – no,' witness passed a hand across his forehead. 'I made a mistake. They were not at my lodgings, They were—'

'Yes?' helpfully encouraged Mr Grice.

'They were,' blurted Dixon, 'on – on Putney Heath.'

'On where?' from the Judge, inclining an ear.

'On Putney Heath, my lord,' repeated Counsel aside, and wishing he had avoided that question followed by his lordship's inquiry:

'What were they doing on Putney Heath?'

'They –' his hand had left the sweating brow of witness and was attached to the walrus moustache to impede the agitated fall of his top teeth – 'I, er—'

'Well?' rasped his lordship.

'I –' removing his hand and in palpable fright – 'I threw them into a – gorse bush.'

'Into a what?' from above.

'A gorse bush, my lord,' another aside from Mr Grice.

'When was this?'

Witness: 'On the Sunday morning, my lord.'

The Judge leaned forward, his old eyes blinking, his old voice wheezing:

'Where, on the Sunday morning, were you going?'

'I was on my way to hold a service in my chapel, my lord.'

'So, to sanctify the Sabbath you threw those incriminating bottles into a gorse bush.'

The Court appreciatively cackled; and his lordship, allowing that to pass, asked: 'Is there anything more, Mr Grice?'

'Nothing more at present of this witness, my lord. I thank you, Mr Dixon.'

But as with bowed head the wretched Mr Dixon turned to leave the box the Defence was up and at him.

'Terms of intimacy have been mentioned between yourself, the deceased, and his wife. Did these intimate terms include an understanding between you and Mrs Todd with regard to marriage?'

'No, none – that is to say,' faltered witness, 'not really.'

'Whatever your relations with regard to Mrs Todd they were known and approved by her husband?'

'Yes,' with confidence restored. 'Most certainly.'

'Were you aware that Mr Todd, as we have heard, had peculiar views on marriage in that he believed a man should have two wives – one for use and one for pleasure?'

'I – I, yes, I think he did, er, mention something of the sort,' was the answer with a scared look at the figure on high who poked forward his wigged head to ask:

'What did he mean by one for use and one for pleasure? Household drudgery for one, and for the other conjugal relationship – or were both to be his bedfellows?'

Witness, with adequate shock as befitting his cloth: 'No, my lord, oh dear, no! He never mentioned *that* to me.'

'Come. Mr Dixon,' bayed Sir Henry, 'did you or did you not understand, as has already been suggested, that Mr Todd had said a man should be allowed two wives in the full and complete sense?'

'Well, I—'

'Did it not strike you, a Christian minister, as an outrageous suggestion?'

'Yer-yes, but he was a man of strange ideas. Something of an – oddity.'

'So it would seem!' was the inimical comment. 'Now, Mr Dixon . . .' with the force of a battering ram was the barrage of questions hammered by Sir Henry at the wilting witness, who admitted that the strange ideas of the deceased included the wish, in the event of his death, that his wife and Mr Dixon should marry.

'A very extraordinary remark,' rumbled his lordship, whereon Sir Henry quick-fired with:

'Did he make this remark at the time he told you he had made a will leaving everything of which he should die possessed to his wife?'

'Yer-yes.'

'Let us hear this conversation relating to the Will.'

Witness, shakily: 'It is a very delicate matter for me to – to—'

The Judge: 'We have long outstepped the bounds of delicacy. Pray continue, Sir Henry.'

'Now then, what did he tell you at that time?'

A silence ensued when, prompted by Counsel, witness was heard to reply that he had told Mr Todd he had become very attached to his wife and as it was disturbing his work he thought it better he should discontinue his friendship with them.

'It was then that he mentioned the Will?'

'Yer-yes – no, he had already mentioned it, but he mentioned it again and said he hoped I would continue to be – to remain friends with them both.'

'I need hardly ask you, as a gentleman,' exquisitely ironical, this, 'that you said nothing to Mrs Todd of your – attachment to her?'

'I – yes – I am afraid I did.'

'You had written letters to her of a sentimental nature

and verses of poetry in which you addressed her by the anglicized version of her name Martha?'

'No.'

'No? Then by what name did you address her both in the verses and in ordinary conversation?'

'Her husband knew—'

'Knew what, Mr Dixon?'

'That I used to call her – Birdie.'

The Court sniggered, witness mopped his damp forehead with his handkerchief, the Judge, busily writing, looked up, his thin old lips mouthing the last word uttered by the shrunken witness, while Sir Henry, mercilessly pursuing his inquisition, reverted to the disposal of the bottles of chloroform.

'Why,' he demanded, 'did you throw them into a gorse bush?'

No answer; and from Sir Henry a trumpet blast:

'Thinking that a gorse bush was the least likely place to find them should a search be made, and you were afraid to retain them from motives of self-preservation?'

'No – I – that was not the reason. I was not – afraid, nor thinking of myself.'

'Were you not? Then what did you mean when you said you were a ruined man?'

From the witness came a stammering bleat: 'I – I – didn't s-say I—'

'Because,' bellowed Counsel, 'you had in mind that you, as a minister, would be ruined were you found to be associated with this buying of chloroform?'

'I – I did see the danger,' was the feeble acknowledgement.

'During one of your conversations with Mrs Todd when you asked her what she had done with the chloroform, did she say, "Why don't you charge me outright with giving it to him –" meaning her husband – "if that's what you want me to say?" Or words to that effect?'

'Well, yes, she – she was indignant – lost her temper with me.'

'Which is not surprising,' Sir Henry said; and sat.

Re-examined by Mr Grice:

'You told both Mr Grimsby and Mrs Grimsby that you had purchased the chloroform?'

'Yes,' tremendous relief at the loosening of the screws, and the application of balm by Mr Grice. 'I made a clean breast of it. I wished to unburden myself to a fellow brother in Christ, and he said –'

'We must not at this juncture hear what he said,' soothingly from Counsel, and from the Judge:

. . . . 'at two o'clock.'

But Sir Henry had not yet done with Dixon when, after the luncheon adjournment, he again took his stand in the box and was in such an evident state of disintegration that the Judge gave him permission to sit while questioned further concerning the 'strange ideas' which Counsel seized upon to gnaw as will a dog with a tasty bone.

'Other than the deceased's curious opinions on married life, did he ever talk to you about this book? It is called *An Esoteric Anthropology*, or *The Mystery of Man* by a Dr Nichols?'

A book was handed up to witness, who after receiving it with something of the same revulsion as if he were presented with an asp, was heard faintly to say that he knew nothing of any such book.

His lordship: 'What is this book about?'

'It is described as –' Sir Henry sonorously read from the title page – '"A Comprehensive and Confidential Treatise on the Structure, Functions, Passional Attractions and Perversions, and the Most Intimate Relations of Man and Woman".'

'Which,' pronounced the Judge, 'if read by the deceased, might well account for his strange ideas in relation to married life.'

By Mr Grice: 'Did you ever see the deceased with this book?'

'No, never.'

'Thank you, Mr Dixon. . . . Sir Henry?'

'No further questions.'

Released at last, and well nigh unconscious, the shattered Mr Dixon was assisted from the box. And now witness after witness was called, the three chemists, each to bear out the purchase of the chloroform by Mr Dixon and labelled by them as Chloroform, Poison; that the purchaser had told all three that he wanted the chloroform to remove grease stains from a suit; that the bottles had all been paid for by him and taken away.

Then Nurse Jennings, the midwife who had attended the confinement of Mrs Todd, was examined by Mr Grice.

While in attendance on Mrs Todd or at any other time, was Nurse Jennings asked by her patient to supply her with chloroform?

To which the answer determinedly was 'No.'

'Were Mr and Mrs Todd living together as man and wife?'

Nurse Jennings, coldly: 'I had no reason to suppose otherwise.'

By Sir Henry: 'You lived in the house with Mr and Mrs Todd during and after her confinement. Was she attentive and affectionate toward her husband?'

'Very affectionate, and always most attentive.'

'She had a difficult labour and a time of great suffering?'

'Yes, and was most courageous – a very good patient.'

By Mr Grice: 'You say you had reason to believe they were living together as man and wife?'

Sir Henry, loudly: 'Do not keep on repeating that phrase or I must ask my learned friend what he means by it.'

The Judge: 'It is a phrase that I shall have to define in due course. Among married people we know what passes in the ordinary relations of married life, but we know nothing of what passes between them in the bedroom.'

More sniggers from the Court and from one of the young barristers behind his hand, '*He* wouldn't know. He's a confirmed misogynist and breeds canaries.'

The confirmed misogynist was saying:

'I have taken a cursory glance at the book you mentioned, Sir Henry. There is one passage that caught my eye. It tells married people how to live together without having children. I have turned down the page and underlined the passage. Would you kindly read it?'

The book is passed to Counsel who reads:

'"There is one way that is natural, simple and effective. It is to refrain from the sexual act. It is also to be observed that the use of the sexual act for mere pleasure and using any means to avoid impregnation is unnatural. . . ."'

The old bewigged head nodded; the shrivelled lips unfastened, graciously to say:

'I am much obliged to you, Sir Henry. I will take further opportunity of looking into the book this evening.'

While in the study of his bachelor chambers his lordship, that evening, looked into the book, she, whose life depended on his direction of the jury, looked into herself.

How was it possible, she wondered, that she, Martha Todd, had come to be here in this prison cell undergoing trial for murder? *Trial by Jury*! . . . Out of a past, in which it seemed she had no being, those words sprang at her with the laughing face of Ted as he strummed at the piano that had replaced the old harmonium. Ted! . . . And those wicked lies told by his father, on oath. . . . And Dixon, too, not lying, no, but every word he spoke gave added length to the . . . rope? O, God, what possible chance of an acquittal with all this evidence against her and more to come! No chance, no hope since it had been proved that she had persuaded him to buy the chloroform. He had been discharged, 'not guilty' and she arrested for – 'wilful murder'.

They had brought her here to this prison cell, how long ago? Weeks? Months? It was April now, they said, but so cold. No warmth from stone walls. Stone walls do not a prison make nor iron bars a cage. That was written by a man in prison almost three hundred years ago. Richard Lovelace. He is only remembered because he wrote that. There are stone walls here and iron bars, and although they had allowed her a bed and a hair mattress with rough horse-blankets, being privileged as not having yet been proved guilty, it *is* a prison and no power of imagination or a poet's mind can make it anything else. . . .

All that had been before this happened, her childhood, her schooldays, her marriage with him, wilfully murdered by her, had a dreamlike unreality. And now she had awakened from that dream to find only this was real. Solid. Tangible. This narrow cell with its iron barred window high up in the wall was the beginning and end of her life in which all time had ceased to be. Today and yesterday, that much of time she knew, hour by hour, that cold crowded room full of faces and wigs and voices of those standing there in the witness box to . . . hang her. Yes, well, one must face facts. *This* is no dream. Did those who spoke answering questions about her and about – him, her husband, did they believe she had murdered him? Did *she* believe it? Perhaps it was true that she *did* do it if she were outside of herself. . . . Did Sir Henry believe it? That interview she had with him here in this cell when he had said he would call no witnesses for the defence for there was none – did that mean he thought her guilty? He had said, as no one had seen her dose her husband with the chloroform, the prosecution's evidence was circumstantial, based solely on suspicion.

'We can only defend,' he had told her, 'on an improbability which I will endeavour to prove is an impossibility.'

There was a doctor in the case. In her dream she had known him as a schoolboy. She had been stung by a wasp. . . . How inconsequent could a dream be! And he had sucked the poison out. Poison! There had been so much talk of poison. And he, the schoolboy in her dream, was the doctor attending her husband. And the doctor had said – had said he loved her. But anything can happen in a dream. . . . Only one thing was certain. The awakening. Here. In this cell. Will they find that she had done it? Who else could have done it? Unless he – who was always talking about dying. Did he want to die? Did she want him to die? It was obvious Sir Henry believed she had wanted him to die. That was why he wouldn't put her in the box. Would they put her in a box when they had finished with her? To be hanged by the . . . and God have mercy . . . But God had no mercy or she wouldn't be here on trial for her life and tortured with hearing them tell . . . how could they have raked it all up? Every little detail, unless she was guilty? Yes, she was, she *must* be guilty. Stupefied him first with the chloroform when he was asleep, and then poured it down his throat. That was how it could be done. She had got the idea from that book, the British Pharmacopoeia, of sprinkling chloroform on a handkerchief for him to inhale and so prevent him from doing *that* to her. His Marital Rights. He was asleep, and snoring, heavily. As he would snore if . . . so easy to make him inhale it while he slept. Or could she have done it while *she* slept? Sleep-walking. Or perhaps she had gone suddenly mad. That outsideness could have been a sign of going mad. If they proved her mad they would put her in a lunatic asylum for life. Far better the other way. All very quick now-a-days, not like in olden times in Foxe's *Book of Martyrs* when they did awful things to you while you were still alive . . . only let it be *soon*. This waiting . . . .

The confusion of her thoughts rushed at her to strike with small incessant demoniac hammer blows. Her hands were pressed against her temples to still the throbbing of them, and sinking on her knees she gazed up at the barred window where a glimpse of sky showed dove-grey shot through with rose from the last of the sun. Up there was freedom from torment and chaos of mind and all disquiet. Only of course no God was up there, no kind old daddy sitting on a cloud and guarding us below. . . . He shall give his angels charge over thee to keep thee in all thy ways. That was just a lovely song sung by a shepherd boy who became a king and a saint and had been a great sinner. And was forgiven. As I hope to be forgiven. . . .

Tears, long repressed, smarted behind her closed lids. Her lips struggled with the words:

'You who died for us in torture that we should live with you in everlasting life, told the repentant thief beside you where they hanged *you* on the Cross, "This day you shall be with me in Paradise".'

'Help me. Help me. I believe. Help thou my unbelief. Did I do it? Did I? Only you can know. . . .'

* * *

On the following day the chief witness for the Crown, Dr John Herriott, gave evidence.

As he took his stance in the witness box, the eyes of all female spectators were fixed appraisingly upon him, where, immaculate and debonair, calmly self-possessed, he stood to answer a barrage of questions concerning the deceased whom he found to be suffering from nervous prostration, insomnia and sub-acute gastritis.

After repeating all that had already been said by former witnesses, how that he had been sent for by the wife of the deceased at four in the morning of January the first, to find the patient dead, and had been present at the post-mortem when no pathological evidence as to the cause of death had been established, witness was questioned as to the presence of a bottle of chlorodyne found on the mantelshelf in the room where the deceased had died. . . . Yes, he had asked Mrs Todd what the bottle was doing there and she replied her husband had used it as a mouthwash.

'Is chlorodyne a substance easily detected by its smell?'

'Yes, and if it has stood for some time it smells extremely like chloroform.'

'Did you detect any such smell?'

'No, but I did detect a smell of brandy.'

'In the mouth?'

'No, on the chest.'

'As if it had been spilt there?'

'I am afraid my nose would not have diagnosed that,' was the serene rejoinder to which, lacing sweetness with vinegar, the Attorney-General said: 'I did not ask you, sir, about your nose.'

'Did you not? With what other organ would I be expected to detect a smell?' inquired witness, affably polite.

Counsel thereupon, and with some acerbity, recalled witness's account of a conversation he had with Mrs Todd on January the twenty-sixth when he told her he was the bearer of good news in that the analyst's report found chloroform to be the cause of death.

'Why should this suggest to the prisoner that it was good news?'

'Because,' witness spoke clearly, decisively, 'it would dispel any doubt as to whether a lethal poison had been administered to the deceased without his knowledge.'

'And which would have seriously involved his wife?'

'In view of certain unwarranted suspicions levelled at her – yes.'

'What was her reply when you told her this "good news"?' was the honey-toned query.

'She replied she wished it had been anything but chloroform.'

When asked to explain what she meant by that remark, witness submitted she had made him a statement regarding the marital relationship of the couple which was, in effect, that being married very young she had been induced to enter into a marriage compact without understanding the meaning of the terms; a marriage that, in deference to the husband's peculiar views, must be of an entirely platonic nature; sexual intercourse was not to occur.

The Judge: 'If sexual intercourse was not to occur – what then?'

'What then' was defined as one solitary exception when a breach of the agreement had been forced upon the wife that resulted in a stillborn child. After this one act of coitus the former platonic relationship was resumed. As told to witness by the defendant they lived together on amicable terms until the last few months of the husband's life, when his nature appeared to have changed. 'We became acquainted with a Mr Dixon,' was the defendant's account of it to the doctor, and, referring to his notes, 'she said, "My husband threw us together and made us kiss in his presence. He seemed to enjoy seeing him kiss me . . ." She gave me to understand,' said Dr Herriott coolly, 'she used these words, "that he had given me to Mr Dixon".'

The Attorney-General, with elevated eyebrows: 'Do you mean then and there – or in the event of his death?'

'I do not know.'

'Did you not ask?'

'Why should I have asked?'

Counsel did not seem to be extracting from his witness the conclusive evidence he had thought to obtain, since none of it threw light upon a motive for the crime of which this 'platonic wife' stood accused.

'You have said the husband's nature appeared to have changed. Pray go on, Dr Herriott.'

Doctor Herriott went on to describe how, according to the defendant, the husband, after having transferred her from himself to Mr Dixon, developed a desire to assume the marital rights he had renounced.

'I take it you mean a desire to have sexual intercourse with his wife?'

'She put it in as delicate a manner as she could, but that' – witness allowed himself a glance at the pale frail figure in the dock – 'that, I gather, was her meaning.'

'Did she resent this – ah – desire?'

'I understand she did in view of her husband's state of health and the fact that he had virtually affianced her to another man.'

'A most extraordinary situation,' interposed, creakingly, the voice of the Judge.

Witness then told how in order to quell the urgent demands of the husband, she sought means to subdue them.

'And how,' with saccharin insistence, 'did she seek to subdue his not – ah – unnatural demands?'

Witness was here seen to hesitate before he replied that one of the means she had considered was to sprinkle a few drops of chloroform on a handkerchief and wave it before his face, thinking thereby he would go peacefully to sleep, but she did not pursue her intention.

'Did she tell you why?'

'Yes, she said she was troubled at having the chloroform in her possession and, unable to keep it a secret from her husband, she had shown him the bottle, but she gave me no details of their conversation more than that, having seen the bottle conspicuously labelled Poison, he was at first furious and shocked, but presently they talked sensibly together of her reasons for wishing to resist his claims upon her, and that she had taken the bottle, placed it on the mantelshelf by his bed, when he turned over on his side and, presumably, slept.'

'Having made this remarkable statement regarding a "platonic relationship" with her husband, did you ask her why she waited three weeks before she told you of it when she saw you searching the room with Mr Bridges?'

'I do not think she saw us searching the room, but if she did she was far more concerned with knowing the cause of her husband's death than in the bottle of chloroform which she had not used nor even opened.'

'Did you see a bottle of chloroform on the mantelshelf during your search?'

'No, I did not, nor did I know that chloroform had been a subject of discussion between Mrs Todd and her husband until later.'

'Did she eventually tell you what she had done with the bottle?'

'Yes, she said she had emptied the bottle and thrown it into the Canal in Regent's Park.'

'Did she then give you any indication that she suspected the cause of her husband's death?'

'She did not suspect. She had already been told of the analyst's report.'

'That chloroform had been found in the stomach of the deceased, brought by you to her as "good news"?' Faint sarcasm here; and, deftly circumventing retort to that:

'I thank you, Dr Herriott.' Not so graciously as might have been expected from examination of so important a witness for the Crown. And now it was Sir Henry Doyle up for the defence.

'Dr Herriott, from the tenth of December when you were first called to see Mr Todd and until the day of his death, you had ample opportunity of observing him and his wife together?'

'Yes, I saw them continuously for three weeks or more.'

'During the whole of that time did you know that Mrs Todd was nursing her husband unaided and with unceasing devoted attention not only by day, but night after night?'

'Yes, I could not have wished for a better nurse. She never spared herself.'

'It was obvious to you that she needed rest and that her health was suffering in consequence of her tireless and diligent care of her husband?'

'Yes, but when I ordered her to bed and to take some rest she said he would get up and walk about the room refusing to sleep unless she sat with him and held his toe.'

Amusement from the Court, a faint smile from the witness, indulgently reflected on the face of Counsel, obliterated by his further question:

'You have described his condition as of extreme nervous exhaustion and mental depression. Did he ever allude to himself as a dying man?'

'He did, frequently. I impressed upon him that he was in no danger of dying and advised him to get up and go out. He said if he did get up and go out, it would kill him.'

'I understand you had prescribed a holiday away from his wife, alone?'

'Yes, because he was a hypochondriac, and it would have been better for him to be sent on a sea trip with no one at his beck and call to nurse and pet him and hold his toe, and that sort of nonsense.'

More amusement from the Court, and from Sir Henry, whose three chinned face relaxed to the semblance of a grinning full moon: 'There is doubtless more nonsense than this for us to hear, but for the moment—'

For the moment Counsel was more concerned with the deceased's physical and mental condition, 'which,' boomed Sir Henry, 'indicated that he had taken mercury?'

'It did, but when I taxed him with it, he emphatically denied ever having done so.'

'You believed him?'

'No. I believed he had been treated in the past for a specified disease which he was ashamed to admit. I imagine it preyed on his mind and would account for his nervous depression, which I took to be syphiliphobia.'

Asked if he had been prepared to accept the wife's statement of the singular relationship enforced by the husband, he replied he had accepted a statement consistent with observation of his patient whose attitude to the physical aspects of marriage he believed to be asexual, and whose personality he described as most unusual.

The Judge, looking up from his notes: 'In what way unusual?'

'In his ideas on certain subjects, my lord.'

Witness then disclosed how on several occasions his patient had told him of his inordinate interest in mesmerism, and that he harboured a belief he was under the mesmeric influence of a friend whose name he withheld and who, he said, 'made him do things he didn't want to do' – absurd and unaccountable things that involved him getting up in the night and waving his hands over his wife's head while she dozed in a chair by his bed, drawing what he described as 'her 'fluence' to himself. He appeared, witness said, to be in a highly excitable state while he recounted this incident. 'But,' the doctor continued with that same unruffled calm, 'I was determined to hear more of this mysterious friend and his hypnotic or mesmeric powers, and I followed up the conversation by asking if he heard voices urging him to do this or that, to which he answered that he heard no audible voices, yet he persisted he was under some strong mesmeric influence.'

'Had you any doubts of his sanity?'

'Yes, I believed him deluded.'

'Now, Dr Herriott, just a few questions on a different subject. Have you, in your experience,' was weightily demanded, 'ever seen a case of poisoning from liquid chloroform taken by the mouth?'

'No.'

'It is extremely rare, is it not?'

'Yes.'

'You yourself have administered inhalation of chloroform?'

'About two hundred times.'

'It is an operation that requires the greatest skill?'

'It requires skill and experience.'

'Have you ever administered chloroform orally to a sleeping patient?'

'Never.'

Here followed a lengthy exposition by the doctor on the effects of inhalation, and/or the swallowing of liquid chloroform. In both cases, in the event of death, the post-mortem indications would be similar.

'Thank you, Dr Herriott, you have been most helpful.'

With an air of ineffable content, Sir Henry relinquished him to Mr Grice, rising to open fire on one whom he now regarded as a hostile witness.

'When you told my learned friend you thought the effect of taking liquid chloroform would be the same or similar if taken by inhalation, that is only your opinion?'

Sir Henry was up again to retaliate with a shell-burst: 'My lord! I protest to that remark and its insinuation. Dr Herriott is an experienced and highly qualified physician. My friend seems to resent my acceptance of his opinion and is NOT entitled to tell the witness "that this is only *your* opinion"! The doctor has given us the result of his research into medical science.'

'Which,' was the riposte of Mr Grice, 'is all he knows

about it.' And hastily dodging a further volley from his boiling opponent: 'Now, Dr Herriott,' with laboured irony, 'may we have your *opinion* as to how much chloroform would be a fatal dose if swallowed?'

'Yes,' rapped out the doctor, 'I should say about two drachms.'

And the Judge, whose attention for the last few minutes had been more engaged with the entry of steak and kidney pudding into his hollow stomach than the entry of chloroform into that of the deceased, called for an adjournment.

. . . 'until two o'clock.'

* * *

Said Miss Emma who, with frenzied interest, had been following the report of the case in *The Times*: 'At least half a dozen doctors and the Home Office pathologist, Dr Stevenson, gave evidence yesterday, and every one of them agreed that chloroform *could* be given by the mouth and one of them, a professor of chemistry and forensic medicine at the London Hospital – *he* says it was done to a boy while asleep in 1863. Another cup, Laetitia, if you please.'

She passed her cup to her sister, dispensing tea as was their custom before retiring to bed, and, passing it back again re-filled, Miss Merridew curtly said:

'Which is the only case he has known of and not from personal experience.'

'So you *have* read it, although,' Miss Emma accusingly exclaimed, 'you disapprove of *my* doing so.'

'I glanced through it, but I do not approve of your morbid attention to this trial which,' was the acid rejoinder, 'appears to excite in you a similar reaction as that of a melodrama performed for the benefit of gaping yokels by a company of strolling players.'

'Well, I'm sure!' declared Miss Emma, indignation in

every bob of her curls. 'Would you have me so insensible to the awful implications attached to one of our – our ex-pupils who is being tried for *murder*! Thank God they have not mentioned the name of our Academy, but I see they have located it as in Dover – and there is only *ours* which can be honestly defined as Select. And look what we selected! And now with Maud Doyle's father defending, everyone will know. Maud is certain to speak of it to her fellow undergraduates at Girton. *What* a calamity to befall us!'

'A calamity more likely to befall Martha Todd,' commented Miss Merridew.

'Oh!' gasped Miss Emma. 'You cannot think she will be – hang – I mean – believed guilty?'

'It will take all Sir Henry's rumbustious advocacy to induce the jury to believe her innocent.' Miss Merridew rose from her chair. 'I am going to bed. Kindly see to the lights when you have digested the last morsel of this journalistic patter.'

'It isn't patter, it's the – Oh! Laetitia!' Miss Emma stared round-eyed over her wrappings of newspaper. 'You said Sir Henry is rumbustious. How can you tell from just glancing through the report of his cross-examination? It reads as if he is very cool and quiet.'

'About as quiet as a charging bull,' impassively remarked Miss Merridew moving to the door. 'And don't forget the table lamp. You left it burning all night.'

'Laetitia!' Miss Emma laid aside *The Times* and sprang, with quite girlish agility, to her feet. 'You can't mean – can you – were you *there*? When you went to the dentist – so you *said* – were you – *did* you –' was the italicized query – 'go? Were you in— No, you surely were not in *Court*?'

'I was in Court,' her sister, with shocking nonchalance replied. 'I found ample time to visit my dentist and to hear so much of the case as I could before my train left at five-thirty.' She swept from the room, leaving Miss Emma distinctly deflated.

The case dragged on for another two days while eminent physicians and the Home Office analyst were called and re-called indubitably to substantiate the contents of the stomach as consistent with the swallowing of liquid chloroform. Their unsparing evidence relating to the appearance of the various organs of the body of the deceased under analysis sent squeamish females hurrying away with handkerchiefs to their mouths to subdue nauseated heavings. But the aesthetic susceptibilities of Mrs Ottery, much in abeyance since she had become a staunch disciple of woman's emancipation, stayed unaffected by and deeply interested in the unexpurgated details of these medical findings. Nor did the prisoner, although evincing unmistakable signs of strain, not only in her excessive pallor but in the trembling of her small ungloved hands clinging to the edge of the dock, show any dismay at the report of the doctors. She appeared to be in a dream, her eyes blank, unseeing. It is doubtful if she heard or was aware of the significance of every word dropped from those strictly professional lips.

'I fear –' whispered Mrs Ottery to her nephew who was in waiting, possibly to be recalled by the defence – 'I greatly fear that Froggie, or that other – Grice isn't it? – who is far the better of the two – will find her, or persuade the jury to find her – guilty.'

'They won't,' muttered John close-lipped. He too, despite his outward composure, was feeling the strain.

'Fools!' in an enlarged whisper declared his aunt. 'Over and over the same ground – so boringly repetitive. Froggie Fennell cares less about this case than about his constituents' reaction to Gladstone's Home Rule Bill. It is madness to allow these lawyers to become Members of Parliament. How can they give undivided attention to politics when they are supposed to be trying cases of murder?' She balanced her lorgnette upon her nose, disdainfully to survey 'these lawyers', the leading Counsels for the Crown and the Defence. 'The day will come,' said she, on a rising note that was nothing of a whisper, 'when we are released from the shackles of purdah to be recognized as something more –' her voice rose higher to enunciate in capitals – 'than MAMMALS' – thereby occasioning scandalized flutters among those ladies who had remained to hear the worst of it, and from an usher a peremptory request for silence, while:

'That, my lord and gentlemen of the jury,' the Attorney-General with dulcitude, was heard to say, 'is the case for the Crown.'

Whereupon Sir Henry rose up, or more correctly, bore down like a galleon, black sails outspread, with the announcement to a startled Court:

'I do not propose to produce any evidence.'

'No evidence!' . . . 'Good heavens, why no evidence?' . . . went the buzz of questions from the audience, to be answered by superior male escorts of disappointed ladies: 'Because the prosecution has already subpoenaed any possibles, and the defence has got as much as he can get from cross-examination . . .' 'His only witness is the girl and he can't put her in the box.' . . . 'Why not?' . . . 'Well, obviously. She'd never stand up to cross-examination' . . . 'There'll be a conviction for a cert.' Was the positive summary of one of the briefless young barristers. 'Not a cat's chance in hell.'

Which from the glum expressions on the jurymen's faces was their opinion, too.

'My lord and gentlemen of the jury,' the resonant voice of Sir Henry rang to the rafters as he opened his challenge for the Defence, 'you have heard the evidence which the Crown has put before you in support of the charge, and, having heard that evidence, I, in the name of Thérèse Marthe Todd, claim from you a verdict of – not guilty!'

At this pronouncement each bewigged head jerked up as if pulled by a wire; the Judge wrinkled his grey-tufted eyebrows and bent to his notes; his dry old lips moving to the words he scribbled down. . . . 'It might be thought by some of my friends', a basilisk glance embraced the upturned faces of some of his 'friends', belligerently to rest upon that of the Prosecution, who returned it with the politest of smiles, 'I say,' vociferated the Defence, 'that it might be thought I speak too confidently when I repeat my intention to justify my claim in the most absolute and complete form, and I believe, when I have taken you through the record of suspicion that has pointed to her guilt – and it is suspicion *only*, and, as I will show you, goes to demonstrate –' he raised a fist and banged the air as if it were the supercilious face of the Crown – '*indubitably* to demonstrate her innocence!'

After this explosive gambit, Sir Henry proceeded most forcibly to demonstrate that claim, going over every particle of evidence and in particular that of the doctors, scientists and pathologists who had undergone his searching cross-examination.

He dwelt upon the difficulties – 'I use the word adopted by Dr Stevenson, the Home Office analyst – the *insuperable* difficulties of administering an inhalation of chloroform to a sleeping person which you have heard, from the unanimous opinion of these doctors, is a most hazardous operation requiring the greatest skill and experience. How much more difficult, indeed well nigh impossible, would be the administration of *liquid* chloroform to a sleeping or waking person – an operation which,' the voice of Sir Henry ascended on a strident note – 'is virtually unknown in medical jurisdiction. Yet you are asked to believe that this young wife, alone with her husband at night, and without any medical knowledge whatsoever did perform upon him just such an operation!'

Here Sir Henry, with the careful precision of an expert chessplayer, paused to summon his forces for the next move. Having brought up his medical knights to the attack, he now brought up his pawns to deal with the lesser evidence of Mr and Mrs Bridges, and the maid, Angharad Williams. 'These other matters' – a throwaway gesture dismissed these 'other matters' which his learned friend had thought fit to point in further direction to the guilt of Mrs Todd: the discussion at the supper table between the deceased, his wife, and Mrs Bridges, referring to the effects of chloroform. 'What more natural,' demanded Counsel, 'that such a discussion should have arisen, resultant on Mr Todd's visit to the dentist that very afternoon to have a tooth extracted by gas? . . . As for the evidence of the maidservant regarding the dress worn by Mrs Todd on the night of her husband's death, was the fact that she had changed her gown for one the maid thought to be a day dress, but under questioning agreed it might have been a loose garment more suitable for a long night's vigil by a sick bed; or, according to Mr Bridges, that the fire had been "newly packed" – were these matters for suspicion? Why, when Mrs Todd awakened from a doze to find her husband cold, and not then believing him dead – why should she not have replenished the fire before rousing the maid to fetch the doctor, and to tell Mr Bridges to come at once, daring not to think, but fearing her husband to have died while she snatched some short repose? Could such trivia as these be presented by the prosecution as suspicious?'

Counsel now turned to a matter that *might* be regarded as suspicious: the evidence of the Reverend Albert Dixon.

'Gentlemen, when you are asked to consider the case of Mrs Todd and allow to be used gravely against her certain untruthful statements she has made that have come to you from Mr Dixon's evidence *alone*, does it not occur to you how fortunate is Mr Dixon not to be standing where Mrs Todd stands now? Suppose his case were put before you that, on a Sunday morning as he walked on Putney Heath on his way to preach a sermon in his chapel, someone who knew him as a constant visitor to the house of Mr Todd had seen him fling away sundry bottles and had thought: "How very odd of Mr Dixon to be throwing bottles away on a Sunday morning." Suppose that person had the curiosity to retrieve those bottles from their hiding place in the gorse bush, and had seen them labelled "Chloroform. Poison." And suppose it had been discovered that Mr Dixon had bought those bottles from the chemists whose names appeared on the labels, having told those chemists a falsehood saying he wanted the chloroform to remove stains from a suit, and it had subsequently been proved that Mr Todd had died from the effects of chloroform – what would have been Mr Dixon's position? I do not for one moment entertain the slightest doubt of Mr Dixon's innocence,' was Counsel's bland assurance, 'but I use it to show that a falsehood told for the express purpose of procuring chloroform, might, if proved in the witness box, be considered by the jury as a serious element of suspicion against – Mr Dixon.'

Here Mr Dixon was seen to slither sideways with a face ashen grey, and was revived by an elderly party with sympathetic clucks and smelling salts, who was later identified as his mother, next to whom he had been seated.

The marital relationship of the Todds was again unfolded to a Court that must by this time have been heartily sick of hearing it. . . . 'As to the falsehood told by Mrs Todd to Mr Dixon in order to obtain chloroform, you have heard in her confidential statement to her doctor, that her husband, save for one occasion only, had never enforced his marital rights, but that latterly he manifested urgent desires to assert those rights renounced on his marriage to a child of sixteen. Concerned for his state of health and, also because in the event of his death he had "given" her to Mr Dixon, under these singular circumstances, and perhaps from a natural revulsion to the sexual act with a man who, according to the two doctors in consultation prior to his death, must have been physically repulsive – we have been told how foetid was his breath and that the duties his wife so selflessly performed would have repelled many a trained nurse – because of these various reasons why she shunned sexual intercourse, she, as would any woman of delicate sensibility, resorted to a feasible excuse for asking Dixon to provide her with chloroform in the hope of subduing her husband's unwelcome demands. The explanation she gave Dr Herriott was similar to that she gave to Dixon, but, as patient to the doctor whom she consulted to prescribe for her own health that had suffered under continuous strain, she confided the full reason why she wanted the chloroform – a professional confidence, gentlemen, of the most private and intimate nature, and which Dr Herriott was reluctantly compelled to reveal in the witness box.'

Counsel then referred to the peculiarities of the deceased. Indeed Dr Herriott had doubted his sanity, since he suffered from a neurosis, described by the doctor as 'syphiliphobia', a term, Counsel ventured to suggest, known to none but the most advanced medical opinion. Moreover, Dr Herriott had stated he considered Mr Todd's attitude to the physical aspect of married life and intercourse in general to be *asexual*. . . . 'You have heard,' with booming solemnity did Counsel draw attention to this, 'how that the father of the deceased, whose vengeful malice nourished the idea of murder and, for what venomous motive only he can know, worked to establish suspicion upon his son's wife. This is the man,' that basilisk look was now directed at him who, having been fortified at the nearest pub, had passed into a state of beatific semi-coma. 'This,' repeated Counsel, 'is he who stood in the witness box to declare against the widow of his son the foul slander from which, while he was here, that son protected her. . . . Now, gentlemen, I must pause for a very short time –' the very short time took the better part of an hour – 'to call your attention to the opening speech of my learned friend, the Attorney-General, who suggested three alternative explanations for the death we are investigating. Either that the man took the chloroform by accident in mistake for a sleeping draught, or that he took it with a view to self-destruction, or that it was administered to him by another person with intent to murder.'

Stress was now laid upon the fact of Mrs Todd's desire for an immediate post-mortem. 'If there had been the smallest idea in her mind of poisoning her husband with chloroform, known to be a volatile drug, would she not have welcomed a delay of the post-mortem? Instead she chafes at the delay and asked for the post-mortem to be expedited that the mystery of her husband's death be solved at once. And,' proceeded Sir Henry, pinioning the attention of those twelve on his every word, 'when it had been verified that chloroform had been found in the stomach of the deceased she tells Dr Herriott she wished it had been anything *but* chloroform. She then, gratuitously, admits she had chloroform in her possession on the night of her husband's death, and goes on to confide in the doctor her reasons why she had procured but had not used it. And, gentlemen – note this well – it is from Mrs Todd herself that the first accusation against her is made. When Mr Dixon pestered her to know what she had done with the bottle of chloroform she turned upon him angrily with words to this effect: "If you want to say it – *say* it! That *I* gave him the chloroform!" Gentlemen, apart from all scientific aspects of the case there stands the inescapable fact that from the moment of her husband's death every word and act of this woman, although aware of the awful suspicion she perceived was gathering around her, were the words and acts of innocence!'

There followed a long exposition regarding the possibilities of suicide in which Sir Henry sketched an imaginary and dramatic reconstruction. It would have been perfectly easy, as had been proved by the position of the bed, for the man to lift himself on an elbow and pour a fatal dose from the bottle of chloroform, shown to him by his wife and which had been placed on the mantelshelf within his reach. In his depressed state of mind, and suffering from the after effects of gas for the extraction of a tooth on that same afternoon, could he not, in a moment of mental aberration, have decided to end his life? . . .

'We know he repeatedly spoke of himself as a dying man. Did he wish to hasten his death which he believed to be imminent? Whatever his purpose, we have been told that when his wife came into the room, prepared to pass the night at his bedside, she heard him breathing stertorously. Such breathing would have been the result of swallowing chloroform, which, if quickly gulped, leaves, as is medically confirmed, little or no appearance of the drug after long exposure, in the mouth or throat. When the wife, waking from a doze, finds her husband cold – what does she do? She tries to warm him by pouring brandy down his throat. Her shaking hand spills some of it on his chest. She rubs his chest with it hoping to increase the circulation. You have heard the doctor say he smelt brandy when he examined the dead man. Gentlemen, this was no scientific miracle performed that night by the grocer's wife under circumstances when it could not have been performed by the most experienced doctor who had given himself to the study of anaesthetics. Yet you are asked to believe that this woman, who sacrificed her own rest at the expense of her health to watch over her husband with tenderest care during the whole of his illness, who called doctors in consultation to discover the cause of that illness – was suddenly transformed into a cold-blooded murderess and, without any motive whatsoever, did succeed in committing a crime, the execution of which, you have been told by eminent medical authorities, would have been, even for them, a most delicate and difficult, and well nigh impossible operation.

'Gentlemen, the one man who might have befriended this friendless, widowed and orphaned young woman –' here a sob or two was heard from among the female spectators, and from Mrs Ottery in a hissing whisper to her white-faced nephew: 'Doyle certainly knows how to act up to the gallery. I shall ask Pinero to write a play about it. That new young man, Charles Wyndham, would make a great hit with this speech only it is not a leading part and he won't play anything else.'

. . . 'The one man,' repeated Counsel, 'who could have proved her innocence, is gone, but she is not left entirely friendless.' . . . With histrionic effect a hand was raised, pointing heavenward; his voice, fraught with emotion, echoed through the silent Court.

'The Spirit of Justice is here today to protect her in her hour of need, to clear your eyes and guide your judgement when my lord deals with the evidence which has aroused suspicion, and which I hope and believe has been utterly destroyed. That Spirit, I am convinced, will speak through you when your verdict tells the world that Thérèse Marthe Todd is – innocent!'

* * *

Miss Merridew who, it seemed, had paid more visits to her dentist in the last five days than in the last five years, sat at the back of the Court wearing a bonnet heavily veiled. She arrived half an hour after the Attorney-General had risen to make his opening speech for the prosecution. She was in time to hear him ask his lord and gentlemen in tones from which all trace of saccharin had vanished – 'if there was one scintilla of evidence to support the suggestion that Mr and Mrs Todd were living together on any other terms than the ordinary terms of man and wife? One act of coition only that resulted in the birth of a child and, thereafter, sexual intercourse between them ceased, until the last few weeks of the sick man's life, when, we hear that "his nature appears to have changed".'

Referring to the tale told by the prisoner at the bar to Dr Herriott of the relations between herself and her husband – 'If, gentlemen, you can believe this extraordinary tale it may go some way to account for what is otherwise unaccountable. But let us take the whole of the story' . . . which at considerable length the Attorney-General proceeded to do.

He reminded his lord and gentlemen of his learned friend's argument that the dead man – 'this complaisant husband' – saw a growing affection between Albert Dixon and his wife which, in the possible event of his death in the near future, was to ultimate in a closer relationship, that of marriage. . . . 'The incredible tale recounted by the prisoner is that she refused her husband his marital rights "because you have given me to Mr Dixon". Her husband then turns over on his pillow – the wife having shown him the bottle of chloroform by which she confessed to have thought to frustrate his desire by impregnating a handkerchief with drops of the drug and waving it before his face – he turns over on his pillow, and goes to sleep. Then while his wife is in the next room he wakes to avail himself of her absence in the space of what he could not count upon being more than a few minutes—'

Sir Henry, interrupting with violence: 'Why not?'

The Attorney-General: 'My learned friend asks me why not? I am dealing with the theory which is put forward that while she had temporarily left the room—'

Sir Henry: 'To change her dress for the night.'

Sir Rodney, soothingly: 'Quite so, but I care not whether it were three, five, ten or fifteen minutes during which time her husband was supposed to have gulped down the fatal dose. She is then said to have come back, and, gentlemen, let me remind you that this theory falls to pieces unless you are prepared to accept that the man having poured from the bottle and swallowed this liquid chloroform has made no utterance of pain or distress, and that when his wife returns she finds him quietly asleep. She then sits in a chair by his bed and she too sleeps. It is my bounden duty and not a pleasant one to place these facts before you, since the theory put forward by my learned friend is that the deceased himself had taken the poison with a view to – suicide!'

The Attorney-General then refuted any probable logical or possible motive for suicidal intent. He was prosperous in business. He had recovered his health sufficiently to speak cheerfully of a holiday by the sea in the near future. On the day of his death he had eaten a hearty dinner of jugged hare and an equally hearty supper of oysters. He had ordered his breakfast for the following morning – had particularly wished for a smoked haddock . . . . 'You must ask yourselves if these facts do not entirely negative the probability – I would almost say the possibility – of deliberately taking his life?'

Having flogged that point to its conclusive end, the Attorney-General alluded to the bottle of chloroform stated to have been within the man's reach on the mantelshelf. What became of that bottle? Before the doctor is called, that bottle had disappeared or been removed. By whom? When? Why? Emphasis was laid on the fact that Dr Herriott had searched the room and had found no bottle of chloroform there, and the jury were reminded that when the doctor asked the prisoner if her husband could have taken poison, she said, definitely, 'No'. . . . Not until three weeks later does she give to Dr Herriott this incredible account that you are asked to accept, and in which she explains her possession of chloroform.

'Gentlemen,' the Attorney-General became in his turn dramatic; his tone, charged with solemnity, adjured them: 'How comes it that the prisoner takes such pains to remove from the room the bottle she declares was never used nor opened, and, at a later date, to remove from the house that which, so far from being proof of her guilt, would have built up the story to account for her innocence?'

To her who heard but did not hear him whose every word dragged her nearer to the scaffold, for she was lost to sound, to sense, or hearing, had one thought only uppermost in the darkening chaos of her being: Guilty or not guilty. Am I? Was I, *did* I *do* it . . . Did I? If I could speak and tell them that *I do not know*. . . . All this talk and no one who saw me with him that night, no one to see me give . . . O, God! I can't remember. There was a void, a blotting out of memory, unillumined in the dark of her tormented mind by these interminable speeches, the ghoulish exhumation of a body, as if by feeding on its corrupt remains, done to death by . . . whom? . . . the truth would emerge, and she . . .

Every head of those twelve he addressed was turned to that amphibian wide-mouthed face which John, with an ooze of blood on his bitten lip, saw to be that of the executioner's assistant, as the Attorney-General pronounced his words of doom.

'Gentlemen, my learned friend has said the Spirit of Justice in the jury-box will be the friend and protector of the prisoner at the bar.' A hand fell upon his heart, while his eyes, as if in communion with a celestial presence, were riveted above. 'I pray you to apply your minds to that Spirit and if you come to the conclusion that any doubt remains then, in God's name, give this woman the benefit of that doubt. But, if, when you have heard my lord, you cannot accept this theory of suicide, then, should the conviction remain in your minds that guilt lies at this woman's door, I ask you, by the oaths you have taken and the duty to the country which you represent, not to shrink from the responsibility that will be cast upon you!'

The Court was more than ever crowded when, after a brief adjournment, the Judge rose for his charge to the jury. Once again, he retailed the history of these people whose lives, he said, they had to consider, and the death of one who formed the immediate cause of this inquiry. He referred to the advent of the Reverend Albert Dixon, and the frequent discussions between the deceased and Dixon who, in the event of the husband's death, should succeed him in closer intimacy with the prisoner than that of tutor: namely that of spouse.

With regard to Dixon's evidence his lordship asked if more than the most slender faith could be placed upon his statements. . . . 'For I think,' the quavering voice gained strength to submit, 'there can be very small doubt on the part of any who have seen and heard him that he was determined that the one person in this case to suffer as little as possible must be the Reverend Albert Dixon.'

Having enlarged upon the friendship of the deceased and Dixon which had progressed to the exchange of letters confirming the trust, esteem, and love each entertained for the other, the Judge, after lubricating his voice with sips from a tumbler of water, went on to ask: 'Gentlemen, can you seriously credit that the deceased was suffering from an internal complaint as alleged by the prisoner but *not* by the doctors who attended him, and that in order to alleviate these sufferings, and his insomnia, she goes to the lengths of persuading the gullible Mr Dixon to procure chloroform for that purpose?'

An excuse or fabrication which, in his lordship's opinion was – 'all moonshine'.

Here Sir Henry, bounding up, came out with:

'I hope your lordship will not think I am improperly interrupting but may I remind your lordship that it was on Dixon's evidence *alone* that Mrs Todd had said her husband was suffering from an internal complaint.'

'I am much obliged to you, Sir Henry,' was his lordship's response in anything but a tone of obligation.

The attention of the jury was then drawn to 'a much pleasanter subject' . . . That it was the prisoner who pressed for an immediate post-mortem, a point of extreme importance in her favour. This, however, was modified by the fact, driven home to those in the jury-box with as much force as the husky old voice could achieve, that Mr Todd, as proven by analytical examination, had died from chloroform introduced into the stomach. . . . 'As to the disappearance of the bottle, averred by the prisoner to have been thrown away, I am not anxious to make too much of this, yet there is no refuting the fact that the prisoner admitted chloroform to be in her possession, and that chloroform killed her husband, administered to him either criminally or not criminally. It is for you, gentlemen, to decide. . . .'

After meandering on to examine the suggestion that the deceased, driven desperate by sleeplessness, and finding the bottle within reach of his hand, had seized it and gulped down the contents, such an act, we are told, would have caused excruciating pain and outcries of anguish, but no such cries were heard, his lordship then turned to what he termed 'this mystic union' between the husband and wife.

As related by Dr Herriott the husband held such exalted ideas about matrimony that the woman he elected for his mate was too sacred to be touched save on one occasion only which resulted in a child, stillborn. Not until the last days of his life did the husband manifest desire to resume his conjugal rights, which the prisoner sought to subdue by obtaining chloroform, but having obtained it, she did not use it. And when the analyst's report rendered it impossible for her to keep silence, 'the reason she gives to the doctor for her possession of chloroform, this –' the old man cleared an obstruction in his throat, the better to enunciate – '*this* was a tissue of romance that could deceive no one but the ecstatic person to whom it had been told.'

The 'ecstatic person', to whom his lordship pointedly alluded, sat, elbows on knees, chin in his hands, the muscles of his face contorted with the effort to keep silent and not shout to high heaven his opinion of this prejudicial and damning lead to a credulous jury, while his aunt beside him drove a sharp dig in his ribs with the superfluous whisper: 'He means you! And if there's to be a conviction, which seems likely, we must appeal – fight it to the hilt. The Home Secretary is an old flame of mine. He'll do it for me . . .'

After more mumbling and further reminder to the jury: 'If the facts it has been my sacred duty to point out to you in the interests of society and justice, and if you think these facts are too cogent when you come to balance the probabilities or improbabilities as to leave in your minds *no* doubt as would induce you to pause or hesitate, then, in the face of Almighty God, it is your bounden duty to act on your convictions, however painful the consequence may be. But if you concur with the emphatic appeal made by the learned Counsel for the defence, and if you still remain in a state of honest and conscientious doubt, then the prisoner would be entitled to an acquittal.'

'Gentlemen my task is done. I now dismiss you to yours. Be pleased to retire and perform it.'

During the two hours in which the jury retired to

'perform' their task, Edward Todd betook himself to the nearest pub to be braced for the remote possibility of an acquittal. To those gathered there, newspaper reporters, loafers, and habitués who had either followed proceedings in Court or in the news-sheets, he delivered his opinion of the Judge as – 'obvershly convinshed –' he had partaken of four double gins and several pints of ale – 'tha' she killed 'im. F'I tell you –' he thumped his chest – 'I knew as – hic – as 'ow she was poisonin' my poor son for munss' afore 'e took ill with every sign o' poison in 'im, an' when 'e didn' die from what she was dosin' 'im with, she goes an' does 'im in with chlor – hic – form. An' that doctor with 'is la-dee-da an' 'is private 'ansom an' 'is cloak – a proper masher – an' between you an' me it was *'im* she was 'avin' 'er eye on an' not the minister 'oo she made 'er jupe – thass'why I inshisted on 'avin' 'nother 'pinion. Same again, Miss,' to the barmaid, 'an' drinks round to all of you to shelebrate jusdishdone –' he made an ominous gesture across his scraggy neck, amid assenting 'ahs' and 'ays', and from one youthful reporter, 'Not a leg to stand on. She's for it. The Judge as good as said so.'

'You're righ' there,' agreed Edward, downing his fifth gin, 'she won' – hic – 'ave a leg sh'tandon when they let 'er drop. Me, I saw a 'angin' – almoss' larss' o' them in public, when I was a lil'un – they ought ter be 'ung in public now – give other killers somethin' frigh'nemorf. . . .'

When he returned to hear the verdict, walking with slow and careful steps to find standing room only, he was in time to see the jury file to their pew-like seats.

Outside the Old Bailey a silent crowd had gathered, ten deep. No less silent were the spectators in the Court; a silence terrible in its intensity, broken only by the click of the dock handle turned to allow the entrance of the prisoner. And now, for the first time, did she show tangible signs that during these six dreadful days, she had suffered crucifixion . . . Her face was devoid of all colour, her lips close-pressed, her eyes glazed, that she looked less like a girl than the ghost of one there, supported by her two women jailers. The prison doctor and the chaplain stood beside the dock, and behind her an impassive sturdy policeman. Then was heard the clerk of the Court, in a voice that resounded through that heavy breathless silence:

'Gentlemen, have you agreed upon your verdict?'

The foreman, gloomily:

'We have.'

'Do you find the prisoner guilty or not guilty?'

A long agonizing pause preceded the answer:

'We have well considered the evidence, and although we think grave suspicion is attached to the prisoner we think there is not sufficient evidence to show how or by whom the chloroform was administered.'

The clerk of the Court: 'Then you say the prisoner is not guilty?'

The foreman, with evident reluctance:

'Not . . . guilty.'

At this a burst of cheering broke from those who, motionless, had sat in a torment of suspense awaiting the verdict, to bring from above the husky objection:

'This conduct is an outrage. A Court of Justice is not to be turned into a – a theatre by such indecent exhibition. Gentlemen, it only remains for me to express my grateful sense of the undivided attention you have given to . . .' His final words were lost in a roaring echo of that 'indecent exhibition' from cheering crowds outside the Old Bailey.

That same evening, in the smoking-room of the Athenaeum Club, three or four of the eminent physicians who had given evidence in the *cause célèbre* that was in everybody's mouth, discussed the case over brandy and cigars.

'If Fennell had not been so absorbed in his constituency, he could have put up a better case for the Crown,' was the disgruntled opinion of one who had borne the brunt of Sir Henry's bombardment. 'It was obvious the old man, who should have retired with his canaries long ago, had determined upon a conviction.'

'Yes, and only Doyle's masterly handling of what was a foregone conclusion, saved her neck,' said another denizen from Harley Street.

'Herriott says,' this from Dr Gardiner, 'that he's writing an article for the *Lancet* to indicate Todd took the dose himself, with no intent of suicide but just enough to scare his wife – out of devilment, to punish her for having told him what she meant to do and – didn't do.'

'Why not?' chimed in yet another learned medico, who although subpoenaed had not been called in evidence. 'Her far-fetched rigmarole of one act only deceived none but that ecstatically biassed young man. And now it's all over she must tell us – in the interest of science – how she did it!'

ELEVEN

She was watching the April green tracery of leaves on gently swaying branches against an opalescent sky, as she settled deeper in the cushions of the couch under the window where Mrs Ottery had placed her. . . . 'Relax, dear child,' trailing round and about with obscure admonishment to, 'be at peace – and your tonic – to burn always with this gem-like flame which is the lighted torch of our emancipation. If it had gone against you we – Mrs Pankhurst and the rest of us would have marched but I was going in the carriage, walking tires me – to Downing Street – and petitioned the Prime Minister and the Home Secretary. Great passions lend to our endeavours a quickened sense of life. Read this.'

She had thrust into her hand Pater's *Renaissance*. It lay unopened on the table beside her.

Was it all a dream? A nightmare? Had all her life been centred in this room decorated with starry blossomed Morris wallpaper and subdued Whistleresque greys and mauves and vaguely patterned chintzes? How long had she been here?

Memory searching through the aisles of forgetfulness revealed a transient glimpse of herself borne away between Mrs Ottery and John past cheering crowds, their faces merged into one immense Titanic face with a wide open grinning mouth. . . . And bodies fighting to snatch a closer view of her wrapped and veiled; women blowing kisses as she was helped into the carriage and brought . . .where? To this huge fantastic house set in acres of garden and tree-girdled lawns at Dulwich. Back again to her beginnings or . . . her end?

The afternoon had brimmed and brightened, dying toward dusk. If she could only know! It was torture, this not knowing . . . 'Grave suspicion but not sufficient evidence.' That is what the foreman, a whiskered fat, red-haired man, had said. 'Grave suspicion'. . . . Guilty or not guilty? A sobbing breath escaped her. She turned over, burying her face in a lilac coloured satin cushion, and heard the jingling bells of his hansom in the drive below, as each day she had heard it.

No! Not yet to see and speak to him. She had not the courage – not yet – to destroy all that would make life bearable, not yet to renounce the miracle of love, and of being loved, to take flight, and go her way . . . alone. For it must be just that, for his dear sake, as some day, in some untroubled future time, he would, he must accept it.

A maid was at the door.

'Dr Herriott, madam, has brought you these.'

Roses, carnations, always his flowers. The room was filled with them.

'I will put them in vases, madam.'

'Thank you.'

The maid went out and John came in.

He closed the door and stood with his back to it. So pale he looked; his eyes, that could not hide the hurt unspoken question in them, anxiously seeking hers.

'Dear love. My darling.' He came to her and kneeling, took her face in his hands and her mouth to his. The first time since that last tortured day when they had brought her here.

He gathered her into his arms. Out of some far off vacancy she heard his words, so long unuttered: 'Why persistently do you keep me away from you? Why?'

In that moment of anguished joy at his touch she freed her mouth and whispered, 'John. I can't. We mustn't. I have to tell you. . . .'

'The flowers, madam.'

He got up and went to take from the maid the two

vases, and bidding her, 'I will see to these,' came back to put them on the mantelshelf. There was a silence between them, while she summoned strength to say what must be said. But he had come to her again and knelt to hold her close and closer.

'There is nothing you can tell me that is not already known to do with you – and me. But I've to tell you this . . . No, hear me,' as feebly she shrove to withhold herself, 'I have the licence ready and you'll come with me and be my love on – Monday week!' That well-remembered faun-like smile, lifting the corners of his mouth that regressed him to the schoolboy of another life, another world, came upon his lips. 'And thereafter then – for ever.'

It was what she knew he had come to say before he said it. What she had longed and prayed to hear and – dared not hear.

'No, my love, lie still,' for she was struggling to free herself, weakened, helpless, yet, with all her might she made the effort to rise from where she lay; and stood, one hand on the arm of the couch for support. She was wearing a greenish gown of Mrs Ottery's. The clinging folds enwrapped her small, too slender body. Her hair parted in wings on her forehead, fell loosely to her shoulders. She made her voice firm to tell him: 'John. It tears me to pieces to say this, but I can't – we can never be married. I can't – I must not be your wife. Not now. Not ever.'

A last splinter of light slanted across her burnished hair; and again, with that twist of a smile on his lips, he left her to turn up the wick of a lamp on the table, and was about to set a taper to it, when: 'No,' he heard in a half whisper. 'Leave it. What I have to say must be said in – shadow.'

'There can be no more shadows for you and me.' He made to take her back to him; and again she held him from her. She was now mistress of herself, collected, calm, no longer drowned in the depths of her love and the agony of her renunciation.

'You see . . . the verdict acquitted me but there will always be a doubt. No, let me speak. . . . Not only in the minds of the jury, but in mine. I may have done it . . . outside of me. I don't know. I just don't . . . know.'

'But *I* know. Listen.' He took her hands, her little cold, almost lifeless hands in his. 'You have been under a terrible strain, and under such a strain it is not uncommon to become obsessed by an illusion. Once you are with me away from all this awfulness that you so bravely, so courageously have borne, you will see it in its right perspective. He drank that draught himself. Not with intent on suicide nor in the hope that it would induce sleep, but just to frighten you – to punish you for having thought of it. You *must* believe this.'

'If that were so,' she said in a thin, broken voice, 'it was I who gave him the idea. But wait –' as again he would have stayed her – 'there is another, a more potent reason why I must not let you marry me. My name is known all over England and out of it. I saw a paper in your aunt's boudoir – a New York paper – with headlines: "The Mystery of Martha Todd. Did she or did she not—"' He made an impatient gesture.

'The gutter Press!'

'No matter what it was – I am known as the woman who killed her husband with chloroform, and has been acquitted for want of enough evidence. If you marry me your career will be ruined. You have a great future. But with me as your wife you will *have* no future. It is Caesar, not his wife, who must be above reproach. People would even think that perhaps we had been in league together to . . .'

Her voice dwindled.

'Good God!' He stared at her, stunned. So that was it! He saw the whole fabric of his life, and hers, shattered, torn in shreds by a love that was beyond desire, beyond regret, utterly, incomparably selfless.

She stood before him inaccessible and unafraid on the brink of self-inflicted abysmal desolation. Her sweet ungiven body, exquisitely made for his delight, called to him in an elusive ghost of passion, denied, renounced against all reason, only to increase her dominant resolve.

He let her have her way if only to humour her – for this present. But he would win her yet. This, he desperately told himself, was just an interim postponement. He would *not* release her. He could not let her go!

She said, coolly, firmly: 'John. I am going back to France, where I was born. I will take Lorna with me. I want to find my mother's relatives, if there are any to be found.' Her eyes wandered to the window where twilight spread its bridge of dusk between night and the dying day. A young moon lay on her back in an amethyst sky, and one faint star, like a beacon, beckoned.

'You can light the lamp now,' her voice sank to a whisper, 'the shadows have gone.'

* * *

On the quayside at Dover he waited to see the cross-Channel boat that was taking her from him, weigh anchor. What right had he to stay her whose adorable cussedness – a laugh that had in it something of a choke which suspiciously brightened his eyes, rose to his lips – had outfaced him? But not for long. No, not for long. He would find and hold her to him, undivided, even though it be by force. Brute force.

Yet, while his mind shrank from the thought that she would go her wilful way uncomforted, alone, his heart applauded. O, but she was rare, this girl of his, whose unstained bravery of spirit, bent on sacrifice, would flagellate itself for him!

He recalled the last time he had seen her at her apartments in Devonshire Street where she had returned from his aunt's house; how, when he had taken her and, for the moment felt her yield to his too stormy kiss, she had withdrawn from his arms.

'I could not love you and not want you,' he had told her, and heard her say in a small childish voice, 'As I want you, but I want more for you than – this.'

'What more?' In the heat of desire's frustration: 'You can't do this to me,' he cried. 'You are a sadist or – a masochist, or both!' And at her surprised, uplifted look from those strangely vividly blue eyes under the delicate raised brows: 'Through your indomitable suffering you have taught *me* how to suffer and – have taught me how to love.' Then again, despairingly: 'You can't *do* this to me and to yourself.'

Her eyes, dark now in the pallor of her face, filled with tears, unshed, as she answered him:

'Some day, some time, you will see that what I do is for our greater love, mine for you and yours for – humanity, as a doctor, a great doctor. Yes, you will be great and world-famous some day. I know it. You are needed more than ever we can need each other. Would you have me stand in your light. You who are the light of my life, but . . . I must put out the light.'

That finished him. He had nothing left to say.

Turning, he went from her blindly, and, in uprisen fury, thought: Damn this quixotic sentimental folly and – God give her back to me. I'll have her yet.'

And now, unknown to her he stood with the crowds on the quayside, for he had followed her to Dover having discovered from her apartments in Devonshire Street the day of her departure which she had stubbornly refused to tell him, or to see him.

He saw the ruffled steel blue waters of the harbour widen as the Calais boat, with its holiday-making passengers aboard, it was Whitsun week, steamed slowly out to sea.

His eyes, seeking frantically among those on deck, sighted her at last: a small gallant figure with the wind in her hatless hair, one hand on the head of the dog at her side, the other shading the sun from her face as she watched the silvery white cliffs of the island she was leaving for ever, recede.

And he, that 'ecstatic young man', called to her inly: My perfectly mistaken darling love, you can't escape. I am here to follow and bring you back where you belong – to me!

He waited there until no more could be seen of the clear sun-dazzled horizon save a fading plume of smoke and the wraith of a coast-line that was France.

OBITUARY

Extract from the Lancet, *February 1930*

. . . The death, at the age of seventy, of Sir John Herriott, Bart., K.C.V.O., M.D., F.R.C.P., Physician in Ordinary to His Majesty the King, is an irreparable loss to medicine. . . . Success and honours came to him early in life, but he had the spiritual grace to let neither spoil him, and perhaps no man could have a more fitting epitaph. . . . He died unmarried and leaves no heir to the baronetcy conferred upon him in 1920 as President of the Royal College of Physicians.

Also by Doris Leslie

THIS FOR CAROLINE

'A portrait, vivid, sympathetic, persuasive, of that madcap (to choose the mildest term) Lady Caroline Lamb . . .' *The Scotsman*

PARAGON STREET

'Superbly readable.' Robert Pitman, *Daily Express*

THE SCEPTRE AND THE ROSE

'A vivid, sensitively written tale about Charles II and his sad but determined Queen, Catherine of Braganza . . .' *Sunday Express*